THE SPOILS OF CONQUEST

Other Nathan Peake novels by Seth Hunter

The Time of Terror

The Tide of War

The Price of Glory

The Winds of Folly

The Flag of Freedom

The Spoils of Conquest

THE SPOILS OF CONQUEST

a Nathan Peake novel

Seth Hunter

McBooks Press, Inc.
www.mcbooks.com
Ithaca, New York

Published by McBooks Press 2017
First published in Great Britain by Headline Review, an imprint of Headline Publishing Group, a Hachette UK company, 2013

Cover illustration © collaberationJS
Typeset in Sabon by Avon DataSet Ltd, Bidford-on-Avon, Warwickshire

The Nathan Peake Novels, book six:

ISBN 9781590137215 (softcover)
ISBN 9781590137222 (mobipocket)
ISBN 9781590137239 (ePub)
ISBN 9781590137246 (PDF)

Visit the McBooks Press website at www.mcbooks.com.

Printed in Canada

9 8 7 6 5 4 3 2 1

Apart from obvious historical figures—all characters herein are fictitious and any resemblance to real persons living or dead, is purely coincidental.

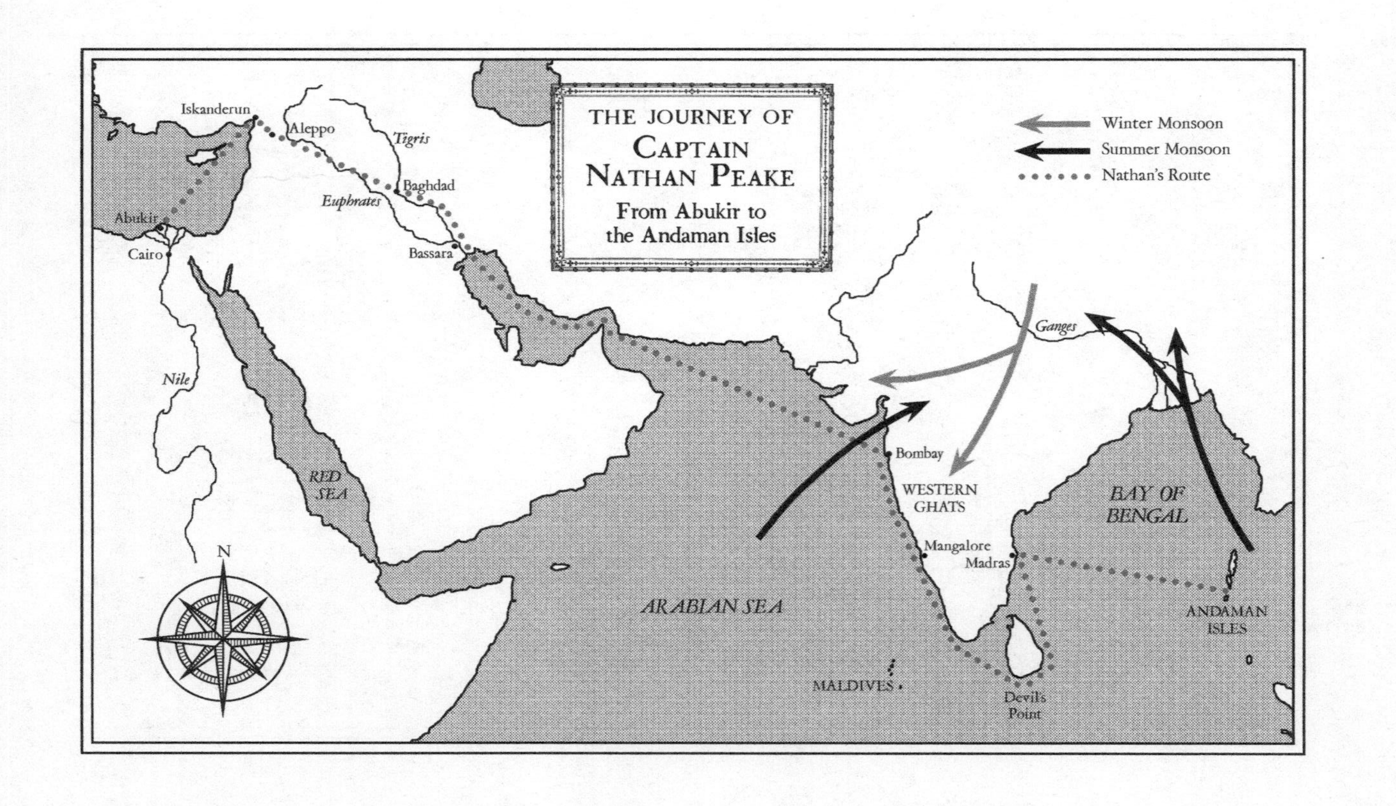
THE JOURNEY OF
CAPTAIN
NATHAN PEAKE
From Abukir to
the Andaman Isles
Winter Monsoon
Summer Monsoon
Nathan's Route
Iskanderun
Aleppo
Tigris
Baghdad
Euphrates
Abukir
Cairo
Bassara
Nile
RED SEA
N
ARABIAN SEA
Ganges
Bombay
WESTERN GHATS
Mangalore
Madras
BAY OF BENGAL
ANDAMAN ISLES
MALDIVES
Devil's Point

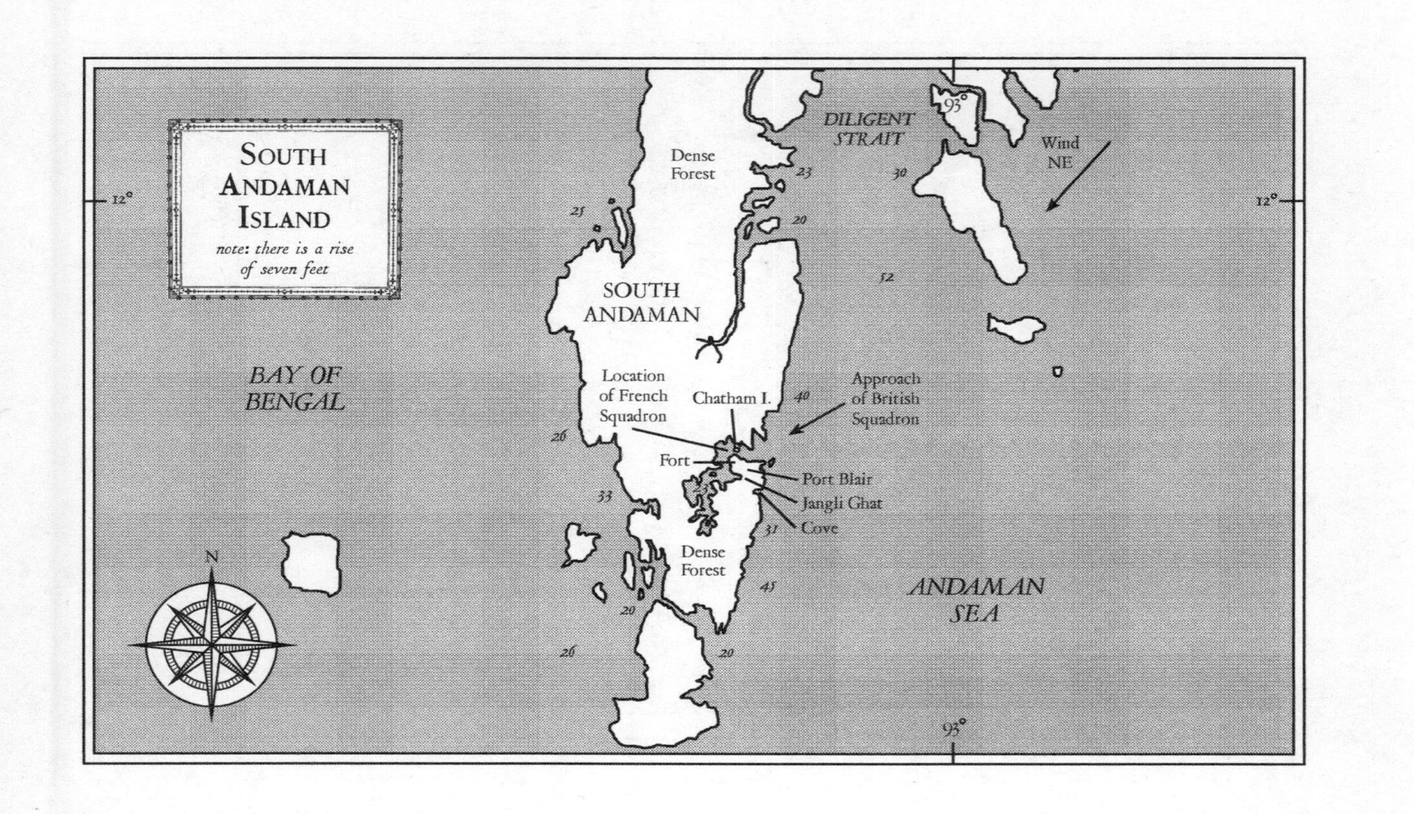
SOUTH ANDAMAN ISLAND
note: there is a rise of seven feet
12°
12°
93°
93°
DILIGENT STRAIT
Wind NE
Dense Forest
SOUTH ANDAMAN
BAY OF BENGAL
Location of French Squadron
Chatham I.
Approach of British Squadron
Fort
Port Blair
Jangli Ghat
Cove
Dense Forest
ANDAMAN SEA
N
25
23
30
20
52
40
26
33
31
45
20
26
20

Prologue

The Admiral's Letter

The two battle fleets lay at anchor, little more than a pistol shot from each other. The great guns were silent now, their muzzles capped, their trucks secured, but not a single ship was without the scars of battle, some shockingly so. Many were without masts, or so mangled about the rigging that they could scarce have moved beyond the sheltered waters of the bay. On several of the most smitten, two or even three of the gunports had been smashed into one, as if by a giant's axe, so that they resembled gaps in a row of teeth, a dribble of dried blood, more black now than red, staining the hulls below.

The haven in which these ruins lay was littered with debris: of masts and spars, torn canvas, shattered timbers, ship's boats – and sometimes bodies. They rose to the surface, propelled by their own noxious gases to appear like ghosts, so many days after the battle, reminding the survivors of the fate they had so narrowly escaped, and the price that had been paid by friends and enemies alike. Whenever this happened the ships would shift very slightly at their moorings, as if moved by some hidden emotion, for there was no wind. The sea was calm. The sky cloudless. The heat stupefying.

In the stern cabin of one of these ships there sat a man writing a letter. He was of middling years, his features gaunt, his complexion bloodless. Apart from the fact that he was not in the least bloated – he was worn to a frazzle, in fact – he might have been taken for one of those ghosts resurrected from the bottom of the bay. There was a bandage about his head and the hair that escaped from under its linen folds dropped grey and straggling to his shoulder. The empty sleeve of his right arm was pinned to his uniform coat, and he wrote clumsily with his left hand, using a wooden T-bar to keep the lines straight and the paper from shifting under his quill.

To His Excellency the Governor of Bombay.
Vanguard, Mouth of the Nile, 9 August, 1798

Sir . . .

That was the easy part. He paused and sat for a moment, thinking of the best way to proceed. There must be no bombast, no vainglory; he would leave that to the enemy. Understatement; that was the English way. The ship stirred again at her moorings. The cables creaked. Pools of sunlight, reflected from the sparkling water, danced on the canvas partitions of the cabin. He moved the T-bar an inch or so down the page, dipped his pen in the ink, and began:

Although I hope the consuls resident in Egypt have sent you an express of the situation here, it is possible you may not be regularly informed. I shall, therefore, relate to you, briefly, that a French army of forty thousand men in three hundred transports, with thirteen sail of the line, eleven frigates, bomb vessels, gun-boats, &c. arrived at Alexandria on 1 July.

On the 7th, they left for Cairo, where they arrived on the 22nd. During their march they had some actions with the opposing Egyptian forces, which the French call great victories. As I have Bonaparte's despatches before me, which I took yesterday, I speak positively . . .

He laid down his quill to search with his one hand among the papers that were piled upon his desk. After a moment or two, he found the despatch in question – or rather, the translation that had been made for him – and sat reading it for a moment with an expression that was not far off a sneer. Then he took up the quill again.

. . . He says, 'I am now going to send off to take Suez and Damietta.' He does not speak very favourably of either the country or its people, but there is so much bombast in his letters, that it is difficult to get near the truth.

From all the inquiries which I have been able to

make, I cannot learn that any French vessels are at Suez, to carry any part of this army to India. Yet I know that Bombay, if they can get there, is their prime objective.

He was obliged to lay down the quill and put his hand to his head for a moment, touching the bandage lightly with the tips of his fingers, fighting the waves of pain that surged through his skull. Bombay. Impossible. Unimaginable. That he should be remembered as the British admiral who allowed the French to march on India, his own great victory forgotten, or, at best, included as a footnote to his rival's triumphant march across Asia . . . This man whom he had never met, but whose lifeline seemed so dramatically to cross his own, like invisible currents in the ocean . . .

Although the stern windows were open, the air was stifling inside the cabin, and his pale features were waxed with a sheen of sweat.

A fat fly had the temerity to settle upon his desk and he flapped at it furiously with his hand. Flies proliferated in the heat, fattened on the plenitude of rotting flesh, for there were bodies still unburied on the shore, but it was rare for them to venture so far into the bay. Pools of light, reflected from the water, danced on the whitewashed bulkheads, and gave an impression of coolness wholly belying the searing, sweltering reality. The ship stank even worse than normal and dark tar oozed from between the timbers of the main deck like old blood.

He began writing again, the sharpened end scratching noisily across the page.

I trust Almighty God will in Egypt overthrow these pests of the human race. It has been in my power to take eleven sail of the line and two frigates; in short, only two sail of the line and two frigates have escaped me.

He read the letter over. This incredible tally. This modest summary of his glorious achievement. *Eleven sail of the line and two frigates. Eleven sail of the line!* Nine taken, two destroyed by fire and explosion. An entire battle fleet reduced to two sail of the line and two frigates.

He thought back over the great sea victories of the past. The Spanish Armada: one Spanish ship taken by gunfire, the rest lost in a storm. Hawke's great victory at Quiberon: seven French ships. Rodney at the Battle of the Saints: five. Jervis at the Battle of St Vincent: four. Only the great Admiral Blake, Father of the Navy, had achieved a greater triumph.

Eleven sail of the line.

He began writing rapidly now, pausing only to move the ruler an inch or so further down the page or to refresh the ink on his pen.

This glorious battle was fought at the Mouth of the Nile, at anchor. It began at sunset, 1 August, and was not finished until three the next morning; it has been severe, but God has blessed our endeavours with a great victory.

I am now at anchor between Alexandria and Rosetta, to prevent their communication by water, and nothing under a regiment can pass by land. You may be assured I shall remain here as long as possible. Bonaparte has never yet to contend with an English officer, and I shall endeavour to make him respect us.

If my letter is not so correct as might be expected, I trust for your excuse, when I tell you that my brain is so shook with the wounds in my head, that I am sensible I am not always so clear as could be wished; but whilst a ray of reason remains, my heart and my head shall ever be exerted for the benefit of our king and country.

I have the honour to be, &c.

Horatio Nelson

He read the letter back. It was in need of improvement, but he did not have the time or the patience. He had at least a dozen other things on his mind, and his secretary would have to make copies before morning. But this brought to mind the one thing he had forgotten to include – and the main reason for writing in the first place. That damned French shot had scattered his wits. It would have to go as a postscript.

The officer who carries this despatch to you possesses my instruction, subject to your approval, to assume command of those of His Majesty's naval forces that are available to him, in order to prevent the despatch of French troops and materiel to India. I recommend him to you unreservedly as an officer of great merit and distinction in whom you may place the utmost reliance should you wish to place your own naval resources at his disposal.

There. It was done. And God help the poor devil who would have to deliver it.

Part One

The Scanderoon

Chapter One

The Captain and the Consul

On the broad platform of the flagship's maintop, some ninety feet above the tranquil waters of the bay, two men were having a picnic. They had made themselves a nest of folded sails, and were shielded from the full force of the sun by a scrap of canvas strung between the futtock shrouds. Between them, on a pewter platter, were the bones of a dismembered fowl and next to it, a bottle of hock, now empty.

This indulgence apart, they seemed an odd couple to find aboard a British man-of-war, even given the exigencies of a service that was obliged to cast its net far and wide in the recruitment of personnel to fight the war against revolutionary France. One wore a blue uniform jacket with a worn epaulette at the left shoulder indicating the status of a post-captain, but it was a shabby, ill-fitting affair, and he wore grubby canvas ducks instead of breeches; he had not shaved for several days, and his naturally dark complexion was further blackened by several months' exposure to the Mediterranean sun. Moreover, he appeared startlingly young for one so senior in rank, though in point of fact he had turned thirty on his last birthday, on the very day of the recent battle, and had been reflecting ever since on his approaching senility.

The other wore the loose-fitting robes of a Bedouin camel herder, which was not a rank normally associated with the King's Navy. He was a man of impressive stature, even in repose, and he had a turban round his head, a dagger at his belt, and a pair of soft camel-skin boots on his feet. He was some several years older than his companion, his complexion even darker, and his beard considerably more pronounced, though shot through with grey.

Both men had their legs stretched out before them, their backs resting against the broad support of the mainmast, and their eyes closed.

This idyll was shortly to be disturbed by a small boy who was ascending rapidly towards them by means of the mainmast shrouds. Declining the open invitation of the lubber's hole, he swarmed upwards and outwards until his head appeared above the edge of the platform upon which the two men reclined. At which point, hanging backwards at an angle of some twenty degrees to the perpendicular, he took a moment of leisure to observe the recumbent forms. They were sufficiently wonderful, in the child's experience of the King's Navy, for his eyes to widen in surprise and his features to contort themselves into a delighted grin. He had not yet seen a crocodile or a camel or any other of the wonders of the Nile but this was almost as good.

'Do you have something to say for yourself or are you just come to gape?'

The grin vanished, to be replaced by an expression more becoming of a junior officer aboard the flagship of the Mediterranean fleet, for, despite his extreme youth, the intruder wore the uniform of a midshipman.

'No, sir. Sorry, sir. Is it Captain Peake, sir?'

'It is, sir.'

With the agility of his brethren, the great apes, the youth propelled himself through the air, briefly defied gravity, and landed upon the platform with a light thud, respectfully touching his hat.

'The admiral's respects, sir, and he would be pleased to see you in his cabin, at your leisure –' His eyes slid to the camel herder – 'and also the gentleman that is with you.'

There was a slight emphasis upon certain of these words that might possibly have given offence to those of a more sensitive disposition, and not wishing to take any chances, having delivered himself of his message, the young man touched his hand to his hat, and stepped backwards into space.

Rather more sedately, and with a brief exchange of glances, the two men picked up their debris and followed.

They found the admiral in his cabin entertaining a civilian, dressed rather like an English squire, and as red-faced and travel stained as if he had been out with his hounds. He rose at their entrance and stood a little diffidently, with his hat held before him in both hands, running his fingers around the brim, an uncertain smile upon his face.

'Ah, and here they are,' the admiral proclaimed. 'Permit me to introduce Captain Nathaniel Peake, late of the frigate *Unicorn*, and Mr Spiridion Foresti, formerly British Consul to Corfu and the Seven Isles.'

If the admiral's visitor was surprised by these titles – being attached to so dishevelled a duo as were presented for his inspection – he hid it well.

'This, gentlemen, is Mr Hudson,' the admiral continued. 'Agent for the Levant Company in Cairo.'

The three men exchanged bows.

'Mr Hudson and I are acquainted,' declared the Bedouin in an English tongue that betrayed a strong flavour of the Levant. Indeed, there were few people of influence in the Eastern Mediterranean with whom Spiridion Foresti was not acquainted. Contrary to appearances, he was in fact Greek, and his business interests had for many years been in shipping. As the admiral had indicated, until quite recently he had represented British interests in the Ionian isles, but since their capitulation to the French and the loss of much of his business, he had focused upon the trade in information. He was, in short, a spy.

'Mr Foresti has been gathering intelligence of the French forces in Rosetta, and thought it wise to take precautions against discovery,' explained the admiral.

'Quite so.' Mr Hudson's expression indicated that if Mr Foresti wished to dress as an Arab that was entirely his own concern. Clearly, he had not felt the need to take similar precautions, despite the presence of above 40,000 French troops in the country.

'Mr Hudson has been telling me about Bonaparte's preparations for a descent upon India,' Nelson confided. 'I am sure he would not mind repeating it.'

Before Hudson could respond to his invitation, there was the sound of a bell – the first bell of the afternoon watch – which was promptly followed by the appearance of the admiral's steward with a bowl of lemon shrub. At the same time, from the deck above came the strains of 'Nancy Dawson', played badly on the fiddle, signalling the mess cooks to attend at the foot of the mainmast, where the yeoman of the hold, carefully watched by one of the ship's lieutenants, was about to mix the grog – a blend of lemon juice, sugar and rum which was held by many to be the principle cause of the British seaman's superiority to all other species of marine life.

The substance dispensed to the admiral's guests contained the same ingredients, but laced with egg white, which was thought to make it more suitable for the consumption of officers and gentlemen, though it was considered effeminate by the lesser privileged. The admiral waited until the servant had departed before nodding for his guest to continue.

'As you are doubtless aware, the bulk of the French Army is currently encamped on the Plains of Giza just outside Cairo,' he reported, 'but shortly after their victory over the Mamalukes, one of Bonaparte's principle agents was despatched to the port of Suez to make arrangements for sending troops to India.'

The impact of this statement upon his audience was muted. If they had not known already, it was clearly no surprise to them.

'Two weeks ago,' Mr Hudson continued, a little put out by their indifference to his news, 'a detachment of four thousand infantrymen marched south from Giza. I think we may assume that this is the first contingent of Bonaparte's advance upon the Orient.'

'Do you by any chance know the name of this agent?' the captain enquired.

'I do, as a matter of fact. His name is Xavier Naudé and his official function is that of representative for the Compagnie du Levant.'

'You are acquainted with this man?' Nelson enquired of Mr Foresti.

'I have come across him in the past,' Foresti replied carefully. 'He is a senior officer of French intelligence who has also served in Venice and in Tripoli. I congratulate you, Mr Hudson. You may think me importunate, but did your informant speak of a woman among Naudé's following?'

Hudson looked startled. His eyes slid swiftly to the admiral, but receiving no help from that quarter he replied: 'Indeed. In fact, I can tell you between these four walls' – he clearly had no concept of the lack of privacy provided by a ship of war – 'that it was she who passed the information on to us in the first place, through an intermediary in Cairo.'

The reaction of his audience was at least as startling. The captain smiled, the consul laughed aloud. They had every appearance of two men enjoying a private joke together.

'This woman, also, is known to you?' Nelson enquired, looking from one to the other.

'Very much so,' replied the consul. 'She was, until recently, our best agent in Venice, though most Venetians knew her as the deputy prioress of the Convent of San Paola di Mare, which, thanks to her, was also the city's best casino.'

Nelson shook his head wonderingly. 'Those who trawl in deep waters net some very strange fish,' he remarked cryptically. The captain and the consul appeared somewhat taken aback by this observation, and he clarified it by explaining: 'The French spy and the Venetian nun. I do not know who is the more to be pitied.'

It was known that the admiral's abhorrence of the French was matched only by his distaste for the Church of Rome.

'Oh, the French spy, without a doubt,' Foresti assured him. 'For she is a very beautiful nun, and the spy is in thrall to her.'

'But she is with him by her own choosing?'

'I think not. In fact, Mr Hudson's information confirms me in this opinion' – he threw a glance at Captain Peake which revealed some previous discussion on the subject – 'and it is good to know that she still has our interests at heart, though I fear she may be in some personal danger as a result.'

'Well, that is as maybe,' the admiral replied, 'but I confess it is the danger that Monsieur Naudé poses that worries me more. I imagine from what we have heard that he may already be on his way to Mysore.'

'Mysore?' This was clearly not on Mr Hudson's horizon.

'The Sultan of Mysore is Bonaparte's principle ally in India,' the admiral explained, 'and an inveterate enemy of the British interest. I think we may assume that Naudé is being sent to liaise with him. Which makes it all the more imperative that Captain Peake completes his own preparations for the journey.'

Conscious, perhaps, that this might be taken as implying a certain tardiness on the captain's part, he turned to his visitor and explained: 'Mr Foresti, among his other concerns, has been making arrangements for Captain Peake's passage to Suez, and thence to Bombay to alert the Governor to the approaching danger, and to take whatever steps he can to alleviate it.'

The merchant was frowning again. 'I wonder if that is wise? I mean, to travel by such a route, with so many French patrols between here and Suez. It is not an easy journey at the best of times. The Bedouin, I am told, are killing every *ferengee* they encounter – after first abusing them most wickedly – on the grounds that they might be allied to the invaders.'

'And yet it does not appear to have caused your honourable self any great inconvenience,' the consul pointed out, with a smile that did not quite take the edge off the remark.

'That is because I travelled by boat upon the Nile,' the merchant replied evenly, 'with a Dutch passport and a *cachet de passage* from the French quartermaster general, which cost me a small fortune in bribes. But I suppose you must have some influence among the Bedouin,' he added, in a clear reference to Mr Foresti's appearance.

'I would not count on it,' the captain interposed briskly, before they resorted to fisticuffs, 'but as for myself, I have passed through French lines before, in one guise or another, and Mr Foresti's tailor might be prevailed upon to fashion me some garments alike to his own, though I would prefer they were not so flashy.'

'And it is rather late in the day to be sending the captain by way of the Cape,' Nelson observed, for this was the favoured route from England to India. 'However,' he exposed Captain Peake to the severe gaze of his singular eye, 'the one thing we must avoid at all costs is these despatches falling into the hands of the French.'

'Well, the direct route is by way of Scanderoon,' Mr Hudson proposed, with an apologetic glance towards the captain. 'If you do not mind the plague, and the Turks, and the brigands on the road to Aleppo.'

Chapter Two

The Flight of the Pigeon

'Scanderoon?' queried Nathan of his companion when they had returned to their eerie on the topmast. 'I take it you know where that is.'

Spiridion looked at him with surprise and some amusement. 'You mean you do not?'

'Not the faintest idea,' the captain admitted blithely. 'I did not like to say, but I knew you would know.'

'I suppose I should be flattered,' the Greek sighed. 'Well, it has several names. Scanderoon is what the English call it, in their vulgar fashion. A crude rendering of Iskanderun, which is its Turkish name. The Venetians call it Alexandretta – little Alexandria – for it is on the site of the port built by Alexander, after his great victory over the Persians at Issus, of which I am sure you will have heard.'

'Of course,' the captain acknowledged with a small bow, 'and I am obliged to you for reminding me. But where in God's name is it?'

'It is on the coast of Hatay, a province of the Ottoman empire, about 400 miles to the north-east. It was once the great port of the world, at the western end of the Silk Road, but now is of little account.'

'Because of the plague,' Nathan enquired coolly, 'or the brigands, or the Turks?'

'All three,' Spiridion confirmed with a smile. 'And some more you do not know of yet.'

They set out early the following morning in a species of coastal trader known by the same name as the port, for it was unique to that region: a form of schooner but rather broad in the beam and blunt in the bow, with three short masts bearing three large, lateen sails. Her given name was the *Peristeri*, which Spiridion translated as the *Pigeon*, a bird she somewhat resembled and which he declared appropriate to their mission.

'And why is that?' Nathan asked him warily, for the pigeon was not the most heroic of images.

'Because there is a particular breed of pigeon – which we also call a scanderoon – used at the time of Alexander to carry messages between his commanders, and still used for that purpose by merchants in the region – and of course, spies.'

'It can talk, can it, this bird?'

'Of course it cannot talk.' Spiridion frowned. Nathan's humour sometimes passed him by. 'The message is attached to its leg.'

'So I am become a scanderoon,' Nathan reflected moodily, 'a carrier pigeon.'

Privately, he was still devastated by the loss of his ship, and had hoped the admiral might have given him one of the French prizes. Even the most battered would have been a considerable improvement on his present transport. The *Peristeri* was a Greek vessel, which had been bound for Cyprus when it was appropriated as a packet for the delivery of Nelson's despatches. She was not built for speed, or for conflict, though she carried a pair of swivel guns in the bow and a 6-pounder at the rear as a deterrent to pirates – or, more likely, as Spiridion said, to discourage inspection by the Turkish Revenue cutters, for she was almost certainly a smuggler. Her present cargo, according to the manifest, was beans, which often disguised a multitude of sins, and she provided a few small cabins at the stern for the convenience of paying passengers, though you would have to be very poor or very desperate, Nathan thought, to pay for a passage on the *Pigeon*.

There were five in his party. Spiridion, of course, who had agreed to accompany him on at least part of the journey; his servant George Banjo – a giant African who had once been a gunner's mate in the Royal Navy and now acted as Spiridion's bodyguard and partner in crime; Nathan's particular friend, Lieutenant Martin Tully, who was to assume command of one of the sloops in his squadron if and when they arrived in Bombay; and a young volunteer by the name of Richard Blunt, who had been recommended to Nathan by the admiral as having expressed a desire to see the Orient. Nathan suspected an ulterior motive for dispensing with his services which would become apparent to him during the course of their journey, but thus far Mr Blunt had displayed no obvious criminal tendencies, and evidenced no mental instability other than a tendency to daydream. He would undertake the duties of a servant – at least until they reached India, when Nathan had promised to find him more suitable employment.

They left Abukir on the morning of 10 August, and for the next few days they made their plodding progress across the Levantine Sea. The prevailing north-easterly obliged them to sail close-hauled on a long tack parallel to the coast, and the wind was so light at times that they scarcely made seventy or eighty miles between each noon sighting. But it was a pleasant enough voyage, at least at the start of it. Lieutenant Tully, despite their disparity in rank, was as close a friend as Nathan had ever had in the service, and he had an easy way about him with men of all stations in life, be they ex-slaves or ex-consuls.

Nathan had lost most of his personal possessions when his last command, the frigate *Unicorn*, had been taken by the French, but he had done his best to replace them from the auction of effects that had followed the battle at Abukir – notably, two uniforms previously belonging to a lieutenant on the *Vanguard* which could, with some alteration, be adapted to his own requirements, an excellent telescope from Dollond's, a sextant, compass and chronometer, a thermometer, a book of maps, and, for his personal protection, a pair of pistols, an officer's short sword and a seaman's clasp knife with a blade as good as any dagger.

Besides these necessities, the *Vanguard*'s purser had provided a quantity of food and wine for the voyage – though not without complaint – and the armourer had supplied a dozen muskets with powder and shot, and an assortment of pikes, cutlasses and tomahawks which would enable them to defend the honour of the service, as he put it, if they had any trouble from 'the local heathen'. At the last minute, he had thrown in a pair of Nock guns – a formidable weapon with seven barrels, issued by the Admiralty to repel boarders, but rejected by most sea officers on account of their tendency to break the shoulder of whoever fired them and to set fire to the rigging.

However, in the absence of either the French or 'the local heathen', their main enemy on the voyage was boredom. They had no duties to perform and there was little in the way of diversion. Nathan spent the days practising with his new pistols, firing at empty bottles of arak as they were chucked overboard by the crew, or taking frequent readings with his new sextant, much to the amusement of the master and his mate, who seemed to know exactly where they were without recourse to any instrument – or, more likely, had no interest in the matter. When these activities began to pall, he idled in the hammock he had had rigged under a canvas awning in the stern, or questioned Spiridion on the finer points of their onward journey from Scanderoon.

'Let us first reach Scandaroon,' Spiridion advised him sagely, composing himself more comfortably in his own hammock.

But Nathan was not to be so easily diverted.

'And what of the British consul there,' he persisted. 'Is he a gentleman of your acquaintance?'

Spiridion turned to face him, with a puzzled frown. 'What British consul?' he enquired.

Nathan felt inside the jacket that he was using as a pillow and produced the folded document which comprised the admiral's written order. Ensuring that no one apart from the helmsman, who spoke no English, was within hearing distance, he proceeded to read it aloud: '"Vanguard, in the Road of Bequier, Mouth of the Nile, 9 August, 1798. Sir – You are hereby required and directed to proceed, with the despatches you will herewith receive, in the vessel that will be appointed for you, to Alexandretta, in the Gulf of Scandaroon, and having furnished yourself with every information *from the consul at that place*,"' – he put great stress on these words – '"you will lose no time in proceeding to Bombay by the shortest and most expeditious route, that may be pointed out *by the before-mentioned gentleman*, delivering the said despatches to His Excellency the Governor of Bombay, on your arrival there, et cetera, et cetera."'

He folded the document with an air of quiet satisfaction and replaced it in his temporary pillow.

'Well, the admiral is misinformed,' Spiridion responded, quite unimpressed. 'Doubtless, by your Mr Hudson.'

'He is not *my* Mr Hudson. I only just met him.'

'Very well. But, I tell you, there is no British consul in Scanderoon, and there has not been for many years. The last one was a Mr Parsons and he died before the last war with the French. Or perhaps he retired,' he considered with a frown. 'Most of them die, however. Usually after a year at most, of the ague or the plague or some such disease.' He thought for a moment. 'Possibly, he means Mr McGregor.'

'And who is Mr McGregor?'

'An agent of the Levant Company. Like Mr Hudson. He sometimes calls himself Consul. Acting Honorary Consul,' he sneered.

'Well, will he not do?'

'No, he will not do.'

'Why not?'

Spiridion sighed. 'Because –' But then he shook his head. 'I have no right to speak ill of the man,' he declared with unusual rectitude. 'I hardly know him.'

'But you are saying he is unreliable?'

'I am sure he is as reliable as any agent of the Levant Company.' This was clearly not intended as the most glowing of testimonials, and the speaker further diminished its value by adding the qualification: 'When sober.'

'Ah. And is he ever sober?'

'Not if he can help it. I am sorry, Nathan, you have induced me into slander, but there it is. Besides, I doubt very much if you will find him in Scanderoon – sober or otherwise.'

'Because?'

Another small hesitation – 'Because there is a possibility that the French party will have established itself in the port. In which case, I suspect Mr McGregor will have removed himself and his family to a less hostile environment, possibly to Cyprus where his mother lives.'

'The French party? In Scanderoon?' Nathan raised himself to a sitting position and observed his companion more closely. 'I thought the French were condemned as infidels and idolaters. Invaders, too, since they came to Egypt. Enemies of the Prophet.'

'Oh, but Bonaparte has recently declared himself to be an admirer of the Prophet, did you not know? No, I agree, it is unexpected,' he added, for Nathan's expression was incredulous, 'but so your Mr Hudson informed me. He has even offered to convert to Islam.'

'But the man is an atheist!'

'Clearly he does not consider this to be a hindrance. I am told he assured the Elders in Cairo that as he had no Christian convictions, it would be of no consequence to him to turn Mussulman, and if they thought it would improve his standing with the local populace, he was willing to oblige them.'

'And this impressed them, did it?'

'As to that, I cannot say, but I am told that when it was explained to the general that he would have to undergo circumcision and forgo the consumption of alcohol, he did not pursue the matter.'

'No, he would not,' Nathan declared dryly. 'He is as attached to his private parts as any Frenchman. More so, indeed, since he is Corsican by birth. And he likes his wine, too, I recall.'

Nathan had known the young Bonaparte in Paris, and had become quite attached to him for a while, the general being under the impression that he was an American merchant by the name of Turner, and an intimate acquaintance of Thomas Jefferson, who had been the American Secretary of State at the time.

'However, infidels or not,' Spiridion continued, 'the French are not as unwelcome in the region as you might care to think. The Revolution has its admirers, even among the Arabs and the Turks. Besides, there is a large population of Greeks in the region who, you may be aware, have a historic leaning towards democracy. There are even some,

I believe, who have read Rousseau. And, of course, you do not have to be a Revolutionist, to wish to be rid of the Mamelukes.'

The captain nodded wisely. There was a time, not so very distant, when the word Mameluke would have conveyed nothing to him. At an educated guess, he would have said it was a species of monkey, but several months in Spiridion's company had acquainted him with a great many of the tribes and factions that flourished – and feuded – within the Empire of the Ottomans. The Mamelukes, he was now aware, had their origin in the Christian slaves taken as young boys from the Caucasus, forcibly converted to Islam, and trained as crack cavalry troops in the armies of the Great Sultan. Originally, they had been sent to Egypt and Syria to fight the Crusaders, but had seized power themselves and established several dynasties throughout the region. One of their many peculiarities was that although they maintained a large harem of African and Arab women, they would only marry women from their own homeland in the Caucasus. But to compound this eccentricity, they refused to entertain the notion of having children by them. If their wives conceived, the babies were aborted. The Mamelukes believed that this avoided the blood feuds and internecine rivalries that had destroyed so many dynasties in the past. Instead, they imported boys of eight or nine from Georgia and trained them as their successors. By such means they had formed an elite of light-skinned, often fair-haired, warriors, at the very pinnacle of Muslim society.

But although they were among the finest fighting horsemen in the world, they had been thoroughly defeated by the French Army, shortly after its landing in Alexandria, and the survivors had fled into the desert to lick their wounds – leaving Bonaparte to march on Cairo and proclaim himself as the Liberator of Egypt, freeing Turk, Arab and Greek alike from the tyranny of the Mamelukes. And the whole of the Levant was waiting to see where he would go next.

'So apart from the plague and the brigands and the evil Turks, we must now anticipate that the French will be waiting for us in Scandaroon,' Nathan remarked dryly, 'sharpening their guillotines and singing the "Marseillaise".'

'I think that would be unlikely,' Spiridion retorted. 'But there is a possibility that one or two of their associates might be sharpening another kind of blade. The art of silent murder is a tradition of these parts. As is the employment of paid assassins. They may prefer garrotting to cutting your throat, but I do not suppose the French will quibble over the means employed, provided you are no longer a threat to them.'

The captain shook his head wearily, as if this was but one more burden on the donkey's back. He was no stranger to violent death, though in his experience it tended to be administered less subtly than by an assassin with knife or garrotte. Nor was he immune to the fear of it, but he had been temporarily deafened by cannon fire and though his hearing had returned, the effect on his mind had been more lasting. He was in that state of apathy – almost of anaesthesia – which invariably followed his experience of a battle at sea, as if some vital nerve had been rendered inoperative, stunned into a kind of acquiescence, a surrender to Fate. Death seemed no more frightful to him than a journey into unchartered waters. Doubtless this apathy would pass and he would be restored to a healthy fear of oblivion – or heaven or hell, or whatever else awaited him beyond the grave – and a desire to make the best of the time available to him, but, in the meantime, he was far more troubled by the heat.

He had a sudden, passionate longing for a beer. A tankard of foaming English ale, drawn fresh from the barrel, cool from the cellar. Served to him in the garden of the Market Inn – his favourite resort when he was home at Alfriston. With his feet up on the table, the apple trees in blossom, the sound of a wood pigeon in the evening air, the sun gently sinking beneath the Sussex Downs, and the shadows lengthening over the churchyard.

It was two years since he had last been in England. He doubted he would ever be there again. Not even to be buried there. A spare piece of canvas, more like, with a cannonball at his feet, a stitch of yarn through his nose, and the deep, dark waters of whatever sea awaited his mortal remains.

He became aware that his companion was regarding him with something like irritation.

'What is the matter?' he enquired.

'You are the matter,' said Spiridion. 'What ails you, my friend? You have a look of doom about you.'

'And this is a surprise to you?' Nathan retorted. 'Is there anything that you have told me that should cause me to be cheerful?'

'Only that when you reach India you will have your own squadron. Does that not cheer you?'

'If I ever reach India,' Nathan conceded gloomily. Spiridion gave him one final, scathing look, turned his back on him and composed himself for sleep.

And so they passed their days. Nathan attempted to shake away his fatal lethargy by indulging in gunnery practice. He formed his party into a gun crew and they fired at a barrel on a long tow, each taking a turn to be gun captain, while the others loaded and swabbed and heaved upon the tackle. They did not hit it, of course, or come anywhere near it, but it was good exercise. They left the gun loaded, for no particular reason save that it was the custom in the service. And Nathan went back to his pistols and his sextant.

On the third day out of Abukir, everything changed for the worse.

It began with a change in the wind. First, it died on them altogether, leaving them becalmed and fretful about twenty miles off the coast of Sinai. Then it began to blow with renewed vigour from East-South-East. A hot, dry wind that had Spiridion scowling and muttering into his beard, and when he caught Nathan's enquiring eye upon him, he said just the one word: '*Khamsin.*'

It was enough. Nathan knew about the *khamsin*. He had experienced it only once, off the coast of Egypt, and had hoped never to experience it again. It was a wind out of the desert, and it brought a good deal of the desert with it, even far out to sea. Apart from the fierceness of the wind itself, which could lay a ship on its beam ends, there was so much sand in the air that you could scarcely breathe, let alone see. It was like navigating in a fog – a fog of stinging sand. Nathan could feel the abrasive dust on his face already, and there was a prominent haze, most dense towards the coast where it had the appearance of a dirty brown cloud advancing across the sea towards them.

Spiridion thought it best to shorten sail and bear due north to take them further out to sea, but they had scarcely agreed on this course, when a shout from the foremast lookout alerted them to the presence of a sail, approaching from the south-west.

Nathan and Tully ascended the mizzenmast shrouds to take a look through the glass. Despite the haze they were shortly able to make out the royals and topgallants of a man-of-war, at a distance, as near as they could judge in the declining visibility, of about three or four miles and on a course which would take her across the *Pigeon*'s bow in little more than an hour. She was almost certainly a sloop or frigate, which was of some concern, for there was not a single ship of that class in Nelson's fleet. The hope was that she was a Turk, but she could just as easily be French – possibly one of the few that had escaped from Abukir.

Nathan watched her grow ever larger in the glass. She did not seem to be flying any colours, which was in itself a bad sign, and she had a predatory look about her. As she closed on them he counted seven black gunports down her starboard side – with a pair of bow chasers beside. Then she broke her colours from the sternpost and he closed the glass with a snap. He exchanged glances with Tully and they scrambled down the shrouds to the deck.

'She is a Frenchman,' he told Spiridion. 'Corvette. Sixteen guns.'

'She may not bother us,' Spiridion suggested doubtfully. 'Not a tramp like this – with a cargo of beans.'

This was certainly a possibility. But it was also a possibility that her commander would send a boarding party to check their papers, or to discover if they had news of the British fleet. It was what Nathan would do in his shoes. He cast a quick glance over his companions. They were in their shirtsleeves, browned by the sun and scruffy enough to pass for members of the crew – apart from Blunt, perhaps, with his sandy hair and a neatness of manner that made him stand out like a virgin in a whorehouse. They might disguise him as a young woman, perhaps, or shove him below with the beans. But no – he shook his head in silent admonition – it would not do. Not that he had any strong objection to serving Blunt in either manner, but there was too much risk that one of the crew might give them away, by word or expression, and besides, even a half-hearted search of the ship would discover their papers, or some other indication of their nationality. Not to speak of a dozen Brown Bess muskets and a couple of Nock guns.

Nathan turned his face to windward and measured the distance to the approaching sandstorm. Five, maybe, six miles at the most. But still too far to be of much use if they held to their present course.

'We will run to the south,' he called out to Spiridion, 'as close to the wind as she will allow.'

Spiridion conveyed this instruction to the ship's master who was standing by the wheel looking fretful. Spiridion's advice did nothing to alleviate his concern. Indeed, he became extremely agitated.

'There is no time to lose,' Nathan anguished, for there were scarcely three miles between the two vessels and they were drawing together with a rapidity that would very shortly bring the Frenchman within firing distance. He was afraid Spiridion would not be forceful enough with his instructions, for he and the master had struck up an acquaintance over the last two days, aided by several bottles of arak, and he might be reluctant to give offence. He need not have worried. Spiridion brought his face up closer to the object of his attention and delivered a riposte that was as stinging as the wind and considerably louder. Then he elbowed the helmsman aside, seized hold of the wheel, and bellowed the instructions himself. As if this was not forceful enough, the massive figure of George Banjo emerged from the hatchway behind him with the two Nock guns in his hands and a look on his face that would have put the Devil to flight. The bemused crew leapt to the braces with startling alacrity, and in a matter of moments the ambling *Pigeon* came clumsily about, her blunt beak pointing towards the advancing cloud and as taut to the wind as even Nathan could desire.

He looked back towards the Frenchman. For a few moments she held to her course and he began to hope that Spiridion had been right and that she would not bother with them. Then he saw her bow shift perceptibly into the wind. It was expertly done, with scarcely a feathering of the sails – a fast, lean predator with a trained crew. She was travelling at almost twice their speed already, by a rough estimate – but she was a square-rigger, and no matter how well handled, she could scarcely sail closer than six points to the wind. Whereas the *Pigeon*, with her lateen sails, could come up almost two points closer. So every mile they ran would increase the angle between them. At least, that was the theory; that was the plan.

But, by God, she was fast. For every few yards she was forced to leeward she gained a hundred on them. And now she was clearing for action. Nathan could see the gunports flying open all along her starboard side. Seven black muzzles, trained as far forward as the ports would allow. It seemed all Nathan had achieved by his manoeuvre was to expose them to her full broadside instead of the two guns at her bow.

He leaned out over the rail, peering forward towards the approaching storm. They were closer now, but it was still three or four miles distant, and the closer they came, the less dense it appeared. It was more of a haze than a cloud, a haze of flying sand, shot through with beams of sunlight. And the wind, too, was dropping. Even the *khamsin* was failing him.

Three days into his mission and he was faced with disaster: inglorious failure. There was nothing he could do about it. Nothing but to consign Nelson's precious despatches to the waves, weighed down with roundshot, so that the French would not have them. And the trunk with his travelling expenses. Six bags of Spanish silver dollars and Maria Theresa thalers to the value of 500 English pounds. He could have cried. He was inclined by nature to despair. Tragedy, as he had oft remarked, was his middle name – but there was a streak of stubbornness in him too. So instead of sending Blunt down to his cabin for his treasure he turned to Tully with an apologetic shrug.

'Damn it,' he said. 'I cannot bear to give up without a fight.'

They looked at the 6-pounder, bowsed up against the stern.

'She is ready loaded,' Nathan pointed out. 'It seems a pity to waste it. And there is always a chance of carrying away a spar.' Even Tully – the eternal optimist – knew this was nonsense, but they crossed to the gun and levered up the port. They had a clear view of their pursuer at a distance of about a mile and a half on their larboard quarter. Within a quarter of an hour or so she would cross their stern, at a range, as near as they could judge, of about a thousand yards, maybe less. Then the gap would begin to widen again, but in the meantime she could bring her whole broadside to bear, probably three or four times.

'To hell with it, let us run her out.' Nathan called to Banjo and Tully to give them a hand with the tackle, but at once, there was a wail from the skipper, and to Nathan's astonishment he threw himself down on his knees at Spiridion's feet, his hands clasped together and the tears rolling down his cheeks. Nathan had no idea what he was saying but it hardly took a genius to guess. And he was right, of course. The *Pigeon* was no bruiser; one well-aimed broadside would tear her apart. Nathan knew he had no right to put the man's life at risk, or the lives of any of his crew, for they had made no vow to fight and die in the King's service; they were not even at war.

He told himself the French would probably aim high, being French, and no one would come to any harm. He could tell Spiridion to haul his wind before any blood was spilled.

They ran out the gun.

Either the French saw this, or they had decided the *Pigeon* had flown far enough, because on that instant the corvette fired. It was at very great distance, and they stuck their heads up over the stern rail to watch the fall of shot. Three waterspouts, widely separated, about a cable's length to their stern. Nathan sniffed disparagingly, but it was a lot closer than he had expected.

'On the next upward roll,' he said.

But it was not so easy from the stern. With a broadside you could see when she started to roll. One moment you were looking at the sea, the next at the sky, and you fired on the way from one to the other. At the stern it called for a different, finer judgement, especially running into the wind. You had to wait for the sea to lift the bow and travel under the hull until you could *feel* it: that exact moment when it began to lift the stern.

Nathan planted his feet like a prizefighter and willed his whole body to sense the movement of the waves through the deck. He had dispensed with his uniform coat and was in his shirtsleeves with a Barcelona scarf tied round his head. 'Wait, wait . . .' he admonished Mr Banjo, who was standing by with the linstock in an agony of restraint, the smouldering fuse inches from the pan. Banjo had served as gun captain on the *Unicorn* and considered himself the greatest gunner in creation. His principle failing was impatience. Never mind seven days – seven seconds was too long for Mr Banjo. Nathan felt the beak dipping into the trough, the rush of sea under the keel . . .

'Now!' A moment's delay as the flame travelled along

the powder. Too soon? Too late? The stern still rising, teetering almost on the brink.

There was a jet of fire through the touch-hole, a far bigger plume of fire and smoke from the muzzle, the carriage shot back to the end of the tackle, and they capered about like the acrobats at Sully's Circus, leaping back from the recoil and then racing each other to the rail to watch the fall of shot.

At least a cable's length short, and a good two points to starboard.

Disappointed, Nathan dropped back to the deck. He did not care to meet Mr Banjo's eye.

'One more,' he said.

But they had to endure two more broadsides from the corvette before they were ready, and on the second, two holes appeared as if by magic in the mizzensail and one of the stays parted with a noise like a snapped violin string, the liberated block crashing to the deck and missing the praying ship's master by a whisker.

'Now!' cried Nathan again, a fraction of a second after Mr Banjo had applied the linstock. Again, the capering clowns and the four heads above the rail.

They distinctly saw the ball strike the sea, no more than a few yards from her bow, a skip and a jump and it crashed into her hull. With no noticeable effect. At that range, it would scarcely tickle the timbers. But it was a hit. Of sorts. Honour could be said to have been satisfied. There was nothing for it now but to put up their gun, haul their wind, and wait for them to come up.

'By God!' Tully said.

Nathan stared, speechless for once. She was falling off

the wind. Falling off the wind and turning away.

They looked at each other in astonished disbelief. Then back at the Frenchman. Still veering to leeward and heeling over so far, Nathan could have sworn he saw the garboard strake all along her side and a glint of her copper bottom. He looked again at Tully. His face was a picture.

'It could not be us,' said Nathan. It was a question, nonetheless. Had they put the fear of God into her, with the astonishing accuracy of their fire?

But no, they had not. And it was not them. It was the phantom figure that had emerged from the haze of sun and sand to the south, and was now bearing down on them under full sail, a great red battle pennant streaming from her masthead and a belch of black smoke and flame erupting from her bow.

'Bugger me,' said Nathan. ''Tis Ben Hallowell!'

Chapter Three

The Band of Brothers

Ben Hallowell was a giant of a man, six feet six in his socks and with the build of a Cornish wrestler, but it would have taken sharper eyes than Nathan's to reveal him at a distance of a mile or more. However, it was certainly his ship. Nathan had seen the *Swiftsure* in action at Abukir. She had arrived late to the conflict and was one of the very few that had survived the battle more or less intact. But he was never more glad to see her than now, with her seventy-four guns and the spritely figure at her prow – of Hermes or Nike, or whatever heathen god or goddess it was that ran swift and sure – setting its wrathful eye upon the fleeing Frenchman.

They gave her a cheer as she passed – and now they could see Ben quite clearly at the con, ignoring them completely, of course, for he doubtless took them for a rabble of Greeks or Turks, and all his attention was directed towards the French corvette, doing her best to escape to the north.

They watched the chase with interest. The corvette probably had the legs of her, all things being equal, but she was compromised by the necessity of falling off from the wind, and although this manoeuvre was executed with remarkable skill, a lucky shot from one of the long nines at the *Swiftsure*'s bow took away her mizzen boom, and before she could sort herself out, Ben had brought his entire broadside to bear.

And after that, as Tully remarked, there was nothing for it but to stow your banter and haul your colours.

The *Pigeon* came up on the *Swiftsure*'s weatherside as she was taking possession of her prize. A couple of midshipmen looked down their noses at them and one of the boatswain's mates shouted at them to sheer off, but Blunt had brought up the Union flag from below and they ran it up the halyard in place of the crescent moon.

This brought her captain to the weather rail and Nathan called out to him, giving him joy of his prize and pulling the Barcelona scarf off his head. He laughed at the look on Ben's face.

'Good God!' he said, reeling a little. 'What the Devil are you doing here?' He looked down from his great height into the stern of the little *Pigeon* with its shabby gun crew still clutching their worms and their spongers, the gun still smoking at the muzzle. 'And what is this? Promotion at last?' He grinned at his own wit.

'Allow me to present Mr Tully, Mr Foresti, Mr Banjo and Mr Blunt,' announced Nathan as they made their bows. 'Of His Majesty's hired vessel *Pigeon*. The admiral sent us to give you a hand with any prizes you might not be able to take on your own account.'

That would wipe the smile off his face. For if the *Pigeon* was in the King's service, she was entitled to half the prize money. Not that Hallowell would fall for that, nor the prize court, not in a million years, but it was worth a try. Ben's grin barely wavered. But then, he was rich as Croesus already. 'Come aboard,' he said, 'and we will discuss it over dinner. And bring your officers with you.'

Nathan dearly loved his dinner – especially when it was likely to be a proper dinner and not the birdseed he had been pecking at on the *Pigeon* – but Admiralty orders were quite clear on the subject. The *Pigeon* was carrying despatches and forbidden to delay for any unnecessary purpose, even to the extent of refusing an invitation to dinner from an epicurean as celebrated as Ben Hallowell.

'Oh, we are in no hurry,' Ben assured him, charmingly – or as charmingly as a bellow can sound at the distance of a pistol shot. 'We will keep you company for an hour or so.'

It was likely to be a good deal longer than an hour, but the *khamsin* seemed to have burned itself out already, leaving a half-decent wind on their starboard quarter, so Nathan and his associates went below to change into their uniforms while the three vessels cruised side by side in relative equanimity under a serene sky. The corvette was called the *Fortune* and she would make a not inconsiderable contribution to Ben's own, for it was certain that the admiral would buy her into the service and she was likely to be valued at not a penny less than £15,000. But Nathan did not press his claim – not wishing to be thought grasping – and they made a jolly dinner party. Hallowell was an amiable host, and he and Nathan were reasonably well-acquainted, having served together with Admiral Jervis off Cadiz. Ben was known throughout the fleet to be Canadian, though he had once, in his cups, confessed to Nathan that he had, in fact, been born in Boston, Massachusetts. His father had been a revenue officer, which had not made him popular among the Americans, and when they took up arms against King George the entire family had been obliged to flee to Canada, including young Ben, who had been fifteen at the time. He was thirty-seven now, and a couple of years senior to Nathan on the Captain's List.

They dined in the great stern cabin with all the windows open to the breeze – which, for once, continued to move them steadily in the direction in which Nathan wished to go – and it was significantly cooler than he had anticipated at four bells in the afternoon watch. Ben had invited the French captain and two of his officers to join them, and though they were naturally a little more subdued than the British contingent, they failed to put a dampener on the proceedings. Possibly they consoled themselves with the thought that they were still alive, unlike many of their comrades in the Bay of Abukir, and that they would almost certainly be exchanged by the first available cartel. The food, too, must have helped.

Ben had just replenished his supplies from the port of al-Arish on the coast of Sinai, and he had barely completed his purchases when the approaching *khamsin* had forced him to put to sea.

'To your good fortune, captain,' he congratulated Nathan, raising his glass; then, recalling his French guests with a faint blush, 'if not yours, gentlemen.'

But the success of the meal owed more to the cook, an individual of Spanish origin, who had been taken as a slave by the Barbary corsairs and had learned his trade in the kitchens of the Bey of Algiers. How he had subsequently come into Ben's employment, Nathan did not like to enquire, but it was a coup worthy of Machiavelli. They began with a cold concoction identified as an Arab soup, made from a combination of stale bread, soaked in olive oil, with water, garlic, and vinegar, and a quantity of fresh cucumbers, lemons and tomatoes, which was served with a pale Jerez, brought up from the depths of the *Swiftsure*'s hold where it had been kept cool in straw and ice ever since its acquisition in Lisbon. This was followed by a quantity of smoked meats and some ox tongue with several dishes of chutney and pickles, followed by a tuna, purchased from the fishermen at al-Arish, and served with fresh vegetables and a dozen bottles of a Sicilian wine. Nathan foolishly took this for the main dish and was startled by the arrival of a whole lamb, roasted over a spit, and served with rice and fruit, in the Arab manner. He loosened his belt, and set himself to the task with his usual resolve, however, going easy on the rice, and confining himself to two glasses of the Spanish red which accompanied the dish. He was beginning to think he had been a little too abstemious when the pudding made its appearance – a concoction of milk and crushed almonds, served with a variation of orange shrub, made of rum, sugar and orange juice, spiced with a little cinnamon. They finished off with some cheeses and an excellent cognac taken from the *Fortune*.

The conversation was inevitably dominated by their recent experience of the battle at Abukir which would doubtless remain the single most spectacular event of their lives. Nathan had served aboard the *Vanguard* during the battle, and as it was fought mostly in darkness, it had been difficult to see the exact part that had been played by the other ships of Nelson's command, so he was interested to hear Ben Hallowell's account.

The *Swiftsure* had been sent off by the admiral to look into Alexandria, and the two fleets had been engaged for some hours before she finally entered the affray. It was properly dark by then, and though the flash of a thousand guns lit up much of the bay, there was so much smoke it was, as Ben vividly put it, like streaks of lightning through thunderclouds. There was sufficient illumination, however, for them to make out the *Culloden*, grounded on a sand-bank north of Abukir Island, and they had given her a wide berth, taking a course that would bring them into the centre of the battle. Then another ship came drifting out of the darkness towards them, without masts or lights, but apparently standing out from the action. Ben took her for a Frenchman and was eager to alter course and give her a broadside in passing, but as she was so battered as to be rendered *hors de combat*, he was persuaded to leave her be.

'Which was just as well,' he told Nathan, 'for we found later she was the *Billy Ruffian*, by God, and we would have near finished her off.'

The *Billy Ruffian* was the name commonly applied in the service to the *Bellerophen*, another 74, which had been so brutally savaged by the French flagship, the 110-gun *L'Orient*, that she had been forced to drift out of the action.

So the *Swiftsure* had proceeded on her settled course, finally dropping anchor between the stem of the *Orient* and the stern of the *Franklin*. Nathan had heard that it was the *Swiftsure*'s guns that had set the *Orient* ablaze, but according to Ben she was already burning when they arrived. However, he had ordered the gun crews to concentrate their broadsides on the poop deck where the flames were at their fiercest. The fire spread and before long the French began to abandon ship. Ben was still picking them out of the water when she blew up.

'Our sails filled and we were almost laid upon our beam ends,' he recalled. 'Then the skies fell in on us. Spars, timbers – the shattered bodies of the dead. I tell you, I have never seen such horror. It was like rain from Hell.'

A silence fell upon the table. Nathan had not been so close when the explosion occurred, but he remembered the exact moment – and the moments that had followed. There had been silence then, too, a terrible silence. And total darkness. The ships of both fleets had stopped firing, as if both sides had been stunned into submission. An almost religious revulsion against the god of war. Then they had started killing each other again.

The *Swiftsure*, aided by the *Defence*, resumed her battle with the *Franklin*. When she surrendered, they moved on to engage the *Tonnant*, eventually helping to drive her ashore. And when the sea battle ended, early the following morning, Hallowell had landed a party of seamen and marines on Abukir Island to take the enemy guns that had been installed there. The *Swiftsure* may have been late to the conflict, but she had continued to the last. And hers had been the last guns to fall silent.

Ben's officers must have heard this story many times, and told it themselves as often, but it clearly moved them as much as at the first telling. And they would continue to tell it, and to be so moved, Nathan reflected, when they were toothless old relics in the care of their daughters, or whatever institution had them in its custody.

'The fortune of war,' Hallowell declared, raising his glass to the French captain.

'The fortune of war,' chorused his officers, raising their own glasses to the enemy with a genuine empathy which Nathan, for one, found impressive, though he did not know what the French made of it. But they all knew it was true and that the boot could so easily have been on the other foot. Had it not been for the timely arrival of the *Swiftsure*, he would have been dining with the French captain by now in the stern cabin of the *Fortune*. If he had not been taken for a spy and put in the orlop deck with the rats.

The French were required to give their own account of the battle and though they did their best to oblige, it was inevitably a much more subdued account, hindered by the necessity for Nathan to provide a translation, for none of them spoke more than a few words of English. Their main contribution to the history was the disclosure that half their crews were ashore when the English fleet was first sighted, foraging for food and digging for water on the beach. It was almost sunset and the French admiral, de Brueys, had not expected an attack until the following morning.

'We were in shoal waters, with sandbanks all around,' the French captain explained. 'Moored in line with every gun pointing out to sea. It was inconceivable to us that the English admiral would attack such a position. And in darkness. Only a madman would have attempted it.'

Nathan had been with Nelson on the quarterdeck of the *Vanguard*, and this had been his own opinion at the time. Nelson had been driven mad with frustration at his failure to find the French fleet over two months of desperate searching. He was immune to reason, or any note of caution. He would not even wait for all his ships to catch up. He was determined to go straight at them. And he had won. The most decisive naval victory of the war – and a good few wars before this.

'It does seem like madness,' Hallowell conceded thoughtfully, when Nathan had translated the French captain's words. 'But one thing you should know about Nelson is that he is a prime seaman – as good a seaman, I think, as any man who is afloat. He knew from the way you were moored how we might reach you – and beat you – even in the dark, even without charts. And we had complete trust in that, trust in *him* – we would follow him into the jaws of Hell. But more than that, he trusts *us*. Not just to follow him, but to think for ourselves, to do what needs to be done, without need for signals or commands. Not just because he is our commander and he knows we will do our duty, but because we are a band of brothers. We fight for each other and we would never, ever, let each other down.'

It sounded vainglorious, especially in the French tongue, and there was a slightly embarrassing silence after Nathan had translated, but he knew the sentiment was sincere and though he might not have expressed it in quite the same way, it was one he shared. But there was something that Ben could not explain, nor he himself. When the English fleet sailed into that bay, with darkness falling, and all those French guns pointing at them, the French had let out a cheer. But it was a very thin cheer. What you might call an apprehensive cheer. And the British had laughed. Not the officers, but the men. A riot of spontaneous laughter had run through the whole fleet. Nathan had seen men on the gun deck of the *Vanguard* throwing their heads back and hooting, slapping each other on their shoulders, punching the air, until called to order by their officers. And this was *before* the battle. In the very face of death. They *knew* they would win. And with men like that, how could you lose?

What made them do it? When Ben – and Nelson – spoke of the band of brothers, they meant their brother captains, not the men. But the men had won that battle. Just as much as Nelson had. They had won it with that laughter. Even before a shot was fired.

It was not until the second dog watch that they came up on deck, blinking in the still fierce light of the setting sun. The wind had backed slightly to the east, but the three ships were holding to their course and keeping pace with each other at a speed of about three to four knots. Nathan was concentrating on putting one foot before the other and wondering how he would contrive to descend into the barge without disgracing himself, when his uncertain gaze fell upon an immense baulk of timber lying upon the main deck. It looked very like a section of mainmast, and a very large section at that, and yet as far as he could see the *Swiftsure*'s mainmast appeared to be intact.

'It is from the *Orient*,' Ben murmured into his ear, moving his head aside to deliver a polite belch. 'I had it fetched up from the sea after the battle.'

'Very good,' said Nathan, nodding wisely, though for the life of him he could not think what use it would be, and he would have thought there were less cumbersome mementoes of the victory that would not get in the way of the guns.

'I am thinking of having it made up into a coffin,' Ben informed him, obviously thinking some rational explanation was required.

'Very good,' Nathan repeated, for want of something more original. 'For yourself?'

'For the admiral.'

Nathan moved his head carefully, the better to fix his eyes upon the captain's features. So far as he could see Hallowell did not appear to be joking. He was regarding Nathan with anxious enquiry.

'I was wondering – how you think the admiral might take it?'

Nathan pondered the subject a moment without inspiration. 'How do *you* think he might take it?' he enquired cautiously.

'Well, as a compliment, I hope.'

'As a compliment?' This required some concentration. Nathan had drunk a great deal of wine. And sherry. And cognac. And rum. 'So you are thinking of presenting it to him before his death?'

'Well, of course, man. How could I present it to him after?'

There was obviously some logic here that eluded Nathan for the time being. 'Is it the custom', he enquired, 'in Canada?'

'The custom?' Hallowell frowned.

'To present a fellow with his coffin before he is dead.'

'No.' The frown increased in intensity. 'But I thought it would serve as a form of monument – to his greatest victory.'

'There is that,' Nathan conceded. 'Well, if you were to accompany it with a few carefully chosen words, to the effect that you neither wish nor anticipate his immediate demise . . .'

'I beg your pardon?'

Nathan's opinion had perhaps not been delivered with the enunciation it required.

'No matter,' he said. 'I think it is an excellent idea. But I would wait until he has fully recovered from the wound he received during the battle – he might be confused else.'

'Well, of course I will. Besides, it will take the carpenter a while to complete.' Hallowell seemed rather annoyed, and Nathan hastened to thank him for the splendid meal and the excellent company he had provided, the which, he said, he would remember with fondness during his trek across the desert.

'Ah yes,' said Ben, recalling Nathan's mission, which had been explained to him privately. 'Yes. Well, I wish you the very best of luck.' His expression indicated that he thought Nathan would need it. A discreet cough at his elbow recalled him to other matters. One of his servants was standing there with what appeared to be a pile of books. 'Oh, I had almost forgot. I thought you might like some reading matter to help pass the time, not having your usual duties to attend to. We took them from the *Fortune*.' The servant passed the books to Nathan, who took them gingerly. 'They are in French, of course, but that should not give you any difficulty.'

Nathan thanked him with a show of appreciation, though they would be an added encumbrance on his journey down the ship's side, and if he was to share in the proceeds of the *Swiftsure*'s latest prize, he would have much preferred to have been given a bottle or two of the cognac they had taken from her. There had been no further discussion of the prize money; nor had he expected it. This was why Ben was a rich man and he was not.

He made it back to the *Pigeon* without loss of either his dignity or his books, and stood propping up the rail until the *Swifsure* and her prize had faded to a wavering memory against the setting sun. He felt a deep sense of loneliness and regret, as if he were watching the passing not just of a ship but of a way of life that had sustained him for many years. And for all the vaunted importance of his mission, at that moment in time he felt he would have given an arm or a leg for command of the little corvette following in the *Swiftsure*'s wake, and his continuing membership of Nelson's band of brothers.

He awoke sometime in the middle of the night in his hammock in the stern with his boat cloak wrapped round him and the night sky full of stars. He lay awake for a while trying to name them, and then slept till dawn.

Chapter Four

On Philosophy and War

'Good God!'

Nathan was sitting upright on the deck of the *Pigeon*, his back resting against the stout bulwark of the stern frame and his legs stretched out before him. He had been reading quietly for the best part of an hour but for the past few minutes his features had shown signs of increasing agitation.

His companions ignored him. Banjo and Blunt were fishing, Tully was cleaning his pistols, Spiridion was apparently asleep. The wind remaining strong on her starboard quarter, the *Pigeon* had made excellent progress northward, advancing some 250 miles in the two days since her encounter with the *Fortune*. But the voyage provided little in the way of either employment or entertainment, and Nathan had turned, in desperation, to literature.

It was clearly not the most relaxing of diversions, either for him or his companions.

'This man', he said eventually, 'should be shot.'

'Which man is that?' enquired Tully politely.

'The man who wrote this book.'

The title of the book in question was '*La Philosophie dans la boudoir*' which had appealed to Nathan partly because of the title and partly because it was dedicated, in a brief note at the front, to 'voluptuaries of all ages and every sex'.

Nathan did not consider himself to be a voluptuary – and would in any case have had little occasion to practise the art in recent years – but he had applied himself to its study in much the same way as he might to any improving piece of literature.

The book was basically about the corruption of a modest and well-mannered young virgin called Eugénie by a gang of reprobates led by an older woman called Madame de Saint-Ange, her younger brother, the Chevalier de Mirval, and a middle-aged roué called Domancé, all of whom combined forces to teach the young virgin what the author was pleased to call the 'Arts of Love'.

Thus far, so French, Nathan had thought, anticipating something similar to *Les Liaisons Dangereuses* by Laclos, which he had read in Paris during the Terror. But it was much worse than that. Much more immoral, much more explicit, much more brutal.

There were many passages to which Nathan took exception, but what revolted him most was the underlying philosophy of the book – that individuals should dedicate their lives to the pursuit of pleasure and the selfish gratification of their own wants and needs. He read out the particular passage that had caused him to exclaim out loud. Tully laid down his pistol and stretched out a hand. 'May I see?' he requested. 'Ah, de Sade,' he declared, after glancing briefly at the cover.

Nathan was taken aback. 'Do you know him?'

'Alas, I have not had that pleasure,' replied Tully. 'But I know of his reputation.'

'Really?'

'Oh yes, we have many an interesting discussion about him during literary evenings in the gunroom.'

'Literary evenings? In the gunroom?' Nathan realised, far too late, that he was being made game of. 'Well, you may find him amusing, I assure you I do not. He is a – what does my mother call it – when you hate women?'

'Misogynist.'

'Quite. Did you learn that in one of your literary evenings?'

'I think we were discussing ethics on that particular evening.'

'Well, anyway, he is one of them. And a sodomite to boot. And I would not be surprised if he was one of those depraved creatures who consort with animals.'

This was one of the most heinous crimes in the Navy and a hanging offence, obliging the poor animal to be thrown overboard so that it could not, in its contaminated state, be served for dinner.

'And what is more,' Nathan continued, 'what is worse in many ways, is that he attacks any decent, human impulse as hypocritical, self-serving and unnatural. The man is a pervert, a scoundrel and a – an anarchist.'

'None of which disqualifies him from being an author, of course,' Tully pointed out.

'Well, it damn well should.' Nathan was outraged. 'And it confirms everything I have ever heard about the Frogs. No wonder we are at war with them.'

Tully looked surprised. He was aware that Nathan was part Frog on his mother's side, while he, as a native of Guernsey, had enough of the breed in his nature to be wary of comparison.

'You are not normally given to prejudice,' he remarked. 'In fact, I believe that is the first uncharitable comment you have ever made about the French, even given the present state of hostilities between us.'

'Then I have been unaccountably naive,' Nathan informed him. 'Clearly, they are a nation of vicious Sybarites.'

'Sybarites, possibly,' Tully considered. 'But not necessarily vicious. I think perhaps you should not judge the nation by the individual. De Sade is a marquis, you know, and was confined to the Bastille in the King's time for abusing prostitutes – which shows some discrimination on the part of the French.'

'So why was he freed?'

'Well, the Bastille, as you will know, was stormed in the first days of the Revolution. There were only six prisoners there, I believe, and de Sade was one of them. I suppose they thought he was a political prisoner, or a victim of injustice. However, I think he has since been re-interred by the Revolutionists, who were as much appalled by him as was the King.'

'Well, that is at least something in their favour,' Nathan

replied grudgingly, 'though I am surprised they have not sent him to the guillotine.'

'I believe they are less enamoured of the guillotine than they were in former days, and have sent him to the madhouse instead. But speaking of the guillotine – the reason we are at war with them, surely, is that they cut off the head of their king, and took issue at our protest?'

'There is that,' Nathan conceded. 'But it is not the only reason. We are always at war with the French, on one pretext or another. I have thought a great deal about this and I think the main reason is a basic incompatibility between the British and the French natures. Or, you might say, our philosophies of life.'

'Do the British have a philosophy of life?'

'You are being frivolous – but indeed there is some truth in this. The British have but one philosophy which is to live and let live. It is a very flexible philosophy, a very tolerant philosophy. Whereas the French have many philosophies – they change as a snake changes its skin, while its essential nature remains the same. And they are forever trying to impose these philosophies upon everyone else – as if they are universal truths. Particularly since the Revolution.'

'Liberty, equality, fraternity.'

'Precisely. These are complicated ideas. One man's liberty is another man's oppression. Freedom may become licence – take de Sade. I have no objection to fraternity, but what do the Frogs mean by it? Fraternity to whom? They can scarce bring themselves to show it to each other, let alone to anyone who is not Frog. Fratricide is more like it. And as for equality . . . am I the equal of a goatherd? I think not – not when it comes to herding goats. Just as I consider myself to be his superior when it comes to commanding a ship of war, though others may have a different opinion.'

Tully made a small gesture of disavowal. 'But surely that is not what the Revolutionists mean by equality,' he argued. 'Surely it is that your goatherd has a right to equality in law – and the right to choose who makes the law, who is chosen to rule over him, in effect. As the Greeks did, in classical times.' He looked to Spiridion for support, but Spiridion was still asleep, or pretending to be.

'That is as maybe, but my point is that whatever philosophy they acknowledge, the French are by nature inclined to take it to extremes,' Nathan insisted. 'They get some half-baked notion into their heads and before they can consider it properly, weighing up the pros and cons, the profit and loss, so to speak, as an Englishman would, they proceed to enact it. It is like the theatre to them. But they are the worst actors in the world. They *over*act.

'I was in Paris during the Terror, as you know, and I have witnessed this at first hand,' he continued as he warmed to his theme. 'I knew Robespierre and Danton, you recall, and many of the other leaders of the Revolution. And Bonaparte, too, though he is not, strictly speaking, a Revolutionist, and he was unemployed at the time. But he was just the same. Actors, all of them. Terrible actors. Bonaparte even wrote a novel. He insisted on reading parts of it to me when we were in Paris. That was terrible, too. And as for their National Assembly, which is what they are pleased to call their democratic parliament, it was the worst theatre imaginable. It was worse than Shakespeare. What is the matter?'

For Tully's polite expression had become uncertain.

'Only that Shakespeare is generally considered to be rather good.'

'Really? Well, I confess I have only seen *Hamlet*. My mother took me when I was in London. But if that is the measure of the man, I am at a loss to know why he is so well regarded. There were one or two good lines. "To be or not to be", that was good – clever, at any rate – but even then, it is a speech about suicide. There is hardly a character who is not deranged or a murderer or both. And most of them end up dead. There was hardly a single player left standing when the final curtain fell. Madmen and murderers and suicides lying in pools of blood. All it needed was a guillotine and you could have been back in Paris. My mother liked it, of course, but then she is half-French. No,' he concluded, 'the French should stick to the stage – and writing novels – and let the British run the world.'

'So is that your own reason for fighting them?' enquired Tully with a tolerant smile.

'Me? Gracious, no. I am fighting them because the King tells me to and pays me to – at the rate of eleven pounds four shillings a month – and would hang me else.'

He spoke flippantly, but, in fact, there was some truth in this: that having taken the King's shilling, so to speak, at the age of thirteen, he was honour bound to serve him for as long as the King desired. There were probably other reasons, but he was damned if he knew what they were, let alone explain them.

He knew why Nelson fought – or at least why Nelson *said* he fought: for God, King and country – for *Glory* – and because his mother had taught him to hate a Frenchman like the Devil. And most officers in the King's Navy would have agreed with him. Possibly adding prize money and promotion to the tally.

Nathan envied them their certainty. He wished he could share it. But he had doubts about God and the King. Particularly since the King had gone mad. He believed in his country but he was not totally persuaded that his country was in mortal danger. The French were a damned nuisance and constantly needed to be put in their place, but for all Billy Pitt's rhetoric he could not see them marching into London and setting up the guillotine in Whitehall. Why would they bother? Which left promotion and prize money, neither of which was to be despised, but they scarcely represented a just cause for war. He told himself, time and again, that the French had to be stopped – but he was not sure he believed it. He was not sure that Billy Pitt believed it – there were rumours that he was engaged in secret negotiations for a peace, even as he sent British soldiers and sailors out to fight and die, provided he would not lose face by it.

In Nathan's more pensive moods, he thought that his own reason for fighting – the main reason, at least – was that he did not wish to appear shy of the dangers it involved, and so forfeit the respect of his fellows. In short, he did not wish to let the side down. Ben Hallowell had put it rather more eloquently, but this was what it amounted to. And a kind of stubborn resilience. A feeling that once he had set upon a certain course, he had a duty to himself and everybody else to see it to a conclusion. It was in his nature.

He only wished he had a better sense of where he was going.

'Now we are in spitting distance, as it were, of Scanderoon,' Nathan challenged Spiridion over a miserable dinner of sardines and ship's biscuit, 'perhaps you would be good enough to share with us your opinion of the route Mr Hudson has proposed, after we are put ashore.'

They had been over the maps, of course, in Mr Hudson's company, but Spiridion had been strangely reticent on that occasion, as if he were keeping his own counsel on the subject, and they had not discussed it in any detail since.

'Well, we will be following the Silk Road of course,' Spiridion replied after removing a bone from his teeth, 'at least for the first part of the journey . . .'

'The Silk Road,' Nathan mused in a tone not far short of wonder. He had seen many wonders in his short life, but most of them had been at sea and never had he hoped to travel in the footsteps of Marco Polo. 'It goes all the way to China, does it not?'

'It does, though we should not go as far that,' Spiridion informed him considerately. 'There are several branches, of course. But the Great Silk Road, which is the one we want, goes by way of Baghdad and then across Persia into Afghanistan, whence it continues along the Hindu Kush and the Karokoram Pass into China. We will get off at Baghdad, so to speak.'

These were the names that dreams were made of – Nathan's dreams, certainly, when he was a boy growing up in Sussex, and he did not think he had entirely outgrown them, if at all.

'And Mr Hudson indicated that we should travel by camel, did he not.'

Spiridion paused a moment and a small smile crossed his face. 'Indeed. There is no other way. I believe the creatures may be obtained without too much difficulty at Aleppo. I take it you can ride a camel.'

Nathan frowned. 'Well, it is not something I have ever attempted. Have you?'

'But of course. I learned when I was in Tripoli. So did Mr Banjo.'

'I see. Well, I am sure it cannot be that difficult.' This was partly in the nature of a question, but as there was no response, Nathan continued: 'I am more concerned with the nature of the terrain we must travel across – and its rulers. It is all part of the Empire of the Turks, is it not?'

'It is. Though we usually call it the Empire of the Ottomans, they being a superior species of Turk. But as you will know from your own experience, the empire is in serious decline. Large parts of it are ruled by satraps who are almost independent of the authorities in Constantinople. This is the case in Baghdad. Many provinces are in a state of rebellion or lawlessness, others waiting for the right opportunity to go their own way. In the opinion of many observers, the entire edifice is on the point of collapse.'

'And is that your own opinion?'

'My opinion is that it has been on the point of collapse for two hundred years or more, and yet it continues in place. However, the French invasion may well provide the final push. It is to be hoped it will not happen in the course of our journey.'

'So tell me about Scanderoon,' Nathan persisted. 'Why is the plague so prevalent there?'

But Spiridion only shrugged. 'Who can tell? Most foreigners who reside there die within a year or two of their arrival. But if we do not stay long, we may escape it.'

This was not as encouraging as Nathan had hoped.

'And the brigands?'

'Wealth will always attract those who wish to steal it. And the Silk Road has seen a great deal of wealth over the years. But the brigands are not as great a threat as they were – as the Silk route has declined in importance, so have they. A single East Indiaman sailing by way of the Cape can carry as much treasure as a hundred camel trains, as I am sure you will know, and the brigands have taken to the sea, changing their name to pirates – or privateers, as many prefer to call themselves. I am told the Silk Road traffics as much in opium these days as in silk.'

'Opium?'

'From the Oriental poppy. A key ingredient of many medicines, including laudanum. Very good to smoke, too, I am assured, mixed with tobacco. You should try it. It would calm your restless nerves.'

With which rejoinder he left the table and went back to sleep.

The following day – their sixth day out of Abukir – they entered the Gulf of Scanderoon and late in the afternoon they sighted the port itself. From a distance, it did not look any more impressive than Spiridion had indicated; nor did it improve on closer acquaintance. Nathan could see why the agent of the Levant Company might be driven to drink. It did maintain a fort, however: a miserable-looking affair, more mud than stone, and without the dignity of a flag. They moored in the shelter of a sandy point on the western approaches, and Nathan instructed Blunt to hoist the Union flag and the blue ensign – which they had brought specially for the purpose. There was no response from the fort or from the town. It did not look as if anyone was at home, in either place.

Nathan wondered about firing a salute. It was always a troublesome business, fraught with matters of proper procedure. There was the question of how many guns should be fired, and even if that could be determined, it was always advisable to send an officer ashore, to make certain the salute would be returned – otherwise it would be taken as an insult to King George which, if he knew of it, might oblige His Majesty to declare war.

He consulted with Spiridion.

'Surely it is unnecessary to send in advance,' advised Spiridion, who possibly knew that as he spoke the language he would be the one who would have to go. 'They are bound to return the salute. What else can they do?'

'So how many guns should we give them?'

Spiridion considered. 'Five,' he said.

'Five?' Five was the number usually accorded to a minor official, such as a vice-consul. 'That's a bit piddling, is it not?'

'It is a piddling little place,' Spiridion pointed out.

Piddling or not, it possessed the dignity of an agha or governor, and though he greeted them with initial reserve

– possibly on account of the five-gun salute – his manner grew more amiable, even deferential, when he heard of the British victory at Abukir. There was no British consul in the town, and the agent of the Levant Company, Mr McGregor, had indeed removed himself to Cyprus.

'It is gratifying to be proved right on occasion,' Spiridion remarked, for Nathan had been ungracious concerning the salute, but the governor was pleased to forward Nelson's despatches to the British ambassador in Constantinople and to provide them with horses for the journey to Aleppo – with a string of mules to carry their baggage and an escort of spahis, Turkish cavalry, to protect them from the fabled brigands.

It was only sixty miles to Aleppo, but it took them three days, largely on account of the road which was bad in most parts and non-existent in others. They rode much of the time through wooded hills, or along rugged, stony ridges with a steep drop on both sides, dismounting to lead the horses, or walking them very slowly. There was no arrangement for changing mounts, as in most of Europe, and they were compelled to rest up at night – and, indeed, during the hottest part of the day. This might not have been so bad had there been any decent inns to rest in, designed on the English model, but there were not. There were establishments known as khans, the caravanserais of the rural areas, but they were mostly run down and inhospitable. The food was poor, the service indifferent and there was no drink: nothing of any substance. As for the accommodation, Nathan had known prisons with better amenities. The rooms were airless and foetid, the bedding suspect, the mattresses infested. Nathan slept on the floor, wrapped in his sea cloak, a folded coat for a pillow. He kept the silver chest with him at all times, and his pistols loaded.

They saw no sign of any brigands, and very few other travellers. It was the wrong time of the year, the commander said. He was a Turk called Sahin and most of his intercourse was with Spiridion – though he did speak some English and French – 'backing both horses', Spiridion reckoned. Whenever he spoke directly to Nathan, in either language, it was to apologise. He apologised for the state of the country, the state of the road, the heat, the inns, the food. And most of all for the time of the year. In the spring and early summer, he said, the hills would have been covered in wild flowers and sweet herbs: sage, thyme, lavender, marjoram and oregano – he took pleasure in naming them all, in English and in French. The sheep fed upon them and the mutton tasted like venison. He kissed his fingers and made a smacking noise with his lips. There would have been many small streams running down from the mountains and turning the wheels of countless watermills. But at this time of the year most of the streams had dried out and the mills were idle. If they had come here just a month earlier, or even a month later, they would have found the hills teeming with wildlife – hares and wild boar, partridge and quail, woodcock, snipe, wild duck . . . they would have had very good hunting. But not at this time of the year.

The only wildlife Nathan saw were vultures, circling high above the mountains. And at night he heard jackals and once, he could have sworn, the coughing grunt of a tiger. When he asked Sahin about it in the morning, he shrugged and said that it had probably been a leopard and that they were common in these parts.

On the afternoon of the third day they emerged from yet another pine forest and found themselves looking down upon Aleppo.

It was one of the oldest cities in the world, Sahin informed them proudly, and had been at the crossroads of several major trading routes for over 4,000 years. From a distance, it certainly looked impressive, even beautiful, with hundreds of minarets and watchtowers rising out of the haze of heat and dust that hung over the plain, and a massive fortified citadel on a steep glacis in the centre. But the haze was not entirely composed of heat and dust. It soon became clear that it was mostly smoke, and as they drew closer they heard the sound of gunfire.

They had arrived in the middle of a war.

Chapter Five

Aleppo

'It started two days ago,' said Mr Abbott, 'but it has been building up for some time – in fact, you could say for over a thousand years.'

They were holed up in the British consulate in Aleppo. It was dark outside and the firing was spasmodic now, only the occasional distant report breaking the almost oppressive silence that hung over the city.

They had ridden in through the Antioch gate during an earlier lull in the fighting, passing through streets that clearly had seen more than their fair share of violence. Several buildings had been burned to the ground, others bore the scars of battle – the walls pitted with the impact of musket balls or grapeshot, windows and shutters smashed, sometimes doors. They saw blood in the streets, even bodies not yet dragged away. Well over a hundred must have died already, the consul estimated, with many more wounded. Large parts of the city had become a battleground – all over a quarrel that had started with the death of the Prophet Mohammed in AD 632.

'I confess that the exact nature of the dispute is beyond me,' he confessed. 'But it seems to have involved a battle for the succession – one faction supporting the Prophet's father-in-law, and the other his son-in-law. Doubtless there are deeper theological differences that evade my poor understanding but they have persisted for centuries.'

'And this is the reason they are killing each other now?'

'My dear sir, Catholics and Protestants have been killing each other in Europe for at least two hundred years over the meaning of a few words that may or may not have been spoken by Our Lord at his Last Supper. I do not think we may claim any intellectual or moral superiority on that score.' The consul's tone was more sardonic than critical. He was not a man given to rebuke.

'I did not mean that we could,' Nathan retorted. 'I simply wondered if there was a particular reason for the fighting to start now. Is it an anniversary or some such?'

'Possibly. I really have no idea. I am a man of trade, not a doctor of theology. And I very much doubt if they know either.'

Robert Page Abbott was in his early seventies, browned and wizened as an old owl, which creature he somewhat resembled with his hooded eyes and his dark complexion, a pair of spectacles perched on the end of his large, hooked nose. Born in Turkey of an English father and a Greek mother, he had spent all of his life in the Levant and was as steeped in the complexities of its business culture as an olive in brine, but he made no pretence to an understanding of its political or religious differences. Save to know how convoluted they were and how impossible to explain.

'The Greeks hate the Turks, the Turks hate the Arabs, and the Arabs hate everyone,' he declared. 'There seem to me to be as many different religions as there are mosques and madrassas – or churches, for that matter – for the Ottomans are tolerant rulers and permit all manner of belief, provided you pay your taxes and do exactly as they say. Not that anyone does, of course. Byzantine it was and Byzantine it will remain until the Apocalypse and beyond – if you believe in the Apocalypse,' he added hastily. 'I mean no offence if you don't, or even if you do.'

'So it could have nothing to do with Bonaparte's invasion of Egypt?' Nathan persisted.

'Ah. Well, there you may have it. There are a great many French agents in Aleppo and it would be very much in the French interest at this moment in time to have the Ottoman Empire in a state of turmoil, with its citizenry cheerfully butchering each other instead of the invader.'

'And where does the army stand in all of this?' Spiridion wanted to know. They had seen little sign of any soldiers in the streets and their own escort had ridden off as soon as their charges were safely delivered to the British consulate. Sahin had said something about reporting to the governor, but Spiridion suspected he meant the governor in Iskanderun, not Aleppo.

'Where does the army stand?' the consul repeated. 'A good question. Unhappily, they have been doing most of the killing – the Janissaries being one of the chief parties in the dispute. Quite why, I have no idea.'

The Janissaries formed the backbone of the Ottoman army. Taken as young boys from Christian communities in the Balkans and the Caucasus, converted to Islam, and trained as an elite force of infantry, they had led the Ottoman advance across central Asia and Europe. But like the Ottomans themselves, they were long past their Golden Age. As the Ottoman Empire had dwindled in power, so had the Janissaries in prestige. Many now regarded them as the scum of the empire, a dissolute, bullying soldiery imposed on the populace by a distant authority.

'They are considerably fewer than the Shi'ites in number,' said Mr Abbott, 'but from what I have heard, they have had by far the better of the fighting. The governor has called on them to return to their barracks but I am not sure they are in the mood to obey. It is not the best time for you to arrive in Aleppo.'

Nathan was aware of this. He was more concerned now with how he might leave it.

He walked over to the open window, taking care to lean his body into the wall so as to present less of a target – though as the window looked down into a gated and guarded compound there was little risk of being shot at. The consulate occupied one side of the Great Khan, the biggest of the city's many caravanserais, built to accommodate the camel trains that passed through the city to and from Baghdad and points East. It was bordered on the other three sides by a long colonnade leading to the stabling for the camels. On the first floor were the rooms for the travellers and the salesmen, who made their living from the goods they transported along the Great Silk Road. But they were all empty now and had been, according to Mr Abbott, for some time.

'So how are we to get out of here?' Nathan said, almost to himself.

'Well, it is no good waiting for a camel train,' the consul advised him. 'We have not had a camel train in Baghdad since early June. Nor will we have until the autumn. It is too hot for the camels.'

'You astonish me,' Nathan confided. 'I thought camels could tolerate the heat. I thought that was what camels were for.'

'Camels have many merits,' the consul assured him, 'but tolerance is not one of them. They do not like hills and they do not like uneven ground on account of their sensitive feet . . .'

This was another surprise.

'They are very sensitive beast,' the consul maintained. 'I think they do not like people overmuch, but God has obliged them to be beasts of burden, and they can do nothing about God, for the present, though they store up resentment against Him and I would not like to be in His shoes when there is a reckoning.'

'So what are we to do?' Nathan demanded. 'I must reach India long before autumn.'

'Well, a camel train will not help you there. They can take as long as two months to reach Baghdad.'

'Two months! But we could walk there in that.' Baghdad was about 450 miles from Aleppo, according to Nathan's maps. He had anticipated a journey of about two weeks.

'Yes, and that is what you do in a camel train. Walk. Pulling the camel after you.' He observed Nathan's look of incredulity with amusement. 'But the camel will carry your baggage for you – and your tent – and more importantly, it will carry your water. You would not get very far without it. No, I believe, we must get together a very small camel train – of riding camels and pack animals – so that you may travel fast and light.'

'And how are we to do that?' Nathan dared to hope.

'We must ask the pasha for assistance,' Mr Abbott declared. 'First thing in the morning. If the war does not resume.'

The war did not resume. Not, at least, in the streets of Aleppo. When Nathan threw back the shutters of his room, he was greeted by the sound of the muezzin, summoning the faithful to prayer, and a view across the rooftops to the towers and battlements of the great citadel on its rocky promontory. There was only a little smoke in the air and no gunfire. The only sound, in fact, beside that of the muezzin, was the welcome clatter of pots and pans from the consul's kitchen.

After they had breakfasted, they changed into their finery for the visit to the pasha. On the Admiral's insistence, before leaving the fleet Nathan had been issued with full dress uniform, hastily knocked up by one of Nelson's servants who had been a tailor in a previous life. He had used the uniforms of at least two smaller officers, possibly victims of the French guns, and its many scars, tucks and seams were disguised by a large quantity of gold lace and cord, so that Nathan felt, as he put it, like Solomon in all his glory. His companions were only slightly less gorgeous. Tully had assumed his own dress uniform, which had somehow survived his various escapades since leaving the *Unicorn*; Spiridion had forsaken his Arab robes for the rather more formal attire of a British consular official; Blunt wore his best blue jacket and white canvas ducks with some very pretty ribbons worked through the seams and a pair of black pumps with silver buckles; and George Banjo astonished them all with the full ceremonial rig of a *Kuroghli* officer in the army of the Pasha of Tripoli, which he had acquired by means known only to himself and its previous owner.

'All we need is a marine guard and a brass band and we could march through Asia,' remarked Nathan as they assembled in the consul's hallway.

The march through the streets of Aleppo promised to be taxing enough, for though the firing had stopped, the atmosphere was charged with menace, or fear, or both. The windows of the houses remained shuttered but Nathan was conscious of many hidden eyes peering down at them. He hoped there were not hidden guns, but if there were, they remained unfired.

'So is pasha the equivalent of governor?' Nathan enquired of Mr Abbott, who was to make the formal introductions. Nathan was often confused by the proliferation of Ottoman titles and forms of address, but he supposed a Turk must feel the same way in London.

'No – the name for the governor is the agha,' the consul replied tolerantly. 'But in Aleppo we have both an agha and a pasha. The agha commands the citadel and the military, the pasha commands the city and the people. And never the twain shall meet.'

'They do not like each other?'

'They hate each other. Do not mention the agha to the pasha, I beg of you, or the pasha to the agha, should you ever meet him. It is going to be difficult enough as it is.'

Being a diplomat, Nathan thought, was a great deal more complicated even than being the captain of a ship. He supposed it was easier if you were born to it. Or if you were of a phlegmatic nature, like Spiridion and Mr Abbott. He was glad they were to do most of the talking.

He was more than a little surprised that the pasha had agreed to see them – if indeed he had, given his current preoccupations. But Mr Abbott insisted that it was necessary, and that it was of the utmost importance to convey the news of Nelson's victory to him as soon as possible.

'It might stiffen his resolve,' he said, 'when it comes to confronting the French party in the city, or even in the empire as a whole. He is cousin to the Great Sultan and may have some influence with him, or then again, he may not. And it is doubtful if the sultan has much influence himself these days. Policy is invariably determined by one of his wives, or one of the eunuchs, but they rise and fall so rapidly, it is useless to try and keep track of them.'

The palace was heavily guarded and there were numerous delays as they were checked through a series of doorways and passageways, but it was clear that Mr Abbott knew his way around – and was acquainted with most of the officials – for they proceeded quite smoothly and were kept waiting for little more than an hour in an ante-chamber before being ushered into the presence of El Sharif Mohammed Pasha himself.

He was a much younger man than Nathan had anticipated, with a dark wisp of beard that conspicuously failed to make him look any older, and an anxious frown that diminished what little natural authority he possessed. He greeted the visitors courteously enough, but if the news of Nelson's victory stiffened his resolve, he disguised it well. Possibly he reflected that Nelson's ships were of little use to him in Aleppo. Not with the city tearing itself apart and Bonaparte waiting next door to pick up the pieces. If he and his troops decided to march on India, very likely the pasha would wish them bon voyage, provided they did not decide to come by way of Aleppo.

The only thing that seemed to cheer him was the news that Nathan was also planning to go to India – and wished to leave the city as soon as possible.

'"A plague on both your houses",' murmured Spiridion discreetly, and a little obscurely from Nathan's point of view. 'Shakespeare,' the Greek informed him shortly. '*Romeo and Juliet*. One of the plays you have not yet seen.'

'He will appoint one of his dragomen to help us find suitable transport,' Mr Abbott reported, after a lengthy discussion in Turkish. 'It is the best we can hope for. Give him your best bow and back out slowly.'

Nathan did as instructed.

The office of dragoman was some way down in the Ottoman hierarchy but essential nonetheless. He was a general factotum, or facilitator, usually with some skills in translation. Nothing much was done in the empire without the dragomen, Spiridion affirmed, or the eunuchs. 'If you want to get on in this part of the world,' he assured Nathan, lest he have some ambition in this direction, 'you either have to use your tongue or sacrifice your manhood.'

The dragoman assigned to them was a Greek – 'they usually are,' said Spiridion – called Grammatico. As well as Greek, he spoke Turkish, Arabic, English, French and Romanian. He was less proficient in the procurement of camels.

'They do not like to travel at this time of the year,' he said, shaking his head regretfully.

'I know,' said Nathan, who was learning fast. 'Because of the heat.'

'Also, they moult,' said the dragoman. 'They do not care to travel when they are moulting.'

Nathan was beginning to form a dislike of camels, even on such a flimsy acquaintance.

He would ask around, Grammatico said, but he feared they might have to wait for the next camel train.

'I hope Naudé is having the same trouble,' Nathan remarked to Tully, 'because at this rate, Bonaparte and his entire army will be in India before we have left Aleppo.'

But on this occasion fortune favoured the British. The very next day, they were interrupted at breakfast by the arrival of Grammatico with astonishing news. There was a camel train approaching from the East.

They hurried to the Baghdad Gate to watch its approach. From the city walls it could be seen stretching far into the distance, a long line of camels and cameleers emerging from the haze of heat and dust. And at its head was the impressive figure of the sheik – the leader of the train – as grand and remote as any prelate or potentate, sitting astride a magnificent dromedary, with a look of absolute disdain for any lesser mortal. 'And that is just the camel,' said Tully when Nathan drew his attention to this marvel. Directly behind him rode his standard bearer with a huge green flag, and then a number of armed guards, riding their beasts with their firearms across their knees and a look that was clearly copied from that of their leader, entirely impervious to the yapping, yelling horde of dogs and young children who had run out to meet them.

The dragoman concluded that the caravan would be heading for al-Joumrok Khan – the customs caravanserai – where all the foreign traders were obliged to conduct their business under the watchful eyes of the Ottoman customs officials, and they followed him through the streets so that they might obtain a grandstand view, as it were, from the balconies. Mr Abbott was already there, having discovered by some mystical means that this was the caravan's destination, and they joined him at the railings. The place was already packed, mostly with foreigners, distinguished by their Western dress and their hats – every foreigner had to wear a hat in public, Mr Abbott had informed them – and he pointed out the French contingent, which was larger, Nathan thought, than any other. He was slightly disturbed that several of them were gazing back with the same rapt attention – Mr Abbott had advised him against wearing Arab clothing for fear he might be taken as a spy, and though he was wearing the drabbest of his uniforms, it was still a uniform and he wished now he had thought of something less noticeable.

But then the caravan arrived, and he stopped thinking about anything else for a while.

It was an extraordinary sight – not even Spiridion had seen the like – and for the next hour they watched as the heavily laden camels swayed and jostled into the compound with an attendant – a camel-puller as he was known – at the head of every file of eighteen beasts. The procession seemed endless. In a very short time the compound was filled and still they came. The confusion was indescribable.

It was impossible to imagine how they might all be stabled, much less watered and fed. And yet, presumably something of this nature had occurred at every resting point on their long journey.

Men and beasts alike were covered in a fine grey dust which rose to air like smoke shot through by rays of sunlight. A smell rose with it that was unlike anything Nathan had encountered anywhere in the world, even in the bowels of a ship of war. And the noise! The jingling of the bells they wore and the harsh, guttural cries of their attendants . . . The entire procession put Nathan in mind of a circus come to town, or the travelling fair, or even the madhouse. But there was also something grander, more dignified, something of the splendour of a royal progress, which he attributed to the imperial presence of the beasts themselves, their strangely elegant, swaying movement and the way they looked about them with an air of great consequence and contempt for every inferior species of the Creator's imagining.

The sheik and his immediate following had taken themselves off to the *mescid*, or house of prayer, which was raised on stilt-like columns in the centre of the compound. Presumably to give thanks to Allah for delivering them safely to Aleppo.

It was normal, Mr Abbott said, for the camels to be rested for several weeks after such a journey, but it was quite possible that the sheik and his followers would not wish to tarry in the city, given the current state of hostilities, for they were likely to break out again, the consul said, at any time.

The dragoman was despatched to find out if this was so, and to offer whatever inducement might be necessary for them to contemplate an immediate return to Baghdad.

While he was gone they watched the unloading of the camels and Mr Abbott gave them a catalogue of the goods they had brought.

'Coffee from Mocha, tobacco from Persia, muslins, shawls and suchlike from India, some jade from China – and silk, of course. And I expect there will be a quantity of opium, which is my own particular interest at the moment. It is much in demand in England, war having had the usual adverse effect upon supplies, and will fetch a very good price if only I can get it back there.' He smiled kindly upon Nathan. 'But that is now far more likely than it was, thanks to you fine fellows – and your Admiral Nelson.'

Nathan acknowledged his appreciation with a small bow. He said he was sure that Admiral Nelson would be pleased to have been of service.

He recalled that Spiridion had mentioned the trade in opium while they were on the *Pigeon*. 'It is used for medical purposes, is it not?' he enquired of the consul.

'Well, you might say that,' Mr Abbott acknowledged, though his smile had become cynical. 'It is the chief ingredient of laudanum, which, I am told, is an excellent panacea for the troubled mind. Indeed, I believe half the gentlewomen in England would be lost without it.'

Now he came to think of it, this was a complaint Nathan had heard uttered by his mother on occasion, though with more sympathy to her sex.

'But here is your man,' the consul concluded, as the dragoman made his way along the balcony towards them. 'Let us hope he brings the news you desire.'

Surprisingly, he had. The sheik was by no means eager to remain in Aleppo and was willing to conduct the foreigners to Baghdad for the sum of 1,000 Turkish piastres – which included a dozen camels to carry them and their baggage. But he would need three days to rest the camels, he said.

After some calculation, Nathan worked out that 1,000 piastres came to about 80 English pounds, a considerable sum for a journey of 450 miles.

'One can travel poste from London to Edinburgh for five pounds,' he assured the consul, 'including tips.'

'But then one would be considerably further from Baghdad than one is now,' Mr Abbott pointed out reasonably.

'I suppose we can trust this fellow?' Nathan enquired, meaning the sheik.

'With your life,' Mr Abbott replied simply. 'His good name is everything to him.'

It was only when the deal was done and a dozen camels had been allocated to their personal use that Nathan recalled that he had not the slightest idea of how to ride one.

Chapter Six

Ships of the Desert

'There cannot be too much to it,' Nathan assured Tully as they viewed the beasts from a safe distance. 'Not when you can ride a horse. I am sure a few hours' practice will be sufficient to get the hang of things.'

For another small outlay, a period of tuition had been arranged for them in the courtyard of the Joumrok Khan, and Nathan, Tully and Blunt had duly presented themselves for the first lesson. Spiridion remained adamant that neither he nor Mr Banjo were in need of lessons, having had as much experience of camels as they should ever desire in the deserts of Tripoli and Egypt.

'Evil-looking brutes, ain't they?' remarked Blunt, as they approached a little closer.

'That is because they have split lips to assist them in grazing,' Nathan informed him, with a great air of knowledge, having spent the previous evening in discussion with Mr Abbott. 'But as a point of interest, their name is derived from the Arabic word, *gml*, meaning beauty.'

'Gummel?'

'Slightly more guttural, I think. From the depths of the throat.'

'And is there anything else you feel we should know about them?' Tully enquired sardonically. 'Before we embark upon the exercise.'

'Only that they have the ability to kick with all four legs and in almost every direction, and you should not approach them head on, as it were, as they have a reputation for bringing up a kind of green bile and spitting in your face, which can be very unpleasant.'

'Yes, I imagine it would,' declared Tully faintly.

'They are called the ships of the desert, you know,' Nathan informed him.

They approached obliquely, from the starboard quarter.

'They seem considerably larger than they did yesterday,' Tully observed.

'That is because yesterday we were looking down upon them,' Nathan advised, 'and now we are looking up. But if it were not for the hump, I do not think they would be very much larger than your average horse.'

'And yet the hump is a significant feature of the animal's physique,' Tully pointed out. 'And it is the hump that we will be riding upon, is it not?'

Nathan confirmed that this was indeed the case.

'And, at a rough guess, I would say it is about seven or eight feet from the ground,' Tully estimated, looking up.

'This is true. But you must not display any nervousness,' Nathan instructed him. 'Camels are very intelligent creatures and can detect nervousness with great acuity. It makes *them* nervous, and, believe me, you do not want a nervous camel.'

'Good God!' Tully stopped in his tracks, clapping a hand to his nose as it was assailed by a most noxious smell. 'Is that them?'

'Well, it is certainly not me,' Nathan assured him, frowning a little, for it was indeed a remarkable stench. 'I suppose it is the sulphur,' he proposed.

'The sulphur?'

'They are sometimes treated with a substance to protect them from infestation. Especially mites. A mixture of olive oil, turpentine and sulphur. It is a powerful deterrent, I am told.'

'It would stun a bilge rat,' Tully confirmed, 'at forty paces.'

Nathan overcame his own repugnance and advanced towards the beast of his choice.

'Good morning to you, sir, and how does one come aboard?' he enquired of the gentleman who was holding the brute's head. He being a Bedouin and lacking a single word of the English tongue, gazed back with a blank expression, but Grammatico, who was in attendance, explained that the animal would be induced to sit so as to enable the rider to mount.

'And so must the mountain come to Mohammed,' Nathan remarked to his companions cheerfully as the beast obligingly lowered itself to the ground. It was not a very good joke but it was the best he would make for some considerable time. There were no stirrups and nothing that could reasonably be called a saddle, save a kind of wooden stool with a leather cushion that was placed athwart the camel's hump. Nathan settled himself upon this convenience, took the reins in his right hand, and signalled to the groom that he was ready.

He was wholly unprepared for what happened next, the camel's method of rising being first to ascend at the stern and then at the bow, a manoeuvre which pitched Nathan head first upon the brute's neck, momentarily threw him back upon the hump, and finally deposited him heavily upon the ground.

'I expect you made it nervous,' Tully remarked when he had ascertained that Nathan was not crippled. 'There seems to be more to it than you proposed.'

His own performance bore out this wisdom, though he did manage to cling to the brute's neck for a few seconds longer than his captain.

'You are supposed to be riding it,' Nathan advised him, 'not making love to it. There, now you have made it angry.' The camel, having finally divested itself of its load, delivered a quantity of green bile in the direction of its tormentor.

Blunt, despite having had the advantage of observing these manoeuvres, fared no better, and complained that he had sprained his wrist.

'Do not be a baby, Blunt,' Nathan instructed him coldly. 'How are you to travel in the Orient if you cannot ride a camel?'

Blunt had no answer to this, but possibly he had reviewed his ambition, for after another tumble he refused point-blank to mount the animal again on the grounds that his wrist was so badly swollen he could no longer grip the reins. Nathan sent him back to their quarters to have it attended to, while he and Tully continued with the lesson. After several tries they successfully mastered the art of remaining seated while the animal was standing. When it was moving, however, it was a different matter.

The animals moved in the manner of certain vessels Nathan had known whose construction inclined them, in anything but the calmest of seas, to roll at the same time as they pitched. But though he had accommodated himself to this motion on the deck of a ship, he was unable to do so whilst perched upon the hump of a camel. He obeyed the injunction of the dragoman to dig his heels in, but found this to be of little assistance. For the first time in his life he began to sympathise with those unfortunate creatures known as landsmen who, having been pressed into the King's service, were exposed to the ridicule of their more accomplished fellows as they were thrown about the decks of a ship of war.

They persisted with fortitude but their continuing failure had an injurious effect upon the body and a depressing one upon the spirit. News of their venture seemed to have spread about the neighbourhood and before long a substantial crowd had gathered, leaning down from the balconies to shout advice and encouragement to the two foreigners while deriving a great deal of pleasure every time one of them fell off.

After one such upset, Nathan observed Spiridion looking down at him from the balcony, with Mr Banjo beside him. Even at this distance Nathan could see there were tears in his eyes and he suspected they were not of sympathy.

'Your seat is all wrong,' Spiridion called down. 'Do not try to struggle against the camel's natural motion. A good seat will enable you to stay upon the hump without rolling off to either side.'

Mr Banjo murmured some words in his ear.

'Oh yes, and you must show confidence.' He took a moment to compose himself as Mr Banjo turned his back, his shoulders shaking. 'Camels admire confidence in the rider. You must not show – a lack of confidence.' He too turned away.

Nathan waited for the camel to sit and then climbed back on again.

'Hup, hup,' he commanded with as much confidence as he could muster. But he fell off again within a few steps, and lay in a winded heap upon the ground.

The dragoman suggested that he might consider using a tartavan.

'And what, pray, is a tartavan?' Nathan enquired, when a part of his breath had returned to him. He had hopes that it might prove to be a more stable animal, equally suited to travel in the desert, but it was not. It was a form of covered litter which fitted upon the camel's hump and was usually provided for women of substance and their maidservants. Or invalids. Or the very old.

It said much for Nathan's state of mind that he did not reject this out of hand. 'How would it play with the gallery?' he enquired, glancing upward. The dragoman did not understand. 'Would it be considered effeminate? A weakness, the mark of an effete foreigner?'

The dragoman thought this was not improbable. Nathan looked up at the brute that had been the source of his discomfort. 'Well, what about the animal itself?' he enquired. 'Is there nothing smaller? Just while we are learning.'

'I do not think there is a camel much smaller than the one you are attempting to ride,' the dragoman replied bluntly. 'Not one that would bear your weight. But you could try a horse.'

Nathan stared hard at him. 'What do you mean, "a horse"?'

'It is an animal very like a camel,' replied the dragoman, 'but without the hump.'

'I know what a horse is, damn it,' said Nathan. 'We rode them from Scanderoon.'

'Forgive me, *effendi*,' said the dragoman, 'I do not understand.'

'I was not aware that horses were an option.'

'An option?'

'I did not know that horses were on offer.'

'But of course. We do not have a great need for them in Aleppo. But there are many in the surrounding area. Very fine horses.'

'And we are permitted to ride them?'

The dragoman's bemusement increased. 'But of course, if that is your wish.'

'I mean in the desert,' Nathan persisted, with considerable restraint. 'I was under the impression that horses could not be used in the desert.'

'Oh but it is only a little desert between here and Baghdad,' the dragoman assured him. 'You will need to carry water for them, but it can be arranged. For a price.'

'Why did you not tell us we could ride horses?' Nathan demanded of Spiridion when they were reunited.

'You never asked me,' replied Spiridion. 'I thought you wanted to ride a camel. I thought you had set your heart on it.'

'The horses are delivered,' Grammatico announced grandly, when he joined them for dinner the following day, 'and you are to leave at dawn.'

Nathan's pleasure in receiving this news was diminished somewhat by the stiffness of his joints. He felt as if he had been beaten with staves and enveloped in a wax dressing. His smile, too, was waxen. Tully was no better. Blunt had his arm in a sling. But it was clearly unwise to allow for a period of convalescence. There had been a further outbreak of gunfire in the city, and though it was quiet now, Mr Abbott advised that the war between the two factions might resume at any moment.

His servants had purchased a considerable quantity of equipment and provisions for the journey including tents, bedding and camp furniture, even a generous supply of rum, beer and wine from merchants in the Christian quarter who, considered by the locals as already damned, were permitted to deal in alcohol. The sheik's men would provide fodder for the camels and there was additional barley for the horses and a dozen skins of water – the horses, unlike the camels, would have to be watered twice a day and the distance between wells or watering holes was likely to be greater than the distance they could travel. 'You should also take a cook and one other servant,' Mr Abbott advised, 'given Mr Blunt's present incapacity.'

But this would require more camels – and more money.

'Pay,' said Nathan, waving a weary hand, 'pay.'

The consul had a final warning before they parted: 'I employ my own spies in Aleppo,' he told Nathan, 'and they have reported that the French mean to stop you, or at least make the journey as difficult for you as they can.'

'You are saying they mean to attack us?'

'I do not know what they plan, exactly. And I do not think the French will be involved directly, for they lack the means. But there are many robbers on the route to Baghdad. They move in great bands, they are heavily armed, and they take what tribute they can from the camel trains. It is possible that French agents have offered to pay them for delaying you as much as they can, or even stopping you altogether. This is what my spies have reported. It may not be true – but you should carry arms at all times, and never stray far from your escort.'

Chapter Seven

The Assassins

Dawn over Aleppo was more a withdrawing of night than a coming of day: a creeping back of the darkness into the desert, leaving a sky the colour of a freshly opened oyster that lightened perceptibly as the sun rose, its golden image mirrored in the many domes and cupolas of the still-sleeping city, a flight of snow-white doves soaring about the minarets of the Great Mosque, and the cries of the muezzin ringing out over the rooftops: '*Allahu Akbar, Allahu Akbar* . . . *As-salutu Kahrun Minan-nawm* . . .' 'God is the greatest, God is the greatest . . . Prayer is better than sleep . . .'

There was no sleep in al-Joumrok Khan, nor much in the way of prayer, so far as Nathan could see. Just a moaning, groaning cacophony of complaint as the camels were loaded up for their long journey. From time to time one of them would move at exactly the wrong time – or exactly the right time, as far as the camel was concerned – and the load would slip, and the cameleer would unleash a torrent of abuse. The camel would respond in kind, from either or both ends of its anatomy: a belching, farting eruption of rage and derision, celebrated by the fiendish, braying approval of the donkeys in the surrounding stalls.

This had been going on for more than an hour.

'They will never be ready in time,' Nathan declared from his usual vantage on the balcony. 'We will still be here by nightfall.'

He was wrong. The sun had yet to reach the top windows of the khan when the sheik emerged from the sanctity of the *mescid* and miraculously, with one final chorus of moans, groans, curses, farts and belches, all was ready. And suddenly everyone was praying. The camels were strangely still and silent. Even the donkeys were quiet. Nathan glanced guiltily at his fellow 'infidels'. Stiffly, like a very old man, he lowered his knees to the ground. It seemed disrespectful – unlucky – not to. The others followed suit, though not without surprise – Nathan was not noted for his religious observance. In fact, his views on spiritual matters were less sceptical, more complicated than they might have thought, and he was at least familiar, as the captain of a ship, with the form. Unhappily, the prayer he chose, one of the very few he knew by heart, was not the most appropriate to the occasion.

'Eternal Lord God, who alone spreadest out the heavens, and rulest the raging of the sea, be pleased to receive into thy Almighty and most gracious protection the persons of us thy servants, and the fleet in which we serve. Preserve us from the dangers of the sea, and from the violence of the enemy; that we may be a safeguard unto our most gracious Sovereign King George and a security for such as pass on the seas upon their lawful occasions . . .'

Halfway through the second sentence, Nathan knew it was not right. He could hardly change it now, though, and he was damned if he could think of any other. Not one that was any more appropriate at any rate. He increased the pace and gabbled on to the end:

'. . . that the inhabitants of our island may in peace and quietness serve thee, our God; and that we may return in safety to enjoy the blessings of the land, with the fruits of our labours, and with a thankful remembrance of thy mercies to praise and glorify thy holy name; through Jesus Christ our Lord. Amen.'

And in the end it was not so bad. Tully congratulated him gravely, and even Spiridion gave him an approving nod. It was to be hoped that God had also.

They left while most of the city still slept, moving with commendable speed through the streets of the old city and out through the Baghdad Gate. Sixty camels and five horses, loaded to the gunwales, as Tully put it, and armed to the teeth.

In truth, they looked more like brigands than guides. In the interests of personal comfort, and in hope of deceiving any French spy who might be observing their departure, Nathan's party wore the turbans and flowing white robes of the Bedouin, with an assortment of weaponry that would have done credit to a Mameluke: a short-pattern naval musket slung at the shoulder; a rifle in a holster on the right side of the saddle; two horse pistols, also in holsters, on either side of the pommel; a sword or sabre at the left hip, and a curved and ornamented dagger – their parting gift from Mr Abbott – hanging from a cord around their necks. They rode in a group, near the front of the column, with their camels immediately behind them, laden with baggage and equipment, including powder and shot and what weapons they did not carry about their persons.

Nathan was secretly proud of their appearance. They looked, he thought, as determined a bunch of desperadoes as ever rode the desert – even poor Blunt with his arm in a sling – and he pitied the poor robbers so foolish as to accost them.

Immediately ahead of them was the leader of the expedition. The sheik. He had a whole string of names but the only one Nathan could remember was Rashid. Abu al-Rashid something something something. He paid no attention whatsoever to his following. He neither addressed them, nor bestowed a single glance upon them, but stared fixedly ahead as at some distant horizon or destiny. It was impossible to associate him with the chaos and confusion of al-Joumrok Khan. Not for him the chivvying and chastening of lesser mortals. They might follow him or they might not; it was all one to him. He was Rashid the Magnificent, leader of men and of beasts; the hopes and dreams of humankind, the victories and defeats of armies and of navies, the despatches of admirals were as the dust of the desert. Behind him rode his standard-bearer with the great flag Nathan had first seen at the Baghdad Gate. Green silk trimmed with red, ten feet long and six feet broad, with a white circle in the middle emblazoned with the words, in black Arabic characters: 'There is but one God and Mohammed is His Prophet.' What else mattered in life or death but this?

'Old Jarvey ain't in it,' remarked Nathan irreverently to Tully – a reference to his former commander, Admiral Jervis, since ennobled as the Earl St Vincent, and as proud and pitiless as any Tartar. But even Old Jarvey would have struggled to match the splendid assurance of the sheik. Nathan wished he could command a ship with such confidence, permitting of no doubt, either in himself or his followers. There was no discussion about the route they were to take, or the speed at which they were to travel. And when he had determined the point at which they would stop and make camp, he instructed his standard-bearer to place his pole in the ground, and that was where it was.

Unfortunately, from Nathan's point of view, their first halt was barely three hours after they had left Aleppo – on the banks of the River Coic, just a few miles out of the city.

'Why are we stopping?' Nathan demanded of Spiridion as the camels milled and pressed around him in an approximation of the earlier scene at the Joumrok Khan.

Spiridion shrugged.

The beasts were permitted to graze on the branches of the camphor trees which grew in profusion on the banks of the river. Then they were assembled in a great circle and made to lie on their bellies, hobbled by the thigh and foreleg, forming a rampart of camel humps. Within this protective circle the goods were unloaded, tents erected and fires lit for the preparation of food and coffee. Nathan was almost beside himself.

'How long are we to stay here?' he demanded of Spiridion.

Spiridion gave him a look. He did, however, enquire of the sheik's followers and returned with the news that they were to remain here for most of the day and would resume only when the sun was low in the sky. There was nothing to be done, he said, in answer to Nathan's protests. For eight hours of the day it would be too hot to travel; they were lucky to be travelling at all.

Nathan sank to the ground and put his head in his hands. His new servant, Ahmed, kindly erected a sheet of canvas over him to shelter him from the sun and gave him a few camphor leaves to rub on his face as a deterrent against the flies.

For breakfast they had a kind of pancake with honey and yoghurt and as much coffee as they could drink. It should have been enjoyable, sitting in the circle of camels in the shade of the camphor trees by the river, but Nathan was tortured by a gnawing agony of impatience. He felt that they had delayed long enough. He wanted to be constantly on the move. This was the practice at sea. You might retire at night and arise in the morning to find that you had advanced forty or fifty miles towards your destination, even with a light wind. Admittedly, there were times when you were travelling in the wrong direction, or the ship was becalmed. At such times Nathan would be in the same fever of impatience as he was now, striding the starboard side of the quarterdeck with his hands clasped behind his back and a brow like thunder. Now, he could not even do that; it was too hot. He sulked in his tent; even when Tully and the others went for a splash in the river, he could not be persuaded to join them. He just sat there, thinking of the French soldiers marching, marching – southward across the desert to Suez and the ships that Naudé must by now have waiting for them there.

Spiridion assured him that no one, not even Bonaparte, would attempt to risk an ocean crossing during the south-west monsoon, when the Arabian Sea, in particular, was lashed by sudden, violent storms and cyclones. And the monsoon would not be over until the end of September.

'They said he could never cross the Alps,' Nathan reminded him. 'And look what happened to Italy.'

Besides, it was already the end of August and the greater part of the journey still lay before them.

Part way through the afternoon, as they huddled under their scraps of canvas, four horsemen rode in from the East and were ushered into the tent of the sheik.

'I expect they are the Horsemen of the Apocalypse,' Tully conjectured, 'and we must prepare for locusts.'

Spiridion made enquiries and returned with the information that they were scouts, sent in advance of the caravan to report on any problems that lay on the road ahead.

Nathan was impressed. His admiration for the sheik increased. He approved of scouts. He was less impressed with the news they had brought. There was a great tribe of Rushwans camped across their route.

'They inhabit the wastelands of Syria and take tribute from those who travel through it,' Spiridion supplied in answer to Nathan's query. 'Not so much robbers as sturdy beggars. Still, they are to be avoided.'

'Can we not pay them a bribe?'

Spiridion shook his head. It was a matter of pride, apparently. The sheik would rather die than pay tribute to a tribe of beggars – his reputation was at stake. So, as the sun began to sink below the foothills, he mounted his camel, his standard bearer in attendance, and they were off again – on a great diversion to the south-east.

It was a remarkable journey. They began with the setting sun throwing long shadows of men and beasts upon the parched earth, then continued under a brilliant canopy of stars. They rode without pause and for the most part in silence, the only sound the steady shuffling tread of the camels and the rhythmic jangling of the bells they wore on their saddles so that they could be found more easily if they strayed. A little before midnight they came upon a great salt lake, at least two miles wide and more than thirty miles long: dry now, as it was for eight months of the year, gleaming white under the stars so as to give an illusion of snow, and Nathan indulged himself in thoughts of the Three Wise Men who must surely have followed this same route from Jerusalem as they fled the wrath of Herod. Did they feel the same need for haste, he wondered, or did they accept that whatever they did would make no difference, as it was all written in the stars?

Nathan wished he had a similar philosophy: one that was more phlegmatic, more accepting of the whims of fate; such a philosophy as Spiridion appeared to have, even Tully. But it was impossible. It must be the Englishman in him, he thought, forever driving his own fate, as if it was a ship or a horse that must do as it was bid, take him where he wished to go. And always with that constant refrain in his brain, like the jangling of the bells on the camels: *There is not a moment to be lost.*

At midnight, to Nathan's immense relief, the sheik called a halt. The standard was once more planted in the dry earth and they made camp for what was left of the hours of darkness. Nathan crawled into his bivouac and was asleep in an instant.

At dawn they were off again – for the three hours the sheik would allow until it became too hot. This formed the pattern of their existence for the next two days. They moved at the pace a camel could walk, which was about four miles an hour by Nathan's reckoning, and covered about forty miles a day, making camp in the same circle of camels, always by a watering hole or well.

Then, on the fourth day out of Aleppo, they reached the desert.

Ironically, it was safer for them here, for robbers did not care to linger in the desert any more than the travellers they were resolved to rob; they preferred to wait at the approaches or to attack the caravans as they emerged on the far side. But the main problem of the desert, for Nathan and his band, was the obvious one. The camels could go up to twelve days without water, it was said, but the horses needed to drink at least two or three times a day, and the skins they had brought with them from Aleppo, and filled at every watering hole, were emptying at an alarming rate. Spiridion advised leading the beasts for part of the time, but this placed an added strain upon their own endurance. They could all ride well enough but sailors did not do a great deal of walking – Nathan's pacing of the quarterdeck covered a great many miles in the course of a day, but it was on solid timber, not shifting sand – and by the end of each trek they were quite exhausted, fit only to collapse under the thin scraps of canvas that were their only shade from the baking sun. And even exhausted, they found it difficult to sleep in such heat. It was a shallow, restless sleep at best.

An added problem for Nathan was the mystery of where they were, and where they were going. To begin with, he took readings with his sextant but, without a chart, it was of little use – he did not know where the desert began or where it ended – and after the first two days he gave up. He was too tired, besides, to even take the instrument out of its box. He was incapable of anything much, save sitting in a saddle or putting one foot in front of another or collapsing under his shelter. He could only trust in the knowledge of their guide, much as his own crews put their trust in him. But it was an uneasy comparison, for he was damned if he knew what he was doing for much of the time, even at sea, and even when he did, he was greatly dependent on luck.

It was especially hard for Blunt, who had less stamina than the others and was further handicapped by his sprained wrist, but he made no complaint and Nathan's regard for him increased as they journeyed on. He spoke to him only once at any length – they were mostly too tired for conversation – beginning with an apology for the farce over the camels.

'It is I who should apologise to you, sir,' Blunt replied, 'for not being able to serve you as I should.'

This had the effect of making Nathan feel even worse about the incident. He had a slightly awkward relationship with servants. It was fine when he was on a ship – they were all his servants there, just as he was a servant of King George. He lorded it over them with a total lack of concern. But for some reason it was different on land, especially when there were only one or two of them. Nathan had grown up in Sussex with a household of servants – his father was at sea most of the time while his mother enjoyed the delights of fashionable society in London. So it was just Nathan and the servants for most of the time, and they treated him like the brat he was, chivvying and scolding him, and giving him the occasional box on the ear. The relationship changed, of course, when he grew up but he still felt perfectly at ease with all of them, and even with the more taciturn shepherds and drovers on his father's estate. But it was different with the likes of Blunt. Partly because he was not a normal kind of servant, if such a creature existed – born to the trade, as it were. He was a captain's servant, which was something else entirely: a gentleman's son – Volunteer First Class – enrolled in hopes of advancement to a commission. Again, this would not have mattered if they had been at sea. Most of his rank, along with the midshipmen and even the master's mates, were gentlemen's sons and you treated them like bilge rats – kicked them if they got under your feet and threw them overboard if they gave you any nonsense – or had them beaten by one of the boatswain's mates, if you were feeling particularly indulgent. But when you were trekking across the desert together, and there were just the two of you, and you had almost broken a fellow's wrist making him ride a camel, you felt constrained to treat him with more civility.

'Still eager to see the Orient?' Nathan remarked, hoping to draw him out a little.

'Oh yes, sir. In fact, I had just been looking at the stars and thinking about Sindbad the Landman.'

Nathan regarded him cautiously, lest he was being made game of, but it was too dark to see his features clearly.

'From the *Arabian Nights*, sir,' said Blunt, detecting his concern.

'Really? I did not realise Sindbad was a landman. I thought he was a seaman. Rated able, that is – able to hand, reef and steer.' In the King's Navy landsmen were the lowest of the low: the pressed men who had never previously been to sea and would much preferred to have kept it that way.

'That was Sindbad the Sailor, sir,' rejoined Blunt diffidently. 'But there was another Sindbad who was a landman. A porter, in fact. He just walked about Baghdad with a load on his head, but he would look at the stars and dream. And one day he met Sindbad the Sailor, who told him about all his adventures. Which is how we get the stories. And then he gave him a hundred gold pieces. I always thought Sindbad the Landman might then go and have adventures, too.'

'I see,' said Nathan after a moment. He was not sure that he did. It sounded a very confusing story to him. 'And was this why you told Admiral Nelson you wanted to see the Orient?'

'I suppose it might have been part of the reason,' replied Blunt cautiously.

'You come from Norfolk, do you not?' Most of Nelson's following came from Norfolk. There was a large clan of them and usually they were as close and tight as the Clan Macdonald.

'Yes, sir. My father is a parson, sir, like Admiral Nelson's.'

'Is he indeed?' They rode along in silence for a moment while Nathan digested this information. There was not a great deal he could find to say about parsons.

'And did you ever think about becoming a parson yourself, Blunt?' he ventured at length.

'Yes, sir. I went up to Cambridge with that in mind.'

'So you were at Cambridge?'

'Yes, sir, at Pembroke College.'

Nathan had not been up to university. Like most naval officers, he had gone to sea as a young boy – though at thirteen he had been older than most – and he had been at sea ever since, apart from a few short periods of leave. There were moments when it bothered him that he had not had a more general education. He thought he might have liked to study history, or music, or even philosophy. But the moments passed.

'So what made you change your mind?' he asked.

'I am afraid I stopped believing in God, sir,' said Blunt.

'Oh.' Nathan was taken aback. Not many would admit that, even if they felt it. 'That is a pity, but it don't seem to stop most parsons.' This was tactless, but it was out before he could think better of it. 'I do not mean to say that your father . . . I mean, there are obviously exceptions,' Nathan blustered. He thought of another way of putting it. 'I mean, it does not entirely disqualify you, does it? Not in the Church of England, at least.'

'I think it does, sir,' Blunt asserted diffidently. 'I think you would have to be a great hypocrite to serve the Church if you did not believe in God.'

'Hmmm.' Nathan nodded to himself a little, thinking of Reverend William Judd, who had been the local parson when Nathan first came to Alfriston and had been there ever since. Even after attending several hundred of his sermons, Nathan could not, with any confidence, say what the Reverend Judd believed in. Certainly it was not 'Judge Not, Lest Thou Be Judged'.

'Well, there are gods and gods, are there not, Blunt? That is to say, men – and women – have very different ideas of the meaning of the word. Parsons too, I dare say.'

'Yes, sir,' Blunt exclaimed with sudden enthusiasm. 'That is exactly what – well, one of the reasons I wanted to travel to the East, sir. I thought I might find something that made me – that is, that gave me something else to believe in.'

'You mean become a Mohammedan or a Hindoo?'

'Oh no, sir, I don't mean that. Well, I don't think I mean that. Only, well, to see if – if there is anything else,' he finished lamely.

'Oh. I see. Well, I hope you find it, Blunt,' said Nathan, 'whatever it is.'

This time neither of them cared to break the silence and they rode their own ways until the sheik planted his standard and it was time for them to crawl under their scraps of canvas again.

On the morning of the fifth day, when they were down to the last skin of water, the terrain began to change. The sand gave way to shale and small patches of vegetation began to appear. It was little more than withered scrub but it encouraged them to hope for improvement and in the distance they could make out a range of foothills and some quite tall mountains beyond. Even better, the scouts came riding in with the report of a watering hole little more than a few miles distant.

This was when they had to be most on their guard, however, for it was a notorious haunt of robbers, Spiridion warned, and they mounted their ponies and rode with their guns at the ready. Happily, there were no robbers, none at least of the bandit order. Instead, there was a small garrison of Janissaries under a *cavus basi* – a kind of sergeant, said Spiridion – who charged 'protection money' of two piastres a camel. But this was normal practice apparently, throughout the Ottoman Empire – a bit like prize money in the service of King George – and they were able to draw water from a small well, enough for themselves and their animals, though the foreigners had to pay another fee to fill the skins they had brought for their horses.

They rode on more cheerfully, for the country was much less arid and there were small hills on either side, some of a dark-hued stone, others resembling chalk cliffs which reminded Nathan of the Seven Sisters in Sussex, though what little grass there was remained parched and withered. However, there were a great many holes in the ground, rather like rabbit burrows – so much so that they had to proceed with great caution for fear of the horses stepping into them and breaking a leg. They were mostly made by lizards, Spiridion informed him, or hares, which had assumed the practice in this part of the world of burrowing into the earth like their lesser brethren, the rabbits. Nathan suspected this was one of his tall stories, but, sure enough, as they rode on he was astonished to see several creatures, very alike to hares, watching from a slight distance with their ears up. He was so moved by this – and by sentimental memories of his boyhood on the Sussex Downs – that he rode off a little way and shot at one with his carbine. Rather to his surprise, and doubtless the hare's, he hit it. The rest took instant refuge in their burrows, but as they rode on, over the course of the morning, Nathan shot three more, and Tully and Spiridion one each.

'We will have a feast,' Nathan exulted as he and Tully rode out to pick up the sixth. 'Jugged hare was always one of my favourite dishes in Sussex. It was a regular treat in autumn.'

'I was wondering if perhaps you should not make a present of them to the sheik,' Tully proposed.

Nathan regarded him with concern. But it was probably a good idea. Tully had an instinct about such things – it was one of the qualities that made him such a good officer. The sheik's remoteness was beginning to bother them; the two groups, though they had been travelling together for some time, had no form of contact. They even travelled slightly apart – the foreigners in a bunch on their horses, and the sheik and his escort twenty or thirty yards ahead – and the rest, after a similar gap, behind. Spiridion said this was because horses and camels did not like the smell of each other, but Nathan thought there might be other reasons beside. Reasons of religion and culture, the long years of enmity between Christians and Muslims, their sense of *otherness*.

Five times a day at a signal from the sheik, the expedition halted for a few minutes for the Muslims to say their prayers. Nathan's party always dismounted respectfully on these occasions and preserved a considerate silence. But it underlined the difference between the two groups. And when they made camp, they slept and ate apart. It made Nathan uneasy. He would have liked to establish more of a rapport, if only to ensure that if they did encounter robbers, or any other enemy, he could rely upon their support.

But he was not sure if he wanted to sacrifice his dinner to achieve it.

'I suppose we could give him three,' he said.

It had the desired effect. Shortly after midday, Spiridion appeared in the mouth of Nathan's tent and reported that the sheik had invited them all to join him for dinner.

'Excellent.' Nathan beamed. 'Tell him we would be honoured. And give him the other three. But make sure he knows how to cook them. I suppose it is too much to ask him to jug them, but if he is to spit them over the fire they should be turned and basted every few minutes – ideally with a little wine poured over . . .'

'I think perhaps we should leave the cooking to him,' Spiridion replied firmly.

'You are probably right,' Nathan acknowledged. But after a moment's consideration, he remarked that whenever they were roasted, rather than jugged, his father's cook had always wrapped them in bacon to preserve the juices and served them with a sprig of parsley.

Spiridion did not trouble to respond.

They usually ate at four, just before setting off again – much later than the practice at sea – and by two o'clock, Nathan was invariably ravenous. The smell of roast hare drifting across the encampment made it far worse.

'I suppose we should not bring wine,' he said to Spiridion, hopeful of being contradicted, 'as they are Muslims.'

'It is probably better not,' Spiridion advised.

'And are we to dress for dinner? I dread the thought of wearing a uniform in this heat.'

'I think you will probably be excused the uniform, provided you wear a clean shirt and wash your hands,' said Spiridion.

A little before the appointed hour, an attendant arrived to tell them that dinner would shortly be served and they duly presented themselves at the sheik's tent, as clean and spruce as circumstances allowed. There was a carpet spread upon the ground for the food and a number of cushions for them to sit upon. Nathan was invited to sit on the sheik's right side and Spiridion on his left. The others placed themselves wherever there was an available space, along with four of the sheik's followers who were also present at the feast. There were some appetisers to start with, none of which met with Nathan's unmitigated approval, and then the main course was delivered, all six on a large platter, heads and all, ungarnished with either bacon or parsley. Nathan was courteously invited to take the first helping. Denied any means of carving, he wrenched off a piece of leg and watched with an unhappy smile as the company dismembered the creatures with their bare hands. The only accompaniment was a large bowl of rice which everyone was expected to share, also using their hands.

The conversation was no better. Nathan tried, but was inhibited by the need for Spiridion to translate and the fear of asking any questions which might be construed as offensive. The sheik appeared to have no interest in the war between the English and the French, and Nathan resorted to the subject of husbandry, asking him a great many questions about the rearing of camels and supplying a good deal of information, which he had not thought he possessed, about the breeding of sheep on the South Downs. It was possibly as interesting as a conversation between two farmers on market day in Lewes, relayed via an interpreter. He attempted to engage him on the subject of brigands, which was uppermost in his mind, but the replies were short and obscure. In the end, he let Spiridion gabble on without him while he gnawed silently at a bone.

When they left, with expressions of mutual esteem and relief, Nathan asked Spiridion if he thought it had been worthwhile.

Spiridion shrugged. 'I suppose it did no harm,' he conceded.

'I was surprised he was not more interested in the war,' Nathan remarked.

'Why should he be?' Spiridion demanded. 'What is it to him?'

'Well, with Bonaparte in Egypt – and Egypt being a part of the empire . . .'

'Egypt might as well be the far side of the moon as far as he is concerned. And I doubt he could give a toss for the empire.'

'I see. So. I take it he is not a Turk.'

'Never say it.'

'A Bedouin?'

'Or that.' Spiridion shuddered. 'You know what Bedouin means in Arabic?'

Nathan did not.

'It is from the word *badiyah* meaning those in the desert. Nomads, tramps, like your Irish tinkers. The sheik holds them in contempt.'

'So what is he, then? He and his tribe?'

'Well, it is difficult to say. They are Nizari, but I am never sure if that is a tribe or a religion or both. They are from the Jabal Amariye, which is the mountain range south of Aleppo. The sheik himself claims to be a direct descendant of Rashid ad-Din Sinan, the Old Man of the Mountain.'

He said this as though it should mean something to Nathan. It did not.

'He was the leader of the Hashishin,' Spiridion informed him, 'who you probably know as the Assassins.' There being no indication that this was the case, he continued: 'They were a professional association of zealots who hired themselves to the highest bidder and were expert at the various forms of murder. The most feared were based on the Nizari stronghold of al Masyaf at the time of the Crusades. I had no idea they were still in the region, but apparently they are.'

'You are quite serious?'

Spiridion looked surprised. 'Why would I not be?'

'And still – practising, as it were?'

'I really have no idea. I doubt it, but then, Arabs are very big on tradition. I think I mentioned to you that the art of silent murder was very much a speciality in these parts.'

'And these are the people to whom we have entrusted our lives and our mission?'

'Nathan, just because they are of the same race does not mean they are of the same inclination – or occupation.

The English are noted for their dedication to the hunt, but you would not say that all Englishmen were fox hunters, would you?'

'Only because they do not possess the means or the mount. But given the opportunity of killing an animal for sport they will happily oblige you – be it bull, bear, or badger. I have no doubt that when you were in Billingsgate, for instance, most of your associates kept a terrier and devoted a large part of their leisure time to the killing of rats.'

Spiridion had spent a part of his youth in this part of London, about his father's business. 'Well,' he said, 'if they were going to kill us, why have they not done so already? They have had plenty of opportunities, from the moment we left Aleppo.'

'Perhaps there is some ritual involved,' suggested Nathan. 'Perhaps they are waiting for the right time and place. Or they have made a rendezvous with others of their kind.'

They mounted their horses and took their places behind the sheik for the next stage of their journey. And a little before midnight, with a small wind whipping up dust devils, they came to an ancient walled city with a gatehouse and a great tower rising up out of the plain. It was entirely in darkness and as they came closer, it became apparent that it had long been abandoned and was mostly in ruins.

They rode in through the gatehouse and the sheik's standard was planted in the centre of a compound surrounded by the ruined facades, their vacant windows like empty eye sockets in a skull. It had an eerie, haunted quality: like a city of lost souls.

'What is this place?' Nathan asked Spiridion in a hushed voice as they began to unload the camels.

'I have no idea,' replied the Greek. 'It looks like one of the ancient cities of Byzantium.' His voice was almost as hushed as Nathan's, for the Byzantium Empire had been largely run by Greeks and was part of his own heritage. He enquired among their escort and returned with the news that he had been right – it was the city of Taiba, once part of the Byzantium Empire but destroyed in one of its many wars against Arabs and Turks. Apparently, there had been such slaughter here that the belief had formed that the place was cursed or haunted, or both, and no one had ever cared to return.

Nathan nodded, looking around the hollow skulls as if he had known this already.

'There used to be a well here, with fresh spring water, but it dried up years ago,' Spiridion informed him. 'But it is still the place where the Silk Road divides, one branch going east to Baghdad and the other south through Bassara.' He might not have been able to read Nathan's expression in the darkness but he guessed what he was thinking and told him to think again. 'The southern branch crosses the Great Desert and we could never make it on horseback,' he said. 'But we have enough water for the night and we will reach the Euphrates Valley by mid-morning. It will be plain sailing from then on,' he declared confidently.

Nathan frowned. In Nathan's opinion there was no such thing as plain sailing. To even speak the words was an invitation to disaster.

They settled down for the night in the open space between the buildings – for there were scorpions and other creatures among the ruins, Spiridion reported. Nathan slept fitfully, waking frequently and lying in the darkness staring at those empty eye sockets staring back. The walls should have made him feel more secure, but there was something ominous about the place, something threatening, and he wished they had camped as usual in the open.

But perversely, at dawn, instead of leaving as fast as they could, he and Tully were sufficiently curious to explore the tall, square tower beside the gatehouse, which rose seventy or eighty feet above the city walls. It had once been the tower of a Byzantine church, Spiridion reckoned, and had then been turned into a mosque. There were few signs of either religion now, but the building clearly had value as a watchtower – there was a stone staircase which had withstood the ravages of time, and they decided to climb to the top, or at least as far as it would allow, for it would give them as good a view as any mainmast over the surrounding area, and they thought they might be able to see the Euphrates, even, far to the east.

They did not see the Euphrates or any other river. What they did see was a large dust cloud advancing on them from the north at a distance of about two or three miles. At first they thought it was a sandstorm, like the *khamsin*, but it was too small, too confined for that. As it came closer, among the swirling cloud, they saw the shapes of men and camels. A large number of them, riding hard, and carrying guns.

Chapter Eight

The Citadel of Ghosts

'They are brigands,' Spiridion confirmed, after his brief conference with the sheik, 'but apparently they do not want our money.'

Before his audience could take any satisfaction from this astonishing claim, he added tersely: 'They want us.'

This was the message they had apparently conveyed to him by the sheik's son, who had been sent out to treat with their adversaries at the camp they had made in the desert, at a distance of about half a mile.

'Us alone?' Nathan enquired, 'or the whole caboodle?'

'Us alone,' Spiridion informed him. 'The *ferengee*. The foreigners.'

'Alive or dead?' enquired Tully.

'This was not specified. Either way it would not be to our advantage.'

'And do we know why?' Nathan asked him.

'To be foreign, I suspect, is sufficient reason, but as they normally prefer to exact tribute, we must assume the French have a hand in it.'

'And tribute would not help?'

'No. The sheik suspects they have been paid a substantial sum already and will be paid more when they provide evidence that their mission has been accomplished.'

'So what are we to do?'

'We will have to fight them, of course,' Spiridion replied, 'unless you propose to surrender.'

'How many of them are there?'

'About two hundred, according to the estimate of the sheik's son. Armed mainly with muskets.'

'Well, there are near forty of us, counting the servants,' Nathan pointed out, 'and I would rather be defending the citadel than attacking it, even in its present condition. You seem doubtful,' he added, for Spiridion's expression was not encouraging.

'The sheik points out that we have very little water,' he explained, 'while the brigands appear to have plenty. They would only have to wait a day or two and we would have to give ourselves up, or cut our own throats and save them the trouble.'

'So what does His Eminence suggest?' put in Tully, 'that we give ourselves up now?'

'No. He says we should defend ourselves to the best of our ability, while he and his men ride for help.'

'Be damned to that,' Nathan cried indignantly. 'We paid him to provide us with an escort, not to make off at the first hint of trouble. We even shared our rabbits with him.'

'Hares,' Spiridion corrected him. 'I put that to him – if a little more tactfully. But he insists it is the only chance of saving our lives.'

'And you believe him?'

'I am not normally of a trusting nature, but on this occasion I think we have no alternative.'

'So we must fend for ourselves,' said Tully, already looking about him to see how this might best be achieved.

The watchtower was clearly the most defensible position available to them. It had stout stone walls, with slots for firing from, four storeys, and a single means of access, the only drawback being the absence of a door. To remedy this deficiency, the sheik supplied them with a number of woolsacks – part of the cargo he was carrying to Baghdad – which his men helped to pile up in the doorway, leaving two gaps to fire through. Nathan derived some small comfort from the discovery that the wool came from England. It was possible even that it originated in his native county, though it would have been too much of a coincidence if it had been supplied from his father's sheep.

The sheik also left them most of the water which, carefully conserved, might last two or three days – always assuming they lived that long – and they retained one of the horses – Nathan having resolved that if all seemed lost, one of them should attempt to break out with Nelson's precious despatches.

The one thing they were not short of was weapons. They had the dozen muskets supplied them by the armourer aboard the *Vanguard*, with twice as many pistols, a wicked array of pikes, swords, daggers and tomahawks, half a dozen grenades – and, of course, the two Nock guns.

Nathan gave one of these to Mr Banjo and kept the other for himself, though he was apprehensive at the prospect of using it, given its reputation for breaking shoulders. 'We will guard the doorway,' he assured him. There being no other firing points on the ground floor, the others were positioned at the various loopholes on the spiral stair, each supplied with three muskets and six pistols, all primed and loaded. Then they settled down to wait.

As the day advanced, the heat grew ever more intense. The pony, tethered in a corner of the ground floor, gave voice to her distress. They gave her some water and took a little for themselves. No one was hungry, not even Nathan, but as the afternoon wore on they ate some dates and a little flatbread, moistened in water, just to keep their strength up.

It was almost dusk when the attack came. Nathan was sitting on the stair with Tully, on each side of the loophole. The sun had dropped below the buildings of the citadel, and they were watching the shadows lengthening across the courtyard when there was a sound not unlike the cry of the muezzin. A moment later, without any further warning, a great horde of men came charging through the gateway, yelling their savage battle cries.

Tully snatched up his musket while Nathan leapt down the spiral stairway to stand beside George Banjo at the barricade. Banjo was there already and as Nathan reached his side he discharged all seven barrels. The report was deafening. Even Banjo, massive as he was, reeled back with the force of the recoil. The mare went mad with fear, rearing and kicking in her makeshift stall. Nathan applied his eye to the gap in the barricade. The blast had cut a swathe through the ranks of charging men, and the attack appeared to have come to a halt. There were no more than five or six men down, out of at least ten times that number, but the fact that the defenders possessed such a weapon was clearly discouraging. Instead of pressing on with their attack, they were hanging back and firing towards the tower with their muskets. But Nathan's companions were keeping up a steady rate of fire from the loopholes, and with brutal effect. Before long, there were at least a dozen corpses stretched upon the ground, and the rate of fire clearly gave an impression that there were far more than five men in the tower.

Nathan could no longer delay his own contribution. He thrust the Nock gun through the gap provided for him, brought the stock into his shoulder, winced in expectation, and pressed the trigger. He had taken the precaution of padding out his shoulder with wool, but it still felt as if he had been kicked by a mule. He was hurled flat on his back, shocked and deafened by the report, the gun still in his hands and the interior of the tower filled with black smoke and the frantic screams of the mare. Nathan felt his numbed shoulder, but nothing seemed to be broken or dislocated, and he picked himself up and rejoined Mr Banjo at the barricade, clawing a pistol from his belt. But there was no need of it. The attackers were in full flight, leaving a score of dead and wounded lying on the bloodied stones of the gateway.

They reloaded the guns, but there was no further attack. They calmed the poor animal, and gave it some water, then drank sparingly themselves. Night fell. Nathan climbed up to Tully's level on the stair and peered out through the loophole. The citadel was in darkness. He could see very little, but he could hear the moans and groans of the wounded. Then, as it grew darker, he saw shadowy figures moving stealthily among them. He let them be – and after a while, the cries ceased.

The moon rose, and the stars came out. The only sound they heard now was the distant howling of jackals from across the desert.

They ate some more dates and bread, and made beds for themselves on the spare woolsacks left by their escort. Nathan took the first watch with Blunt, climbing the tower to the loophole nearest the top, which gave him a view over the city walls and across the surrounding desert. He could see the flickering fires of the brigand camp to the east, but no other lights. Just a great expanse of blackness stretching for many miles in every direction. He could hear the jackals again, but closer now. Probably in the city itself, smelling death. He had no expectation of the sheik returning, or of any outside help. Nor did he have much hope of surviving. The only reason the brigands had not pressed home the attack was because they did not have to. All they had to do was wait; the sun would do the rest.

Death inevitably occupied much of his thoughts during the night. He felt its presence, like a black, hooded figure on the stair. As if it had followed him across the desert, for all his life, in fact, and found him at last. Or else had been waiting for him here. A grim recruiting officer for the army of ghosts that roamed the haunted citadel.

He saw plenty of ghosts that night. Ghosts of men he had sent to their deaths in far-off places, in the chops of the Channel and among the islands of the Caribbean, in all those distant seas, sliding the dead into their watery grave with a few cold words of comfort from the Book of Common Prayer. Young boys of eleven or twelve, and hardened old seadogs. And the others, who would soon join them: Spiridion and Banjo, Blunt and Tully. His companions through all eternity. *Mea culpa*, as the Papists rebuked themselves, *mea maxima culpa.* He felt most guilty for Tully, who had followed him through thick and thin across three continents, sharing his victories and his defeats, only to be led here, to die among the old ruins and the jackals and the scorpions.

It was barely six years ago since they had first met, on the old *Nereus*, chasing smugglers in the English Channel. Tully was a Channel Islander, the son of a fisherman from Guernsey, but his mother had been a seigneur's daughter who had fallen in love beneath her station and had been cast out for it. She had died in childbirth, and the family had taken the boy in and brought him up as a gentleman. But when he was of an age to choose, he had gone back to the life his father led, fishing and smuggling, until he was taken by a King's ship and given the choice of transportation or serving His Majesty. He was a master's mate when Nathan met him, for he had a talent for maths and navigation, and what with that and the manners of a gentleman, he had advanced rapidly in his new profession.

Despite the differences in their rank, Nathan had never felt so close to anyone in his life. No one of the same sex and age, at least. Perhaps it was because they were both outsiders. Though Nathan was the son of an admiral and the heiress of a shipping dynasty, he had been born in New

York, and his mother, for all her family wealth, was as much a rebel and a reprobate as any smuggler or runaway.

And now they would die together.

He wondered if anyone would find their bodies. He doubted it. The jackals would have them. Though he supposed the brigands might pack them up and cart them off – or their heads at least – to show to their French paymasters to claim the rest of their reward, and the French might give them a half-decent burial; they might even notify Mr Abbott in Aleppo so that he could send news of their demise to England.

Nathan felt a sudden vicarious grief for the grief of his parents, for he knew they both loved him, and he loved them. For all the quarrels between them. His mother and father had lived apart for many years now, and it had never particularly bothered him, but the last time he was home in Sussex, his father had told him he planned to obtain a divorce and marry the daughter of one of his neighbours. Nathan knew the girl well – rather too well, in fact. Her name was Frances Wyndham and she was the natural daughter of Lord Egremont, one of the biggest landowners in the county. A boisterous girl, rather too horsy to be considered handsome, but with a fine seat and an outstanding bosom. Once, while the rest of the hunt was otherwise engaged, she and Nathan had enjoyed what was described in hunting terms as a 'tussle' in Windover Wood. There had never been much more to it than that, but you did not really want your father marrying a woman your own age, particularly not when you had enjoyed a tussle with her in Windover Wood. Besides, there was his mother to be considered. Divorce was always a messy business, much reported in the press. All their dirty linen aired in public, and, God knew, there was enough of it: his mother had enjoyed a host of liaisons over the years and kept a number of young men as pets, though she called them her protégés. All in all, they were a disreputable couple. Still, he would have liked to have written to them before he died. Not that he had much to say to them, except to say how much he loved them.

And to ask them to look after Sara and her boy.

That was the other business he would regret – not having settled the business with Sara. Sara de la Tour d'Auvergne, the woman he should have married.

They had met in Paris, when he was on a confidential mission for William Pitt in the first year of the war. She had married into one of the noblest families in France, but she kept that quiet, or as quiet as she could, for it was a time when even a minor title could mean a ride to the guillotine. Her husband, a much older man, had died in exile with the French court in Koblenz, and when Nathan met her, she was living quietly in Paris with her young son, Alex. She used her maiden name of Seton, which was sufficiently obscure to evade the attentions of the authorities, though her father had been a noble of the sword, a Scottish soldier in the service of the King of France.

Sara. Nathan gazed out over the desert, his head filled with memories of another time and another place. Paris at the time of the Terror. The tumbrels rolling down the rue d'Honoré. The studio of Jean-Baptiste Regnault in the same street where Sara had trained as an artist. The house in the rue Jacob where they had first made love.

And now she was in England, living with William

Godwin, the widower of her best friend Mary Wollstonecraft, who had died in childbirth.

Nathan did not know if they were living as man and wife, or if she was his housekeeper, looking after Mary's child. It hardly seemed to matter now; she was so far out of his reach. But he would have liked to have written to her, too. Or to turn up at her door and feel her arms about his neck, her lips pressed upon his, and her body, the lovely, soft warmth of her – all the old clichés. And that other old cliché, that dark, hooded figure on the stair, smiling and waiting, as patient as only Death can be.

Dawn came as it had at Aleppo, a creeping back of the darkness into the cracks, like the scorpions and the other creatures of the night. The yellow fingers creeping across the earthen floors, as if taking the measure of the day, and then the sun itself, heaving its old, fierce face over the walls to take a look. And the sky a bright mockery of hope.

The brigands had taken up their positions during the night, working their way into the ruins, and they kept up a spasmodic fire through the long, broiling day. It was impossible to do more than sneak the occasional, brief glance through the loopholes or the gap in the barricade. But the fire from the guns was nothing to the fire in the heavens. It was probably cooler in the tower than it was outside, but it was hot enough. Nathan felt as if the life was draining from him, that he was in his tomb already. And perhaps he was.

At night, he thought, they would make a gap in the barricade and he would send Tully off on the pony. And if he refused to go, as well he might, he would send Blunt. He was the lightest of them by far and a good rider, even with his sprained wrist. If they left it any longer, the beast would be past running. He doubted if they would make it, but he had to try, though a part of him thought, why bother? The French would either march on India or they would not. It was Bonaparte's fate that would determine it, not his. And perhaps even Bonaparte was as much a plaything of the gods.

He did not expect another attack. Not in daylight, at least. But about halfway through the afternoon, the rate of firing suddenly increased. At least a hundred men must have been shooting at them from the surrounding buildings. Bullets were smashing into the stones and through the loopholes, screaming off the walls. They were even coming in through the gaps in the woolsacks, forcing Nathan and Tully to crouch down with their Nock guns and hope the men above would be able to give them warning of an attack. But no warning was given. The first Nathan knew of it was when a musket barrel was thrust through the gap above his head and fired into the interior. He grabbed a hold of it and wrenched it away. Banjo was similarly employed, roaring in impotent fury at the attackers. Hands were pulling away at the sacks. The barricade was being dismantled before their eyes.

'Up the stairs,' yelled Nathan, and they fell back, taking their guns with them.

Tully was on his way down, the others close behind.

'They are too close to the walls to fire on them,' said Tully. 'And we have used all the grenades.'

They waited there, all five of them, with their guns levelled as the gap widened. Bright spears of sunlight pierced the gloom of the tower. The mare screamed and plunged in her makeshift stall.

'One volley,' Nathan said, 'and then a charge.'

They might hold them off for quite a while on the stairs, but Nathan's fear was that they would light a fire and throw the woolsacks on. Better to die fighting, hand to hand, than choke to death on a black cloud of burning English wool.

But then the gap stopped widening. The hands disappeared. And there was gunfire. Even more gunfire than before.

Nathan peered through the loophole. The courtyard was empty, save for the dead and the dying. He ran up to the top of the tower and looked out over the desert.

The surviving brigands were in full retreat pursued by a small army of mounted men. There must have been at least 500 of them, on camels and on horses. And at their head, on his racing camel, was Rashid the Magnificent, his sword stretched out before him and his standard bearer at his side, with the great silk flag streaming in the wind.

'*There is but one God and Mohammed is His Prophet.*'

Part Two

The Malabar Patrol

Chapter Nine

The Good Little Bay

The brig came out of the dark skies to the west, running before the wind. There was a battle raging out to sea, but it was a battle of gods not of men: a distant flash of lightning, a rippling roll of thunder. The sky ahead was brighter, but it was a misty, eerie light, as of sunshine after rain. Off the larboard bow there was an island – Old Woman's Island, it was marked on the charts – with a lighthouse on a small promontory, and as the brig came up a little into the wind, more islands began to emerge from the haze: so many that they gave the impression of one great landmass of rolling hills, densely forested, but as if sculptured into the shape of birds and animals so that Nathan's first impression was of some exotic topiary in an English country garden. But no English garden could boast such foliage, such tropic display of palm and peepul and other trees for which he had no name – and among them such buildings – such turrets and towers with conical roofs, battlements, flags, blockhouses and palisades . . . They seemed to have arrived in fairyland, or to have been transported back into the medieval past. For a moment, Nathan thought of Venice, that misty, magical city in its muddy lagoon, but a more exotic Venice, a Venice in the jungle, set about with palm trees and creepers, garlanded with jacaranda and oleander and laburnum. Then the brig rounded a small headland and a different forest appeared – a forest of masts and yards, bare poles, square and triangular sails, so many they bewildered the eye, and, beyond them, a more familiar waterfront – severe, square-jawed, almost brutal – a massive fort, bristling with guns, a colossal custom's house and a long line of solid, stone warehouses – a waterfront that had eschewed the baroque for the businesslike, a city of trade, like Venice, but a city of the future, not the past. Bombay. Journey's end.

It was the tenth day of October, sixty-one days since he had left Abukir.

Other cities appeared through the mist of his memory. Scanderoon and Aleppo, and Baghdad, where the crowds had cheered them as they rode through the streets, hailing them as victors over the French, the common enemy who had dared violate the sanctity of their fellow Mohammedans in Egypt; and where the pasha had presented Nathan with a handsome pelisse and, more practically, a boat to take them down the Tigris to Bassara.

And Bassara itself, on the Persian Gulf, a more melancholy stopover, where he had taken leave of Spiridion Foresti and George Banjo, for Spiridion was heading back to Egypt on business of his own, and doubtless of Nelson's. He would not say which route he was taking, but Nathan suspected it was by way of Suez. Spiridion's last words to him had been: 'Look out for yourself – and look out for Caterina.'

The brig began her salute and a string of signal flags broke from the halyard to inform the port authorities that she was carrying despatches for the governor and had not a minute to waste on their petty constraints; the hands were already trimming her yards for the last stage of her journey across the harbour entrance and up the seaway to Parel Island and Government House.

'The good little bay,' said a voice at Nathan's ear and he turned to see the ship's captain – Captain Hale – genial and relaxed for once, his duty almost done. He had been taut as a spring cable on the voyage from Bassara, rarely off the deck night and day, and, even as they entered the gulf, Nathan had seen him glaring at the clouds massing at their stern, as if they would deny him his goal even at the last. Nathan smiled and nodded, though he was surprised at the sentiment, for Hale was a lugubrious soul at the best of times, and his first lieutenant a veritable Jonah. Hale and Hearty, Tully called them, with sardonic humour. But the good little bay was not an expression of personal attachment.

'That is what the Portuguese called it,' the captain continued. '*Bom bain.* The English had another name for it, less gracious: "that hole of a place where the Portuguese come to mend their ships". Not such a hole now, though, eh?'

Nathan looked across the water towards the crowded waterfront. What little knowledge he had of Bombay had been picked up from a book that had been lent him by one of his fellow passengers, an Anglican curate returning to India after a year's furlough back in England. It had been a fishing village when the Portuguese first came here, over two centuries ago. They had built a factory and a fort, even a shipyard, but their principle occupation was the building of churches – churches and monasteries, and even a cathedral. The good little bay. But the King of Portugal had so little regard for their devotions that he gave the place to Charles II of England as a dowry for his daughter, Catherine of Braganza – and the Merry Monarch thought so little of this offering, he promptly rented it to the East India Company for ten pounds a year.

The return on that meagre investment would have bought all the kings and princes in Europe.

'There you go,' said Hale, handing Nathan his glass. 'Up on the knoll beyond the quay.'

Government House had been a Franciscan monastery when the Portuguese owned the islands, but to Nathan it looked more like a Mughal palace, with its ornate balconies and arched windows, the palm trees bowing gently in the breeze and the Union Jack waving a lazy greeting from the flagstaff on the lawn.

They took the launch ashore, Nathan clutching the bag with his precious despatches and the chest full of silver coins at his feet. He thought it would make a good impression to hand it over to the governor for safekeeping: if he took it as a bribe, then so be it – Nathan had no objections to a bribe in a good cause. He was a long way from home; he needed all the help he could get.

He had given little thought to the problems he might

encounter at the end of his voyage, but now he was here the full weight of his office descended on him – not so much fear of the French as a renewed apprehension of his own side. There were some who might be disposed to resent the instructions of a British admiral in a faraway place, and the imposition of a man whose only knowledge of the place came from a book he had borrowed from a fellow traveller. Jonathan Duncan, thirty-fourth Governor of Bombay, might well be among them.

'Odd fish,' Hale had said. 'Not everyone likes him. But he knows India, I'll say that for him. Been here a lot longer than most. If he takes to you, you will be up and running. If he doesn't . . .'

He had left the sentence unfinished, but the implication was obvious. Nathan could make his bow, deliver his despatches, and take the next ship home by way of the Cape.

A part of his mind was still attached to the journey he had just made. It was filled with golden images of the Tigris: the women washing their clothes at the side of the river, the men in the fields, the perpetual motion of the earthen jars on the waterwheels. And crossing the desert, his eyes filled with sand and sun, his nose with the smell of the camels, his ears with their raucous, groaning bellow. He could hear it now, and the curses of their attendants, so that it was as if he was still there, making camp for the night. Save that he was sitting in a barge with the company ensign at the stern, among the sounds and the smells of the sea, the slapping of the wavelets on the hull, the cries of the gulls. And there was something very English about the little harbour below Government House with its jetty and cottages, even something that looked very like a tavern, and a small fort on the headland with another Union flag. There was even a church – God and Mammon, united in awesome majesty. It felt as if all the time he had been moving forward, the earth had been moving back – in time and in space – and suddenly he had been deposited in a small fishing village in Sussex, before the war.

Then, as if his mind and his ear had been searching for it, he heard the tinkling sounds of a harpsichord, and a woman's voice raised in song. He could not hear the words clearly – it might even have been another trick of his imagination, or his memory – but the lyrics echoed in his head:

I wish I were a scholar
And could handle the pen
I would write to my lover
And to all roving men
I would tell them of the grief and woe
That attend upon their lies
I would wish them have pity
On the flower when it dies

It was as if someone had reached out and stabbed him; he could hardly breathe, so strong was the sense of melancholy, and loneliness and desolation he felt.

'You are always looking at the stars, my love. You forget the flowers at your feet.'

Who had said that to him? It was even sadder that he could not remember.

The launch had muscled into a small space among the vessels on the quayside and made fast. Hale had already stepped onto the wooden jetty and was looking up at him questioningly. Nathan took a tighter grip on his bag, filled with a horror of dropping it overboard at the last minute and watching helplessly as everything it contained, his own future with it, sank to the bottom of the harbour, and stepped across the narrow gap and followed the captain ashore.

Chapter Ten

The Tiger and the Goat

His Excellency the Governor of Bombay stood in the window of his study and looked out across the neat lawns of Government House towards the black storm clouds on the distant horizon.

The monsoon should have been over by now, and its lingering presence seemed ill-omened, a sign of heavenly disfavour. Even as he looked a flash of lightning lanced out from the centre of the storm – as sudden and venomous as a striking cobra – and he flinched, as if he had been singled out personally for the retribution of the gods.

He grunted impatiently at his own foolishness. The church bells were still ringing in celebration of the great victory that had been won 2,000 miles to the west. If the gods were not celebrating with them, then be damned to the gods.

'You arrived just in time,' he said, still gazing out to sea. 'It seems the Elephanta still has one last kick left in her.'

'The Elephanta?'

'You have not heard of the Elephanta?' Now he turned from the window and regarded the figure in the easy chair at the far end of the room. His tone was brusque, bordering on rude. 'Name of the wind. Comes with the south-west monsoon. Been the death of more than one ship, even in Bombay harbour. Hits you at sea, you'd soon know about it.'

He sat at his desk and laid his hands on each side of the despatch that had been delivered to him, drumming his fingers on the smooth, polished surface of the wood: solid Indian teak intended for the garboard strakes of a gun-brig and presented to him by the shipbuilders of Surat in appreciation of his continuing patronage. His enemies would call it a bribe. Be damned to them, too.

> *It has been in my power to take eleven sail of the line, and two frigates; in short, only two sail of the line and two frigates have escaped me.*

Yes. The fingers continued their brisk tattoo, beating to quarters. It had been a great victory. And even if it had not been so great, even if the numbers had been reversed, with just two sail of the line taken and the rest escaped, the governor would still have ordered the church bells to be rung, for, God only knew, they needed something to cheer about; some good news from home to boost the morale of his people – and remind his enemies who they were dealing with. He had already had the letter copied by his clerks for despatch to the governor-general in Calcutta, and he would make damned sure that bloody usurper in Seringapatam heard of it too, even if he could not send it to him by courier. Not if he did not want the courier fed to his tigers.

And yet . . . He set his spectacles on his long nose, the better to read that other paragraph, the one that concerned him personally:

> *From all the inquiries which I have been able to make, I cannot learn that any French Vessels are at Suez, to carry any part of this army to India. Yet I know that Bombay, if they can get there, is their prime objective.*

'If they can get here,' he repeated dryly. He shot his visitor a look from under his shaggy brows. 'Think you can stop them?'

'Well, I will do what I can. I am at your command.'

The governor regarded him over the top of his spectacles. He was a dark-looking cove, almost as dark as a native. You might have taken him for one if it had not been for the uniform. Dark as an Arab. All that gallivanting across the desert, the governor supposed, all that mucking about in a sambuk on the Tigris. But it did not look as if it had been too tiring a journey. In fact, he looked as if he had just strolled in off the Bombay Island ferry to pass the time of day. But then he was young – too damned young, in the governor's opinion. Give him a month or two in this fever swamp – that would age him, that would take the shine off him. Turn him into as much of a walking corpse as the rest of them.

Jonathan Duncan had been out in India for twenty-six years and he knew it showed. He was forty-two and looked and moved like an old man, even by the standards of Bombay where men could age ten years in an evening – and be dead by morning. Old Duncan, they called him, 'the Guvnor', if they had a fondness for him, 'the Old Goat', if they did not, and most did not. He knew what they said about him.

Spends all day shuffling around Government House in his slippers and dressing gown, with his hair hanging down to his shoulders, like a miser in a counting house.

That was the commander of the garrison, in his journal, a few days before the fever took him and his effects were delivered to the man he despised. He had even had the nerve to write to the company directors in London to make a formal complaint. *Shows no respect for the dignity of his office*, he had written.

Much good it had done him. Much good it would do any of them. Duncan did his job and he did it well. The directors weren't complaining.

He had come out to India as a boy of sixteen, back in 1772. Just after Clive had won Bengal for the British and made the Honourable Company the greatest power in the land. Duncan's role in this triumph was less spectacular. He had been a lowly clerk, the lowest of the low, grafting away in the company's service for fifteen years – until Cornwallis made him supervisor in Benares and he showed what he could do.

And now he was Governor of Bombay.

He had been in the post for three years now. Longer than the average lifespan in a place like Bombay. For a

European, that is. Two monsoons and you're dead, people said. If the climate didn't carry you off, the cholera would, or the typhus or any one of a dozen other diseases endemic to the place. But it was not going to happen to him. It might age him, it might turn his skin yellow and make his hair drop out, but it was not going to kill him; he had too much to do.

He was presently engaged in building a wall to hold back the sea. Then he was going to drain the land and turn seven islands into one, with a causeway linking it to the mainland. The Duncan Causeway. Bombay was going to be the greatest city in Asia one day, maybe the world. He might not live to see it, but he was damned if he was going to let some jumped-up tart of a French general put him off his stride, before he had barely started.

'Trouble is, now you've sunk his fleet, he's got nowhere to go,' he grumbled. 'Can't go back. Might as well go forward.'

'Sir?'

'This – Bonaparte.' He glanced again at the admiral's letter. 'Italian, ain't he? They run out of generals of their own?'

'He is from Corsica,' the newcomer drawled. 'You have not heard of him?'

'Of course I have heard of him,' the governor snapped. He might play the fool all he liked, he was damned if he was going to be taken for one. 'We may be damned colonials but we can read despatches. We even have newspapers. I read all about his romp through Italy. Just didn't expect him to come knocking at my door.'

'Well, I hope we may be able to prevent that.'

Duncan regarded the speaker thoughtfully. Yes, I heard you the first time, he thought. He knew what was on the fellow's mind. He adjusted his spectacles on his nose and studied the last paragraph – the postscript – the sting in the tale.

> *The officer who carries this despatch to you possesses my instruction, subject to your approval, to assume command of those of His Majesty's naval forces that are available to him in order to prevent the despatch of French troops and materiel to India. I recommend him to you unreservedly as an officer of great merit and distinction in whom you may place the utmost reliance should you wish to place your own naval resources at his disposal.*

The governor was not sure he liked the sound of that. He was not sure he liked it at all.

Possesses my instruction . . . to assume command of those of His Majesty's naval forces that are available to him? What was that supposed to mean? His Majesty's forces in Bombay consisted of just one ship – the old *Pondicherry*, captured from the French in 1793 and on her last legs, by all accounts. She had just emerged from the shipyards at Surat after her latest surgery, having her knees mended, or something like that – the fourth or fifth time she'd been in the yard since they had taken her from the French. It would be far cheaper to scrap her, but she kept the flag flying, he supposed. The only other naval forces in the region were the company's own – the ships of the Bombay Marine. It was true that the directors had applied to the Admiralty to recommend a 'serving officer of distinction' to act as commodore, but this was just flannel, a diplomatic gesture to ensure the Admiralty's continuing support for the policies of the Honourable Company. The officers of the Bombay Marine were servants of the company. They were paid by the company and pensioned by the company and they swore an oath of loyalty to the company. And if they needed a commodore, the company would provide them with one. They were not at the beck and call of the Royal Navy, no matter what this Nelson fellow thought. Who the Devil did he think he was?

Well, the answer to that was plain enough. He was a British admiral. A *victorious* British admiral. A bloody hero. He had just won one of the greatest victories in the annals of the Royal Navy. The church bells would be ringing out for him all over the British Empire, never mind Bombay. If they had made Jervis an earl after the Battle of St Vincent, it was very likely that they would make this fellow a duke. King, Parliament, the whole country, would be singing his praises. What was the Governor of Bombay to a man like that? Jonathan Duncan? Who was Jonathan Duncan? He could hear them now, if he as much as raised a whimper of protest.

Even so. It was a damnable piece of impertinence. And he wasn't going to roll over for them. He owed it to the company to make a stand. He owed it to himself. He owed it to the officers and crews of the Bombay Marine. He was not going to subject them to a gibbering idiot who had never heard of the Elephanta. No matter how many admirals he had in his corner. And if he did, he was going to make it perfectly clear who was in charge here – and it wasn't Sir Horatio-in-the-Mouth-of-the-Nile, or even their lordships of the Admiralty.

'We have our own Bonaparte over here, you know,' he said. 'I wonder if you have ever heard of *him*?'

The fellow frowned a little, inclining his head in polite enquiry.

'Tipu the Tiger,' said Duncan. 'Mean anything to you?'

The frown cleared. 'The Sultan of Mysore.'

'Indeed. The Sultan of Mysore. So what do you know about him? Because he is a lot nearer to us than Bonaparte at the moment and a damn sight more dangerous.'

The fellow nodded. 'I am aware of the danger he poses. I confess I know little of his character or his power . . .'

'Well, let me endeavour to inform you before we go any further. Fatah Ali Tipu, to give him his proper name, Sultan of Mysore – we call him the Tiger, not on account of his military prowess, but because he has a passion for the brutes. Keeps them in cages in his palace and lets them wander around the palace when the mood takes him. Even got a mechanical one that eats a British soldier. No, I am quite serious. It's an organ. Play a tune while it's doing it, by all accounts.'

'A *live* British soldier?'

'No. Good God, man. A *wooden* soldier. Tiger eats it while it's playing. Tiger growls, soldier screams. No, he's got real tigers for eating people. So they tell me. Feeds his prisoners to them. Oh he's a charmer, no mistake. His father was Hyder Ali. Never heard of him? Well, never mind, we've only fought two wars against him. He was an army officer but the old rajah made him commander-in-chief, which was more than a little foolish of him, because

Hyder Bloody Ali locked him up and took the crown himself. Though, of course, being a Musselman, he called himself Sultan. Brought in the French to train his army for him and set about making war on his neighbours. When he died, his son took over – this is Tipu. We've only fought one war against him – so far. Which we won. Trouble is we didn't kill him. And you know what they say about a wounded tiger?' He doubted if the fellow did, but he could probably guess.

'So when you say, he is your own Bonaparte . . .'

'Well, I confess I was thinking more of his "bombast" – as your admiral puts it. Not so clever in the military line. But with a bit of help from the French he could surprise us all. In a year's time he could be sitting where I am now.'

'And he thinks he can trust them? The French, I mean.'

The governor eyed him shrewdly. 'Good question. I wonder. I would not have thought he was that naive – but he knows enough to make use of them, put it that way. Professes to have a great enthusiasm for the Revolution. A few years back he was calling himself Citizen Tipu.' He gave a bark of laughter. 'Oh yes. There was even a Jacobin Club in Mysore, would you believe? Man's a bigger tyrant than King Louis and he supports the Revolution. Still. I suppose you could say the same for the men running France these days.'

'Does he have any communication with them?'

'With Paris? Well, that is another good question. It would have to be overland, of course, by way of Persia and the Ottoman Empire. Much the same way you came. He has sent envoys to Paris, we know that. And the French have sent officers to train his army. Two or three hundred of them.'

'And is it any good?'

'The army? Hard to say. Until we start fighting them. Most of his troops are Hindus, which may be a good thing from our point of view.' Duncan noted the raised brow. 'Nothing against Hindus – as soldiers. We have plenty of our own. But I am not sure how they feel about fighting for a Musselman. Especially one who has usurped their own rajah. He takes care not to offend them, mind, in the matter of religion. He has about 30,000 troops at his command. Not much in the way of artillery, from what I hear. Uses rockets, instead.'

'Rockets?'

'Things that go whoosh. Lots of sparks. Got blades on them. Scares the pants off the elephants. They'd put the wind up me, too, I don't mind telling you, if I saw one coming at me. I hear Cornwallis took a strong dislike to them in the last war.'

'And what about the sea?'

'The sea?' Duncan was puzzled.

'Does he have any naval forces at his command?'

'Ah. Big plans as far as a navy is concerned. Not reached fruition yet. He built a massive dockyard at Mangalore. Plans to build a navy to match our own, he says. Given time, he might. At the moment it is mostly grabs and gallivants. You won't know them. Local craft. Gallivants are big row boats, galleys, I suppose you might call them, grabs are more in the sambuk line but bigger – two-masted dhows, lateen-rigged – coastal craft; useful on the rivers, too. Eight or ten guns at most.'

'And they are based at Mangalore?'

'They are. Mysore, as you may know, covers a good deal of southern India – from the west coast almost as far as Madras. Managalore is their biggest port, halfway down the Malabar Coast. Tipu has renamed it Jalalabad. It is on the backwaters, just behind the shore – very narrow entrance – and they have built a massive great fort there. We will talk more of that later.' The governor glanced out of the window. The storm seemed to be moving out to sea. Good. The gods were on his side after all. Today, at least. He came to a sudden decision, or half of one.

'Well,' he said, reaching for his hat. 'You had better come and see your squadron.'

Chapter Eleven

The Bombay Buccaneers

They were moored in a long line in the deep-water channel between two islands – Elephanta Island and Butcher Island, according to the chart – seven or eight ships of war, perhaps more, the end of the line lost in the thickening haze. A battle fleet in miniature, for most appeared to be gun brigs or even smaller vessels, built to fight pirates and catch smugglers, not to fight the French. Nathan doubted if they had one decent broadside between them, though they looked capable enough for the job they were designed to do, with their sleek lines and their chequered gunports, the company standard flying proudly at their sterns.

As the little *Fly* cruised down the line, a cable's length to windward, the governor provided Nathan with a summary of their principle features and fighting abilities.

'*Antelope*, brig, fourteen guns, just under two hundred tons. Captain Henry Blake. Had her since she was built in 1793. Built of teak – they all are. In the yards at Surat. Best yards in India, best in the world, so far as I am aware. Knock your Deptford and your Chatham into a cocked hat. I know what you Navy fellows think of teak. Splinters turn septic. Oak gives you a clean wound, teak you're a dead man. All my eye. Oak or teak, they'll both kill you, if the splinter goes in deep enough – and if the splinter don't, the surgeon will. Better than oak any year, teak. Stronger, sweeter-smelling and lasts longer. She's not been out the water since 1793, the *Antelope*, and look at her. Fastest ship in the squadron and she'll still be going strong when she's fifty. Can't say that for many of your royal ships, if any. What's this?' As they approached the next in line they could see her name painted across her stern, but Duncan told him anyway: '*Comet*, brig, ten guns, sister to the *Fly*, one hundred and fifteen tons, built this year. Not been in action yet. Captain Thomas Cutler, came out in 1796. Ex-Navy man. Lost a leg at the siege of Calvi. Faster than the *Fly* – Hale won't thank me for saying so, but she is. *Eagle*, snow-brig, sixteen guns. Jethro Foley. Another ex-Navy man. Threw a strop when his admiral called him a whoremonger and came to us – we get a few like that. Nothing wrong with him except his temper. Fine seaman. Navy's loss, our gain. Ah, now this – *this* – is our flagship. *Bombay*, frigate, thirty-eight, just over six hundred tons.'

Nathan's interest grew apace, for this was a proper fighting ship, though he doubted if Duncan had got the tonnage right; she looked bigger than that to him – she'd be a fifth-rate in the service. Thirty-eight guns made her the equal of any frigate in the King's Navy, though he wondered what calibre they were; the ports were closed so he couldn't see from where he stood. If they were 18-pounders she would pack a considerable punch.

Duncan was still rattling away. 'Biggest in the fleet – and the oldest, built in 1773. Picket is commodore. Charles Picket. He won't be aboard now, though. That fellow waving his hat at us is his flag captain, Bevis. We had better wave back at him. Yes, very good. That will do, captain, or your arm will fall off. Bit of creep, Bevis, but a good enough seaman.'

Nathan waved dutifully, while wondering where he fitted into all of this. This was not his navy, nor His Britannic Majesty's. These were gunboats of the Bombay Marine – the Bombay Buccaneers, the Navy called them, not entirely without respect, but with the inference that they were little better than licensed pirates. HCS was their prefix. Honourable Company Ship. This was the company navy, just as Bombay was a company port, like Madras and Calcutta. And the officers and crews swore allegiance, not to the King of England or their lordships of the Admiralty, but to the merchants of the Honourable East India Company – Hale had shown him his papers with the oath he'd signed when he'd joined.

'I, William John Hale, being appointed an Officer of the Marine on the Bombay station in the service of the Honourable Company of Merchants of England Trading in the East Indies, do swear that I will be true and faithful to the said company and will faithfully and truly execute and demonstrate the trust reposed in me, to the utmost of my skill and power, so help me God.'

Nathan had nothing against that. The company had a monopoly on all British trade between the Cape of Good Hope and the Straits of Magellan: dangerous waters, far from the shores of Britain and the protection of the Royal Navy. They needed their own ships of war. Their own army, too. The biggest army in India, by all accounts. And why not? Nathan shared the view of almost every naval officer of his acquaintance that the East India Company was one of Britain's finest assets. The Honourable Company, as it was widely known, had been given its royal charter in the closing years of the reign of Queen Elizabeth and it had been a bulwark of British power and influence ever since. It was nonsense, in Nathan's opinion, to talk of divided loyalties.

But people did. The company's success had made it a great many enemies, and not just in India. Nathan could hardly fail to be aware of the voices that had been raised against it in recent years; the most violent were frequently to be heard in his mother's drawing room.

Nathan's mother, Lady Catherine Peake – Kitty to her many friends and admirers – had made her home a debating chamber and a sanctuary for the most outspoken critics of government policy. Nor was she averse to speaking out herself. Nathan put this down to the misfortune of being American – a citizen of New York – and therefore incapable of restraint. Others were not so charitable. The First Lord of the Admiralty, Lord Spencer, whose good opinion was a matter of some concern to Nathan, had publicly condemned her as a harridan who should be whipped at the cart's tail, and though Nathan was naturally offended by this slander and would have taken exception to it had it been uttered in his hearing, First Lord or no, the provocation was no doubt considerable.

To Nathan's embarrassment and dismay, his mother devoted much of her energy and a large proportion of her income to the torment and confusion of the King's ministers, while providing encouragement and support to as infamous a bunch of scoundrels and rebels as were ever gathered under one roof. Even the House of Commons could scarce compete. One of Lady Catherine's greatest friends was Charles James Fox, Spencer's mortal foe and leader of the Whig Opposition. Another was Thomas Paine, though he had been forced to flee to France so that he would not be hanged for treason. And another was Richard Brinsley Sheridan, the dramatist.

Unfortunately, Sheridan did not confine his vitriol to the stage. He was also a Member of Parliament who had singled out the East India Company as the particular target of his invective. He had denounced its directors from the floor of the House of Commons. He had called them pirates and brigands. He had brought charges of dishonesty and corruption against the Governor-General, Warren Hastings. He had accused the company of making war upon the people of India and using the spoils of conquest to corrupt the entire British political system – purchasing seats in Parliament and bribing others to support them; making it impossible for any government to survive, let alone conduct its business, without the backing of the Honourable East India Company.

This was farcical, of course. Sheridan was a writer. Of farces. He made things up. He was not a bad writer. Some of his plays were quite good. Much better than

Shakespeare's in Nathan's opinion. Much funnier, anyway. But his political opinions were appalling. It was embarrassing to admit an acquaintance with the fellow. Almost as embarrassing as having Lady Catherine Peake for a mother.

However, there was no doubt that the East India Company had its own way of doing things and it was not necessarily the way Nathan would want to do them. Rather more to the point, it might not be the way Nelson would want him to do them.

Nathan's instructions were perfectly clear. He was to do everything in his power to prevent the French from landing troops and supplies in support of their Indian allies. This meant stopping Bonaparte from shipping men and materiel over from Egypt. It was reasonable to assume that the governor would give his wholehearted support to this enterprise. But would he?

From the moment he had met him, Nathan had been troubled by a sense of unease. As he knew little of the man's character, he could only assume that this was down to his appearance, which, frankly, was unprepossessing. He wore a hat now, crammed down over his forehead so it would not blow off – strands of grey hair whipping around his face like seaweed, or the tendrils of a very thin octopus – but when Nathan had first seen him at Government House he had been hatless, his long, greasy locks hanging down to his shoulders, while exposing a completely bald crown, as if the thinner it had grown on top, the more he had grown it at the sides. The effect was rather of a sheep with the mange. Nathan was not generally in favour of wigs, but if ever a man should be advised to wear one it was the Governor of Bombay. Nor did his clothing help.

He wore a shabby old frock coat and a dirty linen stock and his stockings bagged round his scrawny ankles like the saggy skin of an elephant. He looked less like a governor of the East India Company and more like a miserable old miser in a counting house. Perhaps there was not much difference.

In a strange way, he reminded Nathan of Napoleon Bonaparte – the first time he had met him, when he was an out-of-work artillery officer down on his luck in Paris. Bonaparte had been much younger of course, but he had been just as shabby and as threadbare, and with the same madcap schemes in his head, except that where Bonaparte dreamed of world conquest, Duncan dreamed of turning back the sea. Making the seven islands of Bombay into one and joining it to the mainland by a great causeway which would bear his name.

Well, good luck to him. So long as he focused his energies on the land and left the sea to those who were best equipped to deal with it.

'*Cornwallis*, snow, 14 guns. Named after the last governor-general . . . fine man, fine general, fine administrator. Best we've had in my opinion . . .' This was the man who had surrendered at Yorktown, Nathan reflected, and lost the American colonies. Then they gave him India. He supposed they must know what they were doing . . . '*Stromboli*, bomb ketch—'

'A bomb ketch?'

Duncan took Nathan's surprise for ignorance. 'A specialist craft – the only one we have at our disposal at present. You not got them in the Navy? She carries a thirteen-inch mortar – you cannot see it from here, it is housed in a well on the foredeck. Fires an explosive charge – a *shell*.'

Nathan knew the purpose of a bomb ketch. He also knew what a shell was. He had assisted in the bombardment of Cadiz after the Battle of St Vincent. It had succeeded in killing several priests of the Catholic Church and a baby girl in her mother's arms. Nathan had written a letter of protest to the admiral, expressing the view that a British naval officer had no business to be firing shells at women, children and unarmed priests: Spanish, French or otherwise. Old Jarvey – Admiral Jervis – had taken such strong exception to this that Nathan had been relieved of his command and confined for several months in the Moorish Prison on the Rock of Gibraltar. The memory still rankled.

'But what use is a bomb ketch to the East India Company?' he enquired, with an air of amiable bemusement, which he hoped would remove any suspicion of censure from the governor's mind.

'Of very great use,' the governor replied, 'for it enables a fleet to stand well out to sea, beyond the range of shot from the shore, while the bomb ketch lobs its *bombs* over the walls of a city, do you see? We call it a *bombardment*. We employed her at Pondicherry in 1793, when we took the city back from the French, and again in Ceylon in 1795. She might prove equally useful at Mangalore.'

'At Mangalore?'

What in God's name was he talking about? Mangalore was halfway down the Malabar Coast. Six or seven hundred miles to the south. Why would they wish to bombard Mangalore? With 40,000 French troops waiting to descend on them from the north?

But the governor either did not hear or chose not to respond. He was pointing across the water as yet another vessel emerged from the haze, the last in the line, right up under the guns of the fort on Salsette Island.

'There she is – the *Pondicherry*.'

She was standing at some distance from the *Stromboli* – and hence the rest of the line – as if she shared some of Nathan's own reservations at the company she was keeping. A big two-decker – big, at least, compared to what had come before – with the Union flag at her stern instead of the company standard.

Nelson had told him she had once been a French ship, but Nelson had told him quite a few things which turned out not to be true. In fact, her history was more complicated than that. Duncan had told him some of it on the way from Government House. She had been built in England – at the Henry Adams yard in Buckler's Hard – as a fifty-gun fourth-rate for the Royal Navy, and had been called the *Hannibal*. It was just at the start of the last war and she had been sent out East to join Admiral Hughes in the Indian Ocean, only to be captured by the French off Sumatra.

The French had dropped the H and renamed her the *Annibal* – or the *Petit Annibal*, to distinguish her from a larger ship of the same name – and she had taken part in five fleet actions against the British. The French kept hold of her when the war ended and she had become guardship of their colony in Pondicherry on the Coromandel Coast. Bowing to requests from the locals, the French Admiralty had agreed to rename her after the port, and she had remained there, gently rotting, according to the governor, until the beginning of the present war when she was recaptured by the British.

'I suppose we should have given her back her old name,' Duncan said. 'But we never got round to it. Everyone calls her the '*Cherry*, even the crew. But she's yours now – you can call her whatever you like, I suppose,' he added doubtfully.

The *Hannibal*. Nathan rather liked the sound of that. He certainly liked it better than the *Cherry*.

She was lying stern-to and Nathan's first impression was of a grand old lady who had slapped on a bit too much paint and varnish. There was always a certain amount of artwork at the stern of a ship of war – anything over forty guns at least – but in Nathan's view it was better to go light on the colouring; let the carvings speak for themselves. Gold and black was his own preference. Here they had gone for gold, red and blue, with a line of dancing nymphs along the transom, picked out in white. And as they came up alongside her he saw that the theme had been continued to some extent down the length of her hull, for though she had the classic white stripes with black gunports, the strakes at the waterline had been painted red and there was a thin band of yellow between the two gun decks. It should have looked menacing, as it did on a wasp or hornet, but, combined with the other colours, it gave her a rather raffish look, as if she was dressed for a carnival.

Paintwork apart, she belonged to a different age – a time when the British Admiralty had succumbed to the conviction that the Navy needed heavy cruisers – bigger than a frigate, faster than a ship of the line. But the thinking was suspect. They had ended up with a class of ship that was slower than a frigate and too lightly armed to stand in the line of battle; neither thoroughbred nor warhorse. And there were other complaints. They were top heavy, their critics said, they rolled badly in a storm and tended to drift to leeward in the lightest breeze. Britain's chief naval rivals had got rid of them twenty years ago. The ones Britain still had were used as guardships or troopships, or convoy escorts. Or they were *razéed* – cut down to a single deck and converted into very large, heavily armed frigates.

But Nathan had come a long way for this – and whatever her detractors said about her, and the class to which she belonged, the *Pondicherry*, or the *Hannibal*, as he preferred to think of her, was probably the most powerful ship of war in the Indian Ocean. In the right place, and with the right support, she could stop Bonaparte from moving a single ship, or a single regiment, beyond the Gulf of Aden. But she could not do it in Bombay and the sooner they were at sea the better.

What troubled Nathan, after what he had learned of her history, was whether she could ever put to sea. She had been laid up in Bombay harbour or the shipyard at Surat ever since she had been brought from Pondicherry, as far as he could gather. And for most of that time she had been without a captain. He had been taken ill, apparently, and sent back to England but had not survived the voyage. Since when her first lieutenant had been in charge – a man called Joyce. Duncan had said little else about him, but Nathan had detected a strong sense of disapproval. He had said nothing at all about her other officers, or her crew.

* * *

The *Fly* hove to a half-cable's length off her starboard quarter and they stepped into the waiting launch. This time Nathan took Tully and Blunt with him – for it was quite possible that they would stay aboard and they could send back for their kit later. They exchanged few words. Nathan had a good idea what Tully must be thinking, for if Nathan's role was ambiguous, Tully's was even worse.

Whether the ship had been forewarned of their visit by signal or had divined it by some other means, they were clearly expected. Or at least the governor was. Side steps had been lowered to the water's edge and as they ascended them they were greeted by the reassuring wail of the boatswain's call and the stamp and crash of the marine guard as they presented arms. There was a file of redcoats drawn up on the gun deck under the command of a lieutenant. But they were not marines, it became apparent to Nathan as soon as he stepped aboard. They were soldiers – with the badge of the 12th Regiment of Foot on their crossbelts. It was not so unusual on a ship of war for soldiers to fulfil the function of marines, but it added to Nathan's sense of things being not quite right. And then his wandering eye fell on something else that added considerably to his unease – the heads of several women, regarding him with apparent amusement from the level of the deck. As they encountered Nathan's astonished gaze, they disappeared but he could have sworn he heard an explosion of girlish giggles.

With an effort, Nathan recalled himself to the necessity of greeting the ship's officers. A lieutenant had stepped forward, taking off his hat and making his bow to the governor, though his eyes flickered across to Nathan in his captain's uniform with barely disguised alarm.

'Troy, is it not?' the governor addressed him. The lieutenant confirmed that this was indeed the case. 'Lieutenant Joyce aboard?'

'I am afraid not, Your Excellency. He is gone ashore.'

'Is he, indeed?' Nathan gathered from the governor's tone that this was not unexpected. In fact, Duncan's manner revealed a certain wicked pleasure in the situation. 'And when is he due back?'

'I am not entirely sure, sir,' the lieutenant replied uncomfortably. 'He said he would be a day or two.'

'I see. Well, I have brought a surprise for you, Troy. This is your new commodore, Captain Peake.' The lieutenant did not look so much surprised – he looked as if he had been shot. It might have been Nathan's imagination, but he thought he heard a collective gasp from those other of the ship's officers grouped behind him.

'I will shortly leave you to become better acquainted,' Duncan continued blandly, 'but in the absence of the first lieutenant, perhaps you will be so good as to conduct us to the great cabin where we may converse in private.'

The lieutenant flinched, the blood draining from his countenance. For a moment he was rendered incapable of speech or movement.

'If that is convenient,' the governor added pointedly.

Troy delivered a stammering apology to the effect that the great cabin was presently unprepared, and perhaps the governor would be more comfortable in the wardroom. Nathan decided this had gone far enough.

'The great cabin, if you please, Mr Troy,' he instructed him briskly. 'And let us not keep His Excellency waiting.'

For a moment he thought the lieutenant was going to

argue. Nathan engaged him with a look he had copied from Old Jarvey, but he was startled by the horror in the officer's eyes. What in God's name was going on here? Troy's shoulders slumped and he lowered his head in what might have been shame or an apology of a bow.

'If you will follow me, sir.' His tone and the set of his features betrayed the grim fatality of a man leading the way to the gallows.

The *Pondicherry*, in common with all of her class, was equipped with a poop deck, the large space beneath being reserved entirely for the convenience of the flag officer, if she possessed such an object, or her captain if she did not. It was entered through a pair of double doors at the rear of the quarterdeck, immediately abaft the helm. These led to the dining room which, in turn, led to the great cabin. It was of generous proportions. So too were the several women who were its present occupants. They were lying on a number of couches or divans spread upon the floor and conversing amiably while they took turns at a number of hookahs or water pipes. They looked up in surprise when the doors opened. Something – perhaps a gesture or expression of the lieutenant, who stood resolutely in the entrance – alerted them to a potential problem. Swiftly and without a word, they jumped to their feet and fled to the sanctuary of the state room on the starboard quarter. Nathan had the impression that they had a monkey with them.

The lieutenant stood to one side and held himself stiffly to attention, his chin extended and his eyes fixed on an immeasurable distance.

Nathan stepped inside the cabin. It occupied the entire space at the stern of the vessel from one side to the other. A pair of double doors opened on to the stern gallery, another to the quarter gallery. It was not much smaller than the great cabin of the *Vanguard* where Nelson had given him his final orders before he had embarked for the East and would normally have been furnished in much the same manner. Indeed, there were several objects that were by no means out of place: a desk for the use of the flag officer and a table for his charts; a number of upright chairs and a pair of leather easy chairs; a globe and a mounted telescope, and a few other objects of nautical interest. But these were far outnumbered by objects of a far more frivolous and intimate nature.

The deck was covered by a large Oriental carpet, richly patterned and coloured. The armchairs had been pushed up against the bulkhead and the centre of the cabin was occupied by the several brightly cushioned divans, upon which the women had been taking their leisure. A large decorated chest displayed a great many silks and satins and items of female apparel which they had apparently been inspecting, or perhaps trying on. There were a number of footstools and copper trays and water pipes scattered about the remaining area. The bulkheads supported about half a dozen mirrors with richly ornamented and bejewelled frames, reflecting the light that poured in through the stern windows, splintered into rays by the smoke from the hubble-bubbles. There was a strong smell of scented tobacco and other, more exotic odours. In one corner stood a large harp, reaching almost to the deck above; in another was a perch containing a large parrot. Its measuring eye met Nathan's. 'Who's a pretty boy, then?' it uttered in a tone of creaking menace.

Nathan looked at the lieutenant.

'I am very sorry, sir,' said Troy. 'I regret that our standards have been allowed to slip.'

In truth, Nathan was less surprised than he might have been and not such a hypocrite as to be shocked. It had been common practice in the Mediterranean fleet for the captains to take a woman aboard. In fact, 'mistress' was the polite term, for most of them were courtesans, supplied on a regular basis to officers of the fleet by a Mr Udny, the British consul at Leghorn. Nelson himself had possessed one of the most handsome, who had presided as his hostess at formal dinners aboard the old *Agamemnon* when it was his flagship in the Gulf of Genoa. Indeed, when the British fleet had been forced to evacuate Leghorn, Nathan himself had entertained Signora Correglia and a number of her companions aboard the *Unicorn* on their passage to Corsica. His own stern cabin had pretty much resembled that of the *Pondicherry* at the time; there had even been a number of songbirds and a harpsichord. But the circumstances had been exceptional and at least it had been his own cabin, not that of an absent flag officer.

'I will speak with you later,' he told the lieutenant. 'In the meantime, we will adjourn to the dining room – and perhaps you would be good enough to send me whatever charts you possess of the Arabian Sea.'

He caught Tully's eye as they left the cabin. He looked amused.

'I would be glad if you would show Lieutenant Tully around the rest of the ship,' Nathan instructed Troy coldly, 'while the governor and I discuss some matters in private.'

When they alone, Nathan made his own apologies to the governor, though he had an idea that Duncan had known exactly what they would find, and took pleasure from the embarrassment it had caused. Certainly it could only strengthen the governor's hand in whatever game he was playing, and he held all of the half-decent cards already.

'So far as the ship's discipline is concerned, I am sure you will take whatever measures are necessary,' he addressed Nathan smoothly. 'I am more concerned with what measures you propose to take with regards to the French. Or perhaps you have yet to consider the matter.'

'I have thought of little else since leaving the Mediterranean,' Nathan assured him, with scant regard to the truth. But whatever else had been on his mind, the means of stopping the French advancing to India by sea appeared so obvious as to require very little deliberation. 'If Bonaparte is to support his friends in India, he must open up a line of supply from Suez – down the Red Sea and then across the Arabian Sea to the west coast of India. In fact, we know that one of his principle agents – a man called Xavier Naudé – was despatched to Suez for this very purpose at about the same time as I was sent to India.'

He was interrupted in this exposition by the timely arrival of a young officer with the charts he had requested. He found the one he wanted and spread it on the table for the governor's inspection. 'The only way the French can reach India is through the Gate of Grief,' he explained, pointing to the narrow strait at the southern end of the Red Sea, between Aden and the Horn of Africa. The Bab-el-Mandeb, the Arabs called it – the Gate of Grief or the Gate of Tears – possibly because of the number of vessels that have been lost there, for it was notoriously difficult to navigate.

'As you can see, it is only twenty miles wide,' Nathan continued, 'and it is divided by an island – Perim Island, here, forming two distinct channels. If we were to station the squadron at the southern end of the strait, just south of Perim Island, I am confident we could stop even a single French vessel from entering the Arabian Sea.'

'So you are proposing a blockade?'

'I am. The French have no ships of war available to them at Suez. It would be impossible for them to force a passage. With even a small squadron we could bottle them up in the Red Sea.'

'And what about the Île de France?'

'The Île de France?' Nathan frowned.

The governor stabbed a finger on the map. 'Here, to the east of Madagascar.'

Nathan knew where it was. He was at a loss to know what it had to do with stopping the passage of French troops from Egypt.

'You are aware that the French have a garrison there,' Duncan persisted, 'and a squadron of frigates?'

'I am aware that it is a French base. I was not aware that they had any significant naval forces there, beside a few privateers. And it is a long way from Suez – or Bombay.'

'I don't care how far it is. It is on the direct route from the Cape. The route taken by our trading ships between England and India.'

'I appreciate that this may be a problem for you.' Nathan conceded, 'but I would suggest that it is not as great a problem as the danger of a French advance from Egypt. My instructions are very clear in that respect. If you are suggesting an expedition against the Île de France . . .'

'What I am suggesting is that the French may have other means of aiding Tipu Sahib than by way of the Bab-el-Mandeb, or any other Bab you care to name.'

Nathan struggled to keep his voice even. 'You think they plan to support him from the Île de France?'

'I do. Indeed, I have precise knowledge of it. The governor of the Île de France is a man called General Malartic – or, to give him his full name, Anne-Joseph-Hippolyte de Maurés, Comte de Malartic. General M'larky, I call him. I expect he has dropped the title since the Revolution but he is one of the old guard. Professional soldier under the old regime. *Gardes Françaises*. He has a large naval squadron at his disposal – privateers, admittedly, but quite big ones – up to thirty-six guns, from what I have been told.

'According to our intelligence, in January of this year one of these corsairs – the frigate *La Preneuse* – picked up two of Tipu's envoys in Mangalore and took them back to the Île de France for talks. Shortly after their arrival, M'larky posted notices across the island calling for volunteers to go to the aid of Tipu the Tiger – Pasha Tipu the Victorious, he called him – against the aggressions of the British East India Company. Impudent rogue. There was, I am told, an enthusiastic response. They have been formed into a legion under the command of a cove called Louis August Chappuis – Colonel Chappuis – and are ready to leave as soon as conditions are thought to be right.'

Nathan studied the map to give himself time to think. This was as bad as anything he had feared. The Île de France was in the bottom corner of the map, about as far away from Bombay as Bonaparte was – further, in fact, but in the opposite direction.

'I understand your concern,' he began carefully, 'and I confess that I am not as informed as Your Excellency regarding the Île de France. However, I doubt very much if the entire garrison is much more than a thousand troops.'

'One thousand, two hundred.'

'One thousand, two hundred,' Nathan conceded this estimate with a polite nod. 'Whereas Bonaparte has over forty thousand in Egypt, with heavy artillery and a formidable amount of military equipment.'

'But no ships.'

'No ships of *war*. However, there are plenty of merchant vessels in the region which he can utilise as troopships. And if we were to divert our own naval forces to the Île de France at such a time—'

'As I have said, I am not proposing to divert a single ship to the Île de France.'

'Then – forgive me – but what are you proposing?'

'That we intercept them off the Malabar Coast.'

'But with no precise knowledge of where they are to land . . .'

'We know precisely where they are to land. Our intelligence is first rate. They are to land here – at Mangalore.'

The bony finger stabbed once more at the map. Mangalore. On the Malabar Coast. Six hundred miles south of Bombay. Even if the governor's intelligence was correct, and the winds were in Nathan's favour, it would take him the best part of a week to sail there – and how long would he have to wait, off a hostile shore, for this phantom squadron to arrive? If it ever did. He opened his mouth to point this out.

'Mangalore is a hundred and fifty miles from Seringapatam, where the Tiger has his lair,' Duncan continued. 'General M'larky has promised to send help before the advent of the north-east monsoon. Which gives you two weeks at most. I suggest you had better get started.'

Chapter Twelve

The Happy Ship

'I know that you will think me a hypocrite,' Nathan began, ignoring Tully's mild expression of protest, 'but I am not at all relaxed about having women at sea. And if I am perfectly honest, I do not like having them in port, either.'

'Well, they are all gone now,' Tully replied soothingly.

'And the monkey and the parrot?'

'All gone.'

Nathan sighed. It had been a fraught day. He stretched his long legs under the table and looked about him. The great cabin had been restored to a condition resembling what you might expect of a ship of war: all polished wood and gleaming brass, though there was a persistent hint of perfume in the air, even with the stern windows open to the fresh sea breeze. But it was a cabin Nathan might come to like, even love. He particularly liked the two galleries at the stern and starboard quarter which permitted him to walk up and down in perfect seclusion in the open air just a few feet above the sea. He could even pee into it, if he wished. Though there was a perfectly comfortable privy for his exclusive use. The fifty-gun ship might have its drawbacks but it provided excellent accommodation for a flag-officer, which was presumably why it was so often used for showing the flag. You could entertain fifty or sixty guests quite easily in a cabin like this.

There were other considerations, however.

The surface of the table was almost entirely covered with the ship's books and whatever other documents the purser had considered pertinent to Nathan's enquiries. He had spent the best part of the day going through them. On paper, at least, the ship seemed to be in excellent order. She had recently undergone a complete refit at the shipyard in Surat. Her hanging knees, her rudder, and much of her copper sheathing had been renewed. Several suspect strakes had been removed and replaced with new ones. She had been supplied with a new foretop and bowsprit and many square yards of pristine canvas. In addition, her rigging had been given a thorough overhaul and she had received several coats of paint – though in rather more lurid colours than Nathan would have preferred. She was, according to the carpenter, Mr Pugsley, as good as when she had left the Adams Yard in Hampshire, as long ago as 1778. 'Probably better,' he had added, for Mr Pugsley was a Devon man.

So far as supplies went, the ship was more or less ready for sea. Among the papers on Nathan's table was a list of provisions sufficient for a three-month cruise. Nathan was very much taken with lists. Most men he knew were the same. There was something very satisfying about a list. It spoke of order and regulation, the opposite of the chthonic disorder he had encountered upon first entering the great cabin. This was not to say that you could trust it, any further than you could trust the man who had drawn it up. But it was something tangible, something you could get your teeth into. You could learn a lot from a list.

On the other hand, it sometimes raised as many questions as it answered. Why, for instance, had the governor ordered the *Pondicherry* – and presumably the other ships in the squadron – to be provisioned for a three-month voyage? The order had been given over a week ago, when Nathan was still on his way to Bombay. It was possible that Duncan had heard of the French invasion of Egypt but highly unlikely – and why should he dissemble? It was far more likely that he had already been preparing for a long blockade of Mangalore – or somewhere even further afield. Despite his assurances, Nathan was convinced that Duncan contemplated an invasion of the Île de France and he was determined to resist it at all costs.

Before him lay the document the purser had presented to him detailing the weight of provisions, ordnance, powder and shot in tons, hundredweight and pounds. Pursers' lists were notoriously inaccurate, but according to this information the Pondicherry carried 75 tons of water – or approximately 20,000 gallons – either in the ground tier or in casks, 12,000 gallons of beer, 1,000 gallons of rum and 1,000 gallons of lemon juice. No wine was listed – perhaps they did not grow grapes in India – but it would be surprising if they could not get hold of a few bottles. The crew would not care, provided that they had their rum and their beer, but Nathan would miss his wine. There was coffee, though, and tea – and 18 barrels of Virginia tobacco. As to more basic provisions, it looked as if they could sail to Africa and back without taking on fresh supplies.

Unhappily, there was no list of private stores for the captain – or commodore – but Mr Harrison had assured him that the deficiency could be remedied by the next delivery, with the expenditure of only a small portion of Nathan's fortune.

The next list was concerned with the ordnance. Nathan scanned it with a more critical eye. The main armament consisted of forty-four long guns, equally divided between 24-pounders and 12-pounders, and half a dozen 6-pounders – two in the bows, four on the quarterdeck. The greater surprise was the amount of powder and shot at his disposal. Three hundred barrels of powder, five thousand rounds of round shot, six hundred of grape and four hundred of chain.

Nathan had never seen such a satisfying list in all his time in the King's Navy. They had enough powder and shot to indulge in gunnery practice every day if he wished, and still have enough for a major action. And as for provisions, they would need to practise at the guns – and climb to the top of the mainmast ten times a day – if they were not to become fat as eunuchs. In addition to the items on his list, the purser had assured him that they had a quantity of livestock: goats, hens, even a milk cow.

The muster roll was rather less agreeable. The official Admiralty establishment for a ship of the *Pondicherry*'s class was for 370 men and boys including 5 commissioned sea officers, 2 officers of marines, 10 midshipmen and 6 senior warrant officers.

In fact, the muster roll told a slightly different story. The captain had died of a fever and there were only three lieutenants, one of whom was 'gone ashore', while the two marine officers had been replaced by officers of the 12th Regiment of Foot – a lieutenant and an ensign. The ship's master, like the captain, had been carried off with a disease, and his place had been taken, temporarily, by one of the master's mates. The ship was lacking a chaplain and a schoolmaster, neither of which Nathan considered too great a loss, and there were only six midshipmen. Again, this was no great problem, and it gave Nathan the opportunity to keep his promise to Blunt.

The crew was almost up to full strength but the list included an inordinate amount of French names – sixty-six in all. Nathan was aware that a great many French Royalists served in the British Navy, but he had not heard of quite so many in a single ship. It would not have bothered him quite so much if the rest of the crew were British. But they were not. Ninety-two of them were from a Danish frigate which had been wrecked on a voyage to the Nicobar Islands in the Bay of Bengal. They had all volunteered to serve in His Britannic Majesty's Navy, according to the purser, and though Nathan had no reason to doubt his account, he thought it was quite possible that they had been told that this was the only way they would ever get back to Denmark. Denmark was at present neutral, but this situation could change – as it had in the case of Spain and the Netherlands, and several of the German and Italian states who were now allied to Revolutionary France.

Of the remainder, thirty-four were Irish Catholics, and while Nathan did not share the prejudice of many officers about Catholics, it was a fact that large parts of Ireland were currently in active rebellion against King George – or, at least, they had been when he had last read the newspapers six months before. This left just fifty-nine men from mainland Britain – including most of the commissioned and warrant officers. And, of course, the soldiers, who were mostly from East Anglia.

The Navy had relied on foreigners to man its ships for most of the present century, but it was unusual for there to be quite so few Englishmen among them. And there were other issues to consider.

One of them was Nathan's own legitimacy. He had no official Admiralty commission to command the *Pondicherry*. His authority as commodore came from Admiral Nelson, with the approval of the Governor of Bombay. In the circumstances, the governor's approval was the more important. And this meant that he had to do pretty much as the governor ordered. He had an idea that Duncan had played him for a fool – giving him the illusion of power while telling him exactly what to do. Which was worryingly close to the way the East India Company treated the British Government.

Then there was the problem of the missing lieutenant – Lieutenant Joyce. The story that he had 'gone ashore' was somewhat disingenuous. It had later emerged that he had gone to Surat – about a hundred miles to the north – and that he had taken the thirty-two-foot pinnace with twelve men, including the ship's coxswain and a midshipman. The official reason for this expedition was to bring back a spare set of rudder braces from the shipyard there. Nathan doubted this very much. Partly because the carpenter had assured him that there was nothing wrong with the rudder braces, and partly because the lieutenant had taken his wife with him.

And that was another thing. The lieutenant's wife was apparently Indian – and the women Nathan had encountered in the great cabin had been *her* women. Either her relatives or servants or both. It seemed that the lieutenant and his wife had taken over the whole of the stern cabin as their private lodgings. Some might view this as perfectly reasonable when there was no flag officer or captain aboard – but it seemed to Nathan to be something of a cheek. He would have to have words with Mr Joyce – if he ever met him. If he had not returned by noon tomorrow, Nathan planned to sail without him. He was most unhappy about this – more for the loss of the pinnace and twelve men than for the loss of Lieutenant Joyce.

He had an idea that there was a lot more to this than met the eye. He thought Tully probably knew more about it than he was prepared to say – either because Troy or one of the other officers had told him in confidence, or because he did not wish to be thought of as an informer. However, Nathan was determined to get to the bottom of it, not least because he might have to replace Mr Joyce as first lieutenant, and this had implications both for himself and for Tully. He turned his head away and raised his voice, frowning in some embarrassment.

'De Fournier,' he shouted. 'De Fournier there.'

This was the name of the captain's steward – a rather unfortunate name, in Nathan's opinion, a little too close to

'Fornication' for his comfort. He was one of the Frenchmen, of course. Possibly of noble origin. Certainly he gave himself the airs of a nobleman, though quite what he was doing as a steward was anyone's guess. On their brief acquaintance, Nathan had taken an unusual dislike to him. He would rather have had Blunt, for all his failings as a servant. But the man he missed most – of all his old shipmates – was his previous steward, Gilbert Gabriel, a former highwayman, known ironically to his fellows – from his short temper and his propensity for violence – as the Angel Gabriel. Gabriel had been saved from the hangman by Nathan's father and had repaid the debt by serving both father and son faithfully for many years. He had been Nathan's guardian and mentor during his childhood in Sussex and had continued in this role when Nathan first went to sea, initially as a shipmate when Nathan was a humble midshipman, and then as his steward when he was made post. But he had been taken captive by the Venetians during one of Nathan's previous ventures ashore, and not been heard of since. Nathan had spent a good deal of money in an effort to trace him, but thus far his efforts had been in vain.

'Sir?' It was remarkable how much derision and disdain De Fournier could inject into that one simple syllable. Sooner or later Nathan would have to do something about De Fournier, but not now. He had too many other things to think about.

'Pass the word for Mr Troy,' Nathan instructed him, with as much courtesy as he could muster. 'And while you are about it, perhaps you would be good enough to fetch us some wine – some white wine, chilled, if possible – and three glasses.'

'The De Fourniers would be *noblesse oblige*, I suppose,' he remarked to Tully, when the steward had departed on this errand.

'I doubt they are nobles of any description, obliging or otherwise,' Tully replied. 'The "De" is a recent addition. He was plain Fournier when he was in the French service. The literal translation is "man of the oven", as you probably know. His occupation was steward's mate.'

Nathan raised a brow. 'How do you know that?' He never ceased to be astonished at Tully's insights, especially where members of the crew were concerned. He suspected his friend's rise from the lower deck had enabled him to tap into lines of communication denied the more privileged of his associates. But the answer, in this instance, was more prosaic.

'By looking in the French muster roll,' Tully explained. 'The purser has a copy.'

'Does he, indeed? He did not tell me that. And why were you looking at it?'

'A natural curiosity. Also, if we are to live in such close proximity with sixty-six Frenchmen, I would prefer to know something of their history.'

'And is there any cause for alarm?'

'I think not. Most of them are from Brittany or the Vendée.'

This would explain their reluctance to return to France. Both regions had risen in rebellion against the Revolutionary government and had been brutally repressed. Nathan had some personal knowledge of this which even now caused him some pain. But from a practical point of view, they probably hated the present French government even more than Nelson did.

'You sent for me, sir?'

'Ah, Mr Troy, come in, come in. Take a seat, take a seat.' Nathan realised, a little too late, that the grand surroundings were having the undesirable effect of making *him* appear grand. He would be strutting about like Old Jarvey next. He quite liked Troy, from what he had seen of him. He seemed to have been running the ship more or less single-handedly since the first lieutenant had gone off on his jaunt. Admittedly, he had the support of one other lieutenant – or rather *acting* lieutenant, Mr Bowyer – but here Nathan was less impressed. Bowyer had been a midshipman well into his thirties, having failed several examinations for lieutenant, and Nathan was inclined to think he had been promoted out of necessity, rather than from any show of promise on his part. But Nathan had only known him a few hours; the man was probably nervous.

Troy, too, was nervous, but at least he was not gibbering. He was presentable, he had an engaging manner and, more important than either of these facilities, he appeared to know what he was talking about. But it was time he came clean about the first lieutenant, and Nathan was not prepared to put up with any more nonsense about rudder braces. Perhaps a touch of Old Jarvey was not misplaced.

'Everything seems to be in very good order, considering,' he said, with a careless wave at the purser's papers. 'But I am more than a little concerned at the continuing absence of Mr Joyce. I am very much afraid that if he has not returned by the start of the afternoon watch, we shall have to sail without him. This would have serious consequences, not only for Mr Joyce himself, but also for those who accompany him. It is quite likely that they would be classed as deserters and exposed to the full rigours of a court martial.'

Troy chewed his bottom lip. 'But Mr Joyce is not a deserter, sir,' he protested. 'And the men are under his orders.'

'Then what are his orders? Come, sir, out with it. You cannot be accused of breaking a confidence. Mr Joyce could have had no notion, when he left, that the ship was about to receive a new commanding officer – could he?'

'No, sir.'

'Well, then?'

Troy looked miserably at Tully who may have made some small gesture of encouragement, for after a heavy sigh he poured out the story.

'He has gone on a pilgrimage, sir.'

If Troy had said Mr Joyce had taken up piracy, this would not have been more surprising.

'What – to Jerusalem?'

Troy could not restrain a smile. 'No, sir. Not quite so far, sir. He had only gone to Udvada, about a hundred miles to the north.'

'And what is Udvada?' He thought for a moment it might be one of the places St Thomas had visited after his arrival in India. But it had nothing to do with St Thomas, or, indeed, with Christianity.

'It is a shrine of the Zoroastrians, sir. A fire temple. Containing the oldest burning fire in the world.'

Nathan slid his eyes over to Tully to see how he was taking this. His face was impassive. Possibly he had heard it before. 'And who, pray, are the Zoroastrians?'

'They are the followers of the Prophet Zoroaster, sir. Otherwise known as Zarathustra, or the Magi. He lived in Persia, in the sixth century before Christ.'

'I see.' This was an exaggeration. 'However, what I do *not* see, Mr Troy, is why Mr Joyce has gone there.'

The troubled look returned. 'The fact is, sir, I would rather Mr Joyce told you that.'

'Mr Joyce is not here, Mr Troy. So I am asking you.'

'Well, Mr Joyce is a student of the philosophies of Zoroaster, sir.'

'A what? Who?' Nathan shot another glance at Tully who only shrugged.

'I believe – that is – well, his wife is a follower, sir. And I believe that – that Mr Joyce has undertaken something in the manner of a conversion.'

'Good God. So what *are* the philosophies of this – Zoro – what did you call him?'

'Zoroaster, sir. From what Mr Joyce has told me, they believe in one universal and transcendental God and in the struggle between good and evil. Between truth and order, on the one hand, and falsehood and chaos on the other. That the soul is sent into the mortal world to collect experiences of life and that the avoidance of – of such experiences – is a shirking of the moral responsibility and duty to oneself, one's soul and one's family.'

Nathan's gaze was unblinking, but he felt the corners of his mouth begin to twitch. He did not dare to meet Tully's eye. He cleared his throat.

'But Mr Joyce is an officer of His Majesty King George . . .' It was no good. A hysterical laughter bubbled up in his throat. He attempted to disguise this by a fit of coughing. A glance at Tully showed him apparently deep in thought, his chin cradled in one hand, but a certain strain about his features revealed his own inner struggle. Nathan rallied. 'He must, by law, be a Christian. Indeed, a member of the Church of England.'

'Lieutenant Joyce would argue that being a Zoroastrian is not incompatible with membership of the Church of England, sir.'

There was a small explosion from Tully. Nathan gave in. For a moment the two officers sat silently shaking. Mr Troy watched them with concern. Nathan made another attempt at sobriety. 'Would he, indeed? And how does he come to that conclusion?'

'Well, sir, you may not like this, sir –'

'Go on, Mr Troy.' Nathan tried to ignore the strange noises from the far side of the cabin.

'Well, sir, he argues that if killing people is accepted by the Church of England, in certain circumstances, then nothing in the Zoroastrian philosophy—'

'Wait a minute, wait a minute.' Nathan felt it incumbent on him to correct this delusion. 'The Church of England does not condone killing people. Only in time of war.'

'Yes, but—'

'And we are presently at war with the French, who are – or at least whose government is composed of atheists and anarchists and – and—'

'Sybarites?' put in Tully.

Nathan quelled him with a glance. 'I am surprised at you, Mr Troy. You seem to be sticking up for this man.'

'Well, he has been my commanding officer, sir, for some considerable time.'

'Yes. I suppose that is true. You are not yourself a follower of this Zoro fellow?'

'No, sir. I am a practising member of the Church of England, sir.'

Which was more than Nathan was. He feared he was lapsing into hypocrisy. Even so.

'Well, it is one thing to be a scholar of ancient religions –' he began. He paused as Tully stood up and left the room, his gait uncertain.

Nathan took a moment to compose himself. 'But it is quite another to go off on some pilgrimage to a pagan shrine when on active service, and to take a pinnace and twelve men with you.'

'I know, sir. But what was I to do, sir? I did attempt to remonstrate with him. But he said he would be back within two or three days, sir.'

'Did he? And when did you say he left?'

'Four days ago, sir.'

'Well, as I say, if he is not back by noon tomorrow, we are leaving without him.'

'Yes, sir. I am sure he will be back, sir.'

'Otherwise, Troy, you will assume the role of first lieutenant. Which you have been performing very commendably, it seems to me, in the meantime.'

'Yes, sir. Thank you, sir.' Troy looked perfectly miserable at the prospect.

'That is all, Mr Troy. Oh, except that I wish the ship to be restored to its original name – the *Hannibal*.'

Troy paused in his retreat towards the door. 'Sir?'

'The *Hannibal*. That was its name, you know, when it was in the British service. Perhaps you would be good enough to have the name *Pondicherry* painted over, and the name *Hannibal* inserted in its place.'

Troy appeared to be struggling for an appropriate response. Finally, he spoke. It was, however, far from appropriate. 'But – I am sorry, sir – but is that wise?'

'Is it *wise*? What can you mean, sir?' This time Nathan did not have to act the Old Jarvey.

'I am sorry, sir,' Troy said again. 'But many of the ship's company are attached to the present name. It is by way of being a unifying influence, sir. Given that many of them are not British, or subjects of King George. Their loyalty has been very much to the ship, sir.'

'Are you telling me that they will cease to be loyal if the ship's name is changed back to what it was when she was launched – and in the British service?'

'No, sir, but – it – it may cause some – some agitation, sir. They may think it is bad luck. I know that things are not quite as you would have ordered them, sir, and there are certain irregularities, but it has been a very happy ship, sir.'

Nathan sat back. His expression remained stern, but he realised with surprise that it *was* a happy ship. There was something *cheerful* about it. Cheerful, or lackadaisical? But he could not fault the discipline, not at present at least.

'Very well, Mr Troy. There may be something in what you say. We will leave things as they are for the present. I will wait to see just how happy a ship she is when we are at sea. And how efficient.'

'Thank you, sir.' Troy beamed. It transformed his somewhat pinched and anxious features and made him appear about twelve years old. 'You will not be disappointed, sir.'

'I am disappointed already,' Nathan confided when the lieutenant had gone and Tully, apparently sober and once more in control of his emotions, had taken his place. 'I had been quite hopeful about *Hannibal.* There is something much more . . . warlike about it, much more manly. Like the figurehead.' The ship's figurehead was of a bearded and helmeted warrior. 'The *Pondicherry* does very little for me, I am afraid. And as for the *Cherry* . . .' he shook his head. 'What sort of a name is that for a ship of war? And what are we to call the crew?'

'I am not sure I understand,' Tully confessed.

'You understand very well,' Nathan corrected him sternly. The crew of a ship were invariably known by the name of that ship, in its plural form. Hence the *Swiftsures* and the *Unicorns.* 'I cannot speak for others, but personally I would be loath to lead a boarding party onto the deck of an enemy with the cry, "Follow me, Cherries!" Or am I being unduly sensitive?'

'No, but then I would be as loath to refer to them as Hannibals,' Tully assured him. 'And I feel sure the captain of the *Fly* admits to a similar inhibition. Personally, I would revert to the simple, "Follow me, men", but in the passion of the moment who knows what I might utter.'

Nathan reflected on this for a moment as various alternatives occurred to him. 'But seriously,' he resumed, 'what do you make of this Zoroastrian business?'

'I cannot say I would lose any sleep over it,' Tully shrugged, 'provided he puts the requirements of the service before those of his religion, like most members of the Church of England.'

'Yes, but the signs are not good in that respect.'

'I suppose we will have to wait until we have met the man, before we make any judgement against him.'

'If we ever do meet him,' Nathan replied caustically. 'I mean it, you know. I will not delay our departure for him.'

'Of course not. I can take over as first lieutenant if necessary. I am senior to Troy by about three months, apparently. Provided you wish it, of course.'

'And what if I do not wish it?' Tully looked at him in surprise. 'What if I wish you to be captain?'

The smile froze. 'Can you do that?'

'Of course I can. I am a commodore. I can do anything. We do not have a captain and you are the most senior officer present, apart from myself. You have been a commander. You are entirely competent. You have no unnatural vices. Besides those I am acquainted with. And you are a member of the Church of England, are you not?'

Tully did not deny it. 'And you do not wish to be captain yourself?'

'I could never bring myself to captain a ship called the *Cherry*,' Nathan assured him. 'If it were restored to the *Hannibal* I might consider it.'

'But you could insist. You are a commodore. You can do anything.'

'Then I am making you captain, and that is all there is to it.'

'Well, thank you. I will do my best not to disappoint you. But what if Mr Joyce comes back? He is senior to me by several years.'

'Makes no difference. It is my decision. Subject to the approval of the governor, of course. But I cannot see that he will make any objection. I do not think Mr Joyce is a favourite of his.'

'No. So. Very well.' It was hard to tell if he was pleased or not. Nathan thought he probably was. 'And you wish the ship to be ready to sail by the first bell in the afternoon watch.'

'I do.'

And so it was. The last of the provisions were taken aboard some two hours before this, but Nathan waited until the sun was exactly overhead before he gave the order to weigh anchor.

Slowly, but with commendable style, aided by a light north-easterly wind and in brilliant sunlight, the squadron threaded its way through the pattern of islands, past Bombay Castle, and out into the deep water channel leading to the open sea. From the unfamiliar vantage of the poop deck, Nathan looked back at the rest of the squadron – *his* squadron – led by the frigate *Bombay*, stretching back in a long line towards Parel Island and the watchful eye of the governor.

Nathan had taken leave of him at nine in the morning after confirming the appointment of Tully as captain and receiving his sealed and written orders, which were not to be opened until they had cleared the 18th parallel. Nathan was slightly suspicious of this precaution, but it failed to diminish the enormous sense of pride and pleasure he experienced as the squadron headed out into the open sea. He felt that not only the governor but also the entire population of Bombay, all 60,000 of them, had taken time off to watch their departure – seven men-of-war, under a full press of sail, led by the *Pondicherry*, the blue ensign of

Admiral Nelson at her stern and the broad pennant of a commodore at her mizzen.

They were almost abreast of the lighthouse on Old Woman's Island when a small boat was sighted on the starboard bow, under oars.

It was the missing pinnace and unless Nathan was very much mistaken, the figure standing up in the stern and frantically waving his hat was the missing first lieutenant and Zoroastrian, Mr William Joyce.

Chapter Thirteen

The Malabar Patrol

'What the Devil is going on? Are we at war or something? Have the French landed?'

The lieutenant glared about him as if they were lurking aboard his ship, but he must surely have noticed the commodore's pennant flying from the mizzen, and his eyes flew uneasily to the quarterdeck where Nathan now stood watching him, with Tully and the other officers at his side. Joyce was a great bull of a man with a bellow to match. Almost as tall as Nathan but much broader in the girth and at the shoulder. He would have made a fine wrestler or prize fighter and he was clearly as popular with the crew as any Mendoza. There had been a spontaneous cheer from them when the cutter was first sighted and though they had been swiftly restored to order by Troy and the petty officers, it left Nathan in no doubt of the esteem in which the first lieutenant was held.

The *Pondicherry* had backed her sails to allow the boat to come alongside, and the rest of the squadron was obliged to follow suit so that Nathan had the ludicrous impression that the world was holding its breath for Joyce to make his entrance. And Joyce milked it for all it was worth.

His first gesture upon stepping aboard had been to doff his hat and bow to his supporters. It could not be called the customary salute to the quarterdeck by any means. Then came the bellow and the glare, and Nathan braced himself for conflict. Joyce was the heavier by a good two or three stone but he carried a fair bit of that about the waist and he would tire more easily. Keep your distance, Nathan thought, and dance round him, hit him a good few blows to the face and then, when he is losing it, in at the belly hard and fast and dancing away before he can grab you.

Remarkable. That it should even cross his mind for an instant. Officers in His Britannic Majesty's Navy did not conduct themselves like prize fighters. Or wrestlers. Their contests were much more refined, and far more deadly.

Troy was down there talking to him quietly, presumably informing him of recent developments and conveying the commodore's instructions to wait upon him in the great cabin. Joyce squared his massive shoulders and touched his hand to his hat, but the look that accompanied this gesture might be thought challenging. The diminutive figure who had appeared at his side must be Mrs Joyce. She wore Indian dress, with a scarf covering her hair and most of her features. An added complication, but it must be dealt with – and soon. The pilot cutter was about to leave and as far as Nathan was concerned, Mrs Joyce would be aboard it.

The rest of the absentees came aboard more warily than their leader, looking questioningly at their shipmates. Nathan turned away and strode through the door into what had once been the lieutenant's seraglio, Tully at his heels. Let battle commence.

'If it will help matters . . .' Tully began as they entered the cabin.

Nathan shook his head sternly. He had not a moment's regret for his appointment of Tully, but now he had taken the measure of the man he had replaced, and been given an indication of his popularity with the crew, he could not help wishing that they had left an hour or so earlier. He would have sacrificed the pinnace and all twelve men to avoid the present confrontation; not that he feared confrontation, but the last thing he wanted was to give the crew the impression that there was a serious division between their officers.

When Joyce entered the cabin, however, there was a very obvious change of mood. He appeared contrite, even sheepish. He was very sorry, he said, not to have been here when the commodore came aboard, but he trusted everything was in order – his eyes flitted from Nathan to Tully and then about the cabin as if he was looking for something he had left behind, or, more likely, wondering where it had all gone.

'And I was sorry to learn of your absence,' Nathan told him evenly. 'But now you are here, let me introduce you to Captain Tully, who is your new commanding officer. I trust the rudder braces made the journey worthwhile,' he added, with a hint of irony, as he saw the officer struggling to come to terms with this intelligence.

'Ah, well, as to that . . .' They had not got so far as Surat, the lieutenant explained, having taken longer on the journey than he had anticipated. With the wind remaining steadily against them, he had decided to return prematurely to Bombay.

Nathan listened to this explanation in a patient but discouraging silence. Joyce was an Irishman, a Dubliner, in fact, with all the easy charm of that race, but he must have been aware that it was having little effect on his present audience. Nathan had been concerned that Joyce would demand to see Nelson's order, and even challenge its authority, but either he did not think of it or Nathan's remark about the rudder braces entirely took the wind out of his sails.

'Well, I am glad that you were able to join us before we sailed off without you,' Nathan assured him insincerely. 'It would have been a great loss.' But as he felt more in command of the situation, he experienced a corresponding need to put Joyce more at his ease and to leave the subject of fire temples for another occasion. 'As you may have gathered, we are embarking upon a cruise down the coast of Malabar,' he informed him. 'I regret that we will have to wait until we pass the 18th parallel before I am at liberty to reveal the governor's orders in their entirety, but I can tell you that we will be absent for some weeks.' He allowed a small pause for the lieutenant to take this in before he lobbed the next bombshell. 'So I expect that you will wish to take your leave of Mrs Joyce before she is set ashore. Her ladies, she will find, have already preceded her – with all their belongings.'

He observed the flush spreading from the lieutenant's bulging neck, though whether of anger or embarrassment it was impossible to judge. Probably a degree of both. 'She may avail herself of the pilot cutter, which I am assured will be ready to leave in a few minutes.'

Joyce opened his mouth, closed it, opened it again, and finally settled for a curt gesture that was something between a bow and a nod before taking his leave.

Nathan came out on the quarterdeck to make sure that Mrs Joyce did not miss the boat. He found the couple locked in a passionate embrace. Mrs Joyce was weeping. So, too, was Mr Joyce. This was distressing but not unusual. Most men of Nathan's acquaintance wept on occasion, even when parting from their wives. What was the more surprising was that so many of the crew were weeping. Mrs Joyce was clearly as well-liked as her husband.

Nathan felt uncomfortably like Captain Bligh when he dragged the wretched Mr Christian from his Polynesian lovely. When he had first read of this incident – and viewed the dramatic illustration that accompanied it – his sympathies had been mostly with the master's mate. But he had not been a commanding officer then. Now he assumed as stern a visage as any despot, hands clasped firmly behind his back, as the pilot cutter headed back to Bombay with the diminutive figure waving, and doubtless still weeping, at the stern.

Lightning and heavy clouds, but without rain . . . Nathan reviewed his first entry in the commodore's log and found it wanting. The words had been written without much thought to posterity – or, indeed, any thought at all – and as he viewed this single line on the otherwise pristine page, he wondered if he might not have contrived something a little more heroic, portentous, even, to mark the start of his first voyage as a flag officer. As portentous, perhaps, as the dark thunder clouds and the violent flashes of lightning which continued to track them along the western horizon and provided an epic backdrop to the progress of the seven men-of-war as they rode on the back of the brisk north-easterly down the Malabar coast.

'Lightning and heavy clouds but without rain' did not really cut the mustard so far as posterity was concerned. Certainly it fell far short of Homer. But he could hardly write what was truly on his mind, for Nathan was a seriously worried man.

What if they sailed all the way to Mangalore and all the way back without encountering a single Frenchman? How would that look in his journal or – more worryingly – in the report he would have to write to their lordships of the Admiralty? Especially if Bonaparte took the opportunity afforded by his absence, and the prevailing winds, to send a large part of his army across the Arabian Sea and land them on the unguarded shores of India.

It was all very well to talk of Mangalore being the obvious place for a French landing, but it was only obvious – a word Nathan distrusted on principle – if the French were intent on sending troops and supplies to the Sultan of Mysore. What if they made straight for Bombay, the commercial hub of the East India Company, with nothing to defend it but a garrison of 1,500 troops and a 12-gun brig – the little *Fly* being the only vessel they had left behind?

But it was too late to do anything about it now, except fret. And indeed, there was little else to occupy his mind. Tully and Joyce ran a tight ship between them, and with an apparent minimum of effort. *Lightning and heavy clouds, but without rain.* This summation might as well have been applied to the first lieutenant as to the weather. A massive, brooding presence on the quarterdeck, he was clearly nursing a grievance, and there was the occasional flash of something in the eye that threatened to erupt into violence, but in public, at least, he kept himself under a tight rein. And you could not fault him as an officer. He was easy in his manner, at least in so far as the junior officers and the crew were concerned, and confident in his authority. It must have helped, of course, that his voice carried effortlessly from one end of the deck to the other and that he looked as if he could pick up a man with one hand and break him in half – but, happily, he was never obliged to perform such a feat. The crew went about their business with admirable efficiency and no apparent need of instruction. There was no call for the boatswain's mates to chivvy them into action or resort to their starters – in fact, the absence of the notorious knotted rope was another point in the lieutenant's favour so far as Nathan was concerned. It was undoubtedly an advantage that so many of the crew were trained seamen, of course. Danish, French or British, there was scarcely a landman among them. They could hand, reef and steer as well as any crew Nathan had ever commanded, and a good deal better than some. They had weighed anchor, set sail, and led the squadron through the tortuous maze of islands and shoals that comprised Bombay harbour with admirable composure – and the *Pondicherry* was not an easy ship to handle, by any means. For all her airs and graces, she was a damned awkward brute, even in a moderate wind.

In fact, all Nathan's complaints, in those first few days, were reserved for the ship. She responded quite slowly to the helm and she drifted alarmingly to leeward. Nathan would not have called her an old slug – an indictment he had heard levelled at the *Leopard*, which was one of her sister ships – but he very rapidly came to the conclusion that she possessed all the vices of her breed – speed and manoeuvrability sacrificed for an extra layer of guns.

The one thing he could not complain about was his accommodation. Sometimes he would just sit there admiring the play of light from the stern windows on all that polished woodwork and brass. Or he would go out onto the stern gallery to lean upon the rail, and gaze out upon the rest of the squadron under a full press of sail in line astern. And as if this was not enough for any man, he had a separate dining room and sleeping cabin as well – and a vast private larder on the orlop deck, which he had not been niggardly in stocking before they left Bombay. But his pleasure was tarnished by the knowledge that he had almost as much space reserved for his exclusive convenience as that provided for the rest of crew. It was not too bad for the officers who shared the space immediately beneath him, and had the advantage of their own stern windows – with a quarter gallery for Tully – but most of the men were accommodated on the lower deck where they had to find whatever space they could between the guns – 257 men and boys crammed into a space not much bigger than that provided for the commodore. Each of these individuals was permitted just fourteen inches of space to sling his hammock – though of course he had the luxury of twenty-eight inches when one half of the crew was on watch. Yet they seemed in good spirits and there was no muttering or black looks. Even the routine tasks such as the daily ritual of scrubbing the decks and lashing and stowing the hammocks were performed with cheerful efficiency. In fact, if they had not been so cheerful, Nathan might have thought they were automatons, as well drilled and inhuman as Prussian infantry.

He was less impressed by their gunnery. On the morning of the second day, before the sun was at its most merciless, he had the whole squadron practise at the great guns. It was a fairly perfunctory practice – there was no time for manoeuvres or for firing at a target – they just blazed away for an hour or so in line ahead, and afterwards they collated the rates of fire. They were not good. Good would have been three rounds in just under five minutes. The *Bombay* came closest to that, with three in just over six. The *Pondicherry* was by far the worst and there were several injuries. Men began to run into each other, tempers frayed, mistakes were made. One man dropped a twenty-four-pound shot on his foot; one lost a finger on a touch hole; there were two serious burns. Joyce's thunder threatened to erupt. The ship had been in dry dock for the best part of a year, he explained later to his two senior officers, and there had been no opportunity to practise in Bombay harbour. They would do better with more practice.

Nathan said nothing, at least in public. But afterwards he and Tully held a post-mortem in the privacy of the great cabin.

'Three rounds in nine minutes!' Nathan held his head in his hands. 'We might as well command a transport ship.'

'It was not quite as bad as that,' Tully demurred. 'And I am inclined to blame the guns at least as much as the crews.'

There was something in this. So far as Nathan could tell, most of them were the original guns issued to the ship when she was launched in 1778, and they were the old Armstrong pattern which had been standard during the American War – instead of the new Blomefields which were a lot easier to handle and were fitted with flintlocks in place of the old-fashioned slow matches. And this was not his only complaint.

'Why have we no carronades?' he demanded of Joyce. The short, stubbly smashers forged by the Caron Company of Falkirk had become a standard feature aboard most King's ships since their introduction in '82. Nathan was not entirely enamoured of them for they were notoriously inaccurate, but they were very handy at close quarters and as far as he was aware they had replaced the quarterdeck 6-pounders on all ships over a certain size, even the old fourth-rates.

'She was in French hands when they were issued,' Joyce pointed out. 'And we have not received any from England.'

'But the *Bombay* has them and so does the *Cornwallis* – and the *Comet* has nothing but carronades.'

Joyce inclined his head in appreciation of this intelligence but had no comment to make. They were the Bombay Marine. They could have what they liked.

'But I do not think it would matter what guns we used,' Nathan confided now to Tully in the privacy of his cabin. 'It is the gun crews. They are altogether too rigid, too *precise*. I know one must take care with powder and shot and so forth, but I could have had my dinner in the time it takes them to sponge and worm out. And when you hurry them, they run about like headless chickens.'

Tully frowned at the comparison. 'Some gun crews are better than others,' he pointed out. 'If they were to fire at will, it would be a much better performance. And I doubt there is a ship in the Indian Ocean that could stand up to a single broadside, let alone three.'

'So long as it can be brought to bear,' muttered Nathan ominously.

'Is there any reason why it should not be?' Tully demanded. 'They handle the ship well enough – you said so yourself.'

For answer Nathan stood up and fetched a bundle of papers from his desk. They were the Sailing Quality Reports filed by her last two captains and they listed a catalogue of complaints. Nathan skipped over most of them as carping but the one that he found most damning was the reference to her exceptionally low freeboard. When she heeled to leeward, even in a moderate wind, it was impossible to open the gunports on her lower deck – a serious disadvantage in a fighting ship. Nathan was not the least bit reassured by the suggestion that she should always attack to leeward.

'Well, I cannot argue with you about that,' Tully agreed, 'it is a bad fault. But she sails as well and as fast as most frigates when the wind is on her quarter – and I am sure that not even you could fault the sailing qualities of her crew. She has the best topmen it has been my privilege to serve with.'

This was probably true, but it reminded Nathan of something else he had noted.

'I could have been mistaken, but after dinner, when the midshipmen were larking about in the rigging, I could swear I saw an ape up there.'

'Many of the midshipmen look like apes,' Tully remarked, but in such a way as to alert Nathan's suspicions.

'This was a very small ape, a great deal smaller even than a midshipman.'

'Well, it might have been the monkey.'

'The monkey?'

'The midshipmen have a monkey. It belonged to Mr Joyce's women but it was left behind when they were thrown off the ship. They call it Hannibal. It lives with them in the gunroom. It is a kind of ship's mascot. Do you wish them to get rid of it?'

This would mean throwing it overboard, though being midshipmen they would probably eat it. Tempting, but Nathan dismissed the suggestion. 'Perhaps we should put it to one of the guns,' he remarked. 'It could scarce do worse than the men.'

A tightening of Tully's features revealed that he had gone too far. For the rest of their discussion he was coldly polite, and Nathan conceded that he should let Tully and Joyce deal with the handling of the ship while he confined his attention to strategic concerns.

This presented sufficient problems on its own account.

When Nathan opened the governor's written orders, he received an unpleasant surprise. He had expected them to confirm the verbal agreement made between them, and to repeat Nelson's injunction to prevent French troops and supplies from reaching India. His previous experience of official orders should have alerted him to the probability that it would never be as simple as that.

To Commodore Nathan Peake,
His Britannic Majesty's ship Pondicherry, *on the Bombay station*

12 October, 1798

Sir,
In accordance with the authority conferred upon me by the Directors of the Honourable East India Company and His Majesty's Board of Control, and following the instruction of Admiral Nelson, I hereby confirm your appointment as Commodore of the vessels that have been put at your disposal, and request and require that you take whatever steps may be necessary to prevent the landing of French troops and materiel in India and to seek out and destroy those vessels of the King's enemies as may be operating in the region.

You are to consult and combine with the Commodore of the Company Marine operating out of Bombay, in protecting the trade and other interests of the said company and of His Majesty. You are especially required to seek his advice on all matters appertaining to company policy, with particular regard to relations with the native princes, respecting the neutrality of those princes not engaged in the current hostilities, whilst undertaking everything in your power to prevent the intervention of foreign powers opposed to the interests of the company and of His Majesty.

I remain &c.

Jonathan Duncan
Governor of Bombay

There were a number of reasons for Nathan to feel uneasy about this missive. Despite the encouraging introduction, it was not at all clear that Nathan was, indeed, commander of the combined squadron. Yet, at the same time, it was phrased in such a way as to ensure that he would be the one singled out for blame if anything should go wrong. The last sentence was particularly worrying. Was the Sultan of Mysore included in the stricture about the native princes? If so, and it must be assumed that he was, what were they supposed to do if French ships were found under the protection of the Sultan's flag? Sit outside Mangalore until the French came out – or encourage them to do so by shelling the port? What else was a bomb ketch for?

It seemed to Nathan that the governor had 'set him up'. Was Duncan genuinely concerned at the possibility of provoking a war with the Sultan of Mysore? Or was it exactly what he and the Honourable East India Company wanted?

He wondered if the commodore of the Bombay Marine could tell him. He sent a note over in the launch inviting him to dinner.

* * *

Charles Picket was in his fifties, quite small and dapper with the powdered wig and courtly comportment of an older generation. In fact, he looked more like a lawyer than a seaman – he reminded Nathan a little of Robespierre, the little lawyer from Arras who had become leader of the French during the bloodiest days of the Revolution. He had the same sharp eyes and precise manner and a fussy way of dabbing at his mouth with his napkin. And the same artful way of waiting for you to say the wrong thing, or make the wrong move.

There were just the two of them for dinner and Nathan fussed a little over the menu and the preparations, wanting it to be just right. They began with a soup made from a freshly caught turtle, flavoured with brandy; followed by a chicken, cooked in the Breton style, with cider and Calvados; and then a custard tart with dried fruits for pudding. Nathan made sure there was plenty of wine to go with it, but Picket drank abstemiously. A small sip of wine between courses, dabbing at his lips with his napkin, while they talked pleasantly enough of Nathan's life in the Navy and Picket's in India.

He had been with the company since he was sixteen, he said, and had first come out to India as master's mate on an East Indiaman forty years ago. The company had made him what he was; he was a company man, from head to toe. He said nothing to suggest it, but it was clear to Nathan that he did not trust any man who was not.

Nathan waited until they were on the cognac before he asked him what he really wanted to know.

'Have you thought,' he said, 'of what we are to do, if we

come upon the French while they are landing troops upon the shore?'

'We would attempt to stop them, of course,' replied Picket, easily enough, 'according to our instructions.'

Nathan nodded, as if he had come to the same conclusion. 'But what if they were to land in Mangalore itself?' he said.

'I believe that would be for you to decide – would it not?'

'If we were to attack the French in the Sultan's own port, it would be an act of war,' Nathan pointed out.

'That would be for the Sultan to determine,' said Picket with a smile. 'But we could hardly stand by and do nothing, could we?'

So now Nathan knew. This was why they had given him the command of the Bombay Marine. This was why they had sent the *Stromboli* along. Duncan must have summed him up at a glance. An arrogant hothead, out to prove himself. Just the man to provoke a war. And if there was an inquiry by Parliament afterwards, they would throw him to the wolves.

Chapter Fourteen

Enemy in Sight

'There are four of them. I see them with my own eye. Close under the guns of the *castelo*. Three *brigues* and one *fregata*. The *brigues* are privateers, I think, but the *fregata* is *da Franca* – a French national ship, of forty guns or more.'

The Portuguese captain sat in Nathan's cabin, with a glass of Madeira in his hand and the satisfied look of a man who is the bearer of important news, especially if it is bad news for the men he is telling it to.

They had encountered him and the barque he commanded just over a hundred miles north of Mangalore. The French had arrived in the port four days ago, he said, while he was taking on cargo. No, he had not seen them unloading troops or munitions, or anything else of a military nature. They had moored round a bend in the river, too far away for him to see very much at all, except for their flags and their guns. The brigs, he thought, counted between twenty and thirty guns apiece, the frigate – well, as he had said, a very large frigate indeed. He had even seen its name across the stern – *Forte*. Strength. It was reported that they had come from the Île de France and he had no reason to doubt it. Where else would they have come from – a French squadron in the Indian Ocean? The British had taken every Indian base they had ever possessed. He knew nothing of their presence in Egypt.

'Thank you, captain,' said Nathan, standing and extending his hand. 'I am sure you will wish to be on your way. You have been of great assistance.'

As soon as he had gone, Nathan sent a message over to the *Bombay* requesting the honour of another visit from Commodore Picket.

They consulted the chart together. Mangalore was on the Gurupur River, which ran parallel to the coast for several miles before veering westward to enter the Arabian Sea, river and sea being separated by a narrow strip of low-lying land that looked to be mostly marsh and jungle. The castle which the captain had mentioned dominated the harbour and the town – a massive modern fortress built by Tipu's father, Hyder Ali, with the advice of French engineers – and there were several additional batteries covering the mouth of the river.

'Is it possible, I wonder, to send the *Comet* in to reconnoitre?' Nathan enquired.

'It is possible,' Picket conceded. 'We are not yet at war. Though they might instruct her to moor in the mouth of the river. But what would it tell us, other than what we already know?'

'We might discover whether the French have landed troops. And now many.'

'And if they have? Is that a *casus belli*?'

This was the problem, of course. It was for Nathan to determine whether it was cause for war or not, and to act accordingly. No one else was going to. Not Picket, certainly.

'Even if it were,' Nathan retorted, 'I doubt we have the resources to act upon it. And we certainly do not have the authority.'

He thought a slight shadow crossed his fellow commodore's face at the use of the word 'we', though it might have been the reflections from the water. The skies had been clear for the past two days and with the wind remaining in the north-east they had made better time than Nathan had anticipated. If the wind held and they kept to their present course, they would be within sight of Mangalore by the following morning. Little enough time to decide on peace or war.

'Well, we have the *Stromboli*,' said Picket, diffidently.

'You propose shelling the port?'

'I merely make the suggestion,' Picket replied smoothly. 'It is you who command. But the mere threat may be sufficient to incline the French to leave of their own accord. Or the authorities may pressure them to do so.'

'Having already done what they came to do.'

'Quite. But it would be a victory of sorts.'

Yes, but whose? Nathan thought. He did not wish to be considered shy, but the fact remained that the presence of a forty-gun French frigate shortened the odds considerably in the French favour. The *Pondicherry* had some small advantage in guns, but none at all in speed and manoeuvrability. She would win in the end, of course – she *had* to win – but she would not be able to help the rest of the squadron. How would they fare against three large French corsairs? The ships of the Bombay Marine were crewed by Lascars – Indian seamen, from the Laccadive Islands, for the most part. Good seafarers, no doubt about it – Picket said the best in the world, but then he would. It was when it came to fighting the guns that the doubt crept in.

Nathan did not for a moment suppose that they were more lacking in courage or any worse at gunnery than British seamen – certainly in practice they had been better than the crew of the *Pondicherry* – but this was not their war. They had signed up in the expectation of fighting pirates, not the French. They would fight for their ships, probably, and for their shipmates, certainly. And if it was backs to the wall, they would fight to the death. But it was not backs to the wall. If Nathan was the French commander, he would make a run for the open sea. Cut and run to the south-west, with the wind behind him. After all, he had achieved his purpose. And if Nathan was an Indian seaman, or even an officer of the Bombay Marine, he might be tempted to let him go. Good riddance and a fair wind for the Île de France.

He came to a decision. 'We will set up a blockade,' he informed Picket. 'And we will let them know we have the option of shelling the port, if it should come to it.'

He spoke with an assurance he was far from feeling. It was a poor compromise, and he had a strong suspicion that he was doing exactly what Duncan and Picket wanted him to do. Everything now depended upon the French.

* * *

The wind dropped off a little during the night and it was mid-afternoon before they came in sight of Mangalore, or rather the entrance to the river, for the port was beyond sight from the sea. Nathan was in no doubt, however, that the arrival of the British squadron would have been noted from the shore and very swiftly conveyed to the French. It was now a question of what they would do about it.

He had considered tempting them out by placing the brigs and the bomb ketch close to the shore while the *Pondicherry* and the *Bombay* stayed further out to sea. But it was far too risky, and Picket would never agree. They might lose half the squadron, and still let the French get away. So he compromised again by placing the *Bombay* in the mouth of the river, while the rest of the squadron cruised up and down the coast in an elongated figure of eight, dropping off the wind and wearing at the end of every tack.

And so they began the long, laborious, thankless task of a blockade. Which was what the Navy did, most of the time. Off Brest or Toulon, Bordeaux or Cadiz, Leghorn or Genoa – anywhere the enemy kept a fleet or a squadron. Pinning them in harbour to keep the sea lanes open for British trade – and closed to the enemy. At least that was the theory. In practice, it did not always work out that way. Adverse winds could force a blockading fleet far off station and allow the enemy to sneak out the odd cruiser, sometimes the whole fleet. But it was the strategy their lordships of the Admiralty had decided upon, and it was the strategy Nathan employed now, even though it condemned the blockading crews to days, weeks, months, even years of idleness and boredom, ploughing a seemingly endless furrow up and down the same heartbreaking stretch of ocean with just a distant smudge of enemy coast to remind them of why they were here. Not for them the glamour of cruising for prizes, or even the risk of death in battle. Instead, they performed the routine, repetitive tasks of keeping the ship afloat. They scrubbed the decks, practised at the guns, did musket drill and cutlass drill; they lowered the boats and took them in, climbed the rigging, hauled at the braces, took in sail or let it out; they changed the watch every four hours, night and day, slept and woke, lashed and stowed; they bickered and quarrelled, were punished for it, ate their food, drank their wine and their grog, played the fiddle, danced a jig, while the ship turned and turned about, and the glass was turned and turned about, and the ship's bell tolled the precise passage of time, hour after hour after hour . . .

Nathan did what he always did. Played chess with the midshipmen and the officers, wrote letters, kept his journal up to date, paced the quarterdeck or the poop or the stern gallery – a novel luxury – watched the stars, thought about home, thought about Sara, and thought about what he would do when the war ended, if it ever did. Once he invited the other captains over for dinner. He decided he did not much like them, apart from Cutler, the captain of the *Comet*, who had lost his leg at Calvi. He had been a midshipman on the old *Agamemnon* under Nelson, which Nathan remembered from his time on the blockade of Liguria, though Cutler had departed by then. He had been invalided out of the service, but family connections had secured him a commission with the Bombay Marine.

He was a modest, unassuming fellow, but Nathan had the impression that he was tough as well as steady, and he had the technical interest Nathan approved of in an officer.

It was partly this that inspired Nathan to talk to Blunt. He had seen little of him since they joined the *Pondicherry*, surprisingly little after such a close acquaintance on their long journey to India. Tully had taken on the task of schoolmaster, along with his other duties, instructing all the young gentlemen in mathematics and navigation and those other facilities required of a sea officer. But Nathan suddenly took it into his head that he should do a spot of mentoring. Make sure the boy was all right, broaden his outlook a little. Seafaring was not just a matter of mathematics and navigation. Nathan had spent much of his time as a midshipman aboard a survey vessel in the South Seas before the war, and had been fortunate to escape many of the restrictions and formalities that were the norm in the King's service. Certainly he had never had to endure the tedium of a blockade. And he had been privileged to have James Johnston, the captain of the *Hermes*, as his tutor – the finest man he had ever served under, a legendary explorer and a kindly, accomplished gentleman of considerable intellect. He had taught Nathan not only the finer points of seamanship but encouraged him to share his own interest in many other things – philosophy, music, poetry, astronomy and the natural world – he had even, for a while, managed to interest Nathan in birds. So on the fourth day of the blockade, lacking any other diversion, Nathan decided he must do the same for Blunt.

He began by suggesting they climb into the tops to spy out the lie of the land, such as they could see of it from three miles out to sea. But when they had reached the crosstrees he spotted something closer to hand to which he drew the boy's attention.

'Have you noticed the birds?' he said.

Blunt indicated politely that he had. Indeed, it was impossible for him not to have noticed them unless he had lost the use of both eyes and his hearing – there were several hundred of them in the immediate vicinity – and in case he lacked either facility they had been trying to shit on him for the last five minutes.

'Not those birds,' said Nathan, noting the direction of his gaze. 'They are only seagulls –' thus dismissing up to a dozen different species, 'those down there.' He pointed them out, close to the surface of the water. 'Those nasty little black things, more like bats than birds. Those are storm petrels. Named after Saint Peter, because they look like they are walking on water. We call them storm petrels because they hide in the lee of a ship during a storm. Mother Carey's chickens, sailors called them in the old days, from *Mater Cara*, a name the Papists have for the Virgin Mary – and it was believed she sent them to warn of an approaching storm.' Nathan let his gaze roam the distant horizon – cloudless as it had been for days. A storm was all they needed in this situation.

But they had come to see the shore, not the birds. Nathan trained his glass upon it. From this far out it presented an unbroken line of jungle, shrouded in a haze – he could not even see the mouth of the river, let alone the port beyond. No sign of a human presence. They would be there, though, looking back at him and making their own reports.

'They can get word to the Sultan, you know, within hours,' he said.

'The birds, sir?'

'No, not the birds, Blunt, the people, the Sultan's people. They can send a message from Mangalore to Seringapatam – one hundred and thirty miles away – in ten hours. They use runners. Professional runners, like the Greeks. They have teams of them, stationed in watchtowers at ten-mile intervals and they run in relays. They can run ten miles in less than an hour – through jungle. What do you think of that?'

Blunt said nothing but doubtless he was storing it away for future reference.

'That is better than Philippedes, you know,' Nathan informed him. Blunt frowned enquiringly. 'You must know who Philippedes is, Blunt. He was the first marathon runner. He carried the news of the Greek victory over the Persians from Marathon to Athens – twenty-six miles in three hours. Then he died. They were tough in those days. You don't know you're born, Blunt.'

He put his eye back to the glass. 'They are probably on their way already. Ten hours and Tipu will know we are here. Better than the Royal Mail. Bristol to London. Same distance. Sixteen hours. And that is on a good day. I went to Portsmouth once on the Mail, when I was a midshipman, and we had to get out and walk most of the way. And push. Took half a day. They use coconut oil.'

'Sir?'

'For their joints. Give it to you fellows, you'd eat it. Rat cooked in coconut oil. Ever had rat, Blunt?'

'No, sir.'

'Don't know you're born. I used to cook it spatchcocked when I was a midshipman, with a bread sauce. I was famous for it.'

He regarded his protégé thoughtfully. He appeared to have lost weight since their sojourn in the desert.

'Are you getting enough to eat?' he enquired.

'Yes, sir.' Nathan did not believe him. Midshipmen never had enough to eat.

'Made any friends since you came aboard?'

'One or two, sir.' Supplied with caution.

'Who?'

'Well, Mr Vivian is one, sir.'

'Mr Vivian? He is the one who went with Mr Joyce to the temple of fire, is he not?'

'Yes, sir.'

'Talk about it much?'

'Not much, sir.'

Liar. Fair enough, though. You did not want to be considered an informer, even by yourself. Nathan recalled their conversation when they were crossing the desert, and how Blunt had been going for a parson but had lost his faith in God. He wondered if he had found it again, after his experiences in the Tower of Taiba. But apparently not.

'Not that I did not pray when we were under attack,' Blunt confessed, 'but I did not know quite what I was praying to.'

'No. Well, that is nothing to be ashamed of,' Nathan assured him. 'We all pray in times of extremity.'

'Even you, sir?' He appeared startled.

'I am not sure how to take that, Mr Blunt.'

'I did not mean that . . . It is just that . . .'

'I pray to my clockmaker,' Nathan told him.

'Your clockmaker, sir?'

'Mr Harrison. The inventor of the marine chronometer. Surely you have heard of Mr Harrison.'

'Yes, sir. Mr Tully told us about him. But I did not know he was someone people prayed to, like the Papists and their saints. Not that I mean—'

'People don't. Only me. As far as I know. Of course he may have a following I do not know about. A kind of cult. The Harrisonians. But it is a private thing. Have you never thought of the universe as a chronometer?'

'Not really,' said Mr Blunt doubtfully.

'Well, if you think about it, it makes a great deal of sense. A universal chronometer, run by magnetism. The universal clockmaker is a whimsical notion on my part. But if there is a God, or any kind of Supreme Being, it would be nice to think of him as somewhat resembling Mr Harrison, do you not think? A being of endless patience, setting his mind to improvement, and perfection. And making everything run smoothly.'

'But it never does, does it, sir?'

'No, Blunt, it never does.'

'Ahura Mazda is a bit like that,' Blunt said after a moment of silent reflection.

Nathan looked at him. 'Who?'

'Ahura Mazda. It is the name of the deity worshipped by the followers of Zoroaster, sir.'

'Did Mr Joyce tell you that?' Nathan had a moment of panic at the thought of Mr Joyce going around converting the ship's complement, one by one, starting with the officers, until they had taken over the whole ship.

'No, sir.' Blunt blushed, realising he had been trapped into an indiscretion. 'Mr Vivian did, sir.'

'He is not a follower of Zoroaster, is he?'

'No, sir. He is Church of England, sir.'

'So this – Ahuro what?'

'Ahura, sir. Ahura Mazda.'

'This Ahura Mazda is like Mr Harrison, you say?'

'Only that – well, the followers of Zoroaster believe that the motion of the planets and astral bodies and so on conforms to a master plan.'

'So do the Christians,' Nathan pointed out. 'So do all religions, do they not?'

'Possibly, sir. But the Zoroastrians believe that this order is threatened by a destructive spirit who represents chaos and falsehood. Angra Mainyu. And that we have the freedom to choose between one or the other. That is why things keep going wrong.'

'Because so many people choose Angry Mainoo?'

'Yes, sir.'

'But that is not unlike the Devil in Christian belief.'

'No, but Zoroaster came before the Christians, sir. Six centuries before.'

'So, do you think this is the religion you are looking for, Blunt?'

'No, sir. But it is interesting all the same.' Then after a pause. 'But I like some things about it. They say that before you are born your soul is united with its guardian spirit which they call the *fravashi* and that during life the *fravashi* acts as a kind of guardian and protector. After death the soul is reunited with the *fravashi* and the experiences it has collected during life enable it to continue the battle against evil. In the spirit world.'

'Yes,' said Nathan after a moment. 'I suppose that is quite comforting.'

'But your body has to be eaten by vultures.'

'I beg your pardon?'

'When you die, your body cannot be buried. It has to be left out in the open to be eaten by vultures and other carrion.'

This was not something Nathan could condone. If death was not to be avoided, and most learned opinion tended to concur on that point, he would rather take his chances with the Reverend Judd and be buried in Alfriston churchyard.

They both stared into space for a while, lost in their private thoughts, until the bell tolled the end of the second dog watch.

Nathan dismissed Mr Blunt to the squalor of the midshipmen's berth, to his obvious relief, and returned to the quarterdeck. It was around the time he usually had a little light supper in the privacy of his own quarters, but feeling something of the loneliness of command, he invited Tully to join him.

'The commodore's dining room,' he remarked, gazing about his surroundings. 'What luxury.' His tone was sour. 'I suppose some people think I was born to this.'

'You were born to it,' Tully commented, as he poured the wine. 'So was I.'

Nathan was stunned. 'How can you sit there, you rogue, eating my cheese and toast and drinking my wine and tell me I was born into a life of luxury? And that I have done nothing to earn my status.'

'I did not say that,' Tully replied equably. 'As a matter of fact, I believe you have more than earned it and should be an admiral at least. Then we should have a 74 and I would have a decent cabin instead of a cupboard.'

'A cupboard! I have seen your cupboard. It is a palace compared to what you had on the *Unicorn.* You should see where Mr Blunt berths and the rest of his kind. There is a cupboard. Eight young gentlemen in a space barely half the size of where we are now sitting – and a monkey. And they are lucky compared with most of the crew.'

'Well, that is the Navy for you,' agreed Tully complacently, reaching for another piece of toasted cheese.

'Well, it is not good enough.' Nathan relapsed into a brooding silence.

Tully filled his glass. 'We have all been there,' he said. 'And some of us have had worse accommodation.'

'This is true.' Tully, of course, had served before the mast, and Nathan recalled certain quarters he himself had been obliged to tolerate on occasion. 'Well, I am glad you consider that I have some merit on my own account, and have not been counting on my father's influence all these years. Not that he has any – not any more – and even if he had in the past, my mother has done her best to deprive me of it. I have been in prison eight times, do you know that? And I am barely out of my twenties.'

'Eight?' Tully frowned as if he was impressed, but he was only counting. 'I thought it was only four.' He began to tick them off on his fingers. 'Paris, Cuba, Venice, Gibraltar . . .'

'Three times in Paris. Three different prisons. And you are forgetting the Bridewell in Holborn.'

'I do not think I know about the Bridewell in Holborn. Why—'

'No matter but you may take my word for it, it was my mother's fault.'

'And how was Gibraltar her fault? If I remember, you wrote a letter to St Vincent protesting the shelling of Cadiz.'

'Yes, well, I must take full responsibility for that, but the reason I stayed there for three months was because my mother was entertaining rebels and dissidents in her house in Soho. It was bad enough when she was in St James's but at least she counted the Prince of Wales among her guests. Since she has been in Soho she has been consorting with all manner of rogues and reprobates. Coleridge has been there, you know. Even Sheridan.'

'What is wrong with Sheridan? I thought you preferred him to Shakespeare.'

'I say nothing against him as a writer, but he is Member of Parliament, you know, and a great critic of the East India Company. In fact, I sometimes wonder . . .'

He thought better of finishing the sentence. What he had been going to say was that he wondered if certain officers of the company were aware of his mother's relationship with Sheridan and other of the company's critics, and might find it very convenient, even droll, to use her son as a scapegoat for their more disreputable activities. But he was aware that he had a tendency to become unreasonably suspicious. He blamed his mother for that, too.

'I am sorry,' he said. 'I am become a poor companion. You know what I am like when I do not have enough to do.'

Tully raised his glass. 'You have done very well, despite your lamentable parentage – may you continue to thrive under adversity.'

They could scarcely see each other in the fading light and Nathan had opened his mouth to shout for De Fournier to bring the lamps when Tully's features were suddenly illuminated by a flash as of lightning striking through the connecting door to the stern cabin – a multiple flash followed, revealing the whole interior in flickering relief, very like a magic lantern. But it was not lightning, not this time, and had there been any doubt in their minds it would have been instantly dispelled by the rippling roar of a broadside.

'It is the French,' said Joyce when Nathan reached the quarterdeck. 'They are coming out.'

Chapter Fifteen

The Chase

Nathan's appearance on deck was greeted by another rippling broadside and in the fierce, flickering light Nathan saw them. About a mile to the south-east, outlined against the night sky. Two of them at least, under full sail, and he had no reason to doubt the others were there, still hidden in the darkness towards the shore. It looked like they had tried to break out to the south on the flood tide, hugging the coast as closely as they dared, but they had been spotted, probably at the last minute, by the *Bombay* in the mouth of the river and she had moved to intercept them. And now there was a running battle to the south, with the *Bombay* engaged at close quarters with the lead ship, which must surely be the big French frigate, the *Forte*.

By the curse of fortune, the blockading squadron had been on the starboard tack when the French came out, nearing the top of their long loop to the north. So they were a good mile or so from the action when the *Bombay* fired her first broadside, and the distance lengthening with every minute until they could come about. Aboard the *Pondicherry* there was a frantic sense of urgency, the air filled with the fiendish wail of boatswain's pipes and the decks packed with running men as the off-duty watch tumbled up from below. Tully had four men heaving at the helm as the bows began their laborious journey through fifteen points of the compass and Joyce was bellowing with all his considerable might, as if the power of his lungs alone could trim the sails.

Nathan watched in a fever of impatience, hugely frustrated by his inactivity. In the *Unicorn* he would have swung the ship's head right up into the wind and beyond, until the sails filled on the opposite tack, and she would have been hurtling into battle by now, clearing for action. But the *Cherry* was not the *Unicorn*, and Tully would not risk laying her in irons. So he let her fall right off, swinging her fat stern to the wind.

Slowly, slowly the bows came round. Nathan had never seen anything so slow, not so much Hannibal as a great lumbering elephant; it was all he could do to restrain himself from adding his voice to Joyce's, for all the good that would do. But at last they were round, the sails luffing and then filling on the larboard tack with a crack that echoed the sound of the distant guns.

Tully was already calling for more canvas. The sailing master, Mr Olafson, aimed his speaking trumpet at the tops, and the marine drummer – but no, Nathan had to remind himself, they had no marines – the drummer of the

12th Foot, was beating to quarters. But they had fallen way, way to windward, further even than Nathan had feared. He could not see Tully's face in the darkness but he knew how he must be feeling, for his last command had been the *Bonaventure*, a fast French corsair they had taken off Corfu, and she could have turned on a sixpence. They had near a mile and a half now to make up, and the battle was still moving away from them. Worse, and to Nathan's despair, the rest of the squadron was following them round as if they were still on blockade duty, maintaining their course until they reached the exact position from which *Pondicherry* had begun her own turn. Nathan raged inwardly as he watched them, sailing steadily ahead in their perfect line but *away* from the battle. It did not matter if they reached the battle like a mob on the rampage, so long as they reached it as fast as they possibly could.

'Can you believe it?' he said aloud as his impatience got the better of him. 'Why do they not turn?'

'They think you mean them to keep the line,' said Joyce unhappily.

'Obviously,' Nathan snapped. 'But is there not one among them who realises it is not the line that matters but the bloody battle?'

'We could fire a gun,' said Tully.

But Nathan feared a gun would only confuse them further. The *Antelope* was already beginning to wear with the *Cornwallis* coming up behind her; it was best now to let them be. But the *Cherry* was still coming round and she was about to cross the loop, just abaft the *Eagle*. Nathan grabbed the voice trumpet off the master and ran up onto the poop, a lone figure at the weather rail with the Union flag streaming out behind him. He raised the trumpet to his lips and shouted with all the force at his command, if not quite the full venom: 'Mr Foley there!' *Foley, you damn fool, you whoremongering son of a bitch* . . . 'Turn! Turn now! Turn at once!'

But it was useless. Pissing into the wind. The *Eagle* sailed serenely on. But then he felt Tully's hand on his shoulder and he saw the ship behind her breaking out of line, her bows turning to starboard. The little *Comet*. Nathan watched anxiously lest she be laid aback, but she continued to swing round, right into the teeth of the wind. Further, further, until the slack sails filled out and she was on the larboard tack, about a cable's length off their weather side and pushing ahead of them already, towards the distant battle raging to the south.

'Good man!' Nathan cried. Cutler, of course. One man, at least, with a mind of his own.

The *Stromboli*, the last ship in the line, went sailing on in the wrong direction as if she had all the time in the world. And to be fair, she had little reason to hurry. The bomb ketch was about as useless as her skipper in this kind of a battle.

The *Pondicherry* was moving well now, with the wind on her quarter, but she was far, far too late. The guns had fallen silent – there were no more broadsides to guide them – and they came up on the *Bombay* alone in the darkness, lit by nothing more than the great lantern at her stern and the tiny glow of her binnacle light. But there was enough light in the sky for them to see the state she was in. She had clearly had the worse of her encounter with the *Forte* and the brigs must have given her a pasting as they went by.

The French had been firing high, as was their wont, and most of the damage they could see was aloft, but if it had spared the lives of the men, it had made a hopeless shambles of the ship. Nathan took in the shattered rigging, the torn and flapping sails, the mainsail yard hanging all cock-a-hoop like a ship in mourning, and most of her mizzen gone over the side, a great sea anchor holding her by the stern. She looked like a hulk on washday. But as the *Cherry* passed by, Nathan saw men with axes hacking to free themselves from their unwanted anchor, and Commodore Picket in the light of the stern lantern, doffing his hat in a courteous bow and then waving it to urge them on, his mouth opening and closing in soundless exhortation.

Nathan could see nothing of the French. All he could see was the *Comet*'s stern lights in the distance, but even as he looked she fired with one of her bowchasers. The flash was too small, too brief for Nathan to see what they were firing at, but presumably the *Comet* could, unless they were firing blind into the darkness.

And so they began the long chase to the south. The *Comet* in the lead and the *Cherry* hurrying after her with every scrap of canvas she could carry. The *Antelope* passed them within the hour, and vanished into the murk to windward. The other three ships were presumably labouring behind. Nathan could see nothing of their quarry. He could only hope that the two fast brigs would give him some warning if the French changed course.

They must be following the line of the coast southward, but sooner or later, if they were heading back to the Île de France, they would have to break to the south-west. And if the squadron stayed on their heels, if they did not let them get too far ahead, this would give the *Cherry* a chance to bear down on them. A small chance, fast diminishing. And yet Nathan dared not lose them. He felt a dull ache in the pit of his stomach. He would be blamed for letting the French reach Mangalore and now he would be blamed, with more justice, for letting them leave. Certainly he blamed himself. Why had he not set the squadron to cruising south of the river? It was obvious that, with the wind from the north-east, this was the direction the French were going to take. But Nathan was ever wary of the obvious – a consequence of his own devious nature.

But if the French had broken to the west, he would have been left beating against the wind. At least with the squadron to windward there was that small hope of catching them. What he should have done, of course, was place the *Pondicherry* in the mouth of the river, not the *Bombay*. But it was no good bewailing his past errors. What he should be doing was figuring out the route the French were most likely to take to the Île de France and how to stop them getting there.

He and Tully spread out the relevant chart and studied it as best they could in the light of an overhead lantern. The Île de France was to the west of Madagascar, about 2,500 miles across the Indian Ocean.

'So if this is their destination, sooner or later they will have to bear to the south-west,' Nathan mused. 'But probably not for a while. If they change course now, or in the next twenty-four hours, they will have to thread their way through the Laccadive Islands.' He pointed them out on the chart, a long chain of pearls strung along the south-west coast of India, the original homeland of the seamen they called Lascars. 'More likely they will head further south and make for the Mamala Channel.' He indicated the gap between the Laccadives and the Maldives, a little further to the south, between two and three hundred miles off the tip of India.

'It is certainly what I should do,' Tully agreed. '*If* I were heading for the Île de France.'

'Where else could they be heading?'

Tully shrugged. Nathan sighed. This, of course, was the problem. There were many other ports along the South India coast – Alleppey, Cochin, Calcut, Trivardrin – any one of which could provide them with a temporary haven. Or they could seek refuge in the Maldives themselves – a series of atolls spread over several hundred miles of ocean. They had been claimed by the Dutch until the fall of Ceylon two years ago. Now, presumably, they had passed into British hands. Although, as far as Nathan was aware, none of the locals had been concerned in this transaction, and very few of them could have ever met a Dutchman, or an Englishman. He was fairly sure there was no English presence there.

'The fact is we have no idea where they are heading,' he admitted. 'All we can do is stay in the chase.'

They stayed in the chase all through the murky night, heading ever southward, following the stern lights of the *Comet* and the occasional discharge of her bowchasers into the darkness. The *Cherry* was moving fast, by her own standards – between eight and nine knots – with the wind steady on her larboard quarter, but they were constantly having to compensate for that exasperating drift to leeward. All ships had such a tendency of course, but

Nathan had never known it so extreme as with the *Cherry*.

'They should have fitted her with a pair of reins and a bit,' he remarked to Tully after yet another correction when they lost the *Comet* for an anxious half-hour.

Towards the end of the middle watch the wind freshened to such an extent that Tully was obliged to take in canvas as fast as he had been putting it out, and they were heeling so far to leeward the lower gunports were permanently under water. Dawn broke over a heaving sea, the air filled with so much spray and flying spume they lost the *Comet* altogether, at least from deck level, and they were only reassured of her presence by the lookouts high in the tops. There was no sign whatsoever of the French, or the rest of the squadron, not even the *Antelope*. It felt like madness, hurtling through an increasingly violent sea in pursuit of an invisible foe with Mother Carey's Chickens skulking and skittering to leeward.

Then, a little after six bells in the morning watch with Nathan thinking about his breakfast, the situation changed. There was a cry from the foremast lookout, relayed from the waist and up to the quarterdeck. A strange sail, two points on the larboard bow *behind* the *Comet* and closing. It could be the *Antelope,* or one of the other ships of the squadron, but Nathan feared the worst. The flash and rippling roar of the broadside confirmed it. One of the French ships had slipped behind in the darkness and come up on the *Comet's* stern.

Nathan ran up the ratlines to the foretop and braced himself against the futtock shrouds as he struggled to hold the glass steady. For some frustrating moments he could see nothing but the heaving grey-green mass of sea, but then he caught a glimpse of sail and focused on the French ship. She was the *Forte*. Even at this distance he could just make out the long row of gunports. Tully had edged the *Cherry* two, perhaps three, points into the wind and they were beginning to close on her, but they were still a half-mile or so distant when they saw the frigate cut across the *Comet*'s stern and rake her. Twenty guns, most of them 24-pounders, firing at point-blank range into her stern. The brig seemed almost to stagger with the force of the blow and her mizzenmast came crashing down across her gun deck bringing the spanker boom with it and a mass of billowing canvas. Her ensign was gone too, so she could not haul her colours even if Cutler was minded to surrender, and the *Forte* came sharply up in her lee, keeping pace with her as they ran to the south, and firing at will.

Nathan was no more than a spectator in this fight, and it was a fight the *Comet* could not possibly win. The mainmast followed the mizzen and then the foretopmast. Nathan could not see if she was firing back – but she was heeling over so far to leeward he doubted if Cutler could bring a single gun to bear. The *Forte* had backed her mizzen to keep from racing ahead and the two ships were almost dead in the water with the *Cherry* closing rapidly. The end could not be long delayed, but when it came it was worse than Nathan's worst imagining. Through the smoke of battle he saw a flicker of flame on the *Comet*'s gun deck, too broad, too sustained to be from her guns. Even in these conditions, with so much spray in the air, it had enough combustibles to feed upon, and there was a violent explosion as it reached the cartridges for the nearest 6-pounder. The *Forte* fired again and again into the smoke and flames.

It was no more than the *Swiftsure* had done to the burning French flagship at Abukir, but *L'Orient* had been a great monster of a three-decker with over a hundred guns and both ships had been locked in mortal combat. There was something particularly chilling about the *Forte*'s action when it was perfectly clear that the *Comet* was out of the fight, and Nathan was in as cold a fury to pay her back for it. But she fired one final broadside and then clapped ahead, leaving her opponent burning fiercely along half her length with the strong wind fanning the flames that were likely to consume her.

The *Pondicherry* had made up a lot of ground during the fight and she was barely a cable's length off the *Comet*'s starboard quarter when the flames reached her magazine. She had loaded up with forty barrels of fresh gunpowder in Bombay and the explosion was like a starburst on the ocean, a boiling blister of red, white and orange fire that was just as suddenly gone, leaving nothing but the memory seared on Nathan's shocked retina, and a black pall of smoke already shredding in the wind. He felt the blast in his swaying perch in the foretop and the air was filled with a black rain of debris. A great splinter of mast came down like a spear just off the *Cherry*'s plunging bow and there was human debris, too, that made him sick in the stomach. Not a single member of the brig's crew could possibly have survived such a blast. Cutler and his fifty-two officers and men were gone in an instant.

Nathan had known how vulnerable the brig was, out on her own in front of the squadron, and his bitter self-reproach was matched by a savage desire for vengeance. But it was a wish that was unlikely to be granted, for the frigate was moving steadily away from them, and at an angle that made it impossible to fire a single shot worth the powder. He could see Joyce up forward frantically trying to point one of the 12-pounders, but it was as far up against the gunport as it could go, and from Nathan's vantage he could see that they did not have a hope in Hell of hitting her.

Even so, an alternative plan was forming in his mind. On their present course, the *Cherry* would cut across the frigate's stern well within firing range. Unfortunately, she would be to windward, heeling so far over that even the guns on her upper deck would be pointing into the sea. But if they were to cut back again, with the wind on the opposite quarter, there was a slim chance of raking her – a very slim chance, indeed, for the frigate would be so much further away by then, and if the French saw what he was about, they had only to alter course themselves to deny him even the satisfaction of a long shot. But it was surely worth a try.

He returned as swiftly as he could to the quarterdeck. Tully was at the weather rail staring out after the departing frigate with a look that mirrored Nathan's own feelings on the subject, and the younger officers were staring at Nathan as if he had recently joined them from a travelling fair. It was possibly the first time they had seen a commodore sliding down a backstay in a near-gale, he reflected, but any satisfaction he might have derived from this was swamped by more urgent considerations. He explained his plan to Tully who grasped it with his usual alacrity.

'Pass the word for Mr Joyce,' he said to Blunt. Then he barked a series of instructions to the acting master and the men at the helm that had the *Cherry*'s bows edging even further into the wind and heeling so far to leeward that there was a danger the seas would break over her gunwales, never mind the lower gunports.

They were making their first pass across the frigate's stern, at a distance of about a cable's length, when Mr Vivian, who was commanding the quarterdeck 6-pounders, began to shout out and point towards the chase. His voice was so thin, the wind so strong, neither Nathan nor Tully could hear what he was saying at first – but he seemed to be indicating something at the frigate's stern. The rudder broken loose? Another fire? Then Nathan saw the object of his interest. A pale figure outlined in one of the stern windows, just below the huge tricolour streaming from the flagstaff. The window was open and it was apparent, even at this distance, that a woman was standing, or rather crouching there, braced against the window frame, and that she was practically naked.

'What in God's name . . . ?' Nathan looked at Tully to share his bemusement. 'Is she mad?'

He looked again. The woman was wearing some kind of shift or camisole, but her legs and arms and most of her chest were bare, and her long black hair was flying in the wind.

The French captain's wife, maddened by the sound and fury of battle, exhibiting herself to the enemy? These and other equally fantastical notions crossed Nathan's mind as he moved to the rail and brought the glass to his eye, hooking his arm through the mizzen shrouds while he searched for the focus. But nothing in his wildest imaginings could have astonished him more than the sight that greeted him when he found it.

He had seen her only once – though in circumstances etched in his memory – but even across the gap of 200 yards there was no mistaking the face framed in the lens of his Dolland glass.

'Good God,' he announced to the startled midshipman, 'it is Sister Caterina!'

And then she jumped.

Chapter Sixteen

The Nun's Story

Nathan swore an oath and turned away, pausing only to grab Mr Vivian by the seat of his pants as he threw off his coat and prepared to climb the rail.

'Idiot,' he told him. 'Get some men forward and throw her a line.'

'She might as well have put one round her neck afore she jumped,' declared Mr Olafson, who was clearly of a more practical disposition.

Olafson was an oaf, but he was right. No one could possibly survive such a leap into such a sea. But they could see her dark head above the waves, her bare arms rising and falling as she fought to stay afloat.

Nathan crossed to Tully at the con. 'We have to try,' he insisted urgently. 'Not just for her sake. She may have some intelligence for us.'

Tully read the message in his eye, but his own was doubtful. He looked aloft at the taut sails and then at the angry sea.

'We could lose the ship,' he said. But it was more in resignation than protest. He was already moving away, barking a stream of orders, and they heaved to the wind and backed the main topsail so that she lay to, pitching and rolling like an abandoned hulk.

'We cannot hold her long,' Tully shouted above the noise of the flapping canvas. Nathan did not doubt it. There was no possibility of launching a boat. The best they could do was drift down upon her until they were close enough to throw a line, and hope she stayed afloat that long, and the ship was not broached by the heavy seas. Not a man aboard would have bet on either.

But the swimmer had seen something they had not – a broken spar or even part of a mast, almost certainly from the wreck of the *Comet* – hurled like a javelin after her killer. It rose on the swell and they saw it at last, a skirt of trailing rigging spread about the timber like the tendrils of a giant jellyfish. She caught hold of a part and gripped it in two fists, resting a moment, and then she began to haul herself in. When she reached the spar she threw one arm over it and raised the other towards them. It might have been Nathan's imagination, stirred by what he knew of her, but it seemed more a gesture of defiance than entreaty.

The *Cherry* was slowly drifting down upon her, still rolling violently but more or less holding her station, and a dozen men were running forward with their lines. The first two fell short but the third dropped close enough for her to let go the spar and swim for it. She caught a hold of the end with both hands and slowly they began to reel her in.

Nathan made his way forward to be there when she reached the side. There were two men hanging from ropes to help her up the tumbledown, and well they might for she was in the last stage of exhaustion when they finally heaved her aboard: a lovely wet silkie of the seas, her long black hair straggling like seaweed about her breasts, but a silkie with legs, kneeling, coughing and retching upon the deck. The sodden shift did little to hide her charms, and half the crew that was not fighting to keep the ship afloat, gawped and grinned like spectators at a fair. Nathan almost heard the sigh when he wrapped his boat cloak round her. He helped her to her feet and she gazed up at him with a weary smile, which swiftly changed to a puzzled frown as if she struggled to remember where she had seen him before.

Now was not the time to remind her. He led her aft to where his officers were doing their best not to stare in the same besotted fashion as the crew. It was a miracle to Nathan that the ship had not foundered while they gawked, though there were some disapproving looks too, he thought, notably from Joyce, who may have questioned his priorities in the matter.

Tully had the ship in motion, but the *Forte* was beyond their reach; they could barely see her topsails across the heaving sea and she might have been halfway to Ceylon for all the hope they had of catching her. But now a shout from the lookout alerted them to another sail, crabbing up from the south-east. She proved to be the *Antelope*, struggling belatedly to their assistance and so close to the wind that she was in mortal danger of being taken aback. Why she had been so far to windward was a puzzle to Nathan, but he would have to wait for Blake's explanation of that. His other concerns were more pressing.

'Permit me to present to you Sister Caterina Caresini of the Convent of San Paoli di Mare in Venice,' he said, taking great pleasure in observing Tully's expression. She looked shocked enough herself, that he should know. 'You have Captain Tully to thank for holding the ship steady in such a sea,' he informed her, 'while we fished you out.'

'I thank you, *capitano*.' She blushed, performing a modest curtsey and laying on the accent. Her English, Nathan knew, was almost perfect. But Caterina, whatever other talents she possessed, was ever the actress.

He took her into his cabin, which in the *Pondicherry*'s elegant terminology, was known as the state room, and called for De Fournier to bring brandy and towels.

'Clothes, too,' he ordered, as an afterthought. 'Clean clothes.'

'We have no women's clothes,' replied De Fournier primly, 'clean or otherwise.'

'Come, sir,' Nathan rebuked him sternly. 'Are you telling me we have no women aboard?'

There were always women aboard, whatever the strictures against it. Every captain knew it and every crewman knew he knew it. But this time, it appeared, there were not. His turning out of Joyce's harem had scourged the entire ship clear of the female presence before they left Bombay.

'I am happy enough in men's clothes,' Caterina assured them and De Fournier departed with a scandalised expression in search of the purser's slops.

'I will leave you to your wardrobe, such as it is,' Nathan told her, 'but when you are ready I would welcome an opportunity to talk.'

'Of course.' But she was still regarding him quizzically. 'It *is* you, is it not? My avenging angel from the sea?'

It is what she had called him in Venice. The avenging angel, who came to assist her in her fight against the French – and her own private enemies among the Venetians.

'Captain Nathaniel Peake,' she announced with sudden remembrance. 'Of the *fregata Unicorn.* Venice. Just before the French came and put an end to us. And now you are here. Do you always come when I am most in need of you?'

'I will tell you about it,' said Nathan, 'when you are dressed.'

The Caterina he had known in Venice was a woman of some consequence, and even greater infamy. The most beautiful woman in Venice, the English ambassador had called her, and the most dangerous. He did not know the half of it. Later Nathan had learned more of her background from Spiridion Foresti, who was her mentor in the world of intelligence and more than a little in love with her.

She had been born the daughter of a shepherd in the Veneto – the mainland territories of Venice – but had forsaken her family and flock for the precarious life of a player in a travelling theatre company, from which humble beginnings she had risen to become the most famous actress in Verona. But, like many an actress, her name was linked with scandal, and her indiscretions had attracted the attention of the Inquisition who had obliged her to enter a nunnery – Nathan gathered that it was either that or prison

– whence, by means too devious for him to contemplate, she had risen through the ranks of the religious to rule the most prestigious convent in Venice. Had she been a man, Nathan had little doubt that she would have worn a cardinal's hat, or even a pontiff's. As it was, she had made the Convent of San Paolo di Mare into the best and most notorious casino in Venice. When he had met her, she was at the peak of her powers and the occasional lover of the Admiral of the Venetian fleet. She was also, and rather more discreetly – so much so that not even the British ambassador had known of it – a leading intelligence agent for Spiridion Foresti.

Although Spiridion had asked him to look out for her, Nathan had never seriously thought to make her acquaintance, and certainly not in circumstances as bizarre as these.

When she entered the great cabin she was wearing the canvas ducks and striped shirt, the waistcoat and blue jacket that passed for the uniform of a British seaman, not that anyone with half an eye could ever have mistaken her for such. Her long dark hair was still wet and glossy from her swim and she had let it hang loose to dry, but she would not have been unconscious as to the effect. She wore no make-up, but she had a face that needed no artifice. She must have been about thirty-three or thirty-four, Nathan reckoned, but only because Spiridion had told him so – she looked ten years younger to him; it must have been all that sheep's milk as a child, he thought, or some more potent brew. It was rumoured that her mother had been a witch.

'This is very nice,' she observed, looking about her. 'You have risen in the world since last we met. Are you an admiral?'

'Only a commodore,' he told her, a little regretfully, as he poured wine for them both. He was aware of her penchant for admirals.

'You were posing as an American sea captain, I recall, when you were in Venice. Captain Turner, was it not?'

'Very good, but rather more than a captain. I was a merchant and shipowner and in good repute with Thomas Jefferson, who had sent me to buy the Venetian fleet.'

'Ah yes.' She smiled. 'And you thought the Venetians would believe that.' But then she frowned as another memory came. 'You disappeared. We heard that you were taken by the French.'

'By the Venetians, in fact. I spent a night in the Doge's prison and they were about to throw me into the Canal of the Orphans with an anchor round my neck when the French came to my rescue.' The frown deepened. Caterina was no friend to the French; she would rather he had stayed with the anchor. 'They thought I was who I said I was – and a friend to the cause,' he added, by way of an apology.

The frown went. She shrugged. She was herself no stranger to deceit.

'So where did you learn to swim?' he asked her. 'Not the convent, I think.' Though, in fact, it was such a convent, an indoor pool such as they had in the seraglio of the Great Turk would not entirely have surprised him.

'In the streams of the Veneto when I was child.' She eyed him thoughtfully as if deciding what he should know and what he should not. 'I was the daughter of a shepherd. Chodeschino was our family name. It means sheep's head in English.'

'I know,' he said. 'Spiridion Foresti told me.'

Spiridion had told him many things about her, but had said that for the most part she was a mystery and that you could not rely upon what Caterina herself told you because she invariably lied. But in matters of intelligence, he had found her totally reliable – though for reasons he could not entirely explain.

'I think it is partly pride,' he had told Nathan when they were in the desert. 'A feeling that she should give value for money – and certainly I paid an exorbitant price for her services. Also, she would know that an agent who is unreliable is of no use to anyone, and is very likely to meet with a swift and violent end. But I do not think it was that alone. Whatever she tells you to the contrary, and whatever frivolous airs she gives herself, she is an idealist and a patriot. I think she would like to see Venice as the capital of a united Italy which makes her an inveterate enemy of France, at least for the time being. If ever France were to support the notion of a unified Italy, she would be for France. As it is, she is for England. It is as simple as that. Not that anything is ever simple with Caterina Caresini.'

'Spiridion Foresti,' she said now, in the same tone, in fact, as Spiridion would say, 'Caterina Caresini', as if reflecting on the equal measure of pain and pleasure they had brought each other. From what Nathan knew of them, he thought they deserved each other, and that they would probably end up living together, with the same degree of mutual exasperation and admiration, on Spiridion's beloved Zante, or some other island, a pair of old spies, recalling foul deeds and old tricks played upon a wicked world. 'Do you know what happened to him, when Corfu fell to the French?'

'He went to Tripoli,' Nathan told her, 'and then to Egypt to look for you.'

He saw the look of surprise – unfeigned, as far as he could tell.

'Tripoli? So he –' But whatever she was going to say, she thought better of it. 'To look for me?' She said it doubtfully, but with a measure of hope.

'He had information you were with a French agent called Naudé. Xavier Naudé.'

'Did he, indeed?' She reflected upon this for a moment. 'And did he know *why* I was with him?'

'He thought you must have had your reasons.'

'Well, you can tell him from me it was not from choice.' She looked angry now, though this too might be an act. 'Did Spiridion think it was by choice?' Nathan shook his head vigorously; it would be unwise not to. 'So where is he now – Spiridion?'

'Went to Suez, to see if you were still there – and told me to look out for you in India. I never thought to find you, of course, least of all in the Arabian Sea.'

She gazed at him in frank astonishment. 'There must be a God,' she said.

He thought he would leave the theological discussions for a more appropriate time. 'So where is Naudé now,' he asked her, 'and how came you to be aboard a French frigate?'

'Because Naudé would have it so.'

'I think you had better tell me the full story,' Nathan advised her.

And so she did. It was a story like an adventure from the *Arabian Nights*, and he would not have believed a fraction of it, had he not known it to be true. The first part at least.

She had left Venice before the French came – on an American ship called the *Saratoga*, but they were taken by Barbary corsairs off Sicily and brought as hostages to Tripoli.

'Was that where Spiridion saw me?' she asked Nathan, who shrugged, smiling, not wishing to give too much away. 'So was I not worth the hostage money?'

'You would have to ask him.'

'I would, believe me, if I saw him again. Though I might cut his throat first, to save him the trouble of lying.' She was capable of it, he thought, and looked angry enough. 'They made me a slave,' she said indignantly, 'in the seraglio of Pasha Yusuf Karamanli.'

'Really.' He looked properly shocked, though it was an effort not to smile. He had been sent to Tripoli himself to rescue her, along with the other hostages, but had been beaten to it by Naudé, at least in her case. 'Clearly you did not remain there long.'

'No. I have Naudé to thank for that.'

'Out of the frying pan,' he said, but she only frowned, clearly not familiar with the expression. It was said that she had learned English as the lover of Sir Richard Worsley when he was Minister to the Serenissima, but more lies were told of Caterina than she told herself, and it was probably not an expression the ambassador was likely to use.

'Naudé took me with him to Egypt to see General Bonaparte.'

This was something Nathan had not known. 'Bonaparte? In person?'

'Bonaparte in person,' she mocked. 'Does he impress you, the little general? You admire him?'

'As a general, there is surely much to admire.' He shrugged. 'But then I do not know him.'

In fact, he had come as close to knowing him in Paris as any man who was not of his own family, and had saved his life when his horse had bolted in face of the royalist rebels. It would not have been wise, of course, to admit this to Caterina. Bonaparte was the destroyer of her beloved Venice – he had brought an end to its thousand-year history as an independent republic, and then handed it over, like so much plunder, to the Austrians. She would not warm to a man who had saved his life.

'I hope he rots in hell,' she said, 'or in Cairo, which is worse, and his army with him.'

'Well, this would save us all a great deal of trouble, certainly,' Nathan assured her. 'Were you with him in Cairo?'

'For a whole month.' She had clearly not enjoyed the experience.

'And did you see much of Bonaparte in that time?'

He was surprised she had not found an opportunity to stab him, or poison him, or to contrive some other form of revenge. She was, after all, a Venetian. But, apparently, Bonaparte had been too preoccupied even to spend time with Caterina Caresini.

'And you had no opportunity to escape?'

'If I had, do you not think I would have taken it? Or do you think I was waiting for the opportunity to throw myself into the sea and hope that some passing British admiral would find the time to stop for me?'

'I only wondered. And I am only a commodore,' he reminded her. 'I only mention it in case . . .'

'Pah. I was kept under lock and key all the time we were there, or if they let me out it was with Naudé himself and his assassins. *He* was under no illusions about my wish to escape, even if you are. I gave that man hell, believe me.'

He did. 'But what did he want with you?'

She gave him a look. 'What do all men want?'

He had the grace to blush. 'Forgive me, I should not have asked. And then? I mean, after Cairo?'

'We crossed the desert to Suez.' Her shoulders slumped for a moment, staring into her glass of brandy, and then flicked him a glance. 'Have you ever been in the desert?'

'It is not my natural element.'

'No. Nor mine.' She shuddered. 'Camels. Scorpions under every rock. Blankets smelling of . . . the flies, the filth, the people . . . My God. And the sand. It gets everywhere, even—'

'And you were heading for Suez, you say?'

'Yes. Not that I knew that at the time.'

'Did he not say anything to you of his intentions? I do not mean towards you, but . . .'

'No. Only that we were going to India. To make his fortune, he said – and I would be a princess, with a palace and servants, and jewellery and silken dresses, and elephants. Pah. Did he think I was still Caterina Chodeschino, the shepherd girl from the Veneto, to be bought with trifles? I had all that in Venice before the French came, saving the elephants, and was beholden to no man for it. Men. The things they think will impress you. Elephants, though. I had never heard that before.'

'And at Suez?'

'Oh. Yes, Suez. We spent a week there. It was worse than Cairo. But something happened . . .' She sank into reflection. Nathan wondered if she was trying to remember, or if she was deciding whether or not to tell him. He had the sense to keep quiet. 'I decided to be nice to him. Or at least not so unpleasant.' More reflection. 'Well, he told me Bonaparte had promised to send him an army and that they were going to invade India.'

'Bonaparte, or Naudé?'

'Bonaparte, of course. Though you will think from Naudé that it was he alone. Naudé was to go with the advance guard and then Bonaparte to follow. I gave this information to a serving woman – in Cairo. I told her she would be rewarded if she took it to a certain person I know. Did Spiridion have news of this?'

'I believe he did, yes.'

'Good. Then he will know I was still – that I am not working for the French?'

'I do not believe he would ever think that. So these men went with you to Suez?'

'What men? Oh, the brigade of guards? No. I did not see them. All we had were a few camels and some goats. And the men who were with them. And Naudé's assassins.'

'Naudé's assassins?'

'Four of them. From Tripoli. They were the ones who freed me from the pasha's prison. But then they became my jailers.'

'So how long did you stay in Suez?'

'Long enough. Then we went to Aden. My God.' She covered her face with her hands in a theatrical gesture of despair. 'Have you been to Aden?'

'No. I regret I have not had that pleasure.'

'Pleasure? Aden? This is a man who promises me elephants. Why Aden, I said? I had rather stay in Tripoli and become one of Karamanli's wives, the fat pig.'

'Well, it is a direct line from Aden to Mangalore.'

'Really?' She regarded him with interest.

'Eighteen hundred nautical miles, near enough.'

'How interesting. Is this why they made you an admiral?'

'Commodore.' He felt himself redden. 'So what did you do in Aden?'

'Well, after a few days playing the casinos and attending the theatre, just when I am looking forward to my first ball, a ship comes for us. A frigate.'

'The *Forte*?'

'No. A Dutch frigate. It comes from the Cape of Good Hope and is using Aden as a base, I think, for raids upon British shipping.'

This made sense, of a sort. The Cape had been Dutch until they joined with the French in 1795, and the British took it from them, and Ceylon and such other colonies as they took a shine to.

'Then we had to wait for another elephant – *the* Elephant, Naudé called it.'

'The Elephanta. It is a wind – a cyclone. It comes—' She gave him a look. 'I am sorry, go on.'

'So we do not leave Aden until the end of September. And in the third week of October we arrive at Mangalore.'

At roughly the time Nathan had arrived in Bombay. He thought of all those weeks plodding across Syria and Mesopotamia, wondering what Naudé was doing and thinking he was being given a hero's welcome by the Tiger of Mysore. Instead, he had been languishing in Suez and Aden with a tigress.

'They fire the guns and wave the flags. They even have a band. And all these men in robes and turbans and beards – they are there to greet us. They think we bring the French army. They do not look so pleased when we march off the ship. Just Naudé and his four assassins and me. Naudé tells them Bonaparte is marching overland through Persia – which is a lie, of course. I do not think Bonaparte will leave Cairo, unless he goes back to Paris. But then two days later four French ships arrive – from the Île de France – with a hundred men. Volunteers, Naudé told me, sent by the governor to help Tipu Sultan fight the British. *Condottieri*, I call them,' she sneered. 'Freebooters.'

'Only a hundred you say?'

'Ninety-nine, to be precise. I can tell you exactly who they are, or *what* they are, if you wish. They are two generals, thirty-five officers, thirty-six European soldiers, twenty-two native troops, and four men who build ships. And two emissaries of Tipu Sultan who were sent to the Île de France. Sheik Abouram Sahib and Mehmet Bismila. I hope the Sultan is pleased with what they achieve for him. Two generals and a hundred men to drive the British out of India.'

If the East India Company wished for a pretext to declare war upon the Sultan of Mysore, this surely was it. Good news, too, for Nathan, if there were no more than a hundred men landed. He regarded Caterina with something like awe. No wonder Spiridion had spoken so highly of her as an agent. If it was all true, of course, and she was not just making it up.

'Two generals? That seems excessive for such a small army.'

'I think they have nothing better to do – on the Île de France. Probably they are retired. The commander is only a colonel – Colonel Chappuys. Louis Auguste Chappuys. He fought in India in the last war. For the King of France. But now he is for the Revolution.' She did not look as if she believed this, or expected anyone else to believe it.

'And the ships from Île de France – there were four, you say?'

She nodded. 'I can tell you exactly what they are, too, if you wish.'

'Please do.' He prepared to make a note of them; he did not have a memory like hers.

'There is the *Forte* – the one you were chasing. A frigate of forty-two guns, but I expect you know that, being an admiral or whatever it is you are.'

He nodded. It was almost possible, he discovered, to feel sorry for Naudé.

'Then there is the *Iphigenie*, twenty-two guns, the *Général Malartic*, named after the Governor of Île de France, twenty guns, and the *Succès*, eighteen guns, all of them corsairs.'

'And the Dutchman – was she with them when they left Mangalore?'

'Yes. She is the *Braave*, thirty-six guns, Captain Van Norden.'

Five altogether, including two heavy frigates. The two squadrons were evenly matched. In fact, the odds – and even the number of guns – favoured the French, especially now that he had lost the *Comet*. It was surprising, in fact, that they had fled so precipitately to the south instead of stopping to fight.

'And who is in command – not Naudé?'

'No. He thinks he is – he has a certain political authority, and since the Revolution that carries weight, I know – but the true commander is Leloup, the captain of the *Forte*, Captain Jean-Baptiste Beaulieu-Leloup – the Wolf.'

Nathan glanced at her a little sharply because she no longer sounded flippant or ironic. She sounded, he might almost have said, whimsical. Perhaps the Wolf had succeeded where Bonaparte had failed.

'I do not suppose you know where he is heading next, this Wolf?'

'Oh, but I do,' she said, smiling sweetly. 'Do you wish to know that, too?'

Chapter Seventeen

The Silver Ship

'Devil's Point?'

Tully appeared dubious.

'You think she is making it up,' Nathan ventured. 'The Devil and the Nun.'

'Not at all, but—'

'She showed me on the chart. Here.' Nathan pointed it out to him: a small promontory on the south-east coast of Ceylon, where the Arabian Sea meets the Bay of Bengal. They were in the little office on the quarterdeck, about the size of a shed which was used as a chartroom by the sailing master. It was the only place on deck where they could talk in some privacy and without shouting. The wind had increased markedly while Nathan had been with Caterina; it was now blowing a near-gale and they were braced against the bulkheads like a pair of great apes in a packing case.

The Devil and the Nun. He had to admit it was a possibility. There was a man in Venice known as the Devil, though he had been named after Christ – doubly so, in fact, for his Christian name was Cristoforo and his family name was Cristolfi. Cristoforo Cristolfi. *Il Diavolo*. The chief agent of the Inquisitors. He had been Caterina's arch-enemy before Naudé had succeeded to the role. No friend to Nathan, either. It was Cristolfi who had ordered his arrest and summary execution in the Canal of the Orphans. He still felt a chill at the thought of him, and their meetings in the *Magistrata alle leggi* in the Doge's Palace, where criminals were brought to answer the charges against them. Their shared enmity of this man was a powerful bond between them. Or some sort of a bond, at any rate. It was probably not wise to count on it.

'You are thinking I am right?' said Tully.

Nathan shook his head. He had been thinking that, but not only that. He had been thinking of a moment in the great cabin, when a violent lurch in the ship's motion had thrown Caterina against him while they were looking at the chart. It had been disconcerting. It still was. Caterina had brought complications into his life before, and could do so again.

'So why are they heading for the Devil's Point?' Tully asked him.

Nathan told him what Caterina had told him: 'There was a Frenchman from India who joined them at Mangalore. He came aboard the *Forte*. An important man. Even Naudé deferred to him. He called him Monsieur le Marquis, but she heard Leloup call him Fabien.'

'Leloup?'

'He is the captain of the *Forte* and the commander of the squadron.' Once more he saw the doubt in Tully's eyes. A glint of irony, too. 'I know.' The Wolf was another name she could have invented. But why would she?

There were so many reasons it was a waste of time speculating.

'She makes things up as she goes along,' Spiridion had once told him. 'It is a talent of hers. She will see a picture on a wall, a name on a map, and she incorporates it into whatever story she is telling at the time. I have seen her do it. It is quite remarkable. There is never a pause in the conversation and you can barely see her eyes move. I only realised when I saw the names once, after she had left the room, written on the cover of a book I had been reading.'

And this from a man who considered her generally reliable.

'How did she hear this conversation?' Tully demanded. 'Or was she included in it?'

'No, she was not included. She was in the adjoining cabin and the stern windows were open. She heard only some of it, but they were talking of two East Indiamen bound for Calcutta with a quantity of silver bullion. The marquis had come from Madras to tell them about it. He said it had been arranged for the two ships to call at Devil's Point to take on water and to rendezvous with a ship of war that was to escort them on the final stage of their journey to Calcutta.'

Tully frowned. 'How could he have known about something like that?'

Nathan shrugged, but it was a fair point. The despatch of silver bullion would be a closely-guarded secret, and even if it had been picked up by some spy in London, the news could hardly have reached India before the silver did.

'And this ship that is to meet them,' Tully persisted, 'does it have a name?'

'The *Shiva*. That is the name Caterina heard. Of fifty guns.'

'But I thought there was not another ship of fifty guns in the Indian Ocean.'

'That is what I was told by the governor of Bombay. It does not mean it is true.'

'So – two East Indiamen and a fifty-gun ship of war. Quite a mouthful for this wolf.'

The East Indiamen were two-deckers and heavily armed. They might carry as many as fifty or sixty guns themselves, though they were usually of a small calibre. 'Even so, if I was the Wolf, I would chance it.'

And so would Tully. 'So what are we to do?' he said.

The ship plunged into a trough and they felt the shudder down the whole of her length as she came up.

'There is not much we *can* do in this weather,' Nathan conceded. 'Save to keep running before the wind.'

Running was hardly the word for it. Tully had reduced sail to a single reefed maintop and it was all they could do to ride out the storm.

Nathan made his way back to the great cabin and knocked politely on the door. Caterina told him to come in. She had made herself at home. She had taken the cushions from the long bench of cupboards that ran along the stern windows and arranged them in the form of a couch on the floor, right up against the bulkhead. When he opened the cabin door she had been stretched out on it with her hands clasped behind her head, but she propped herself up on one elbow and regarded him amiably when he came in.

'I feel more comfortable on the floor while the wind it blows,' she said. 'You do not object?'

'Not at all,' Nathan said. All she needed was a water pipe and the cabin would be more like it had been when he had first seen it. 'But you are welcome to use the state room as your own. I will have the cot made up with clean bedding.'

'Oh but I will not take your cabin. I am very happy to sleep here, unless . . .'

They batted this to and fro for a while. In the end it was settled that she should sleep in Nathan's cabin room and that he would sleep in the small dining room and they would share the state room between them.

He sat down in one of the armchairs for the time being and regarded her thoughtfully.

'I have been wondering why Naudé took passage on the *Forte*,' he began, 'having been sent as emissary to the Sultan of Mysore – in Seringapatam.'

'I wonder that, too,' she said, frowning.

'And did you come to any conclusion?'

'I think Naudé knew the marquis before.'

'Before what?'

'Before he met him in Mangalore. He was in India during the last war with the English – did you not know?'

Nathan had not known. There was no reason why he should. Naudé had largely been Spiridion's concern. The two men were by way of being rivals. Spiridion had been the leading British agent in the region, and Naudé had been the French. There were many issues between them, and Caterina was one of them.

'He was in Pondicherry,' said Caterina, 'as a young ensign in the army of the King of France. Barras was his colonel.'

Nathan had not known this, either. Barras was the leading light of the Directorate – the five men who ruled Revolutionary France. Which made him the effective ruler – the new Fat Louis. Bonaparte's wife – Josephine – had once been his mistress, which was the main reason Bonaparte had been made a general, according to his detractors. Nathan was not of this opinion. Whatever else you said about Barras – and his venality was legendary – he knew a good soldier when he saw one. On the other hand, he was first and foremost a politician, and Bonaparte's success in Italy, though it was useful, had made him dangerous. There were some who thought Barras had sent Bonaparte to Egypt to be rid of him. As far away as possible. India, even.

'I think Naudé knew something of this when we were in Egypt,' Caterina said. 'He was always saying to me: "In India I will make my fortune – and I will make you my princess." I thought it was just the words of a Frenchman, a braggard. But it is possible he knew something of these ships, do you not think?'

Nathan considered. It was just possible that if the silver ships had left England in spring – April or even early May – the news could have been relayed to Paris, and thence to Toulon before Bonaparte's armada sailed to Egypt. There was a regular trade in spies across the English Channel – and smugglers of both sides profited by it. But the silver would have been loaded in great secrecy – and in closed leather boxes or trunks. No ordinary spy could possibly have known about such a delivery.

And then there was the question of dates. The big East Indiamen usually left Britain much earlier in the year – to take advantage of the seasonal winds across the Indian Ocean. The usual schedule was to go out with the south-west winds from June to September, and to come back with the north-easterlies in November and December.

The other question concerned this mysterious marquis.

Barras had been a marquis, too, Nathan recalled. No, not a marquis – a vicomte. Paul François something something, Vicomte de Barras. Nathan had known him in Paris – or at least met him. Several times. Like Bonaparte, Barras had been under the impression that Nathan was an American sea captain and adventurer, trying to interest the Directory in building a new French empire in the Americas at the expense of Spain. Barras was by no means a Revolutionist. His main interest was money – and empires were largely about money.

Barras had talked to him about India when they were in Paris. How he had fought at Pondicherry when it was besieged by the British. So Barras, this mysterious marquis and Naudé had all been in India at the same time.

It was all very murky. He wondered if Caterina knew more than she was saying. Perhaps drink would loosen her tongue. He doubted it somehow, but it would be interesting to see where it might lead. He could spend a happy few hours rolling around in the great cabin with Caterina on her cushions while they rode out the storm. But it would not do. It would not do at all. He excused himself and went back on deck and to the less dangerous embraces of the sea.

They were two days riding out the storm – and another two in search of the rest of the squadron. They found the *Antelope* first, and then the *Eagle*, both a little the worse for wear, but sound enough to resume the hunt. And at the end of the second day, just as night was falling, the *Bombay* came straggling down from the north under a jury rig. So then they were four.

'Signal *Bombay*,' Nathan instructed Mr Blunt, 'and request the commodore's attendance aboard the flagship as soon as it might be convenient.'

'It is impossible,' declared Picket, when Nathan had told him as much of Caterina's story as he deemed suitable. 'How could they have known?'

'Did *you* know?'

'Me? A silver shipment? Only a very small number of people would have known of it, in London and in Calcutta.'

'And this ship – the *Shiva* – which is to meet them at Devil's Point?'

'She is an old East Indiaman,' said Picket thoughtfully. 'Built in Deptford in the late sixties. Her original name was the *Gabriel* but she was sold into the country trade, and for some reason her new owners renamed her the *Shiva* – after the Hindu goddess of destruction,' he added disapprovingly.

They could call her the *Devil's Whore* for all Nathan cared. 'The country trade?' he enquired. It struck a vague chord but he was damned if he could remember why. Something Duncan had said?

'It is what we call the traders that are permitted under licence of the company's monopoly. But it is also a name we use for smugglers – an aphorism, you might say. Like the freetraders and the moonrakers of the English Channel. One who is "engaged in the country trade". The practitioners are mainly British, or Persian. But I am not sure who owns the *Shiva*.'

'But she does have fifty guns?'

'Possibly, but not heavy guns. Twelve pounders for the most part – maybe half a dozen 18-pounders on the lower deck, more for ballast than anything.'

This was not what Nathan would call ballast. 'Is it usual for ships to be so heavily armed,' he enquired, 'in the "country trade"?'

'I believe her trade is mostly with China, through the Strait of Malacca, which is heavily infested with pirates – as are all the China Seas.'

'And she has a French crew?'

'I think they are mainly Lascars and Malays – and some Chinese. Perhaps some of the officers are French.'

He was beginning to look rather worried, Nathan thought.

'So you think we should take this threat seriously, or not?'

Picket shook his head. 'It is very hard to say. But if there is a shipment of this nature, and we have had intelligence that the French plan to intercept it . . . well, I would not care to report to the Governor of Bombay that we failed to act upon it.'

Nor would Nathan.

'It really rather depends on how much you trust your informant,' continued Picket bluntly. He had met Caterina, still in her sailor suit, and had appeared to be impressed. But then this was her usual effect on men.

'Plucky young woman,' Picket had said. 'Very sharp, lots of bottom.'

'I trust she is in good faith,' Nathan responded guardedly. 'And that she has reported accurately what she heard, or thought she heard. But they know she is a British spy, or was, and there is the possibility that the information was fed to her deliberately.'

'In the expectation that she would jump overboard – in a gathering storm – and swim to the nearest British ship of war?'

'There is that.'

'Well, it is your decision,' Picket declared, in his usual supportive fashion, 'but, at the very least, it will give us an opportunity to catch up with these scoundrels and pay them back for what they did to poor Cutler and the *Comet* – and the *Bombay* off Mangalore.'

Picket had lost eight men in the encounter off Mangalore, and his sick bay was still crowded with the wounded.

'But what if it is a *ruse de guerre*,' Nathan put to him, 'and the French plan to bring troops from Egypt while we are far to the south?'

'Good God, man, we are far enough to the south already,' Picket retorted.

This was true, and it was hard to resist the opportunity of surprising the French at their rendezvous and serving them as they had the *Comet*.

'Very well.' Nathan came to a decision. 'Then let us set a course for Devil's Point.'

Chapter Eighteen

Devil's Point

'I do not for a moment believe that anyone would accuse you of being shy when it comes to a fight,' Tully assured Nathan over breakfast in the captain's cabin. 'And if anyone did, and I was made aware of it, I would have them flogged to within an inch of their lives.'

Nathan regarded his friend sceptically. 'Have you ever had a man flogged, Martin?'

'No, but I can only be pushed so far.'

They were discussing the crew's opinion of Nathan's conduct in breaking off his pursuit of the *Forte* in order to pluck a half-naked nun from the sea.

'Well, I am sure they are saying something disparaging about me,' said Nathan, 'for I have observed it in their manner.'

'You have been exposed to insolence? Disrespect?' Tully reached for the coffee pot and found it empty. He raised his voice for his steward: 'Arnaud. Arnaud there.' Tully, too, had a French steward, but a rather more obliging one than De Fournier.

'I will not say insolence,' Nathan allowed. 'I will only say I have seen *looks* exchanged, particularly by certain of the junior officers.'

'Looks? What kind of looks?'

'Knowing looks. Smirking looks.'

'Ah. Well, you know why that is.'

'What do you mean, "Ah"? Said with that – *knowing look*. That is exactly what I mean.'

'I have said to you before, Nathan, and with the greatest respect, that you are sometimes a little too concerned with the opinion of those under your command. You can do as you like. You are the commodore.'

The steward came in with more coffee and toast and the discussion was suspended until he had departed with the empty pot.

'So what are they saying about me?' Nathan resumed, when he had gone, buttering his toast with a great air of indifference.

Tully sighed. 'It is really of no consequence, you know.'

'I do not know. That is why I am asking you. I am – as you have pointed out – the commodore. I am as removed from common intercourse as the Pope in Rome. That is why I rely upon my friends to inform me.'

'Very well. It has not been said to my face, but I believe that there is an opinion, shared by some, that you do not practise what you preach.'

'I have never preached in my life,' Nathan affirmed. 'Save when I am obliged to do so at Sunday divisions by the exigencies of my office, and even then I confine myself to generalities – one might almost say banalities.' Nathan had an aversion to preaching, derived from his sufferings as a child under the brutal regime of the Reverend Judd of Alfriston, who had been known to draw out his sermons for an hour or more. 'What am I supposed to have preached and not practised?'

'Abstinence. From the desires of the flesh.'

'What? Do not be ridiculous.'

'"The women of my people have ye cast out from their pleasant houses – from their children have ye taken away my glory forever."'

'Good God! Who said that? I did not say that.' His brow furrowed in suspicion. 'Is this Mr Joyce?'

'No. It is the Prophet Micah, as a matter of fact, from the Book of Micah, Chapter Two, Verse Nine. But I will admit that it was Mr Joyce who drew my attention to it.'

'The mutinous dog! What is the Book of Micah? How dare he bring the Book of Micah aboard a Christian vessel.'

'The Book of Micah is in the Bible, I believe, albeit the Old Testament. The Prophet Micah being one of the minor prophets of the Jews and a contemporary of the Prophet Isaiah.'

Nathan regarded him with suspicion, for Tully was no more inclined to the study of the Bible than he was.

'I thought Mr Joyce was a follower of the Prophet Zoroaster.'

'He is. But he maintains that this does not prohibit him from reading the Bible and drawing such solace from it as he may.'

'I see. So, I take it that this is a reference to my casting out of *his* women from *my* house – such as it is. And that the suggestion that I do not practise what I preach is a reference to the fact that it is now occupied by a deputy prioress of the Church of Rome?'

Tully smiled. 'This may possibly have been what he had in mind, yes.'

'Where was I supposed to put the bloody woman if not in my cabin? I could hardly stick her in the orlop deck. Or would you rather I had turfed you out of your quarters? Or Mr Joyce from his?'

'I have no opinion on the subject, I have merely told you what it was you wished to know.'

'And you let this – seditious libel – pass without rebuke?' Tully made a noise very like a snort. 'You consider it amusing?'

'I do think it was quite droll, yes. At least I did at the time. I thought you would, too, as a matter of fact, else I would not have mentioned it. Come now, you cannot possibly take it seriously.'

Nathan considered. 'Well, I would not take it *quite* so seriously if I thought Mr Joyce had the slightest degree of respect for me. As it is—'

'Oh but Mr Joyce has the greatest respect for you.' Tully seemed genuinely concerned.

'Does he? Good God, why?' He observed Tully's expression. 'I do not believe you.'

'He said, in my hearing, that he was honoured to serve under the son of Lady Catherine Peake.'

'My mother?' Nathan was stunned. 'What has my mother to do with anything? He has never met my mother.'

'He has, as a matter of fact. In London.'

'Oh my God! You are not saying –' Nathan had gone a little pale. 'He has never had . . . ?'

'Of course he has not. He is far too young.'

'I hope you will never say that in my mother's presence. Besides, he must be all of thirty. My mother would consider that positively senile. Joyce? Joyce?' He frowned. 'Oh my God, there *was* a Joyce. I remember. Not that I ever met him but ... And he was a Dubliner.'

'It was not Mr Joyce.'

'I am sure his name was Joyce and that—'

'It was his brother.'

'His brother?'

'His elder brother. When you were a schoolboy at Charterhouse.'

Nathan journeyed back in his mind to this distant period of his life, just before he had joined the Navy. He had been a boarder at Charterhouse but he had spent a fair bit of time at his mother's house in St James's, when she first set herself up in opposition to King George and was busy filling it with all manner of dissidents and Republicans.

Joyce, Joyce . . . ? A number of likely candidates flitted before his eyes, all young men of a certain age and temperament. Then he had him. Neil Joyce? Noel Joyce? Some Joyce at any rate. A tall, lean, gangling fellow with red hair and a garrulous manner. An associate of John Wilkes and Charles James Fox and other so-called Friends of Liberty, who called the rebel army in America 'our army' and ostentatiously celebrated its victories over the redcoats. Nathan groaned aloud and held his head in his hands. Why did his mother do this to him? He had no recollection of seeing an even younger Joyce about the house, nor could he remember his mother having mentioned such a creature, but then there was no reason why she should have. Nathan had made it very clear to his mother at an early age that the less he knew of her liaisons the better, though at the time she always referred to them publicly as her protégés.

'Well, she certainly made a great impression upon him,' Tully reported. 'He was lavish in his praises. Wise, witty, beautiful, bewitching . . .'

'Yes, yes.' Nathan sighed. 'You told him, I hope, that we have nothing at all in common.'

'I would not be so ill-mannered. I have oft heard it remarked that you have an excellent profile, and as to wit—'

'I mean in terms of our political views.'

'I said you had a great deal of affection for your mother and had been a staunch support in her hour of need.'

'Me?'

'Well, it is true, you know.'

'But you know what I think of my mother.'

'I know what you *say* about her. I also know you have devoted a considerable amount of effort and resources to ensuring her continuing comfort and wellbeing.'

'I have done what any son would do to avoid the embarrassment of having a mother detained at the King's pleasure.'

'Be that as it may, Mr Joyce regards Lady Catherine as one of the most virtuous women he has ever met.'

'Good God, man, she was sleeping with his brother. What does he mean, virtuous?'

'Possibly in the French meaning of the word, of having a deep sense of public duty.'

'Absurd. However, I have nothing more to say on the subject of my mother. I have said enough already. But I do not consider it respectful in Mr Joyce to be quoting the Prophet Micah at me and accusing me of being a hypocrite. I hope you assured him that my relations with Caterina – *Sister* Caterina – are entirely virtuous – in the true, English meaning of the word and none of your French bollocks.'

'I did no such thing. I have no idea what your relations with Sister Caterina are. Nor do I wish to. They are entirely your own concern.'

'Well, I can assure you, as your friend and commodore, that there has been no impropriety between us. None whatsoever.'

He relapsed into a brooding silence. His relations with Sister Caterina had required considerable steadfastness on his part, and he believed he deserved some credit for this. He had spent two nights now in close consort with her, their adjoining cabins separated by only the thinnest of partitions. He could hear every movement she made, every sigh, every murmur she made in her sleep. Or if he could not, he could imagine them. Virtuous he may have been – a true English gentleman – at least in so far as his actions went, but his thoughts had been entirely French.

If the voyage lasted much longer, he was not sure how he would cope. Yet there was no end in prospect. They had been driven far to the south-west by the storm and now faced a long, hard tack across the Laccadive Sea towards Devil's Point on the distant coast of Ceylon. Further, the wind that had so whipped and harried them had died to a warm caress – all Nathan's analogies, it seemed, were now of a sexual nature – and for long periods they had lain practically becalmed. They sweltered under a burning sky the long day through, and the nights brought scant relief; certainly not for Nathan, writhing in his cot, wondering if his tormentor desired him as much as he desired her. He had only to cross a few feet of cabin to find out. But to do so would be to declare himself as much a hypocrite as Mr Joyce and most of the crew clearly considered him to be. The kind of commander he despised, who had one rule for the officers and crew, and another for himself. Not that he had ever said anything, let alone preached it, that was in any way supportive of abstinence. The sins of the flesh, indeed. He left that kind of thing to the Reverend Judd and his like. But he had made it plain that he did not approve of women aboard a ship of war and now most of the crew thought he was having sex in his cabin with a nun of the Church of Rome. He could have wept. Especially as he wasn't.

On the other hand – a small subversive voice whispered in his ear – if they believe it anyway . . .

He could not stop thinking about her. It was like the rustling of silk in his ear. And the thoughts in his head . . . He invited Joyce and several of his fellow officers for dinner, if only to avoid dining alone with Sister Caterina. But he was overly conscious of her presence. He felt her eyes on him throughout the meal. Once he inadvertently touched her hand when they both reached for the salt, and a shiver passed through him. He was dreading the night ahead. Or, to put it another way, he was torn between apprehension and desire.

He need not have worried. The sea had its own agenda.

He was walking his special preserve on the poop deck, in solitary splendour but disturbingly aware of Caterina's presence immediately below his feet. She had gone for a 'lie-down', she said, after dinner and she had given him a look that was very little short of an invitation. He was also aware that he had only to glance through the skylight to catch a glimpse of her. He stared resolutely out to sea and whistled for a wind. They were still over a hundred nautical miles from the rendezvous at Devil's Point with no prospect under the present conditions of reaching it in anything much under two days. Two more days of torture.

But then from the lookout in the maintop came the shout of 'Sail ho! Three points on the starboard bow.'

And within moments, the sound of gunfire came rolling towards them across the lethargic sea.

Chapter Nineteen

Shiva the Destroyer

The lookout had been mistaken: there were two ships, not one. But so close together, it was as if they were joined at the hip. They were running northward, about as close to the wind as it would allow, and pounding each other with their broadsides so fiercely it was like one continuous roll of thunder.

Nathan ran up to the maintop for a better view through his glass. The nearer of them was a two-decker of 1,000 tons or more – and he could just pick out the striped ensign of the Honourable Company at the stern. The other, being to leeward, was masked both by her opponent and by the smoke from the guns, but she looked much the same size, and although Nathan could not see her colours, it was reasonable to assume she was French.

When he slid back down to the deck, Tully had cleared the ship for action and the drummer was beating to quarters. There was a rush of feet and a rumbling of iron wheels as the guns were run out. Powder monkeys were scurrying up from below with cartridges and powder barrels and the redcoats were climbing into the tops with their muskets and their grenades. Everyone but Nathan, it seemed, had something to do. In the absence of more useful employment, he sought out his steward and instructed him to store Sister Caterina in the orlop deck, well below the waterline, with the furniture and other breakables. He considered taking a moment to pass on a word of reassurance, but decided against it, not wishing to appear anxious. He could rely on De Fournier to make sure she was kept out of harm's way, he thought, in as much as was possible on a ship of war. If a spark reached the magazine she was done for, but then so were they all.

The combatants were still some five miles distant and in such a light wind it was likely to be an hour or more before they were within range, even if they did not change course in the meantime. They were still heading almost directly towards the squadron, both ships firing high in the hope of carrying away something vital. It was astonishing to Nathan that this had not happened already, for they were both taking a severe pounding, but as they came closer he saw that the courses and staysails were so full of holes he was surprised they could hold their wind. Still they came on and he could see the tricolour now at the stern of the ship to leeward. A French two-decker, then, in an ocean that was supposed to contain nothing more formidable, according to Governor Duncan, than a small frigate. Either she had not sighted the four ships bearing down on her from the north-west, or she was entirely indifferent to them. She was still partly masked by the East Indiaman, her upper decks almost completely enveloped in smoke, but the lookouts were well above the fog of battle and should have spotted them long before now if they had been doing their job properly. Nathan could only suppose that she intended to keep up the chase until the very last minute.

Closer and closer they came and he signalled Picket to continue on his present course, while the *Cherry* veered a full three points to the south-west so they would have her fenced in whichever way she broke. Closer . . . barely a mile between them now . . . and at last the Frenchman saw the danger.

The commander did what Nathan would have done in the same circumstances – he backed the mizzen to let the chase forge ahead and then began to wear ship, falling off the wind and turning more than twenty points of the compass to bring the bows round to the south-west. Clearly, he had decided that if there was to be a fight, he would rather take his chance with the *Bombay* and her consorts than with the big two-decker to leeward.

Nathan clapped the glass to his eye as she dropped off the wind and read the name at her stern. For a moment he thought it might be some trick of the imagination or a blurring of the vision. But it was neither. She was the *Shiva*.

'What in God's name is she up to?' he wondered aloud as he and Tully studied her through the glass.

'She must have been taken prize,' Tully supposed.

It was the most logical explanation, but she had a hell of a lot of men for a prize crew. She looked like she was preparing to fight the guns on both sides, and she was making an excellent job of wearing ship – and coming much further into the wind than Nathan had anticipated.

'She is going to cut through the squadron,' he cried out as the plan became clear to him.

They brought the *Cherry* back on her old course but they were lagging a good thousand yards behind, and to his considerable alarm Nathan saw that the *Shiva* was heading straight for the gap between the *Bombay* and the *Antelope*. And there was not a thing he could do about it.

But the East Indiaman could. And did. No sooner was she freed from her tormentor than she dropped off the wind and fired a final broadside at a range of three or four hundred yards. It was a long shot but it did more damage than all the close-quarter work that had preceded it. The *Shiva* had just completed her turn when her foretopmast began to topple forward and sideways, with all the majesty of a towering pine lopped by the woodman's axe. Down it came: spars, sails and all, over the side and into the sea.

The effect was as if a giant hand had reached out from under the water and seized her by the head. With nowhere else to go, the stern began to drift sharply to leeward until she was laid flat aback.

And the *Pondicherry* came swooping down on her, like Sister Caterina's avenging angel.

Nathan could see the figures crawling all over the *Shiva*'s forecastle, fighting to free her from the wreckage hanging over her bow, but until they did, she was dead in the water – a sitting duck.

'Let us serve her as we planned to serve the *Forte*,' he said to Tully, 'before Caterina went for her swim.'

Tully understood, but his expression was tense and his eyes shot up to the sails as he weighed up the problems involved. They were carrying a lot more canvas than when they were chasing the *Forte*, and it would be a much more difficult manoeuvre. Nathan opened his mouth to make a suggestion – and then snapped it shut. This was Tully's affair – he was the captain of the ship, and he had always been a far better sailor than Nathan anyway. Nathan would be better employed fighting the guns, but the guns were now Mr Joyce's domain.

There was nothing to be done but cross to the rail, clasping his hands firmly behind his back for fear he might start chewing his nails, and disgrace himself before the crew. The *Shiva* was still firmly held by the head, and the *Bombay* was now closing fast. Even as Nathan watched, the frigate veered sharply to windward and fired her entire starboard broadside at a range of about 600 yards: firing high and wide for the most part, but not without effect. A lucky shot parted the yard from the stump of her foremast and another mass of canvas and timber came crashing down on the men fighting to free her bow.

The *Pondicherry* was also turning to windward to cross the *Shiva*'s stern and Nathan could see the faces of the officers on the quarterdeck staring helplessly back at them. They would have known exactly what they were in for, and that there was not a single thing they could do about it, save to stand there on that exposed deck and brace themselves for the storm that was about to erupt.

Joyce gave the order to fire as you bear, and within seconds the great guns were in action, singly or in pairs, the 12-pounders on the upper deck and the 24-pounders below, with so little a gap between them it was like one long, rippling roar. Some of the guns would have fired high and some would have fired into the sea, but the vast majority fired straight into the *Shiva*'s stern, and it simply imploded – the elegant stern gallery, the windows, the transom – and with them, surely, the vital link between her helm and her rudder.

The *Pondicherry*'s own helmsmen were spinning the wheel, bringing her bows hard a-starboard, with every hand that could be spared hauling on the braces, while the gun crews charged across the decks to the opposite side. The guns there were already loaded and run out, the range so close there was no need for trimming or hauling on tackle. Each gun captain simply applied the match the moment he sighted the target. Fired at almost point-blank range now, the heavy iron shot blew away what was left of the *Shiva*'s stern and travelled the length of the ship, smashing whatever was in its path, guns, carriages and men. The wind was blowing the smoke forward, and Nathan had an almost clear view of the shambles they had made. He doubted if he would ever forget it. He had been in three major fleet actions – he knew the effect of a twenty-four-pound ball of iron on the human body, but he had never seen anything like this. It was as if some demonic hand had ripped a hole in the universe to give him a brief glimpse of hell.

Nathan had no illusions about the nature of his profession, but sometimes illusion was preferable to the terrible reality. Sometimes it was all that kept a man sane.

He turned to Tully and saw in his eyes the same grim acknowledgement of what they were and what they did. It would not stop either of them from doing it. Shiva was not the destroyer here.

'Lay off her stern,' he said, 'and we will pound her until she strikes.'

It was cold-blooded murder but it was the quickest way to end it. The *Shiva* was in irons, caught by the wreckage at her head; she could hardly bring a gun to bear. If her commander had half a grain of sense or humanity in him he would strike.

But Nathan's experience should have told him there was neither rhyme nor reason in a battle at sea. The men were drunk with rum, rage and fear; the officers with glory, honour or shame, blinded by smoke and deafened by the roar of the guns. And you stood there, trying not to flinch, with every nerve in your body screaming at you to run and hide; *standing*, for God's sake, not ducking or cowering or taking the least bit of cover, standing on those sand-scattered, blood-spattered decks, with solid iron shot hurtling through the air at over 1,500 feet a second and smashing into wood, canvas, metal, flesh and bone – seeing what horror such a missile at such a speed will make of a man. You could not stay sane in such a slaughterhouse; you had to be mad already. Any man with half a grain of sense or humanity would not be here; he would be safe ashore, playing hide and seek with his children.

So even as these thoughts passed through Nathan's head, even though he prayed that someone, somewhere, would strike that big bold tricolour still flying from the shattered stern of the *Shiva*, he could see the crew hacking with their axes at the wreckage that still gripped them by the head, the officers up forward urging them on, the men in the tops firing down on their tormentor with small arms and swivel guns, a man with half an arm trying to heave a 12-pounder cannon with the other so that he could train it through the gaping hole that had once been a gunport, and the rest of the gun crew lying dead around him . . . Pandemonium. And worse was still to come.

The *Shiva* finally came free of the wreckage holding her by the head, but with the sails laid flat aback and the rudder gone she began to drift helplessly stern-first down on the *Pondicherry*. There was frantic activity on her upper deck. The men who had been hacking at the rigging came running aft led by their officers, snatching up whatever weapons were available to them. It was a moment before Nathan realised what they were about. And someone on the *Pondicherry* – it might have been Joyce – roared the command: 'Stand by to repel boarders!'

Nathan looked to Tully. It was vital to widen the ever-closing gap between the two ships, but there was precious little room for manoeuvre. The *Cherry* could come no further into the wind, and to fall off would expose her to the same raking broadside she had dealt the *Shiva* – assuming she had guns left to fire and men to fire them. But they did not have to wait like dummies until they were boarded. Two could play at that game.

There were few rules for boarding in the King's Navy – strangely so, given the care and discipline that went into the gunnery. For most captains it was a tactic of last resort, best left to pirates and buccaneers. They preferred to batter a ship to death with their heavy guns. But the crews, being pirates and buccaneers in their black hearts, were all for it, and some of the officers, too, even the younger admirals – Nelson was a great man for boarding.

Mr Joyce had devoted a great deal of time to cutlass drill and the brutal arts of close-quarter combat while the ship was lying idle in Bombay Harbour, and when Nathan took command he had left most of the arrangements as he had found them. Above a third of the crew had been detailed as boarders, in two divisions. The first wave was composed of the most vicious and violent of the hands, mostly waisters and servants (there was a belief among them that they were the men Mr Joyce was most eager to be rid of – and they derived a certain perverse pride from this). The second wave was drawn from the gun crews – one man from each gun – reliable, steady men, for the most part, more endowed with muscle than brain, and possessed of a certain brute force that came from the heaving of heavy cannon. The third division was composed of the redcoats, with their muskets and bayonets – another widespread belief among the crew was that their main role was to drive the other two divisions before them, and consider the killing of the enemy only as a secondary concern.

Their weaponry, with the exception of the soldiers, ranged from short swords and dirks for the officers, to pistols and cutlasses, pikes, axes and tomahawks, marlin spikes and belaying pins for everyone else – anything, in short, that might be employed in the murderous trade of close-quarter combat upon the crowded deck of a ship of war. And as to strategy – there was none. It was a brawl – and British seamen were traditionally good at brawling. It was assumed that they needed little instruction in the subject.

Nathan should have stayed well out it; he knew that. He should have stayed on the quarterdeck to direct the fighting and send reinforcements wherever they were required – but he could not bring himself to remain so detached, so godlike, not after the slaughter he had witnessed on the lower deck of the *Shiva*. It did not make it any better, but somehow it *felt* better, to subject himself to the same arbitrary throw of the dice that determined who was to live and who was to die, even if most of them lived and died by his own command.

'We will go in over the stern,' he instructed Joyce and Dudley, the army captain. 'Marines to the fore – I mean soldiers, of course,' he addressed Dudley with an apologetic bow; astonishing how, even at a time like this, one remembered the niceties. 'Once we have cleared the quarterdeck, instruct your men to line the rail and fire into the waist. If there is any fight left in them.'

This was all there was time for. The two ships came together with a grinding of timbers that sounded very like a groan. And then all hell broke loose. Five or six grappling lines snaked out from the *Pondicherry* and a great hail of hand grenades and smoke bombs – even stink pots – were hurled from the yards of both ships. Nathan grabbed a hold of the mizzenmast shrouds and climbed up on the rail, paused a moment, and then leaped the several feet onto the *Shiva*'s quarterdeck. It occurred to him, too late, that he should have yelled something inspiring.

'Glory or a tomb at Westminster!' Nelson had cried at the Battle of St Vincent.

Nathan had nothing so wonderful in mind, but it might have been an idea to have at least indicated that the rest of the boarders were to follow him.

But they needed no encouragement. Tombs and glory were subjects for admirals to ponder and they were welcome to both. Murder was what they had in mind, and the swiftest, most effective way of going about it. They were already swarming aboard the *Shiva* by every means at their disposal, a homicidal tide of blue and red, apparently led by the fourteen-year-old Mr Vivian with a pistol in one hand and a cutlass in the other and an expression of total savagery on his youthful features.

'*Eagerness and heat in action, especially in a first onslaught, ought never to be the cause of a man putting himself so much off his guard as to lift his arm to strike a blow with his cutlass,*' advised the Admiralty manual on the subject. On the contrary, their lordships proposed, the boarder should rush '*sword straight out*', thus maintaining his guard and watching for his opportunity to make a thrust: '*the slightest touch of the point being death to the enemy.*'

Regarding the use of pistols, they advised the boarder to hold his fire '*to the last extremity, until his life depend upon it.*'

It was not to be supposed, for one instant, that the writer of this missive – or more likely the committee that had, after lengthy discussion, drawn it up – had based their advice upon personal experience. If they had, they would very shortly have made the discovery that an extended arm, even with a sword attached to it, is not anything like as long or as lethal as a pike, and of very little use against a barrage of small-arms fire.

In fact, most boarders discharged their pistols in the first rush and then hurled them at the enemy, before laying about them with every weapon at their disposal. The result was not elegant, but it was effective. It carried the boarders halfway across the enemy quarterdeck, sweeping all before them. Nathan went with the flow. He was half blinded by smoke and the flash of pistols and carbines. He felt the wind of a bullet past his ear, another tore the epaulette off his right shoulder. Men fell on either side. He was hurled into a steel hedgehog of pikes, felt a savage pain in his left side and a warm gush of blood, slashed right and left – ever mindful to keep a stiff right arm – and then suddenly, surprisingly, found himself standing in the clear on a patch of empty deck. Too empty, for he immediately became the target of a hail of missiles from above, mostly discharged from carbines and pistols, but also including at least two grenades which he was obliged to distance himself from with some rapidity.

His retreat brought him into the thick of the fighting again, and he found himself hard-pressed by two opponents, one wielding an axe, the other a pike: a combination which caused him some considerable heart searching, especially as they came at him from two different points of the compass. Fortunately, he still had a loaded pistol in his hand, not so much in compliance with the Admiralty guidelines, as because he had simply forgotten to fire it. He did so now, though, discharging it at the man with the pike while simultaneously plunging his sword into the axeman's thigh. If the pistol shot had the desired effect, the sword thrust proved a less effective deterrent, seeming more to enrage the victim than to disable him. He advanced like a berserker, albeit with a slight limp, swinging the axe at Nathan's head with such dexterity that it threatened to revise the widely accepted proposition that a pointed weapon is more effectual than one that is edged. Nathan retreated with such rapidity he lost his footing on the greasy deck, sliding with comic abandon on a mess of blood and entrails. He rolled immediately to one side as a second blow smashed into the planking at his head, and sprang to his feet – only for a violent kick to send him sprawling in the scuppers. He looked up through a blur of blood and pain to see his assailant poised for one final, murderous blow – and then the point of a sword appeared through the man's throat and he lost all further interest in the proceedings. As he toppled to the deck Mr Joyce appeared in his stead, holding out a hand to help Nathan to his feet.

'I am very much obliged to you, sir,' Nathan acknowledged with a bow, but the lieutenant's gaze was directed at a point somewhat below Nathan's belt. Following its direction Nathan experienced a similar alarm – indeed, he had been conscious for some moments of a not unpleasant warmth in the region of his crotch, but had put this down to something less serious than blood, if rather more embarrassing to explain. He now saw that his breeches were stained as red as a butcher's apron. He felt anxiously about the affected area, but in as far as he could tell, all was intact and the blood was not his own. He looked up to reassure Mr Joyce that this was the case, but found him otherwise engaged halfway across the deck.

'Is everything all right, sir?'

Nathan turned to find Mr Vivian regarding him with polite concern as he groped about his private parts.

'Thank you, Mr Vivian, everything is quite all right,' Nathan assured him, and the midshipman rewarded this confidence with a seraphic smile, gazing about the decks with perfect wonder. 'Eton wall game ain't in it,' he remarked obscurely – and then rushed off to find someone else to kill.

Nathan took a moment to look about him. There appeared to be plenty of fight left in the *Shivas* – more than he had anticipated after the blows they had dealt her with the heavy guns. The crew were mostly Asians and Chinese, and even as he fought for his life, a part of Nathan's mind had been wondering what made them so resolute, for this was no war of theirs. But then his own men were Danish or French for the most part and had as little reason to fight and die for King George or the Honourable Company.

A great many of the enemy seemed to be aloft, either because they had been ordered there to take in sail or because it had occurred to them that it was a much safer place to fight than on the decks. Whatever the reason, they had a great assortment of weaponry up there and they were employing it with murderous effect. Captain Dudley had directed his men to fire into the tops, but they were barricaded with hammocks, and only a few bodies were falling from the sky to add to the confusion and hazards on the decks.

It was quite impossible to tell who was winning. There was too much smoke around, for one thing, and the wind was too light to clear it. Nathan wondered if there was anything he could do to improve the situation, to impose some discipline upon his own side at least, but nothing immediately occurred to him. Then, suddenly out of the chaos and confusion, he saw the masts of another ship, looming up to windward. The *Bombay*. She announced her arrival with a great battle-cry from the boarders assembled on her decks, and the usual hail of grappling hooks and missiles as the two ships ground together.

The advent of a hundred fresh men proved decisive. Picket had half as many again in the tops, adding to the fire of Dudley's redcoats, and with more effect, judging from the sudden increase in the number of bodies falling from the sky. At last, the enemy seemed to lose heart. All the fight went out of them and they began to throw down their weapons. The battle was almost won.

A familiar face loomed up out of the murk. Blunt. And with him another midshipman, whose name Nathan had not yet committed to memory. Slater, Salter, something of that sort.

'Come with me,' he instructed them.

What he had in mind was to find the *Shiva*'s code book, and any other books and papers that might be useful to him. The usual practice before a battle was to secure them in a canvas bag weighted with shot, which was concealed somewhere close by the captain, so that it might be thrown overboard if the ship was in danger of being taken. Quite possibly this had been done already, but it was also possible that it had not.

The two midshipmen guarded his back while Nathan checked the flag locker and the cupboard for the binnacle light. Nothing there, save flags in one and candles in the other. Nathan looked about him. There was no office, or shed, like the one on the *Pondicherry*. Then he saw a man in the blue coat and facings of an officer, lying by one of the quarterdeck 6-pounders. He was clearly wounded but he was propping himself up on one elbow and groping for a pistol that lay on the deck. Nathan kicked it away and lifted him by the collar.

'Where is the chartroom?' he demanded.

The officer pointed feebly towards the stern quarters under the poop deck and Nathan let him fall back and led the way aft. The whole area had been cleared for action and there was nothing obviously resembling a chartroom, but Nathan's eyes were still adjusting to the change of light. He felt oddly disorientated. It was like being on a stage in a theatre, dressed to resemble a forest in some fairytale, with shafts of sunlight pouring through the holes in the shattered stern.

Then he saw a body lying in the far corner with something bulky next to it. He was moving over to it when there was a shout of alarm and he turned to see a dark shape outlined in the doorway they had just come through. He was pointing something at Nathan's head. There was a blinding flash that seemed to come from within his own skull, and then nothing. He did not even feel the pain.

Part Three

Island of the Dead

Chapter Twenty

The Boy in the Front Pew

'A wicked man walketh with a froward mouth. He winketh with his eyes . . .'

Reverend Judd's own eyes scanned the cowed ranks of his congregation with righteous anger . . . and settled at length upon a small boy in the front pew, flanked by two stout female attendants. For some moments he subjected this individual to an intense regard, much as an owl might regard a small cowering creature of the night before swooping to make its kill. There was no apparent reason for this scrutiny or for the perceptible wrath of the beholder. The boy's mouth was not especially stubborn or peevish, and his eyes flickered no more than might be considered normal in an eleven-year-old boy during the interminable progress of the Sunday service. His expression, in fact, was one of the most earnest interest and innocent candour.

'He deviseth mischief; continually he soweth discord.'

Nathan registered the rebuke and stored it away for future reckoning. His immediate concern, however, was to catch the attention of another small boy in the front row of the choir and cause an explosion of inappropriate mirth. Thus far he had been unsuccessful, the individual in question staring resolutely ahead, though the strain about his features betrayed a certain weakness in this regard.

Nathan allowed his gaze to travel briefly to the large stained-glass window above the altar. It depicted the cataclysmic events of Judgement Day, with the righteous being led to eternal solace, and the wicked to the fires of Hell. But the sunlight, dimly visible beyond this panorama was a constant reminder of more urgent matters requiring the boy's attention once he had escaped his present confinement. The Sussex Downs might have been appropriated by the adult world for the rearing of sheep, but it still possessed a great many amenities for the diversion of small boys. In the two or three miles between Nathan's house and the sea were several woods, countless streams and ponds, a river, a great many barns filled with rats and other vermin, two villages and endless opportunities for the mischief against which the parson so weightily inveighed.

Nathan was aware, of course, that Reverend Judd had singled him out for particular attention. It was not the first time he had been the subject of the parson's invective, and it would almost certainly not be the last. It was partly for this reason that he had led the village boys in a raid upon the parson's orchard the evening before, stripping it of its considerable bounty only a few days before it was due to be harvested. Reverend Judd was extremely protective of his orchard and partial to the cider it produced. What he did not imbibe personally, he sold to the local inn-keepers at a considerable profit, so this assault represented a serious personal and financial loss. To add insult to injury, the commander of the raiding party had left a note thanking him for his generosity to the poor of the parish, signing this missive 'Robin the Hood'.

Despite this subterfuge, Reverend Judd had clearly discerned Nathan's hand in this enterprise, but he had not a shred of evidence to lay against the perpetrator. Hence this morning's sermon, which had now reached a pitch of intensity and venom that was causing serious disquiet to his parishioners.

'Therefore shall his calamity come suddenly,' he bellowed, slamming his fist down upon the open bible and glaring down from the pulpit upon the object of his censure. 'Suddenly shall he be broken without remedy.'

The parson's unseemly passion and the principle direction of his gaze was not lost upon Mrs Madison and Mrs Moody, the two female attendants who had been deputed to see Nathan through the weekly ordeal of the church service. They shifted uncomfortably in the pew; they exchanged the briefest of glances over the head of their charge; they looked down at him with deepening suspicion. Their charge appeared perfectly oblivious to their apprehension and met the parson's gaze with unflinching complacency, but as the sermon drew to an end, and the congregation stood for the Creed, he caught the eye of his confederate in the choir and deliberately winked.

It had the desired effect. The chorister's glee could no longer be suppressed and he exploded in untimely mirth.

The parson's normally choleric complexion turned a shade darker. For a moment, Nathan thought he might interrupt the affirmation of the faith and leap down from the pulpit to seize him by the collar and administer a brutal flogging before the eyes of the entire congregation. This would not have been entirely unwelcome – driving the parson into a public display of lunacy was one of Nathan's private ambitions – but the Reverend managed to control his emotions and continue with the service, and Nathan allowed his mind to drift off entirely, roaming his beloved Downs at least in his imagination and recalling the adventures it had recently afforded him, not all of which would have met with the unbridled support of his minders. In the past month alone, he had acted as a lookout during the landing of a consignment of French brandy on the shores of Cuckmere Haven, assisted the notorious Black Jack Hinchcliffe in a poaching expedition on the estates of his father's neighbour Lord Gage, and culminated this lawlessness with the previous evening's assault upon Reverend Judd's apples. There was a growing body of opinion among the more respectable of the parish that the boy was running wild and would very likely end his days in a penal colony – if the hangman did not make an end to him sooner and save the taxpayer the expense of transportation.

There was general agreement as to the reasons for this neglect. The boy's father, Captain Sir Michael Peake, was one of the greatest landowners in the shire and a fine upstanding Tory gentleman, not noted for his indulgence to the wicked or profligate. However, he was away at sea fighting for King George against an unholy alliance of American rebels, French scoundrels, Dutch charlatans, and

Spanish idolaters, and to assist him in this enterprise, he had taken his body servant, Gilbert Gabriel, who, despite his own history of criminality, was widely reckoned to be the only man beside the boy's father who could impose a measure of restraint. His mother, Lady Catherine Peake, was a lost cause, being half-American and half-French and therefore doubly damned. She was, besides, almost permanently up in London engaged in the world of fashion and politics, where she lent her voice and her considerable fortune in support of the King's – and her husband's – enemies. As for the rest, the boy's tutor, Dr Urquhart, was a learned gentleman with a degree from Dublin University, but he had as much notion of discipline as an Irishman in an alehouse, while servants like Mrs Moody and Old Maddy, who were expected to take charge of him in the absence of more senior figures, found themselves unable to curb his excesses beyond the boundaries of their immediate domain, and then only with the most vigilant watchfulness and the aid of a switch or such kitchen implements as came conveniently to hand.

It was, in every way, an idyllic childhood for a boy of spirit and initiative. Although he missed his parents, especially his mother, Nathan was perfectly aware of the advantages that accrued from their absence, and quite capable of exploiting them to the full. Even the existence of several enemies wholly committed to his downfall only added spice to his adventures. The only problem, to the boy's way of thinking, was that they lacked focus. In fact, at the present time, he was having difficulty in making them conform to even the most basic rules of time and motion. One moment he was sitting in the front pew of

Alfriston Church while the trees of the adjoining elms waxed golden in the autumn sun, the next he was lying in the long grass on the upper slopes of the Long Man of Wilmington, at the height of summer, playing the flute.

Even more puzzlingly, his toes seemed a great deal further from his head than they had been when he was standing in the pew, and for a moment, indeed, he thought he had exchanged places with the giant who gave the hill its name.

Otherwise, he had little to complain about. It was certainly a great deal more pleasant than being in church. There were clouds of gossamer seeds drifting in the warm breeze and hordes of daddy-long-legs bowling across the grass as if they were off to the Midsummer Ball, while far below the whole of the Cuckmere Valley lay open to his benign inspection. This pleasing vista was further improved by the figure of a young woman advancing towards him up the path from the village. As she came closer, he recognised her as Frances Wyndham, the daughter of Lord Egremont, who was one of his father's neighbours. Though once accounted a great nuisance and cry-baby, she had improved with the years and now must be counted among the shire's finest amenities. Moreover, with a delicious frisson of shock and pleasure, he realised that with the exception of a pair of lace-up boots and a sennit hat, she was perfectly naked. His delight at this unexpected bounty was swiftly checked, however, by the remembrance that she was now his father's mistress. Even more alarmingly, she appeared to be heavily pregnant, although he could have sworn this was not the case only a few moments previously, and that the child in her belly was very likely his little half-brother

– or half-sister, which would, in the circumstances, be preferable.

Nathan had the wit to appreciate that this was very probably a dream – though it was an unusual dream for a boy of eleven, whose wicked imaginings had not previously led him into territory more dangerous than the parson's orchard. The spectre instantly vanished, leaving him with an interrupted view of the village and the square tower of Alfriston church, where Reverend Judd no doubt continued to spit bile at the reprobate in the front row.

He should really get back there, Nathan thought, before his absence was generally noted. But it was very pleasant to lie here in the sunshine, playing his flute and watching the daddy-long-legs dancing to his tune. So pleasant, indeed, that he began to feel exceedingly sleepy. Perhaps if he just dozed off for a few minutes, he could still make it back to the church before the end of the service. But the dream of Fanny Wyndham had left him with the uneasy feeling that all was not well, that the world was – in some undefined way – seriously out of kilter. He even began to wonder if it had not been a dream at all, but some prophetic vision of the future – a future, moreover, in which he did not exist. The child in Fanny's belly was not destined to grow up in his shadow, but to replace him. He had been gazing upon the new heir to the Windover estate – or at least its progenitor. Which was not, in itself, such a terrible blow as the realisation that this injustice could only occur because he himself was dead.

So alarming was this notion, that he left the dancing opiliones and the floating gossamer and hurried back to join his younger self, but when he entered the church he saw that a great many changes had occurred in his absence. A haze of dust and debris floated in the splintered light from the windows. The stained glass was shattered, the Last Judgement lay in a thousand fragments about the nave, and the body of Reverend Judd was draped over the pulpit with a long splinter of oak embedded in his back. While this may not have been too distressing in itself, Nathan's unease was compounded by less edifying sights. The pews were filled with corpses, many lacking heads and limbs, and the stone floor was stained by an inordinate amount of blood and other substances that were best kept within the confines of the human body. The air was filled with shreds of scorched flesh, or paper, which lazily circled, like motes of dust, in the beams of light pouring through the holes in the roof. And someone, somewhere, was ringing a bell.

It was all very alarming, and the worst of it was that it was all his fault. Reverend Judd had been right. *He deviseth mischief; continually he soweth discord.* And this was the result.

With this insight came an intense pain in the region of his left ear, and a sudden change of perspective. Instead of the interior of the church, he was looking upon the recent scenes of chaos on the deck of the *Shiva*. As they flashed before his eyes, they became reduced to one powerful image: the figure standing in the doorway of the captain's cabin with a raised pistol pointing at his head.

Nathan struggled to emerge from these nightmares, as a drowning man struggles to surface from the fatal grip of the ocean. Distantly, he could see a gleam of sunlight. No, not sunlight – more the warm, flickering light of a lantern at the end of a tunnel. He forced himself to move towards it, though his limbs felt impossibly heavy, and in the centre of the glow he discerned a head – not a severed head, but more like the heads in the stained-glass windows of the church, framed by the golden halo of saints and seraphim. Gradually, his eyes found their focus and the head its form, and as it bent towards him he recognised the angelic features of Sister Caterina Caresini.

'Where am I?' His voice was a feeble croak, even to his own ear. From what he knew of the nun's past, he might be in heaven or hell. If it was hell, it did not seem a matter for immediate concern.

'You are in your cabin,' she murmured, 'in your own ship.'

He tried to raise himself from the pillow but the pain that had been lurking in the space above his left ear instantly became severe and took over his whole head. He sank back upon the pillows.

'What happened?'

'I will fetch Captain Tully,' she said, rising from her chair. 'He said to tell him as soon as you were awake.'

'No. Stay.' He tried to reach out a hand, but she was gone.

'You were shot,' Tully informed him. 'In the head.'

Tully mistook his silent stare for incomprehension. 'In the stern quarters of the *Shiva*,' he continued. 'By one of the French officers. With a pistol.'

'I know that,' Nathan's voice was still a croak, but not quite so weak. 'But how bad is it?'

Tully's expression grew a little less concerned. 'Clearly not as bad as I feared,' he confided. 'It creased your skull, just above the left ear. You have been unconscious for four days.'

Nathan raised a tentative hand to his head. He appeared to wear a crown of linen, bulging at the temple.

'The ball – is it still in there?' He kept his voice steady, knowing the answer was like to be a sentence of death.

'No.'

No. Life, then. With its immensity of opportunity, with gossamer seeds and sunlight and the daddy-long-legs dancing. Or a living death? A crippled, drooling sub-existence on the twilight fringe of humanity.

'And Dr Halsey has sewed up the wound. But he does not know if it has done any – that is to say, there may have been some – compression – within the skull.'

'So there may be permanent damage?'

'He said we will have to wait and see. If you appear cogent . . .'

Nathan smiled, though it felt more like a grimace, his dry lips cracking at the edges. 'Do I often appear cogent?'

Tully also smiled. 'It is a rare occurrence, but it has been known.'

Nathan tried to raise himself again, bracing himself against the tide of pain. 'Help me up.'

'No, you must lie still, Nathan – the doctor—'

'I want to see if I can walk.'

But he had to get out of the cot first, a difficult manoeuvre at the best of times and in the rudest of health.

'If I am so ill, why am I not in the sickbay?' he demanded petulantly, giving up on the attempt and falling back in his cushioned tomb.

'The sickbay is fairly crowded at present,' declared

Tully dryly. 'It was thought you would be more comfortable in your own—'

'How many did we lose?'

'Nine,' Tully informed him after a moment. 'Nine dead, twenty-two wounded.'

It could have been worse.

'Blunt, Joyce . . . ?'

'Mr Blunt is quite well. Mr Vivian, I am afraid, has lost an arm – but only the left arm. And the doctor is hopeful of his recovery.'

No more Eton wall game. But he had moved on to more violent pursuits. Perhaps the loss of an arm would be no great hindrance to him.

'But no other officers among the casualties.' Tully's voice betrayed a degree of irony. He might rise to be an admiral but he would always be a smuggler in his soul, and the son of a fisherman, and as much a rebel, in his own way, as Nathan's mother.

'And the *Shiva*? Did she strike?'

'Yes, and is taken prize.'

'What—'

But Tully raised a firm hand.

'Not yet. You must rest. You are lucky to be alive. When you have slept, I will tell you the whole story.'

Nathan's eyes went to the skylight, a myriad of distorted mirrors reflecting the multiplied image of the lantern. There was very little movement in the ship, but he could tell from the creak of timbers and the very slight tilt of his cot that they were underway.

Tully anticipated his next question. 'We are halfway through the middle watch,' he reported. 'The wind is from the north-east and we are on the starboard tack, crossing the Bay of Bengal, bound for Madras. Now—'

'Madras?' Nathan moved his head a little too violently in Tully's direction and winced as the hammer struck a sharp single bell. 'Why Madras?'

'Easy, easy,' Tully said, as if he were addressing a restless horse. 'All in good time. I am going to leave you now so you can sleep.'

'Wait.' Nathan raised a hand. He knew he would not sleep until he knew what had happened and why they were heading for Madras. 'I was looking for the signal book,' he said.

'And it is found. Blunt found it. And some other papers. It is good that you remember this, but you must not tax yourself.'

Nathan did suddenly feel very weak and weary. He could hardly keep his eyes open. 'I will sleep now,' he heard himself say. 'But as soon as I awake—'

'As soon as you are awake I will come and tell you the rest of the story, but the doctor will wish to see you first and then . . .'

But his voice came from a great distance and the darkness had once more descended.

Chapter Twenty-one

The Falcon and the Pearl

'Who is the King of England?'

Nathan regarded the doctor warily. 'This is a trick question?'

'No, sir.' Dr Halsey frowned. 'Why would it be a trick question?'

Halsey was a sharp-featured little man with a long nose and a gloomy countenance. He reminded Nathan somewhat of Dr Fell in the nursery rhyme, who was always depicted in the illustrations that accompanied it as a stooped raven, a bird of ill omen.

I do not like thee, Dr Fell,
The reason why I cannot tell;
But this I know, and know full well,
I do not like thee, Dr Fell.

The pain inside Nathan's head had receded to an occasional throb when he heard a loud noise or was made fractious. On the whole, he felt a great deal better, though still weak and extremely hungry. He had slept round the clock, almost, and it was now nearing the end of the first watch, which was to say near midnight. In Nathan's view the doctor would have been best left in the sickbay to attend to his more needy patients while the commodore was attended by his steward and his cook.

'You want me to say the father, but you mean the son.'

'No, why—' But then Dr Halsey frowned. 'Can you not answer the question?'

'George. The Third.' Nathan was by no means assured by the surgeon's denial. 'But if he were to be declared – incapacitated – by reason of his madness, then it might be that the son, who is also named George—'

'But that would make him the Regent, would it not?'

'I suppose that is true. Very well. George the Third.'

'And the chief of his administration?'

'Pitt. Billy Pitt. This is easy.'

'Very well. What is Canopus?'

'A star. The lucida of Argo Navis. Also the ancient city by which we fought the battle of Abukir.'

'You appear quite *compos mentis*,' the surgeon informed him a trifle grudgingly, Nathan thought. 'It would appear that there is no permanent damage.'

'Good. Now can I have a drink of water?'

'By all means.' The doctor looked for assistance but finding none available to him, he was reluctantly obliged to supply the need himself from a small flask and a leather cup residing beside the patient's cot. 'I will have to raise your head a little,' he said. He stooped over the cot, noticeably increasing his resemblance to a carrion bird pecking at a corpse. But it was only to put his hand behind Nathan's head, lifting it very gently as he brought the cup to his cracked lips.

'I thought I saw Sister Caterina,' Nathan said when he had drunk a little.

'Yes. She has been sitting with you all day. In fact,' he added after a small pause, 'she has been at your side ever since you were brought back from the *Shiva*, more dead than alive.'

'Really?' This required rather more careful thought than the questions the surgeon had asked. Nathan was not sure he was up to it yet, but it promised to be more pleasant than not. 'And where is she now?'

'She was here when I came in,' Halsey replied. 'But she left. Perhaps she thought I wished to be private with you. Shall I have her sent for?'

'No. Not yet.' There was another thought demanding Nathan's more immediate attention.

'Captain Tully said the sickbay was crowded.'

'I am afraid it is, though becoming less so.'

This was unlikely to be because they had recovered.

'How many more have we lost?'

'Four. Their wounds were severe. In a hand-to-hand engagement of that nature . . .'

Clearly Halsey was not going to take a greater responsibility than the man who had ordered the attack. He was very probably right.

'And how many of the *Shiva*'s?'

'Forty-four dead and near a hundred wounded.'

'Good God! That must be near half the crew.'

'They were fighting to the death. By the laws of the sea they may be considered pirates – and would hang for it.'

This would explain why they fought so long and hard. 'But I thought she was taken by the French.'

But this was as far as Dr Halsey was prepared to indulge him.

'I will ask the captain to attend upon you,' he said. 'He gave orders to be summoned as soon as I had finished my examination.'

'Did I pass for a pension?'

'I believe you must discuss that with the proper authorities. As far as I am concerned, you have every chance of resuming your present command, after a due period of convalescence.'

'Can I walk?'

'I see no reason why you should not. Though you would be advised to remain where you are for at least a day or two.'

'What about food?'

'A little broth perhaps . . .'

'Be damned to your broth, sir,' Nathan was stung into retort. 'If you see my steward, ask him to see if there is any cold pie left in the larder and a pint of small beer. If you would be so good,' he added, remembering his manners, 'and thank you, Doctor, for your – your . . .' He was at a loss to know quite what the surgeon had done for him, but it had no doubt played a significant part in his recovery.

'All I did was sew you up, sir, I doubt the gunner's wife could have done a better job.'

'And I doubt you have had a more difficult patient, sir, but thank you, all the same.'

* * *

'You are quite certain you are prepared for this?' Tully enquired.

'Quite prepared, thank you,' Nathan assured him, 'apart from the hunger cramps in my stomach and a growing anxiety gnawing at my breast that you seem determined to prolong. Pray tell me the worst. If you are not too fatigued.'

Tully smiled. 'I am not too fatigued, and the news is not entirely bad. But it is a lengthy tale. Very well.' He settled himself in his chair with a sigh. 'I had better start at the beginning.'

'That is usually the best way.'

'The *Shiva* was hired by the Honourable Company to wait upon the *Falcon* at Devil's Point—'

'The *Falcon*?'

'The chase. That is, the East Indiaman she was fighting when we—'

'The silver ship?' If she was, there would surely be a large reward. The East India Company was not stingy about that.

'If you are continually going to interrupt we will never get through this.'

'I beg your pardon, but if you had added in parenthesis . . .'

'Very well. Parentheses and all. The *Falcon* – an East Indiaman built in Deptford in 1793 by the firm of John Perry and Sons – left London at the beginning of May in the company of another ship, the *Pearl*. Bound for Calcutta by way of the Cape.'

'The Falcon and the Pearl'. Another story out of the *Arabian Nights*.

'The *Falcon* was carrying the usual freight – woollen and metal goods for the most part – but the *Pearl* carried a quantity of silver coin for the use of the Governor-General in Calcutta.' Tully paused a moment, as if weighing the effect of his words upon the patient. 'To the value of one million pounds sterling.'

Nathan pursed his lips and let out a silent whistle. This was the exact amount Billy Pitt put aside annually to pay off the national debt. Spent wisely it would buy a fleet the size of Nelson's at Abukir.

'But it was all in the *Pearl*? None in the *Falcon*?'

'Apparently not.' Tully shrugged. 'They were accompanied by two ships of the line and two frigates, sent to reinforce Admiral St Vincent at Cadiz. They reached Gibraltar at the end of May but they had endured some rough weather and were obliged to remain there a month for repairs. Then they travelled without escort to the Cape.'

This was not unusual. There was little chance of falling in with the enemy off the coast of Africa, not with St Vincent sitting on Cadiz, and it was reasonable to suppose that two East Indiamen had enough guns between them to see off any pirates or corsairs they might encounter. But Nathan wondered if the delay at Gibraltar had alerted the Spanish and, through them, the French.

'They reached the Cape at the end of August, but then there was another problem. There was news of a heavy French frigate that had joined the privateers at Île de France . . .'

'The *Forte*.'

'Quite. Apparently she had a fight with two of our frigates coming round the Cape and our people came off the worse for it. They were supposed to provide an escort for the next part of the journey but only one of them was ready for sea. It was already very late to make the journey out and they were advised to wait until after the monsoon. However, it was decided to take the risk. Apparently, there is urgent need of the silver in Madras.'

'For what purpose?' There were a number of questions that arose in Nathan's mind and this was possibly the least of them, but it might provide some clue that would help answer the rest.

'The purpose was not disclosed. Not at least, to the captain of the *Falcon*. They left the Cape in September with just one escort,' Tully resumed. 'A forty-gun frigate that had been in the Dutch service, sister to the *Braave*, in fact, and renamed the *Bridport*. She was to escort them as far as Devil's Point where they were to rendezvous with another ship of war sent from Madras to meet them.'

'*The Shiva*?'

'They did not know the name, but I think we can safely make that assumption. However, when they finally arrived at the rendezvous, they found an entire squadron waiting for them – six ships, all flying the colours of the East India Company.'

'Leloup.'

'So it would seem. The timing is right. But as they entered the bay, something must have alerted the *Bridport* – possibly someone recognised the *Braave*, or even the *Forte* – but whatever the reason she fired a gun and flew the signal to scatter—'

'Why did they not fight? If they had all fought together . . .'

'I know. But if they were faced with a superior force, the plan was to scatter. The *Falcon* was to act as a decoy. It was felt in London that even if the French knew of the consignment, they would not know which of the two ships was carrying it. Or whether it had been shared between them. As they approached the rendezvous, the *Falcon* was about a mile to the rear. She had been having some trouble with her steering and was hurrying to catch up when she saw the signal. That is how she escaped.'

'And the others?'

'The captain thinks they must have been taken. He heard gunfire but then night fell and he was at a loss to know how to proceed. Then, at break of day, they fell in with the *Shiva*.'

'Which had been taken by the French?'

'As to that, there is some doubt. You will have to discuss it with Commodore Picket.'

'But if she was not taken . . .'

'That is the mystery.'

'But what of the papers that were taken from the *Shiva*? Do they not tell us anything?'

'Commodore Picket has them.'

'You have not seen them?'

'No.'

Nathan reflected in silence for a moment. The ship was rolling rather more heavily than it had been, and he was aware of rainfall upon the deck above. Even in the poor light he could see it dancing on the glass of the skylight.

'The north-east monsoon is upon us,' Tully remarked, noting his gaze. 'We have had a number of violent downpours in the last few hours.'

'And we are bound for Madras?'

'The commodore was of the opinion that we must report what has happened to the governor, Lord Clive.'

'So when do we expect to arrive?'

'Four – perhaps five – more days. Provided the weather holds. We are beating against the wind, of course, but if it does not increase . . .'

'And no more news of Leloup? Or the *Pearl* and her escort?'

'None. Or I would have told you. If you show signs of agitation, the doctor says I must—'

'Be damned to the doctor. So the silver ship is taken?'

'It would appear so.'

'And that is it?'

'That is the gist of it. I am sorry it is not more palatable, but it was hardly your fault.'

'No.' Nathan wondered if the East India Company would share that view. 'What of Sister Caterina?' he asked.

Tully looked surprised. 'What of her?'

'Well, where is she now?'

'I really have no idea. Probably in her cabin. Would you like me to send for her?'

'Well, if she is asleep, of course . . .'

'You should sleep yourself,' Tully counselled him sternly. 'Sleep, the doctor says, is the best cure.'

'I have been asleep for the best part of five days. I think sleep is not the most pressing of my needs at present.'

'I would not advise—'

'I do not mean that.' Nathan sighed. 'I merely wish to thank her for her care of me, but if you have an opinion on the subject, I would, of course, be properly grateful for it.'

'I will see if she is about.' Tully paused at the door. 'But you should not exert or excite yourself in any way.'

'I have no intention of exerting or exciting myself,' Nathan retorted. 'Good God, man.' He paused a moment to let the throbbing in his head recede a little. 'And if there is a possibility of anything to eat . . .'

'It is quite late for the galley,' Tully pointed out.

'Of course, but if—'

'I will see what I can do,' sighed Tully.

Chapter Twenty-two

Wellesley's War

'So, we may have our war, but we have lost the means to pay for it. Thank you, gentlemen. Anything else whilst you are here?'

The governor-general viewed the two commodores with deceptive affability. Though his tone was sardonic, it was clear to Nathan that he was a very angry man; so angry, indeed, that one wrong word was likely to trigger an explosion. Richard Wellesley, Second Earl of Mornington, was a man of middling years with a face that reminded Nathan of the camel he had attempted to ride in the Joumrok Khan, though others, less well travelled, might have chosen a thoroughbred racehorse as a point of comparison. Either way, it was a face designed for winning, or putting people in their place, which often came to the same thing. It was long and narrow with a broad, noble brow which merged on its upper slopes into a mane of powdered hair; an exceptionally long nose, and a mouth perfectly formed for an expression of haughty disdain or smirking contempt. 'He has never forgiven God for causing him to be born in Ireland,' Commodore Picket had advised Nathan on their way here, 'and woe betide any man foolish enough to remind him of this misfortune.'

Despite his poor start in life, Wellesley had been educated at Eton and Cambridge and was generally reputed to be a great scholar, though this had not prevented him from entering the world of politics. Before accepting the office of Governor-General of Bengal, he had been on the Board of Control appointed by Parliament to oversee the affairs of the East India Company.

His Excellency was presently accommodated in the Garden House, the residence of the Governor of Madras some several miles south of the city, having arrived from Calcutta in August – bringing half the Bengal Army with him to reinforce the local garrison. Through the expansive windows of the governor's mansion Nathan could see their tents receding into the middle distance in long, straight lines, with the regimental colours drooping in the humid air and squadrons of cavalry drilling on the governor's lawns. It was widely reported that some 22,000 native troops of the East India Company and 4,000 British regulars were currently stationed in and around Madras, and that as soon as the rains ended they would advance on Mysore. The news that a hundred French volunteers had landed on the western coast had given the governor-general every justification, in his view, for declaring a state of war. However, the loss of the *Pearl* and her precious cargo had clearly robbed him of any satisfaction he might have felt in this pretext, and as was usual in such circumstances, it was the messengers who were likely to bear the brunt of the blame.

'Are you counting them, sir?' Wellesley had remarked Nathan's interest in the view from the window. 'Have you calculated their value in pounds, shillings and pence? Do you know what it costs to maintain an army of twenty-six thousand men in the field? Or to pay their wages, which, I am informed, are some three months in arrears? And now they are expected to march through two-hundred-and-fifty miles of jungle to fight their own people. My God.' His thin lips twisted in disgust.

Nathan was well aware that the great majority of the forces at the governor-general's disposal were mercenaries – native troops of Hindu or Mohammedan persuasion. Their reasons for fighting were even more of a mystery to him than the sentiments which drove his own ship's company to fight and die for King George. He imagined that a great many things came into it – pride, politics, racial and religious prejudice, a passion for soldiering – but like any mercenary army their principle objective was money – pay and the promise of plunder. And if for one moment they suspected the Honourable East India Company lacked the means of providing one or the other, it would be extremely foolish to rely upon any more quixotic sense of loyalty. In fact, they were as likely to vent their disappointment upon their tardy paymasters and exact a bloody retribution for being so ill-used. But if the governor-general did not know this already, Nathan was not going to be the one to inform him.

'One million pounds sterling,' Wellesley reflected. 'Vanished into the wastes of the Indian Ocean. Unless one of you gentleman has some idea of where we should start looking for it.'

He gazed around the subdued faces of his audience: the two naval officers; his two younger brothers who apparently served him in the roles of private secretary and military adviser; the commander-in-chief, General Harris; and the Governor of Madras, Lord Clive, son of the great Robert Clive, whose glorious victories Wellesley wished to emulate, it was said, and in whose shadow he appeared destined to remain. But none of these worthies appeared willing to hazard even a wild guess as to the whereabouts of the governor-general's treasure, let alone incur his wrath by pointing out that it was very likely on its way to the Île de France and so lost to him for ever. The silence lengthened. Nathan stared resolutely at the toes of his gleaming Hessian boots, determined to keep his mouth shut and his powder dry. He was to some extent protected by the bandage around his head, though this was unlikely to carry much weight with an old Etonian. *Floreat Etona.* What was it? Never kick a man unless he is down, and then make sure he never gets up. Something of that sort, anyway; Mr Vivian would know. Nathan had been to Charterhouse, where they preferred kicking a ball to heads. Doubtless Mr Vivian and my lord Wellesley would consider this effeminate. He had nothing useful to contribute in any case. He had no idea where the money had gone, or even if its loss was as disastrous as the governor-general had indicated. The East India Company could ill afford to lose one million pounds, but it was still only a fraction of their annual profits. And doubtless they were insured with Lloyds.

If it was meant to pay for a war against Tipu Sultan, then it was a different matter, of course. But then they should have taken better care of it. The whole plan had been flawed from start to finish. Why had they not spread the load between a dozen East Indiamen instead of loading it onto one ship? Why did they not provide a decent escort? Or better still, why not pay the money to the Rothschilds and let them move it about the globe in their own wonderful way, which seemed to be independent of winds and wars and whatever else mere humans were obliged to take into consideration?

Of course Nathan had no intention of saying any of these things. To do so would in all probability bring the governor-general's rage down upon his head, broken or not. It was said that Wellesley had set his heart on this war; that it was the only reason he had come out to India in the first place, forsaking a position in government; and that he and Billy Pitt had planned it between them, as a decisive step in creating a new empire in the East, which would replace the one Britain had so carelessly lost in the Americas.

'What did the prisoners have to say for themselves?'

Every face in the room turned in the direction of the speaker. He was one of the governor-general's two younger brothers who, though he could hardly have been more than thirty, wore the uniform of a full colonel in the 33rd Regiment of Foot. There was a close family resemblance – especially about the nose, which was even longer and bonier than the governor-general's – but his features were far more youthful and he had a devil-may-care look about him: the look of a rather bumptious schoolboy with an impatient air of showing his elders the right way of going about things. His lips were not so thin as his brother's, and his hair, which was unpowdered, hung in brown, glossy curls almost to his shoulders, but there was nothing of the fop about him. He looked lean and hard and fit, and extremely sure of himself. His name was Arthur, Nathan recalled – the Honourable Arthur Wellesley – and his role was to advise his brother on military affairs. Nathan wondered what General Harris, and his fellow officers, felt about that. Harris had remained a silent presence in the corner of the room but he kept glancing out of the window as if he had rather be in one of the tents.

'What prisoners?' demanded the governor-general with something very like a snarl.

'The prisoners that were taken with the *Shiva*,' the prodigy replied with composure. He looked as if it would take a very great deal to discompose him, even a rocket from his elder brother. 'Particularly the officers – those who survived the encounter. I suppose they have been questioned?' he demanded of the commodore.

'Indeed,' Picket replied, 'but there were only two officers in any shape to be questioned. They maintained that they were French naval officers from the *Forte*, transferred to the *Shiva* when she was taken at Devil's Point, but they would be aware that they would be condemned as pirates else and hanged for it.'

'And the rest of the crew?'

'Oh, they are from the *Shiva*, but they are all Lascars or Malays and claim they had no choice.'

'Is this not the most likely explanation?' Lord Clive demanded.

Picket gave no answer. He was reluctant, Nathan had noted, to challenge the opinion of his superiors, the Governor of Madras in particular.

'What of this Italian woman you rescued off Mangalore,' the colonel continued, having clearly taken on the role of judge advocate, 'do you believe *her* story?'

'Why should she lie?' Nathan felt all eyes turn to him and cursed himself for being provoked into speech, especially as he had his own doubts about Caterina's respect for the truth. 'I can think of no reason why she should make up such a story.'

'Save that she be in the service of the French,' Lord Clive sneered, with a look about the room as if to share his astonishment that anyone should be fool enough to think otherwise.

'Then she would have even less reason to disclose their plans,' Nathan retorted evenly.

'Perhaps we should speak with her,' the colonel suggested. 'Where is she at present?'

'She has taken lodgings in Fort Saint George, awaiting passage to England,' Nathan replied, a little uneasily. He was not at all anxious to have Caterina exposed to an interrogation, least of all by Colonel Wellesley.

'Did she have a name for this mysterious Frenchman she claimed to have overheard?' the governor-general enquired in a voice that suggested he was more of Lord Clive's opinion than not.

'Only that he was referred to as Monsieur le Marquis,' Nathan replied, 'and Captain Leloup once called him Fabien.'

'No one we know, I suppose?' Wellesley drawled in the same sardonic tone, his eyes lazily sweeping the room. He clearly did not expect a positive reply and nor was any forthcoming, but Nathan happened to be looking in Lord Clive's direction, and he saw a look of startled concern, almost of horror, cross the governor's face. It certainly wiped the smirk off it. The colonel had observed it, too. Nathan saw him shoot a glance at his brother, but if the governor-general had noticed, he chose not to pursue the matter. Instead, he addressed another question to Picket.

'You took some papers, I believe, from the *Shiva* after the battle . . .'

'That is right, my lord, but they did not appear to contain anything of significance.'

He had told Nathan much the same thing and Nathan had lacked the energy, or the authority, to press him on the matter. Wellesley lacked neither.

'Perhaps we should be the judge of that,' he informed Picket coldly.

'Well, there was the French signal book,' the commodore conceded with a flush, 'as to the rest –' he glanced towards Lord Clive – 'I had hoped to discuss this in private with His Excellency.'

'Really?' Wellesley's raised his elegant brows. 'You would prefer us to leave the room.'

'I beg your pardon,' Picket looked as if he wished *he* could. 'It is just that – the only other document of interest was His Excellency's order to the commander of the *Shiva*, despatching the vessel to Devil's Point.'

'You are implying there is something improper in that?' Clive bridled, but Wellesley raised a restraining hand.

'Not at all. On the contrary.' Picket's flush had

deepened. 'But as it was marked "Most Secret and Confidential" . . .'

'I assume this was to prevent the location of the rendezvous from being revealed to the French,' Wellesley suggested, 'which would no longer appear to be an issue. Anything else?' He addressed Picket as he might a junior subaltern who had singularly failed to impress.

'There were a few charts – but nothing out of the ordinary.'

'Nothing that might indicate where the French were going next?' the colonel drawled sardonically.

'Of course not. Would I not have said?' Picket was beginning to look like a broiled lobster and it was not just the heat in the room. 'If you wish for a full itinerary . . .' The company waited expectantly – 'Well, if I recall correctly, there was a general map of the Indian Ocean, a few more detailed charts of the Malabar Coast and the Bay of Bengal. And some charts of the various atolls thereabouts.'

'What atolls?' Lord Clive demanded sharply.

Picket ticked them off on his fingers. 'The Laccadives, the Andamans, the Maldives . . .' It was clear that he did not consider any of this important.

'The Maldives?' Wellesley's voice was entirely lacking in its customary languor.

'They are some three hundred miles to the west of Ceylon, Your Excellency, but—'

'I know where they are, damn it. It did not occur to you that the French squadron might have made their base there?'

'I – I had no reason to suppose it, my lord.' Picket threw

another wild glance at Nathan but Nathan was saying nothing. He had been unconscious when Picket had decided to set a course for Madras. Let him take the consequence of that decision. 'I cannot think—'

'They must have had some rendezvous in the area besides Devil's Point, I would have thought.' Wellesley looked about the room for support. 'Surely the *Shiva* would not have gone off in pursuit of the *Falcon* without some arrangement of that nature. And God knows I am no seaman, but are they not likely to seek a safe haven until the monsoons are over? Commodore?' he appealed to Nathan. 'Would you risk a journey across seven thousand miles of open sea in the stormy season with a fortune in silver rattling round in the hold?'

'Probably not,' Nathan conceded. It was not a problem he was ever likely to encounter, he thought.

'But, my lord, there are over a thousand islands in the Maldives . . .' Picket objected reasonably enough.

'But only one port, I believe. On the island of Malé.' Wellesley clearly took satisfaction from knowing every small detail of his dominions. 'The people are Mohammedans, quite possibly in sympathy with Tipu Sultan and the French. The more I think on it, the more I am inclined to think that Malé is the ideal haven for them.'

Any port in a storm, thought Nathan, for it seemed a desperate notion to him. But he left it to Picket to tell him so.

'Possibly one of the *Shiva*'s officers might be able to help us,' Colonel Wellesley suggested. 'If a greater degree of persuasion were to be exerted.'

'You mean string 'em up by the thumbs . . .' General

Harris frowned as if trying to recall if there was anything in the King's Regulations to prevent it.

'I was not thinking of anything quite so medieval. However, if it turns out that they are *not* in the French service, then they are guilty of piracy and may be hanged for it. If it were indicated that a degree of co-operation might incline the governor-general to clemency . . .'

His brother nodded. 'Excellent notion. Where are they now?' he snapped at the unfortunate Picket.

'Aboard the *Bombay*, Your Excellency, awaiting transfer to Fort Saint George.' Picket wiped a hand across his brow to stop the sweat from blinding him.

'Then might I propose they be accommodated there as soon as possible,' the colonel put to him, 'and the situation clearly explained to them, in words they cannot fail to understand.'

'You do that, Arthur, you are good at making yourself clear,' the governor-general instructed his brother. He seemed more cheerful now he had decided on a course of action. 'And in the meantime, we must prepare for every eventuality. How soon can the squadron be made ready for sea?' he asked Nathan.

Nathan thought quickly, though it was not a decision he cared to make in a hurry. The region was notoriously prone to cyclones during the north-east monsoons and there was the problem of the islands themselves. If the French had chosen to make their base at Malé it was reasonable to assume that they had taken the trouble to defend it. He wished he had seen this chart Picket had finally seen fit to tell him about.

'We could be ready for sea within a few hours,' he

declared, 'but, with respect, there is little point if we do not have sufficient force to achieve a result. If we assume the *Bridport* and the *Pearl* were taken at Devil's Point, the French have seven ships at their disposal, including three heavy frigates . . .'

'So what force do you require, sir? I regret we have no ships of the line to hand, and it would be a while before they could be sent out from England.'

Nathan ignored the sarcasm. 'The *Shiva* would be some help,' he replied. 'But she has been badly knocked about and—'

'How badly? Is she seaworthy? She must be, or you could not have brought her here from Ceylon.'

'Yes, but we were lucky there was not a storm.' He glanced at Picket, but he was no help, sitting there in his pool of misery. 'And she is hardly in shape to fight a battle. If we could put her in a dockyard, make some rudimentary repairs to her stern, and her steering, then—'

'How long?'

How long was a piece of string? They were dealing with a dockyard. 'Three, four days, maybe, if they know what they are about.' As many months if they did not, and a considerable amount in bribes, either way.

'Harry – write to the supervisor at the dockyard,' Wellesley instructed the younger of his two brothers who served as his secretary. 'Tell him he is to make it the most urgent priority. I want that ship ready in three days maximum. Three days,' he said to Nathan. 'Then you must take her as she is, or go without her. Anything else?'

'I cannot rightly say until I have seen the position, but if the place is defended . . .'

'You will need soldiers. We have plenty of them, doing nothing in particular at the moment. How many do you want?'

General Harris opened his mouth, but the governor-general raised a hand to still any protest he may have uttered.

'We could scarcely accommodate more than two or three hundred in the ships we have at present,' Nathan began.

'Commandeer any merchant ships you please,' Wellesley informed him blithely. 'You have my authority. My God, we have just brought half the Bengal Army down from Calcutta. Just state your needs, sir, I beg of you.'

'Perhaps the *Falcon* –'

'You have it. And the men? A thousand? Two thousand?'

'I think a thousand would be more than adequate,' the colonel assured his brother with a lazy smile. 'Light companies and grenadiers. I will discuss the details with General Harris, and if I might have the honour of leading them . . .'

'Light companies? Grenadiers?' Harris finally managed to find his voice, though it was clearly under some strain. 'But what of the march on Seringapatam? We could lose our best men.'

'There will be no march on Seringapatam if we do not get our money back,' Wellesley retorted. 'I will leave the details to you, colonel, and we will discuss your further involvement later. I suggest we bring this meeting to an end. There is a great deal to be done. And not a word of this outside the walls of this room.' He seemed to address this more particularly to Picket than to any of the others. 'If the thing is to be done, it must be done with the greatest despatch and in the greatest secrecy. Or we can pack our bags and prepare our excuses for when we return to England.'

Chapter Twenty-three

Jonah and the Whale

'This is madness,' Picket hissed in Nathan's ear as they left the governor's house. 'Utter lunacy.'

Nathan maintained his policy of saying nothing, though privately he was in complete agreement. But if a king could go mad, so could a governor-general. Some might see it as a duty.

'If they are not on their way back to the Île de France, they could be anywhere in the Indian Ocean,' Picket persisted. 'Why did you not protest?'

'Me?' Nathan considered one of a number of replies and settled on the most pragmatic. 'Because it would have served no useful purpose,' he declared, 'other than to enrage him further. Besides, we will have the *Shiva* repaired, anything else we require, and a thousand soldiers at our disposal. If the French prisoners do decide to talk, at least we will be in a position to act upon it.'

They drove into Madras with General Harris, along a road mired from the monsoon rains and clogged with military traffic – gun limbers and supply wagons, bullock carts, muleteers with strings of recalcitrant mules, even elephants and camels, wallowing in the filth and splashing through the puddles, cursing, bellowing and trumpeting their complaints, according to the facilities gifted them by the Almighty. And the fields about filled with tents, and ditches and latrines and horse lines . . . all the paraphernalia of an army under canvas. Twenty-six thousand men and twice as many animals with nowhere to go.

'All ready and waiting to march – just as soon as the rains end,' the general declared, rather more positively. And then, with a puzzled frown as he recalled the conversation in the governor's house, 'or as soon as may be.'

He relapsed into a moody silence. Picket looked ready to weep. Nathan's mind was filled with calculations. He wished he could see the charts Picket had taken from the *Shiva*. It was difficult to make any kind of plans without them.

They pulled into the side of the road to let a squadron of cavalry ride past – 19th Light Dragoons, Harris said, in their Tarleton helmets and blue jackets, looking more like French cavalry than British, he complained sourly. Then there was a skirl of pipes and he cheered up a bit. The 77th Highlanders, he informed his audience, clansmen from the north of Scotland, in their tall black shakoes and swinging kilts, muskets at the shoulder. They looked happy enough, splashing through the puddles, but it could have been worse; they could have been in Stirling. All eyes turned to the right as they marched past their commander-in-chief in his stationary carriage, and Harris sat stiff-lipped and misty-eyed as he returned their salute, dreaming of leading them on the Tiger's lair, no doubt, and hoping it would not remain a dream.

They carried on into Madras, following the line of the River Cooum with the ramparts and redoubts of Fort St George extending for several miles on the farther side. The oldest British fortress in India, it had been built in on swampland granted to the East India Company by the local nayak in 1639, since when the port had grown into one of the greatest in Asia, but General Harris said it was a terrible place for the fevers and was forever flooding during the monsoon. In fact, the river looked close to bursting its banks and the bridge they crossed was barely a foot above water.

They entered the fort through the western gate and dropped Nathan off at the hospital in Charles Street where he was to have his head examined by the city surgeon, Dr Sutherland. He saw no reason to cancel the appointment. Picket could deal with the *Shiva* and the dockyard, and they could leave the other arrangements to General Harris and Colonel Wellesley. But he asked Picket to send the charts over to the *Pondicherry* as soon as he returned to his ship.

Dr Sutherland was a Scot, of course. Most doctors in Nathan's experience were Scots and came in two sizes – craggy or corpulent. Sutherland was one of the craggy sort, so craggy, indeed, that he more resembled a corpse than a surgeon, which could not have cheered his patients much. Not that cheering his patients seemed to be a priority with him. He pushed his long nose close to the wound and sniffed about like a dog smelling for truffles, tapped Nathan's skull all over with a bony finger like a woodpecker drilling for beetles, and made him sit with his legs crossed so he could test his reactions to a small wooden mallet tapped sharply upon his knee. Then he exposed him to a series of mental tests similar to those that Halsey had contrived, save that he required him to name not only the present king but a great many of his predecessors.

'Would it not be more pertinent to ask me some questions about navigation?' Nathan enquired mildly.

'Why should I do that, when I do not wish to go anywhere?' the surgeon enquired tartly. 'Kings and queens will do very well, thankee, unless you have a particular objection to them. You are not a Republican, I suppose.'

Nathan rattled them off with confidence until the Wars of the Roses caused him to lose his bearings a bit, but then, as the doctor conceded, it had caused the kings and queens some confusion, too, and Henry VI himself cannot have been too sure when he was king and when he was not.

'Well, I can find nought wrong with you,' the doctor declared with some reluctance, 'and you might live to be a hundred, if you leave the knocking of heads to others.'

It was raining when Nathan emerged from the hospital, though rain was a totally inadequate means of describing the deluge that poured down from the vast black hole that passed for a sky. He felt unusually glad to be alive, in celebration of which he put on his cloak and hat and ran all the way to the coffee house where he was to meet Tully and Caterina, arriving thoroughly soaked but with his high spirits by no means dampened.

'You look very nice,' he told Caterina, though in truth he preferred her in a sailor suit. She had left that behind on the *Pondicherry*, however, and had assumed the more conventional attire of a respectable Englishwoman, or as respectable and English as Caterina would ever look. 'You look nice, too,' he assured Tully, shaking the rain from his hat and sitting down with them at the table.

'I take it you will live,' said Tully, correctly assessing his mood.

'To be at least a hundred,' Nathan reported, 'if I do not drown or get knocked on the head by the French. But they collected the fee at the door to be on the safe side.'

'And the governor-general?'

'The governor-general was less obliging. He gave me three days.'

'To live?'

'To be ready for sea.'

'Where . . . ?' Tully began, but then snapped his mouth shut.

'I will tell you later. What are we drinking?'

'Well, as it is a coffee house . . .'

'Sure it is,' Nathan looked about him, as if he had at that moment become aware of it, 'just like London.'

'Save for the heat, and the flies – and the punkahwallas.'

This was true. There were flies in the coffee houses of London, too, but not quite so many, and not usually of the bloodsucking variety, preferring to leave this facility to the paying customers. Madras had the same species – of merchant trader, if not of flies – bloated with a good morning's feasting at the exchange. Nathan wondered if they knew about the lost silver. Almost certainly, he thought, for all the governor-general's strictures about secrecy. You could keep very little from the men of money, and sailors were a notoriously gabby bunch. There were a few of them here – though not from the squadron, as far as Nathan could tell – along with a scattering of military men. Caterina was the only woman, though, and was being ogled by every man in the room. She was, of course, quite impervious to it. Indeed, she seemed oddly subdued.

'How are your lodgings?' Nathan asked her politely. Her resumption of female apparel had made him more reserved.

'Quite comfortable, thank you,' she replied coolly.

He wondered if male visitors were permitted, and whether the next three days would afford him the leisure for them to spend any time together. She would almost certainly be gone by the time he returned, if he ever did. She had stated her intention of taking passage on the next ship that was bound for England.

He sipped gloomily at his coffee. The best Ethiopian Mocha, almost certainly as good as anything to be had at the Turk's Head, but it gave him little satisfaction. His good mood was quite gone already. Even if she planned to stay in England, it could be years before he was back there. And England had its own constrictions, so far as Nathan was concerned. Faced with a choice between Caterina and Sara, what was he to do? Marry one, keep the other as a mistress? One in Sussex, one in London? Who would be the wife, though? Sara, probably, she was more the wifely type. Caterina was definitely more of a mistress. But, no, it would not do. It would not do at all. He was by nature monogamous. Or rather, he was inclined to love only one woman at a time. Though he frequently regretted it.

'Nathan?'

He realised they were both regarding him with some concern.

'I am sorry?'

'Are you sure the doctor said you were quite recovered?'

'Absolutely. Why do you ask?'

'Because Caterina has asked you twice how many lumps of sugar you would like,' Tully informed him.

'Oh, I am sorry, two please.' She helped him from the sugar bowl and he stirred his coffee moodily. 'They may wish to see you before you leave,' he told her.

'Who may wish to see me?'

'The governor-general and his brother.' Nathan dropped his voice. 'They want to ask you about this Frenchman you overheard in Mangalore. Monsieur le Marquis.'

'I can tell them nothing that I have not told you already,' Caterina insisted. 'I did not see the man, I only heard his voice.'

'I think, perhaps, they want to make sure you were not mistaken.'

'You mean lying?'

'No, not at all. Just – they just want to meet you,' he finished lamely

She sniffed. 'What are they like?'

'"What are they *like*"?' Nathan frowned. It was as if she were sizing them up as clients. 'They are Irish,' he said. 'Or at least, born in Ireland. You do not want anything to do with them, more than you have to.'

'But the governor-general – he is a lord, is he not?'

'An Irish lord,' he said. 'It is not the same.'

'And are not the Irish Catholics?'

'Not when they are of the rank of the Wellesleys. They are what we call Anglo-Irish horse Protestants.'

'Caterina is looking for a patron,' Tully said by way of an explanation.

I bet she is, Nathan thought. 'I understood you were setting off for England,' he said, 'as soon as you could find a ship.'

'Well, now I think I might stay,' she said.

This should have been cheering but certain things needed clarifying first.

'But why? What is there for you to do in Madras?'

'I am thinking to establish a convent here,' said Caterina.

Nathan smiled at the jest, but her expression appeared perfectly serious. He recalled with concern that her last convent had been judged the best casino in Venice – and some said the best bordello.

'Is that wise?' he cautioned. 'The English are not quite so – permissive – as the Venetians.'

'Not that kind of a convent,' she assured him. She even had the grace to blush. 'It will be to serve the poor.'

Nathan stared at her. 'The poor?'

'The poor and the sick. There are a great many in Black Town.' Black Town was the native quarter and the place where the Portuguese lived, as opposed to White Town where the English lived, and other Europeans of the Protestant persuasion.

'But – what – why?' Nathan was confused. He looked to Tully as if for an explanation. Tully said nothing, but

Nathan judged from his expression he knew something Nathan did not.

'Why me?' Caterina finished for him. 'I know.' She shrugged. 'But someone has to. And I feel it is what God wishes me to do.'

Nathan could hardly believe he was hearing this. He wondered for a moment if he was being made game of, but if so she was making a very good job of it. Her expression remained perfectly grave.

'It is like Jonah and the Whale,' she said.

'I am a little confused,' Nathan admitted.

'God wished to send Jonah to Nineveh,' Caterina told him, 'but Jonah had other plans. So he sailed off in a ship. But God caused a great storm to rise and the sailors threw Jonah into the sea and there was a sea monster—'

'A whale. Yes, I know. Apparently, they had them in the Med in those days. And the whale swallowed him and spat him out in Nineveh. But it was not actually the story that was confusing me.'

'That is what happens to me.'

Nathan wondered if his wits were not quite as sound as the doctor had indicated. 'Are we not in Madras?' he asked Tully.

'Madras is my Nineveh,' Caterina assured him. 'The place where the Lord wishes me to be.'

'But – why would the Lord want you to come to Madras?'

'To do His work. And the work of Saint Thomas.'

'Saint Thomas?'

'You know of Saint Thomas, Nathan,' Caterina assured him firmly. 'Everyone knows of Saint Thomas. The apostle of Christ who did not believe He rose from the dead. It is why we call him Saint Thomas the Doubter. Later, he came here to preach and he was made a martyr, on a small hill near here, by the pagans. The Portuguese have a shrine there and that is where I will build my convent.'

Nathan struggled to come to terms with this. 'But you have no money, no—'

'I have money – much money – from what I did in Venice. It is with Coutts and Company in London. But they tell me I can draw upon it in Madras.'

Nathan put a hand to his head. It had begun to ache again.

'Did you know of this?' he asked Tully.

'She had just told me.' Tully nodded. 'She made a vow. When you were ill. And in danger of death.'

'Captain!' There was a flash of the old Caterina. 'You said—'

'I said nothing. I promised nothing.'

'Oh no,' Nathan groaned. 'Caterina – it is such a waste.'

'A waste!' She said something in Italian, possibly vulgar. 'What else am I to do with my life?'

Marry me? Be my mistress? Better the first, in the circumstances. Nathan opened his mouth –

'I am sorry for intruding, sir. Mr Blunt said I would find you here.'

Nathan looked up. Lieutenant Joyce towered above him, respectfully touching his hat. Nathan regarded him as if he were an apparition, or a whale sent by God. 'Is there a problem?' he enquired.

'No, sir, not a problem, as such.' The lieutenant looked disconcerted by the intensity of Nathan's expression. 'It is just that – there is someone who would like to meet you.'

'Meet me?' Nathan was somewhat confused. 'What, here?' He peered around Joyce's massive bulk but he appeared to be alone.

'Not here, sir, but in Madras. If you can spare the time.' He glanced helplessly at Tully. 'He is – that is . . .'

'Who is it, for God's sake?'

Joyce looked like an embarrassed schoolboy. 'Well, that is to say – it is my brother, sir.'

Chapter Twenty-four

The Confidential Agent

'My goodness, sir, I see you are the great man in the world. And it seems only yesterday I watched you kicking a ball in Saint James's Park.'

Neville Joyce – not Noel or Neil – had grown older and stouter since the days when he had been a fixture at Lady Peake's house in St James's and the red in his hair had mostly transferred to his face. What was left of Nathan's earlier optimism vanished completely. It was always depressing to see one's mother's lovers grown old.

'How do you do, sir?' Nathan greeted him cordially enough, though he was still distracted by his encounter with Caterina. 'What a small world it is.'

'It is to be sure,' Joyce Senior agreed, 'and delighted I am that you are still a part of it. Brother William told me about your wound,' he explained. 'I trust you are quite recovered.'

'Oh, entirely,' Nathan assured him glumly. 'I could name you all the kings and queens of England back to Henry the Fifth.'

'Well, that is a wonder,' Joyce acknowledged. 'Your mother always said you were a sharp one, and quite wasted upon the Navy, though you seem to have done well enough by it. And how is your mother, by the by?'

'Quite well, thank you, when I last heard from her,' Nathan replied.

Joyce had done well enough by himself, too, if his brother were to be believed. He had made his money in the law and had been elected a Member of Parliament, but he had lost his seat in the last election and had come to India with an organisation called the London Missionary Society, though in quite what capacity Nathan had yet to discover. He doubted very much if it was as a missionary, unless he had undergone a complete change of character, but then, after Caterina's conversion, he supposed anything was possible. The first lieutenant had said something about an association with William Wilberforce and the Saints of Clapham, so maybe it was on their account; they had a facility for mixing religion with politics, though their current preoccupation was with slavery, and so far as Nathan knew, the East India Company had no interests in that line of trade.

At any rate, Joyce had not chosen to meet on church premises. Their rendezvous was in one of the private rooms on the first floor of a tavern down by the seafront, with a view through its windows of the shipping moored in the Roads. Nathan could just make out the vessels of his own squadron on the very edge of the crowded anchorage, over towards the mouth of the Cooum, with the *Shiva* tucked in between the *Pondicherry* and the *Bombay*. He would be more than happy to see her moved into the dockyard in the next hour or so, if they were to stand any chance at all of getting her ready in the three days the governor-general had allowed him.

'I am delighted you were able to spare the time to call upon me,' Joyce beamed after he had sent the potboy for some refreshments. 'We saw you come in with the *Shiva* and the *Falcon* and could see you had been in the wars.'

'I am very glad to see any friend of my mother's,' Nathan assured him insincerely. 'But Mr Joyce did say you had some information concerning the *Shiva* which might be of interest to me.'

'Indeed, sir, indeed I do. You are, I believe, presently in the service of the East India Company?'

'I would not say that at all.' Nathan shot a glance at the first lieutenant who shook his head sadly at this misapprehension. 'It is true that I am presently in command of a squadron of the company's ships, but I am wholly in the service of King George.'

'Quite so, quite so. Indeed, I am glad to hear you make the distinction. It is one that far too many people tend to forget.'

Nathan frowned. 'I am not sure I take your meaning, sir.'

'I mean that the interests of His Majesty and of the Honourable Company are not always in accord. Though, to hear some people talk, you would think the King and Parliament were mere instruments of company policy. However,' he added quickly as he saw Nathan's frown deepen, 'I have not brought you here to give you my views on politics. I am sure you hear quite enough of that from your mother.'

The potboy came in with a bowl of some crimson liquid very like blood, if a little on the thin side, which Joyce introduced as Stobart Gin. 'Dutch gin mixed with pomegranate juice and sugar,' he elaborated as he filled three cups with the ladle provided for that purpose.

'Let us drink to our reunion, sir.' He raised his cup with apparent relish. 'And to ours, Brother William. Until this morning we had not seen each other for two years,' he informed Nathan, 'so my thanks to you, sir, for bringing us together again.'

'I believe you must thank the French for that,' Nathan advised him. Their encounter with the French squadron was no secret, though he must be careful to say nothing of the silver.

'Well, it is an ill wind,' remarked Joyce. 'The *Shiva*, I understand, was flying French colours when she was taken.'

'This is true.' There was no harm in confirming it. The tricolour could clearly be seen from the waterfront, with the blue ensign and the flag of the Honourable Company flying above. 'But what, may I ask, is your particular interest in the *Shiva*?'

'In India we say that she is employed in the country trade,' said Joyce. 'In England we would call her a smuggler. Or a free trader. She smuggles goods into China, did you not know that, sir?'

'It had been suggested to me.'

'And was it suggested to you what might be the nature of those goods?'

'It was not. I am sure you can instruct me.'

'Opium.'

Nathan inclined his head in polite interest, but it did not cause him any particular disquiet. He knew that it was a prime ingredient of laudanum and that his mother considered it injurious to the health of women, but, so far as he was concerned, the Chinese were welcome to it. Just as the British were welcome to their Dutch gin and their French brandy, taxed or untaxed.

'Do you know the value of the company's exports from India to England?' Joyce enquired in an apparent change of subject.

'No idea. Substantial, I imagine.'

'On the contrary. It barely covers the running costs. A few years ago the company was close to bankruptcy. What saved it was the China trade. English wool and Indian cotton in exchange for China tea, porcelain and silk. But tea was the main thing. It is said that all the wealth and power of the Honourable Company has come down to the price of a cup of tea. Until the Chinese took it into their heads to demand payment for it in silver.'

'Silver?' Nathan's interest quickened.

'Silver bullion. Shipped out from England. Which the company could ill afford. They came up with all kinds of schemes, including a plan to grow tea in India. No less an authority than Joseph Banks said it could be done, and I have no reason to doubt his opinion – it grows wild in the jungle, I am told, in parts of Assam – but in the meantime the company had no choice but to obtain it from the Chinese, and pay through the nose for it. Then some bright spark – who doubtless knew the names of the kings and queens of England way back to Alfred and his cakes – came up with a new idea. Let us sell the Chinese opium, he proposed. Let me fill your cup, sir.'

Nathan declined. He felt the need to keep a clear head about him and it had suffered sufficient a pounding of late, what with the French and Sister Caterina.

'There was already a large market for opium in China. And the company had plenty of the stuff. It is grown all over Bengal – for medicinal purposes. Bengal opium, I am told, is the best there is. So the Bengal farmers were induced to stop growing rice and wheat and whatever else they grew, and to sow their fields with poppies. But there was a problem. The Chinese Emperor does not approve of opium. Not for the masses. And who can blame him? Millions of his subjects lying comatose, mere skin and bone, no use for anything but filling a pipe and sailing down the River Lethe. No work done. The economy in ruins. So he made the trade illegal – with the death sentence for anyone caught dealing in it. And all their goods forfeit, ships and all. The company could not be doing with that. So they decided they would not trade directly in the stuff – they would sell it at auction in Calcutta, and let the buyers take the risk of smuggling it into China. But – and here's the really clever part – the buyers had to pay for it in Canton – in silver. Which the company could then use to buy China tea. And silk and porcelain and anything else they wanted. Brilliant, was it not? No wonder they are the biggest trading company in the world. Everyone a winner – except the Chinese, of course. And the Bengal farmers who are made to grow poppies instead of food. You cannot eat opium. You cannot feed it to your children. It is only a matter of time before Bengal faces a major famine. And then the company will throw up its hands and say, "Oh, you cannot teach these people anything, they do not even know how to grow enough food to eat!"'

Nathan was silent for a moment. Lieutenant Joyce was sitting with his hands on his knees staring out of the window at the ships in the Roads.

'You make a strong case,' Nathan agreed at length, 'but I was never of the opinion that the East India Company was dedicated to the betterment of mankind. The world is a wicked place and the world of commerce more wicked than most. I am not a member of the London Missionary Society; I am an officer in the service of King George and until—'

'But it is the interests of King George that concern me, sir – you smile, but I am not the man you knew as a schoolboy. I am a lawyer and I have been a Member of Parliament. I, too, have sworn an oath of loyalty to the King. Do you think His Majesty would approve this business if he knew of it? Do you think Parliament would?'

'You will think me cynical, sir, but I do not suppose that Parliament would lose a moment's sleep over it, not while the East India Company makes a profit and distributes some of it in their direction. And as for His Majesty, I am sorry to say that even in his right mind, he would have little regard for the affairs of the people of China.'

'He would when he has to fight a war against them, with all the blood and treasure it would cost him. And believe me, that is what will happen if the East India Company is allowed to persist in this enterprise. Besides, you are wrong about Parliament. I represent a group of members who are very much concerned with the activities of the East India Company.'

'Mr Fox, I suppose, and Mr Sheridan?'

'Yes, they are part of it. But so are a number of Tories. So was Edmund Burke while he lived and he was no friend to the radical cause. Burke believed that the greatest threat to Britain's interests came from the French Revolution and the City of London. And at the heart of the City was the single most pernicious threat of all – the headquarters of the East India Company. The Spider of Leadenhall Street, as he called it, spinning its web about the globe. Not only exploiting the people of India but corrupting the entire political establishment of England.'

Nathan sighed. 'Well, I do not wish to argue with you, sir, or offend the ghost of Edmund Burke, but what would you have me do? I have no more influence with the Directors of the East India Company than I do with the Governor-General of Bengal, or the King of England. Far less influence than you, I suspect, and there is no other service I can do you.'

'There is, as a matter of fact,' Joyce assured him genially. 'I need evidence of what the company is up to. Written evidence that I can present to my friends in Parliament.'

Nathan's expression was cold. 'And you think I can provide you with it? I am sorry, sir, I do not know what or who can have given you that impression, but they did you a disservice.' He glanced at Lieutenant Joyce who was still staring out to sea with a fixed expression on his face, doubtless wishing he were back with his wife and his Zoroastrians in Bombay.

'I understand there were some papers taken from the *Shiva* . . .'

Nathan stood, carefully placing his cup upon the table and picking up his hat.

'I am sorry, sir, but I do not believe there is any point in continuing this discussion.'

'I beg of you, do not take offence. The *Shiva* is a smuggler, sir, and as an officer of the Crown there are some things you should know about her. If you do not already.'

'Such as?'

'Her owner is a Frenchman. Fabien Maurice de Montclair, Marquis de la Marche. He claims to be a Royalist, but he was a close friend of Paul Barras when Barras was in India and it is my belief that he is still in his service. Montclair is a soldier of fortune and an adventurer, but two years ago he set up a trading company with a licence from the Governor of Madras, taking a number of company servants as his partners. This year he bought the entire opium harvest of Bengal. Payment to be made, as usual, in silver – in Canton.' He smiled at Nathan's expression. 'Now I hope you understand what a monstrous spider this is.'

Nathan sat down again. 'Montclair, I take it, is based in Pondicherry?'

'He is, but a year ago he took the lease on an island in the Bay of Bengal. Until a year or two ago, it was used as a penal colony by the East India Company – where they could send those Indians considered a threat to their interests. Unfortunately, a good many of their own employees also died – of the fever. It is not a good place for Europeans who have no resistance to the local diseases. It was widely known as the Island of the Dead. But it suits Monsieur le Marquis very well, being sufficiently remote for him to run his business without undue interference, and conveniently close to the Strait of Malacca, which is the most direct route to China.'

'And what is the name of this island? I assume the Island of the Dead is not how it is marked on the map.'

'So the ship's papers did not tell you?'

'They told us nothing save the name of the ship's captain – and that the ship was under hire to the East India Company.'

But Nathan was wondering now, if there had been other papers that Picket was keeping to himself, until he had enjoyed a private interview with the Governor of Madras.

'Well, that is interesting in itself,' Joyce mused. He appeared to come to a decision. 'Very well. I will tell you. It is one of the Andaman Isles, some seven hundred miles west of here. There is a natural harbour on South Andaman called Port Blair, named after the company officer who made a survey of the islands back in the eighties. If you are looking for the Marquis de la Marche and the silver you have lost – yes, I know about the silver – then you might be advised to look there before you look anywhere else. Before he pays for the company's opium with the company's own treasure.'

Nathan stood up again, reaching for his hat. 'I am indebted to you for your confidence,' he said.

'Not at all,' replied Joyce. 'I suppose you know how best you may repay me.'

Chapter Twenty-five

The Cosmic Dancer

Nathan stood amidst the debris of the *Shiva*'s stern cabin as the carpenter concluded his report. It was not the most encouraging he had heard. The dockyard had done the best they could in the time available to them but in the carpenter's opinion, it was far from good enough. The ship was, he considered, 'barely seaworthy'.

'You could say that for half the ships in the King's Navy,' Nathan remarked dryly, 'it does not stop their lordships from sending them to sea.'

Nor would it stop Nathan. The *Shiva* was his wild card, his one hope of evening the score, if only she could stay afloat for long enough to be of service. He gazed about the cabin, remembering that glimpse of hell afforded him during the battle. They had boarded up the shattered stern windows and reinforced the splintered planking with heavy timbers, so the only natural light now came in through the open gunports. The dismounted guns had been repaired or replaced, but even in the poor light he could see the dark stains in the deck planking from the blood that had been shed by their unfortunate crews. The bulkheads had been restored, but the oak panelling was beyond repair and the beams supporting the upper deck were riddled with shot. The cabin reeked of violent death, but probably more in his imagination than in his nostrils.

As for the rest of the ship, to his own eye, it seemed in reasonably good shape considering the mauling it had received. They had replaced the foretopmast, patched up the sails and the rigging and fitted a new rudder. In the parlance of dockyards, they had performed miracles. But in Mr Pugsley's view, the ship needed a complete overhaul. Either that or a merciful ending. It was forty years since she had left the Blackwall yard at Deptford and there were prison hulks in the Medway, the carpenter insisted, that were in a better condition.

Nathan had a great respect for carpenters but they were not the most encouraging of God's creatures.

'Well, so long as she gets us to the Andamans,' he concluded blithely. 'And she may go out in a blaze of glory.'

Exactly on cue there was a rumble of iron wheels on the deck above, where Mr Joyce, who had been placed in temporary command, was practising the men at the guns. He could do little more than load and run them out, as they were still within the confines of the Madras Road, but Nathan seized the excuse to end his gloomy converse with the carpenter and watch how they performed. The survivors of the *Shiva*'s former crew had been pressed back into the company service on the promise of a pardon if they acquitted themselves well, but to ensure their loyalty they had been joined by a company of the 33rd Foot and several hundred men of the 1st Bengal Artillery who would work the guns. Like most of his kind, Nathan was entirely prejudiced against the employment of soldiers on the great guns – it smacked of Spanish practice – but he had little choice in the matter, unless he wished to strip the rest of the squadron of their gun crews. They seemed competent enough at their drill, but it was a far cry from working the guns in action, and their only experience of the sea had been on the voyage down from Calcutta. Yet another reason to hope for calm weather on the run across the Bay of Bengal.

Joyce declared the practice at an end and dismissed the men to their dinner. The galley stove had been spared the devastation on the gun deck – it was shielded to some extent by the bulk of the fore capstan – and at least they would have hot meals for the duration of the voyage. If they were in a fit state to eat them. The native troops had brought their own cooks aboard and there was a rich smell of mutton curry rising from the galley chimneys. Nathan's stomach stirred in response, but it would be at least an hour before he could satisfy its cravings – unless he offered to sample what was on offer, to ensure it was suitable for human consumption. It was not normally within the province of a commodore, but it might be seen as a noble gesture, a sign that he had the men's interests at heart. He wondered how he might best frame this suggestion to Joyce who was standing uneasily at his side, doubtless awaiting some remark concerning the gunnery practice they had just witnessed.

'Well, they seem to know what they are about,' Nathan

conceded. 'And you may practise with live ammunition during the voyage out. Have you been able to accommodate them to your satisfaction?'

With well over three hundred of them crammed into a space the size of the average taproom, it was doubtful if it would be to the men's satisfaction, but fortunately no one had consulted them in the matter.

'It will take them a little while to adjust to life aboard ship,' Joyce replied diplomatically, 'but they are a stoical bunch and provided they have food in their bellies and a job to do, I doubt they will voice any complaint.'

Exactly the opening Nathan required, but before he could act upon it, the lieutenant continued, 'And the ship itself, sir? Were you satisfied with your inspection?'

'More satisfied than Mr Pugsley, I think, but you know what carpenters are. He is more inclined to think her more *Shiva* the Destroyed than the Destroyer.'

He thought that was rather good on the spur of the moment, but Joyce confined his mirth to a tight smile.

'Shiva is, of course, a masculine deity,' he informed Nathan diffidently. 'And the Hindus think of him rather as the God of Transformation. He has many benevolent as well as fearsome forms. Indeed, he is sometimes depicted as the Cosmic Dancer – dancing among the stars. And in his fiercer forms he is seen as slaying demons.'

Nathan could think of no more intelligent response than to nod wisely. He screwed up his nose. 'What is that smell. Not burning, I trust?'

'No, that is the men's dinner. They are having a mutton curry.' He caught Nathan's eye. 'Would you like to try some while you are here?'

Unhappily, their attention was diverted by a hail from their starboard quarter and they moved to the rail to observe a boatload of Redcoats approaching from the direction of the shore. And with them, sitting composedly at the stern, was the unmistakeable figure of Colonel Arthur Wellesley.

'Good day to you, sir.' The colonel removed the straw hat he wore in place of the customary military shako and delivered himself of a cursory bow. 'You may remember me from our short acquaintance at the governor's house. I have the honour of commanding the troops at your disposal.'

Nathan's formal congratulations masked a strong measure of disquiet. As senior naval officer he was, of course, in overall command of the operation, but in any such undertaking there was bound to be a certain overlap of authority. It was bad enough, in Nathan's opinion, to share command with any soldier, but when that soldier was the brother of the Governor-General of Bengal, it could only add to the complications.

'I trust you have not had too much trouble accommodating my troops,' the colonel remarked, wrinkling his nose in response to the strong smell of curry.

'Not at all,' Nathan assured him, noting the use of the personal pronoun and adding it to his list of reservations. In fact, it had been as much trouble as one might expect to embark 1,500 troops with their weapons and equipment in a matter of hours. Beside the gunners, there were almost a thousand British troops from the light and grenadier companies assigned to the invasion of Mysore; young Wellesley having had his way in that, too, despite the objections of General Harris. Most of them were stowed aboard the *Falcon*, and the rest distributed fairly evenly about the rest of the squadron.

'And how do you find the *Shiva*?' enquired the colonel airily, as if he personally had been responsible for her repair.

'As well as could be expected,' Nathan replied cautiously. 'I have just completed my inspection, and if you would care to accompany me back to the flagship, I will see to your own accommodation.'

Wellesley would have to have the cabin so recently vacated by Caterina, which was a great inconvenience, but probably not the worst Nathan would have to endure in the days and weeks ahead.

'Excellent,' declared the colonel, 'but first I have brought you a little gift – with the compliments of His Excellency, the Governor-General.'

He stretched a languid hand and received a rolled-up document from one of his aides which he presented to Nathan with a small inclination of the head. For a moment, Nathan thought it was a knighthood or some such honour at the governor-general's disposal. It was not. It was a chart – of the Andaman Isles.

'Made in the year '89 for the East India Company,' Wellesley informed him. 'I am told you will find it superior to the one you took from the *Shiva*.'

Nathan noted the name of Lieutenant Blair at the top – the officer Neville Joyce had told him about who had made the first survey of the islands. The port that now bore his name was a large indent on the eastern coast of South

Andaman. A natural harbour projecting inland for a distance of about five miles, roughly the shape of a monkey hanging from a branch and reaching down with one long, grasping paw. There were no buildings marked, but careful soundings had been taken and there was a detailed note of the depths all around the coast and in the harbour itself. It was, as Wellesley had indicated, greatly superior to the chart they had taken from the *Shiva*.

'This will do very well,' Nathan remarked, rolling it up again. 'The only problem with it, is that it is does not show us if the French are there. Or what defences they may have at their disposal.'

'Well, I expect we shall find that out when we get there,' declared the colonel complacently. 'Maps are all very well, but there is nothing like seeing the place for yourself.' He raised his weathered countenance to the heavens as if daring them to oppose this ambition. 'Let us hope the weather is on our side.'

Chapter Twenty-six

The Bay of Bengal

The cyclone struck on the third day out of Madras. In the manner of cyclones it delivered a series of warnings before falling upon them, as if it knew they could take all the precautions in the world without in the least altering their fate.

The first, for Nathan at least, was when he went out onto the stern gallery towards the middle of the first watch. There was a moderate swell running but nothing out of the ordinary and the rest of the squadron was ploughing along quite steadily in their wake with a cable's length between each ship. The sky was clear with a great panoply of stars, and though the wind had freshened somewhat in the last hour or so, they were holding steady on a course east-south-east without the necessity of taking in sail. They would soon have to wear ship but at their present rate, Nathan reckoned they should sight the more southerly of the Andamans before nightfall upon the following day.

The *Shiva* was the next ship in line and she appeared to be riding the swell quite comfortably with no more than a creamy moustache of spray at her bow, the pale figure of the Archangel Gabriel, or, as he was now known, the Cosmic Dancer, clearly visible in the moonlight. Nathan experienced a momentary sense of unease, not quite a premonition but not far from it. It was bad luck to change the name of a ship and it had happened to two of the ships in the squadron. Changing the *Hannibal* to the *Pondicherry* was bad enough, but the *Gabriel* to the *Shiva* smacked of deliberate provocation. He found himself thinking of his old friend and servant, Gilbert Gabriel, and wondering where he was now and whether he could see the stars as clearly as Nathan could, or whether he was rotting in some Venetian prison, or long removed from the torments and afflictions of mankind.

He put the thought aside and began to relieve himself, steadying himself with one hand on the balustrade and taking care to aim between the rails so as not to splash his boots. He was gazing idly at the night sky when, somewhat to his consternation, the stars went out, one by one, as if they had been snuffed.

Besides some divine intervention, which he dismissed as far too much of a coincidence, it could only be caused by the rapid onset of cloud – and an enormous cloud at that, for there was now not a single star to be seen.

He had seen something like this before, just once in the Caribbean, when it had presaged the advance of a hurricane. They did not have hurricanes in the Bay of

Bengal but they had something very like them, and they were invariably preceded by a strong swell.

Making his excuses to the colonel he betook himself to the quarterdeck to find Tully in consultation with the sailing master and the officer of the watch. They were all of the same opinion. They were in for a blow, and in this part of the world, at this season of the year, it was likely to be violent. And with that, the first drops of rain began to fall upon the decks.

Tully took the usual precautions. The watch was summoned from below and all hands were put to taking in sail, sending down the topgallant masts, rigging preventer braces on the lower yards and doubling any gear that might conceivably part. The guns were lashed fore and aft, cow fashion, against the inner planking, and the ports themselves secured with port-bars caulked with oakum.

There was now a considerable swell running but the wind was by no means alarming and, considering the ship was in good hands, Nathan took to his cot on the very sensible grounds that if the weather turned as bad as they expected it was likely to be the last sleep he would have in some days.

He awoke halfway through the morning watch, with a grim, grey light filtering into his cabin and the sound of heavy rain drumming upon the skylight. The swell had increased considerably but the real shock was the barometer. It had fallen so far during the night he suspected a fault, but no amount of tapping upon the glass could shift its stubborn level and he pulled on his tarpaulins with the grim expectation that it would be some while before he took them off again.

When he emerged on to the quarterdeck it was to observe a very different sea from the day before. The waves had increased considerably in size and they were covered in white caps, with streaks of foam skimming across the surface of the ocean like grim outriders of an advancing army. Looking up, he saw that the low clouds seemed to be keeping pace with them, and the wind that drove them both was whistling through the rigging, bringing heavy gusts of rain.

Tully had taken in all but three staysails and a single reefed topsail on the mainmast – his favourite rig for facing down a storm – but Nathan doubted if they would endure for long. His own preference was for running before the wind, scudding under bare poles or with the barest scrap of canvas on the main topmast in an attempt to keep the ship steady. But with the wind in its present quarter this would take them far from where they wished to go, and clearly Tully was of the opinion that this would be to throw in the towel before they had been battered sufficiently to warrant it. He had four men at the helm, fighting to keep her steady into the howling wind.

Nathan looked for the rest of the squadron – and found them spread out over a mile of ocean with no pretence now of sailing in line ahead. His eyes sought out the *Shiva*, the most vulnerable of them. She had set the same storm sails as the *Cherry*, but she was struggling badly, rolling so far that her lower yards were almost in the sea, and the figurehead at her prow was now obliterated by spray. She should take in all but the foresail, Nathan thought, and try to hold her own against the wind. But there was no signal he could devise to convey this opinion, and in any case, he must leave it to Joyce now. He must leave it to all of them.

He spent the rest of the day on deck, a lonely, hunched figure at the rear of the quarterdeck. He was no use to man nor beast, but he felt it gave Tully some moral support – and he was there to be consulted if needs be. Rarely had he felt so miserable or so alone. All his endeavours were at the mercy of the wind. But then they always had been; the wind and the sea and an impenetrable destiny.

He could not think of destiny. The wind and the sea were enough to be going on with; they were certainly frightening enough. The wind was now a legion of demons, howling through the rigging; the grey-green sea a frenzy of monstrous waves, sweeping the decks fore and aft. He could see nothing now of the rest of the squadron. He could only hope they were keeping station, or still afloat. He had appointed a rendezvous in case of separation – in Hut Bay off Little Andaman, the most southerly of the islands. His great fear, though, was that if they held to their present course they should run upon the Nicobars, the neighbouring archipelago to the south. But given the present fury of the waves, they might founder long before that.

Tully had taken in the staysails – as Nathan had known he must – and they were now barely holding their way under a single goosewinged topsail, the weather side made fast and the lee clew set. But even with that little scrap of canvas, there was a very great danger they would be taken aback, driven backwards on themselves, when the very least they might expect was to lose the rudder.

He wondered how the *Shiva* was faring. The soldiers would be battened down below decks, in a hellhole beyond their imagining, until now. Three hundred men rolling in their own stinking piss and vomit. Jesus. And how she would roll. Every roll must appear to be her last, at least to them. They were Mohammedans. Faithful sons of the Prophet in a ship that had once been called the Angel Gabriel and was now named after a Hindu God. Shiva the Destroyer, or the Cosmic Dancer, as Joyce would have it; it was all the same to them. He had done for them with his dancing.

Tully came to him. The ghost of Tully, his features drawn, his face streaming with water and a trickle of blood from a cut on his temple. He shouted in Nathan's ear – it was barely possible to hear a word, even this close, but Nathan gathered he was suggesting he go below. Nathan shook his head firmly. The next question was unbelievable and Nathan had to ask him to repeat it.

'Shall I set you a chair?'

'A chair? Here? In this?'

'We can lash it to the deck for you.'

'No. The men have enough to do, to keep the ship afloat.'

Tully had sent the off-duty watch below – there was no point in keeping them on deck – but it would be scant relief for them. Everything swimming in water, the galley fires doused, no hot food, the ship rolling like a barrel and the water with it. Nathan would rather be on deck.

Suddenly, towards the end of the afternoon watch, the wind began to slacken. The sky was brighter. The rain stopped and the clouds began to break. There was even a glimpse of blue sky. It was like a miracle. The wind fell to a near calm and huge walls of cloud appeared on all sides, brilliant white in the sunshine. The air was warm and humid. Every man on deck stood staring about them, almost in wonderment. There were even smiles, bewildered, wondering smiles. Nathan caught Tully's eye. No smiles there. They had reached the eye of the storm. Or rather it had reached them. It was a pause, not an ending.

The wall of cloud was moving towards them from the north-east and soon it had enveloped them. And as the sky darkened, the wind and the rain returned as violently as before.

And so they battled through the night. All hands now were either on deck or at the pumps fighting to keep the ship afloat, for there was above a foot of water in the well and the ship felt dangerously sluggish to Nathan. When she rolled, a huge weight of water rolled with her, and he could feel her struggling to come up: the old lady wondering if it was worth the effort, and could she not just roll over and die? And all these human parasites aboard, striving not to let her. He lent a hand at the pumps himself, to encourage the men, and for something to do. Anything to feel he might make some contribution, no matter how small, to his own fate.

They lost two men overboard during the night. There was no possibility, of course, of lowering a boat. A lifebuoy had been made fast to the deep-sea lead-line and secured aft to offer a last chance to a man in the water, but in the darkness and in such waves, it was of little use. Nathan stayed on deck with Tully through the long, lonely night. He was practically asleep on his feet, his fingers clasped tight around the knife in his pocket in case he was obliged to cut the lifeline about his waist. He could think of no reason why this might be necessary. If the ship were to founder, he would drown with it, for there was no swimming in that sea, and nowhere to swim to, though he still feared the islands in the darkness ahead and the terrible sound of the sea beating upon the rocks.

Dawn brought some relief. The rain now came in gusts and the wind was dropping with each passing squall. The sky was rising, and so was the barometer, as fast as it had gone down. By mid-morning the clouds were breaking into fragments and becoming whiter. The waves were still large and capped with white foam, but the wind was steadily dropping. Tully clapped on more sail – the staysails reappeared and even a reefed foresail. But there was not a single ship in sight, in all the vast, turbulent ocean.

At noon they sent the hands to dinner – and their first hot meal for several days. Nathan was invited to join the officers in the wardroom and though it was a simple meal of beef hash and pease pudding, washed down with a small beer, it tasted better than any banquet. He joined in the grace with more sincerity than usual.

They reached the rendezvous early in the morning of the sixth day out of Madras. The sky was a cloudless blue, the sea almost calm, gently caressing the rocks Nathan had so feared during the storm. The island was a mass of forest and foliage, rising to a height of several hundred feet, alive with the sounds of birds and monkeys. A stream could be seen tumbling down to the beach. It was a perfect tropical anchorage. All it lacked was ships.

And then they came, one by one over the course of the next two days, like Mary's little lambs, dragging their tail of boats behind them. Bedraggled, broken, missing bits of mast and yard, and one – the *Eagle* – with her bowsprit snapped right off at the stump, but in good shape, considering what they had been through. All but one. The *Shiva*.

By the end of the second day, when she still had not come, Nathan held a council of war in the stern cabin of the *Pondicherry*.

There was no question, of course, but that they must press on with their mission. They still had five ships – and a thousand troops. The loss of the *Shiva* was a blow, but it was not decisive. It was quite possible that the cyclone had done as much damage to their opponents, even in their anchorage on South Andaman – if they were still there. If it had not, well, he would be heavily outgunned but their lordships of the Admiralty had never accepted that as an excuse for ducking a fight, and nor would the Governor-General of Bengal.

'At first light I propose to sail the squadron to the main group of islands,' he announced. 'We will moor in the lee of Havelock Island to the north-east of Port Blair.' He pointed it out on the chart. 'And if Colonel Wellesley is in agreement, he and I will go ashore in the cutter and see what awaits us there.'

Wellesley nodded. But many of his men needed at least a day to recover from the effects of sea sickness, he said. Most of his officers appeared to be in a similar plight, and even Wellesley himself looked a lot less cocky than he had in Madras.

'You shall have at least a day,' Nathan pointed out, 'while we are making our reconnaissance.'

There was the usual quibbling over details. Details which amounted to very little compared to the abiding question of whether the enemy would still be there. Nathan felt an unfamiliar apathy. Or rather, the kind of apathy he felt *after* a battle, rather than before it. Possibly he was drained by the storm. He felt the loss of the *Shiva* keenly. It might not be crucial but it was, he thought, ill-omened. He suspected that he had made the wrong decision in waiting for her to be repaired in Madras – and that everyone present knew it. If they had sailed three days before, they would have reached the islands just before the storm broke – though, of course, this might have been worse than meeting it on the open seas. But he felt as if nothing he could do was right, as if he was pursued by a malignant fate and nothing would prevail against it.

It was almost dark when he finally went on deck to see the officers, naval and military, back to their ships. The moon had risen and it made a shimmering pathway to the distant horizon. The air was full of sounds. Bird sounds for the most part with some outlandish shrieks that were presumably monkeys'. Nathan heard them as jeers.

Then there was another sound, much more welcome to his ears.

'Sail ho!'

And as he looked out to the east, along the silver trail, he saw a familiar shape outlined against the moon. Though it was too far off to be sure, and it was entirely against his nature to be optimistic, he knew at once it was the *Shiva*.

Chapter Twenty-seven

The Island of the Dead

The cutter landed them in a small cove on the south side of the island and they climbed a forested hill – marked on the map as the Jangli Ghat – following the route of a small stream to the top. It took them over two hours and they were soaked through after the first few minutes, either from the rain that dripped down through the forest canopy, or the stream, or their own sweat. The heat was as bad as anything Nathan had ever known, and their stumbling progress was jeered by the usual Greek chorus of monkeys and parrots and other exotic species hidden in the ample foliage of the trees.

The view from the summit made it worth the effort, at least to Nathan. From a height of about 500 feet he could look right down into Port Blair and the inlet in which it nestled. The port itself was little more than a collection of ramshackle huts with a single jetty and a squat little fort perched on the end of a small peninsula. But what made the climb worthwhile for Nathan was that beyond the fort, sheltered from the prevailing winds by the jutting promontory, lay the French fleet.

There were seven of them, moored in a rough crescent in the little bay to the west of the port, much like the French fleet at Abukir with their guns covering the approach from the sea. Nathan applied his eye to his Dollond glass and studied them at length. The big two-decker nearest to him had to be the *Pearl*. She was built along the exact same lines as the *Falcon* and still flew the East India Company flag at her stern beneath the French tricolour. She seemed to be in good shape, unlike the ship next to her, which he guessed must be the *Bridport*, and had clearly been in the wars. Her mainmast and mizzen had been replaced by a jury rig and several of her gunports had been battered into large gaping holes. She had the tricolour flying above the blue ensign. Beyond them, near the centre of the bay, was the *Forte*, with a slightly smaller frigate next to her that was almost certainly the *Braave* – Nathan could see the Dutch flag, or the flag of the Batavian Republic, as it now was, at her stern – and then the three privateers, which Caterina had named as the *Iphigenie*, the *Général Malartic*, and the *Succès* – smaller than the two frigates, but by no means trifling, with sixty guns between them.

He moved the glass back to the *Pearl*. There were a few men about the decks, making and mending or sitting smoking their pipes, but not enough to indicate a full crew, or anything like it, and the same went for the *Bridport*. They must have had prize crews aboard, which was important – indeed, Nathan had been counting on it. Five ships was handful enough; seven, fully crewed and armed, would have been a serious worry.

But probably not as worrying as the fort.

It was on the end of the small promontory which protected the anchorage: a primitive enough structure in the shape of a star with low stone ramparts reinforced with a bank of earth, and the sea coming right up to the walls. But there was nothing primitive about the guns. They were modern 18- or 24-pounders and Nathan counted thirty of them, mostly covering the mouth of the inlet. Almost as worrying, directly opposite the fort, was an island – marked on the chart as Chatham Island – extending right across the harbour, with two narrow channels to the north and south permitting access to the anchorage. The southernmost was barely two cable lengths across, and directly under the guns of the fort; the other was a good bit wider, but an approaching vessel would have to come right up into the wind to round the northern tip of the island, almost certainly requiring a tow, and there was another battery with at least six guns on the far shore, at the very edge of the jungle. The entire length of the channel was navigable by smaller vessels, according to the chart, but even at high tide Nathan could see where the water was breaking over three or four sandbanks, close in to the northern shore.

He took another look at the port. Several of the buildings, he now saw, were in good repair, newly roofed, and big enough to store a large quantity of opium, or silver, or both. Beyond them were a few barrack-like buildings, in much poorer condition and practically falling down in some cases, which had presumably housed the prisoners during Port Blair's short history as a penal colony. There were very few people about. No more than a dozen or so, all on the ramparts of the fort. Almost certainly the crews would remain on the ships. It was said that a fever, like a demon, could not cross water. A man on a ship, even in an enclosed bay, might stay sleek and fit as the butcher's dog, but a few days on land would make a corpse of him. Nathan's party had been ashore for three hours now and he felt as if some fatal miasma was already settling upon him, like the clouds of insects that buzzed around his head.

'Any ideas?' he enquired of Colonel Wellesley, who had been surveying the position through his own glass.

'I was rather hoping you had,' replied the colonel dryly.

Nathan pointed out the problems of an attack from the sea. 'What if we were to land troops on this side of the island,' he wondered, 'and attack from the land?'

The colonel was not overly enthused by this proposal. It had been difficult enough landing with a handful of men – sharpshooters of the 33rd Foot, the fittest men in the regiment. They had almost foundered in the surf, and the climb up the Jangli Ghat with their rifles and equipment had just about done for them. They had been stood down now, and they looked like they might never stand again, sprawling on the floor of the jungle puffing on their pipes to deter the swarming, stinging insects.

'We could lose half the men landing on that coast,' the colonel pointed out, 'and the rest marching on the fort. Pray take a look.' Nathan did, while Wellesley dwelt upon its principle features. 'Walls twenty or thirty foot high, with ten cannon mounted to sweep the approach from inland. Four hundred yards of cleared ground to cross. Then, as I am sure you will have observed, the moat.'

The moat. Nathan had not observed it, in fact, but he did now. It was a simple channel cut from one end of the peninsula to the other. At this distance it was difficult to judge how wide it was, but they would need boats or a bridge to cross it. The only access at present was the drawbridge at the gatehouse.

'Our only chance is to take them by surprise,' the colonel said. 'For I have seen very few people in the fort itself. They probably rely on the men from the ships to fire the guns, and it will take some time for them to come ashore. But they will see us as soon as we emerge from the jungle, with most of the peninsula still to cross.'

And if the ships came out in the meantime, they stood a good chance of escaping to the south-east, taking the *Pearl* with them and its precious cargo of silver. Always assuming it was still aboard and not in the godowns down by the harbour. Or somewhere else entirely.

'What puzzles me is why they are still here,' the colonel mused. 'It is three weeks since the encounter at Devil's Point.'

'They could be waiting for the monsoon to end,' Nathan guessed. It would be difficult to navigate the Malacca Strait against a north-easterly, and the ever-present danger of cyclones. 'Or they could be waiting for the *Shiva* to join them – with the *Falcon* as prize.'

And even as he said it, the idea took shape in his mind.

Chapter Twenty-eight

The Happy Return

They came in on the morning tide – the *Shiva* in the lead and the *Falcon* behind her. Both ships flying the tricolour, and the *Shiva* displaying the recognition signal at her mizzen halyard. A single word signal for La Retour and the letters H, R and X. La Retour Heureux. The Happy Return.

It was more in hope than conviction – the codes were invariably changed every few days – but it might cause some confusion. A delay in the order to fire. Long enough for the two ships to enter harbour.

Nathan stood on the quarterdeck of the *Shiva* watching the distance narrow. They were well within range of the fort now, and still the guns stayed silent. But it could so easily be a trap. A spy might have brought the news of the *Shiva*'s capture from Madras. Or the rest of the British squadron might have been sighted at their anchorage a little further up the coast. The French might be biding their time, waiting for them to step right into the jaws of the harbour, until there was no possibility of escape.

Useless to worry about it now. But Nathan did. He agonised over whether to fire a salute, but he had no idea whether it was expected or not, or even how many guns to fire. Did you salute a marquis who had turned smuggler and pirate? The French prisoners had been no help in this, but they did say that the marquis had been with them during the encounter with the *Pondicherry* and that he had died in the battle. This might explain why their comrades, ignorant of their fate, were still waiting here for him, before they moved the silver out to China.

Nathan clutched at straws. Anything, rather than believe Leloup was gloating from the ramparts of the fort, with his gun crews hidden from sight, ready to leap up at a moment's notice and unleash mayhem. Just like Wellesley's men, lying in the long trail of boats behind the two ships, with the tarps pulled over them, waiting for the moment of release, or death.

Closer they came, between the two headlands now, with the jungle rising up on either side. They could see the parrots flitting about in the treetops, and there was the inevitable screech of monkeys, very like fiendish laughter. The same mocking laughter that had followed them up the Jangli Ghat, as if the creatures of the forest knew something they did not. They were approaching the promontory now, and men were emerging from the barracks – women, too – to stand gawping and waving at them all along the waterfront. At least they were gawping and waving and not running towards the fort. But that, too, could be part of the plan.

It was dead ahead now, at a distance of about a quarter of a mile, and Lieutenant Joyce, who was at the con, told the helmsmen to come a little into the wind. They could see clear through the southern channel now to the anchorage beyond, with the *Forte* moored so that her guns could sweep its entire length. Nathan knew a little more about her now, and her guns: thirty 24-pounders and fourteen 12-pounders on her gun deck, eight carronades on her quarterdeck and forecastle. She was said to be the most powerful frigate ever built. He could see men up in her tops and all along her rails, watching the *Shiva* come in, some of them waving, and Nathan thought he could hear cheering, but it might have been wishful thinking.

Now a boat was pulling away from her side and heading towards them – two officers in the stern, and a dozen men at the oar – but they were pulling against wind and tide; they would never reach the *Shiva* before she reached the fort. Barely 200 yards now and closing; close enough to see the faces of the men on the ramparts staring out at them, and the smoke from the slow matches blowing back in the north-east wind. This was good. The smoke from the guns would blow back in their faces, thought Nathan, still clinging to his crumbs of comfort as he stared back into those unwinking black eyes, somehow looking that much more menacing than they did on the deck of a ship.

He stood on the leeward side of the quarterdeck, with Joyce at his side, and Blunt and Vivian a step or two behind, all trying to look as if they did not have a care in the world. Blunt whistling tunelessly and Vivian shielding his eyes from the sun with the one hand that was remaining to him and the empty sleeve of his left arm pinned to his uniform coat in the style of Admiral Nelson, save that all the officers wore plain blue jackets and hats, like the officers of any merchant ship, and the men on deck or up in the rigging were either Lascars from the Bombay Marine, or gunners of the Bengal Artillery, dressed as seamen.

But someone in the fort did not like the look of them, or had become agitated by their rapid progress towards the inner channel. There was a flash and a bang and a great waterspout rose just a few yards ahead of them. The classic shot across the bows. Heave to and await inspection. The next shot would be right into the hull, and very likely it would be the whole battery.

'Shall I return fire?' Joyce's impatience was palpable. But at least Blunt had stopped whistling.

Nathan shook his head. 'Let us keep them guessing as long as possible,' he said. 'But you may take in sail – let them think we are obeying their order.'

There was someone standing up on the ramparts now, in clear view, waving his hat and hailing them. Nathan took off his own hat, and waved it back, grinning cheerfully. Another few yards and they could bring their broadside to bear. But the officer had seen something – or had finished with guessing. He jumped down from the top of the ramparts, and seconds later they erupted in fire and fury.

This was no shot across the bows, and at that range they could not miss. The heavy shot carried the length of the *Shiva*'s top gun deck, bowling men over like ninepins, splintering timber and screaming off metal. One of them took a deflection off the breech of a cannon and came hurtling up into the quarterdeck, passing right between Nathan and Joyce and taking off the head of one of the helmsmen. And with a noise like a groan, the main yard parted from the mainmast and came crashing down into the waist, bringing the course with it before the topmen could haul it in.

But they were level with the fort now, at a distance of no more than a hundred yards, and Nathan nodded to Joyce to return fire.

The guns were ready, primed and loaded, but it took a few moments for the gunners to run them out. They had trained them twice a day during the voyage from Madras, but the men were small in stature, and the biggest guns they had handled until now were 6-pounder field guns on proper carriage wheels. They lacked the brute strength of a British seaman at hauling the heavy trucks and levering the muzzles of 12- or 18-pounder cannon. And this was their first experience of enemy fire at extreme close range.

Blunt had the topsails counter-braced and they were fast losing way, but not quite fast enough. Within seconds they would be past the fort and into the bay, which was the last thing Nathan wanted. He looked towards the *Forte* and saw her gunports opening all along her starboard side and the topmen swarming into her rigging. Presumably the same thing would be happening all along the French line. If the *Shiva* went much further they would be in amongst them, a single two-decker with a scratch crew against two frigates and three heavily armed brigs.

'Let go the stern anchor,' he ordered. Then as it dropped into the shallow waters of the bay: 'Let go the bower.'

They were moored now at head and stern exactly in mid-channel and barely 200 yards from the fort, with twenty guns staring down at them.

There was another blast of fire and smoke from the ramparts, but only two or three guns firing now. Maybe Wellesley had been right, and they needed the crews from the ships. But they were firing right down into the waist of the *Shiva*, and the heavy iron balls smashed through the thin deck planking to do untold damage to the hull below. Still, it hardly mattered now if she foundered. She was exactly where Nathan wanted her to be. He gave Joyce the nod.

'Fire!' roared the lieutenant, and as the order echoed along both decks the guns went off in turn, a rippling broadside from bow to stern, firing at maximum elevation into the ramparts.

The fort vanished for a moment but when the smoke cleared there was scarcely a sign of damage. Perhaps a chip or two out of the battlements, and just a few small stones and a couple of spent cannonballs, rolling down the earthworks into the sea as if in mockery of their puny efforts. But the *Shiva*'s tops were alive with sharpshooters, sweeping the ramparts with small arms fire and grape from the swivel guns. Even a few grenadiers from the 33rd, hurling their bombs at the fort – and finding it, too, in some cases, though most dropped harmlessly into the sea. And now the *Falcon* fired. Nathan could see the 12-pound roundshot smashing into the top of the ramparts and even if they did not bring the walls a-tumbling down, as the trumpets had at Jericho, they were a mighty distraction to the gunners. There were only one or two guns firing from the fort now, and the boats from both ships had cast off their tow and were pulling for the shore. Twelve boats in all, packed to the gunwales with men from the 33rd and the 12th Foot, the two Highland regiments, and the Swiss mercenaries of the De Meuron Regiment – all handpicked men from the light companies and the grenadiers, the strongest and fittest in the army.

They would need to be both, for if they made it to the shore they had to climb twenty feet of sloping earthworks and another ten of stone wall, and then fight whatever was waiting for them on the far side.

The blue cutter from the *Shiva* was the first to land – or to hit the rocks at the foot of the earthworks. She had more than forty soldiers aboard and they were leaping ashore from the bowsprit, several falling short and dropping into the sea, but most of them made it, and the seamen were hurling grappling hooks high up into the battlements so the soldiers might haul themselves up on the ropes.

Nathan did what he could to help them. The *Shiva*'s guns unleashed one more broadside before they were forced to cease for fear of hitting the soldiers. Most of them had landed now, and those boats that were not stuck upon the rocks were heading back to the *Falcon* for the next contingent. The earthworks were alive with soldiers, like red ants streaming up an anthill, but they were taking punishment. Nathan could see men falling back and sliding down the embankment into the sea.

But then the *Forte* joined the fight and Nathan lost all interest in what was happening on shore.

It was a raking shot, firing langridge and grape at about four hundred yards range, and a hail of lead and iron swept the *Shiva*'s decks and rigging from stem to stern.

'Bring us to bear on the frigate,' Nathan roared at Joyce, though he was barely a few feet away. They were moored on a spring cable and they brought the guns to bear neatly enough, but there were precious few to man them for that one raking broadside had caused havoc among the gun crews on the upper deck. The guns below were still firing, but to no apparent effect, and now the frigate's bows were swinging towards them and she was coming out.

Nathan snatched a quick glance back towards the fort, but the smoke from the *Shiva*'s last broadside still shrouded the ramparts, and he could just make out the red coats moving through it, and the occasional flashes of small arms fire. It was impossible to tell who was winning or losing – and there was nothing he could do about it either way. But the ship's boats were on their way back from the *Falcon* with the rest of Wellesley's assault force and Nathan thought he could see the colonel with them in the commodore's barge from the *Pondicherry*.

He turned back to his own immediate problem. The *Forte* was getting under way with staysails alone, goose-winging towards them, with her spritsail and both jibs at one angle to keep her head up, and the staysails at the other, driving her forward. It was a neat manoeuvre if it worked, but she was dangerously close to the shore and so close to the wind Nathan could see the sails feathering at the edges. He looked along his upper gun deck where Joyce had restored some semblance of order.

'Load up with chain, Mr Joyce,' he called out. 'High into her rigging.'

This was an unusual order on a British ship – it was usually the French who aimed high – but they had to stop her somehow. God help them in their present state, if she came alongside.

Another ragged broadside, but the *Forte* came on. And there were others forming up in line behind her. They were all coming out. Nathan looked back at the *Falcon*. She was hove to with her bows facing down the channel. She had no idea what was heading her way. She was too far off for any voice to carry a warning, and there was no signal he could contrive, no boat left for him to send. Well, she would find out soon enough. Five against two, and neither of them Navy ships. There were times when Nathan thought he could do nothing right. This was one of them.

The *Forte* was almost up with them now, steering for the narrow gap between the *Shiva* and the island so that she could rake them again. They would probably use grapeshot this time, which would sweep the decks of any living soul, himself included. He thought of praying, but the words would not come and he doubted Mr Harrison was listening. He was busy mending his clocks, far from the world of men.

The *Shiva* fired another ragged broadside from her lower deck – and the miracle happened. A chainshot must have sheered through her jib halyards, for both jib and flying jib were carried away to windward, and instantly she fell off the wind and bore straight down upon the shore.

The crew were struggling to trim the staysails when the *Shiva* fired a ragged broadside from her upper deck. There could not have been more than four or five guns firing, but they served their purpose. This time it was the spritsail that went, and with it the last remaining chance of sailing the *Forte* out of her present predicament. Her captain did what Nathan would have done in the circumstances and dropped anchor.

And that gave Nathan the only chance *he* had.

'Cut the cables,' he shouted to Joyce, 'and prepare to board.'

They had over four hundred soldiers aboard the *Shiva* beside the regular crew, and though most of them were artillerymen, they knew how to fight. They grabbed whatever weapons were to hand – handspikes and gun rammers, belaying pins and axes, along with the more conventional pikes and cutlasses, while the seamen hauled on the braces to bring the wind once more on their starboard quarter. With her cables cut, the *Shiva* was moving forward again, bearing down on the frigate's larboard bow, and the French were either too busy trying to keep her off the shore, or too blinded by smoke to see what was coming. Certainly no one fired upon her, and she smashed into the frigate's larboard side just abaft the roundhouse, the bowsprit carrying right across the forecastle and ripping through the foremast shrouds. And the boarders went in after in a great, baying horde of red and blue, the seamen among them running right up the bowsprit and dropping down upon the defenders, lashing about them with their assorted weaponry. It was clear that their rapid change of allegiance had not affected their propensity to violence, or perhaps they thought they had something to prove.

This time Nathan did not go with them. Someone, he thought, had to keep a clear head, and his head had already taken all the battering it would bear. He could see another frigate coming up through the smoke on the *Forte*'s larboard quarter – the *Braave*, presumably, and he had fewer than a hundred men left to work the ship and fight the guns. Not that there was any working to be done for her bows were firmly locked into the *Forte*'s rigging and if it had not been for the frigate's anchor both ships would have run aground. He called out instructions to the men in the tops, causing them to take in sail, and directed the soldiers that were still up there to fire upon the incoming frigate, though there was little they could do with small arms and swivel guns. He was almost sure that the *Braave* would board them – there was little point in firing into them now – and he was determined to defend the colours with the few men at his disposal.

He looked back towards the fort. The smoke had cleared and there were red figures swarming all over the ramparts with more climbing up to join them. The *Falcon* had finally seen the danger from the French squadron and turned into the wind to sweep the channel with her broadside.

But even better, wondrously better – out of the haze to the west – just entering the mouth of the harbour, was the *Pondicherry*, with the *Bombay* and the rest of the squadron behind her.

The *Braave* had seen them, too. She promptly fell off from the wind to bring her broadside to bear. It was the only thing she could do in the position she was in, and not without hope of success, for unless the *Cherry* did the same, she was restricted to firing back with her two bow-chasers. But in the confines of the narrow channel it was a delicate manoeuvre, and the first of the big brigs was coming up fast behind her. Quite what the brig intended was difficult to tell. Possibly she was heading for the slight gap between the frigate and the island, but the frigate was still turning, the wind filling her sails from the north-east.

The bowsprits crossed like two long lances and then the brig's bows smashed into the *Braave*'s. Hopelessly interlocked, the two vessels drifted together onto the mud and rocks at the end of the island, and it was all over, bar the shouting.

The boarders from the *Shiva* had swept the frigate's decks and even as he watched, Nathan saw one of the artillery officers hauling down her colours at the stern and fighting to tie his own regimental flag in its place. It was almost certainly the first time a French ship had been taken by men of the 1st Bengal Artillery. He looked back towards the *Braave*, lying helplessly on the mud with the *Pondicherry* bearing down on her, preparing to rake her with her whole broadside. The Dutch frigate was still flying the flag of the Batavian Republic – very like Britannia with an attendant lion – but even as Nathan looked, someone cut the halyard and it came fluttering down into the sea.

Chapter Twenty-nine

The Mighty Admiral of the World

It was a great day for the hauling down of colours. The last to go was the tricolour on the fort, and one of the Highlanders wailed happily away on the pipes as they raised the Union flag in its place. Nathan found Wellesley watching from the jetty and looking even more pleased with himself than usual.

'Well done,' Nathan congratulated him. 'I give you joy of your victory, sir. May it be the first of many.'

'Yours, too,' replied the colonel, with the ghost of a smile. 'I hope you enjoyed yourself half as much as I did.'

'Must be the Irish in you,' Nathan told him. He never wanted to experience again what he had felt on the quarterdeck of the *Shiva*, when he had seen the *Forte* goose-winging towards them, and the rest of the French squadron coming up behind.

It was the wrong thing to say. The smile froze and the colonel gazed down his long nose. 'Just because a fellow is born in a stable,' he snapped, 'does not mean he is a horse.'

But even a Wellesley could not put Nathan in his place. Not today.

They had found the silver in the holds of the *Pearl*, in fifty stout oak chests, the company seal still stamped in wax upon the locks, save for the two that had been opened, presumably at Leloup's order, to check the contents.

So the governor-general might have his war, and Nathan his reward. Not that he was counting on it. In any case, he had enough rewards for one day. Five French ships taken and their two prizes recaptured. And the Wolf was dead. Leloup had been killed by the *Shiva*'s first broadside, according to the surviving French officers, and Naudé had died in the fierce hand-to-hand fighting aboard the *Forte*. They had kedged the *Braave* and the *Iphigenie* off the mud, and all the French ships were now back at their moorings in Navy Bay, each with a prize crew aboard, and the Union flag flying above the tricolour, as proudly as it did on the fort. There had been some nonsense from Picket about flying the company flag, but Nathan would have none of it. He could fly it on the fort if he wished, he told him, but he would have to fight the colonel first.

Nathan's squadron was moored in the harbour mouth, preparing for the journey back to Madras. Port Blair had never seen so many ships and probably never would again. Thirteen in all. And all under Nathan's command – the mighty admiral of the world, Joyce had called him, and he was too happy to deliver even the mildest of rebukes.

It was Joyce who came to him, towards the end of the long day, and told him about the opium.

'The godowns are packed full of it,' he said. 'Must be the entire Bengal harvest, ready for the run to Canton.'

He wanted to know if he should have it loaded aboard the *Falcon*.

'No,' said Nathan. 'Burn it.'

'Burn it?' Joyce looked startled. 'Is that an order?'

'Let us call it a suggestion,' said Nathan. 'But if you do not care to light the pyre, then I will.'

'No.' Joyce grinned at him. 'I will do it. But I will need a bit of help.'

'Take a few of the Lascars from the *Pearl*,' Nathan told him, 'but do not tell them what they are burning. And in your report, blame the French.'

So they sailed for Madras, with the sun sinking down onto the horizon ahead, and a great black pall of smoke darkening the eastern sky before it was properly night. And even Jonah and his whale, and St Thomas and all his doubts, could not take the shine off Nathan's satisfaction, for he was the mighty admiral of the world and he had done something right at last.

Epilogue

The Spoils of Conquest

In April, 1799, the British troops finally marched on Seringapatam. Nathan was not there to see them go. He was with his squadron in the Arabian Sea, guarding against intervention by the French. His prizes were bought into the service and he moved his flag into the *Forte*, leaving Tully with the *Pondicherry*. Lieutenant Joyce was given command of the *Iphigenie*. He was, to Nathan's knowledge, the first Zoroastrian ever to command a ship of His Britannic Majesty's Navy.

At the end of May, he heard that Seringapatam had fallen to the British. The Highlanders had led the assault, fortified, it was reported, with an issue of whisky and biscuits. Tipu's body was found among the dead. He had been killed while firing on the attackers with a series of hunting rifles, passed to him by his servants. The former rajahs were restored to the throne of Mysore, under the protection of the British East India Company. Colonel Wellesley, Nathan heard, had been made governor of the new province.

Nathan continued his patrol in the Arabian Sea. But the French never came. Not by sea and not by land. At the end of the year, came news that Bonaparte had abandoned his army, sailed back to France in a frigate, and seized power by military coup. Nathan was not wonderfully surprised.

There was also news from England at last. His father wrote that their old servant, Gilbert Gabriel, had finally been discovered in Venice. He had been imprisoned by the French but released by the Austrians and was now living with a former nun of the convent of San Paolo di Mare and working as a gondolier. He sent his best wishes.

Nathan's father made no mention of Fanny Wyndham, or of his proposed divorce. Nathan hoped he had dropped the idea.

His mother penned a short note to say that she was sorry not to write at any length but she was very busy organising opposition to the Seditious Meetings Act. She sent her love. In a postscript she mentioned that she had been burned in effigy on a bonfire in Lewes. 'What a hoot!'

He also had a letter from Sara. She said that she had left the employment of William Godwin and had moved to Sussex, where Nathan's father had been kind enough to provide her with a cottage and a small stipend. She had taken up painting again and was very much in love with the sea. His father was a frequent visitor.

In the summer he had word from Caterina. She had given up on the idea of a convent but had founded an orphanage at the foot of Saint Thomas's Mount. If he was ever in Madras, she wrote, he should drop by. There would always be a bed for him.

And, finally, there was a letter from Spiridion Foresti. He had returned to his native Zante and had been placed under house arrest by the French. He had made friends with the governor, however, and was pretty much given the freedom of the island. When Nathan had done with conquering the East, he should come and stay. There was a house he might like to buy, with an orange orchard, overlooking the sea. It would make a fine home for a retired seaman. And even Ulysses, he wrote, had come home in the end.

Acknowledgements

With thanks to Martin Fletcher, who had the original idea for this series, for his continued support, advice and direction as publisher during its progress from the English Channel to the Andaman Sea; to Emily Griffin at Headline Review for guiding me through the editing process; to the staff at the British Library who helped me search through the extensive archives of the British East India Company and found me many contemporary charts, maps and illustrations; to the staff of the Caird Library at the British Maritime Museum in Greenwich and the creators of the brilliant new East India Company exhibition there; to the geographer Dr George Adamson for sharing the results of his comprehensive work on the effects of the south-west monsoon in the Indian Ocean, including many personal records and journals of eighteenth-century colonial administrators and navigators; and to Emma Donald at Winchester University for assisting with my research into 1790s Madras and the Andaman Isles including the explorations of Lieutenant Blair and Captain Moorsom 1788–1790, and the nautical papers on the Bay of Bengal made by the 18th century explorer and geographer

Alexander Dalrymple – all of which helped me chart my own course through the troubled waters of the period.

Additionally, for their help and encouragement over the whole Nathan Peake series, my thanks to the English Arts Council for their initial award and funding, which helped begin the journey; to Square Sail in Charlestown and the captain and crew of the *Earl of Pembroke*, who provided much of the nautical expertise and hands-on experience of sailing a square-rigger; to Brian Lavery and the staff of the Caird Library at the National Maritime Museum in Greenwich; to Richard Gott and the staff of the National Archives of Cuba; to Cate Olsen and Nash Robbins of Much Ado Books in Alfriston, who came up with so many of the books I needed for my research; Michael and Kitty Ann, my sailing companions and co-owners of the *Papagena*; Ian Tullett of Rye who shared his extensive knowledge of sailing generally and the English Channel in particular; my father, former Leading Signalman Stan Bryers who helped me in many practical ways with his knowledge of the intricate world of naval communications; my children Dermot and Elesa Bryers; Liz Molinari and her uncle Marcello for helping to make my stay in Venice so entertaining and informed; to Bibi Baskin and my hosts at the Raheem Residency in Alleppey, to the owners and staff of La Riserva di Castel d'Appio in Liguria, to Michael Raeburn in Paris, Larry Lamb in Normandy and John and Jackie Fisher in Indre, for providing me with rather more pleasurable places to write than my attic in Balham; and especially to Sharon Goulds for taking leave from her own work for the international aid charity PLAN to join me in my more erratic explorations of the Caribbean, the

Mediterranean and the Arabian Sea, and learn more than she needed to know about wearing under staysails in a moderate gale.

Fact and Fiction

The Australian writer Thomas Keneally said in a recent interview that all fiction is lies.

Well, yes, up to a point . . .

Fiction is by definition 'invention or fabrication; stories about imaginary events and people'. That is, lies. But of course not *all* fiction is lies – fiction can and often does contain some truth, and sometimes quite a lot of truth. However, when a writer or filmmaker says a book or film is based on a true story, I think it's important to say what is true and what is not. Obviously, you can't label it as you go along; that would spoil a good story. But you can include a footnote.

So here it is.

The Spoils of Conquest is based on a true story. After winning the Battle of the Nile, Admiral Nelson sent one of his officers to Bombay to warn the British authorities there that Napoleon was in Egypt with 40,000 French troops and that he planned to march on India.

Nelson's letter in the Prologue is a close approximation of the real despatch he wrote at the time to the Governor of Bombay. It forms part of the collection assembled between 1844 and 1846 by the historian and former naval officer Sir Nicholas Nicolas, and you can see the originals, in Nelson's own handwriting, in the National Archives at Kew.

The principle change I have made is to the postscript. In the real postscript he wrote:

> *The Officer, Lieutenant Duval, who carries this Despatch voluntarily to you, will, I trust, be immediately sent to England, with such recommendations as his conduct will deserve.*

Lieutenant Thomas Duval was an officer on the seventy-four-gun *Zealous*, which had taken part in the battle. He travelled by Scanderoon to Iskanderun and then by horse and camel overland through Aleppo to Baghdad, where he transferred to a sambuk for the journey down the Tigris to Bassara, or Basra. Thence by the *Fly* packet to Bombay where he delivered his despatches to the Governor, Jonathan Duncan.

I've appropriated this journey for Nathan Peake and his companions. The chief of these, Spiridion Foresti, is based on a real-life character of that name who was British consul in Corfu until the French invasion of the previous year and was known to Nelson and others as the best intelligence agent in the region. However, at the time the novel is set, he was held by the French as a British spy and although he was later released, I have no evidence that he was ever in Egypt, Syria or Iraq.

Ben Hallowell is another real-life character – he was the captain of the *Swiftsure*, which Duval encountered on his journey to Iskanderun just after it had captured the French corvette *Fortune*. I've invented the meeting between Nathan and Hallowell, of course, but the rather unlikely story of the mast from *L'Orient* is true. Hallowell did have it made into a coffin for Nelson, who was touched by the gift. He kept it behind his chair in his dining room on the flagship, until his captains and his servants complained about it, and he had it sent to his undertaker in London. On his last leave home, before Trafalgar, he visited the undertaker and had it upholstered in satin, ready for his use. After the battle, his body was brought back to England preserved in brandy and wine. It was transferred to Ben Hallowell's coffin where it was viewed by the populace in the Painted Hall of Greenwich Hospital, before it travelled to its final resting place in the crypt of Saint Paul's Cathedral.

Although Nathan follows the exact route taken by Duval, the events on the journey are either invented or taken from the journal of Abraham Parsons, former British consul in Iskanderun who made a similar journey in 1774.

I've described Bombay Harbour and the ships of the Bombay Marine from contemporary accounts in the East India Company archives kept in the British Library. The landing of the French in Mangalore is also true, but the encounter between the Bombay Marine and the French squadron is a piece of fiction.

The French squadron itself was real enough and I've used the names of the real ships and commanders. However, the events at Mangalore, Devil's Point and the Andaman Isles are imagined.

In fact, the *Forte* was captured in battle with the frigate

Sybille in February 1799 in the Balasore Roads in the Bay of Bengal. An excellent account of the battle by Lieutenant Hardyman of the *Sybille* can be found in the Asiatic Annual Register of 1798/99. The *Forte* was a monster. She mounted thirty 24-pounders on her main gun deck and fourteen 12-pounders, with eight 36-pounder carronades on her forecastle and quarterdeck (which were not counted as 'proper' guns in her rating), and she was crewed by 470 officers and men. The *Sybille* had 38 guns and about 350 men, but she took the *Forte* prize with the loss of almost half the French crew dead and wounded. One interesting detail of Hardyman's account, which I have used in my story, is the crucial role of smoke in a sea battle. The smoke from the guns was so dense that the *Forte* could not see her opponent for much of the battle and fired at a merchant vessel on her starboard quarter while the *Sybille* came up on the opposite side and pounded her into submission.

The battle of Port Blair is my own invention entirely. The port had been a penal colony run by the British East India Company but was abandoned at the time, because of the death toll from disease, probably malaria. Colonel Arthur Wellesley – who later became the Duke of Wellington – was in Madras at the time, preparing for the invasion of Mysore.

The story of Tipu's death in the Epilogue is true – as far as we know. The story of Lieutenant Joyce is not. There has never, to my knowledge, been a Zoroastrian in command of a ship of the Royal Navy, but I am happy to stand corrected.

Most of what I have written about the British East India

Company is true. In 1600, Queen Elizabeth I granted a group of London merchants a royal charter giving them a monopoly on trade between Britain and the East Indies. Shares were owned by wealthy merchants and aristocrats, and over the next hundred years the company established factories in Bombay, Calcutta and Madras, trading mainly in cotton, silk and spices.

India was then part of the Islamic Mughul Empire, but the emperor's authority was in decline and the country was torn by wars between rival factions and dynasties, many of whom established semi-independent provinces. European powers led by the Portuguese established bases in many coastal areas – and the rivalry between them led to more wars.

The British East India Company built up a large private army, initially to protect its trading interests and to expel its European rivals. It formed alliances with native princes and supported them against their own internal rivals. Eventually, it had the biggest army in India and controlled vast swathes of India territory, dispensing justice and collecting taxes. It also established its own navy – the Bombay Marine. It was, in effect, an imperial power. The taxes it collected made far more profit than trade. In fact, by the end of the eighteenth century, the company's profits came down to two things – taxes and tea.

The English love affair with tea began in the 1660s when Charles II's Portuguese bride, Catherine of Braganza, introduced it to the English court. By the 1750s, it had become the national drink.

The British East India Company had the monopoly on the supply of tea, which came exclusively from China, and which they paid for by exporting English wool and Indian cotton.

But in the 1750s, the Qing emperor decreed that as China had all the goods it could ever need, all trade with foreigners must be paid for in silver.

This would have crippled the company. They explored the idea of growing tea in India – where it grew wild in the forests of Assam. But it was too much trouble. They had a better idea. They would pay for their tea with opium.

Opium had been used in medicine in China and other places since at least the seventh century, but in the seventeenth century, the Dutch introduced the Chinese to the practice of mixing it with tobacco and smoking it. Consequently, over the next 200 years, millions of Chinese became addicted to the drug. And this provided the British East India Company with a golden opportunity. They grew loads of the stuff 'for medicinal purposes' in Bengal – and they decided to use it to finance their trade with China.

The Chinese had made the opium trade illegal. Ships carrying the drug were seized and the crews put to death. So the company held an annual auction in Calcutta where the opium harvest was sold to independent merchants known as 'the country firms'. It was these firms which took the risk of smuggling the drug into China. But the company insisted the smugglers paid for it in silver bullion – in Canton.

And they used the silver to pay for their tea.

This is the story I have appropriated for the plot of *The Spoils of Conquest*. The character of the Marquis de la Marche is fictitious, but there were plenty of real-life characters like him. They bought the opium at the company auction and then ferried it to China, where it was stored on hulks moored in Canton Bay and then sold to criminal gangs who smuggled it ashore in Chinese galleys called centipedes or scrambling dragons. Then it was sold at a vast profit to their millions of customers across China. The Chinese called it foreign mud.

It led to two major wars between Britain and China and a lasting legacy of bitterness.

But it was not just the Chinese government who objected. The fact that a British trading company employed a large private army and navy, made war and peace, controlled vast overseas territories, and sold huge quantities of opium to smugglers, did not escape censure in Britain itself. However, the immense wealth of the company directors enabled them to buy a number of seats in Parliament and form a powerful political lobby which for many years blocked any attempt at reform. The company also lent vast amounts of money to the Government, provided troops and ships for imperial wars, and supported their political allies in Westminster against their rivals, just as they did in India.

It took the Indians themselves to bring the company's rule to an end. The Indian Rebellion of 1857, also known as the Indian Mutiny, and the repression which followed, caused such revulsion in England, not least from Queen Victoria herself, that Parliament was forced to take action, and the company's territorial holdings came under the direct rule of the British Crown. The company itself was formally dissolved in 1873.

East India House, the Leadenhall Street headquarters of the company, was demolished in 1861 and the site is now occupied by the Lloyds Building. But there is an excellent permanent exhibition telling the history of the company at the National Maritime Museum in Greenwich, and over 200 years of company archives are kept at the British Library – both of which institutions provided an invaluable source of research material.